TERRY'S CREW

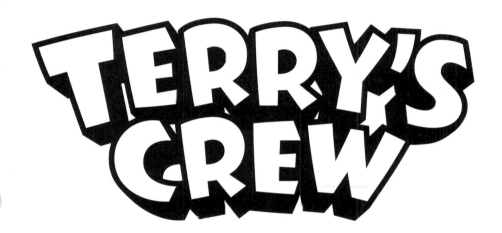

TERRY'S CREW

By TERRY CREWS
and CORY THOMAS

Little, Brown and Company
New York Boston

About This Book

This book was edited by Andrea Colvin and designed by Megan McLaughlin. The production was supervised by Bernadette Flinn, and the production editor was Lindsay Walter-Greaney. The text was set in Collect Em Now BB and Mikado.

Little, Brown and Company
Hachette Book Group
1290 Avenue of the Americas, New York, NY 10104
Visit us at LBYR.com

First Edition: November 2022

Little, Brown and Company is a division of Hachette Book Group, Inc. The Little, Brown name and logo are trademarks of Hachette Book Group, Inc.

The publisher is not responsible for websites (or their content) that are not owned by the publisher.

Library of Congress Cataloging-in-Publication Data
Names: Crews, Terry, 1968– author. | Thomas, Cory, illustrator.
Title: Terry's crew / by Terry Crews and Cory Thomas.
Description: First edition. | New York : Little, Brown and Company, 2022. | Summary: "Inquisitive young artist Terry strives to make space for himself as the new kid at Rock City Academy, a place where he can finally hone his talents. Terry learns the consequences of dreaming big and the value of real friends along the way"—Provided by publisher.
Identifiers: LCCN 2021050369 | ISBN 9780316499965 (hardcover) | ISBN 9780316499958 (ebook)

Subjects: CYAC: Artists—Fiction. | Schools—Fiction. | Friendship—Fiction.

Classification: LCC PZ7.1.C7436 Te 2022 | DDC [Fic]—dc23

LC record available at https://lccn.loc.gov/2021050369

ISBNs: 978-0-316-49996-5 (hardcover), 978-0-316-49998-9 (paperback), 978-0-316-49995-8 (ebook), 978-0-316-27341-1 (ebook), 978-0-316-27586-6 (ebook)

PRINTED IN CANADA

TC

Hardcover: 10 9 8 7 6 5 4 3 2 1
Paperback: 10 9 8 7 6 5 4 3 2 1

To my high school art teacher, Dwight Eichelberg...for believing in me when I didn't believe in myself —TC

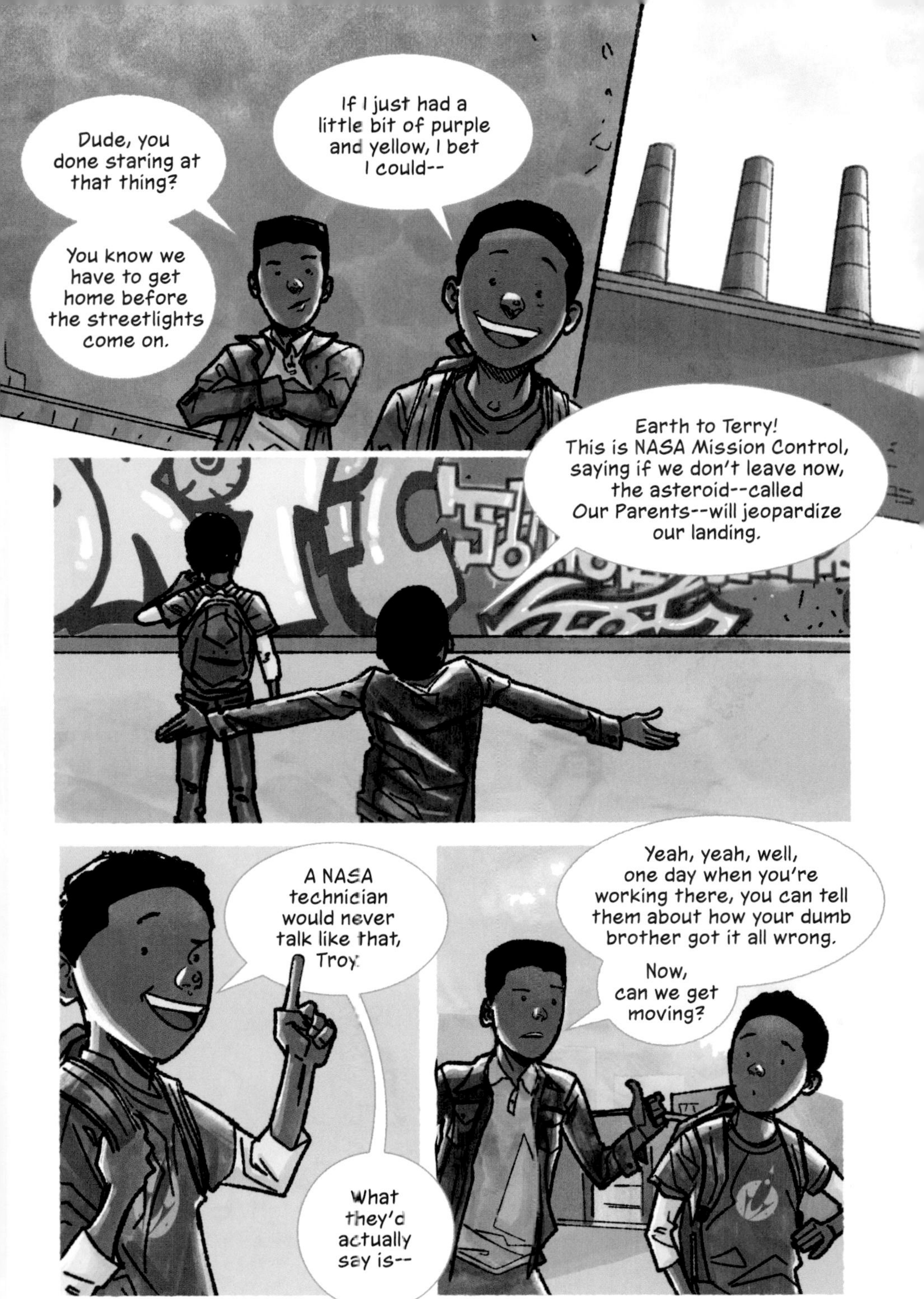
Dude, you done staring at that thing?
You know we have to get home before the streetlights come on.
If I just had a little bit of purple and yellow, I bet I could--
Earth to Terry! This is NASA Mission Control, saying if we don't leave now, the asteroid--called Our Parents--will jeopardize our landing.
A NASA technician would never talk like that, Troy.
What they'd actually say is--
Yeah, yeah, well, one day when you're working there, you can tell them about how your dumb brother got it all wrong.
Now, can we get moving?

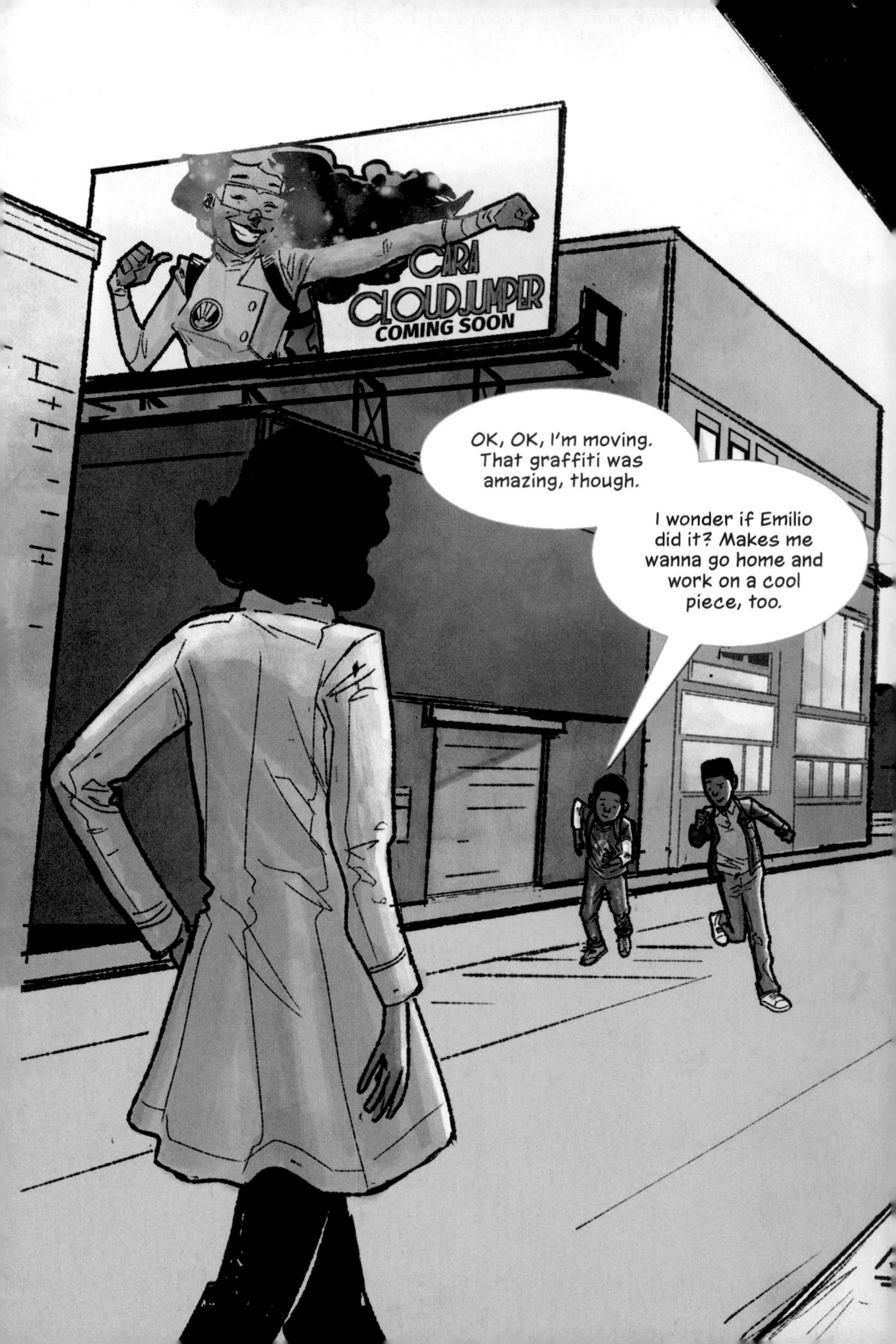
CARA CLOUDJUMPER
COMING SOON
OK, OK, I'm moving. That graffiti was amazing, though.
I wonder if Emilio did it? Makes me wanna go home and work on a cool piece, too.

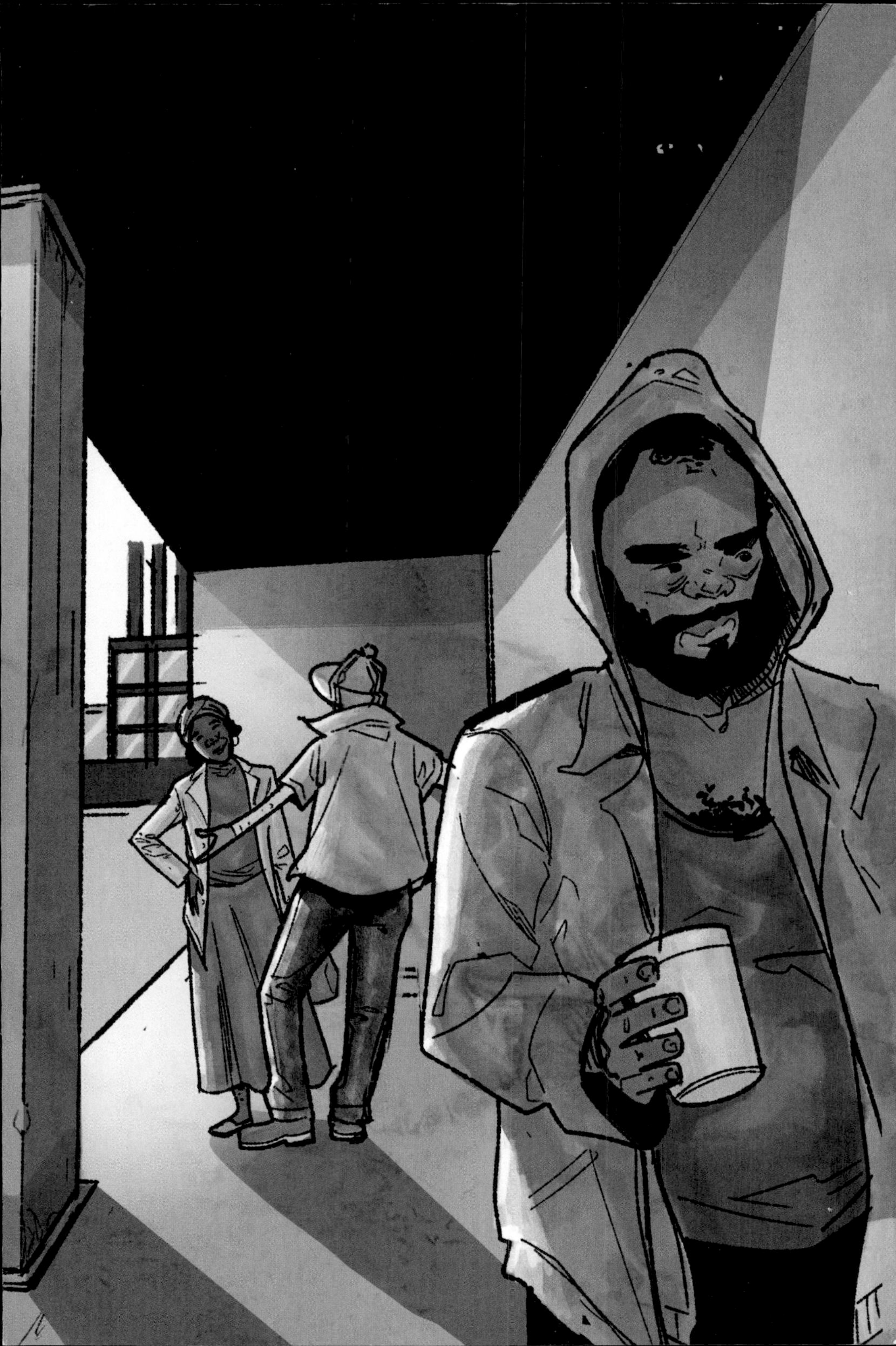

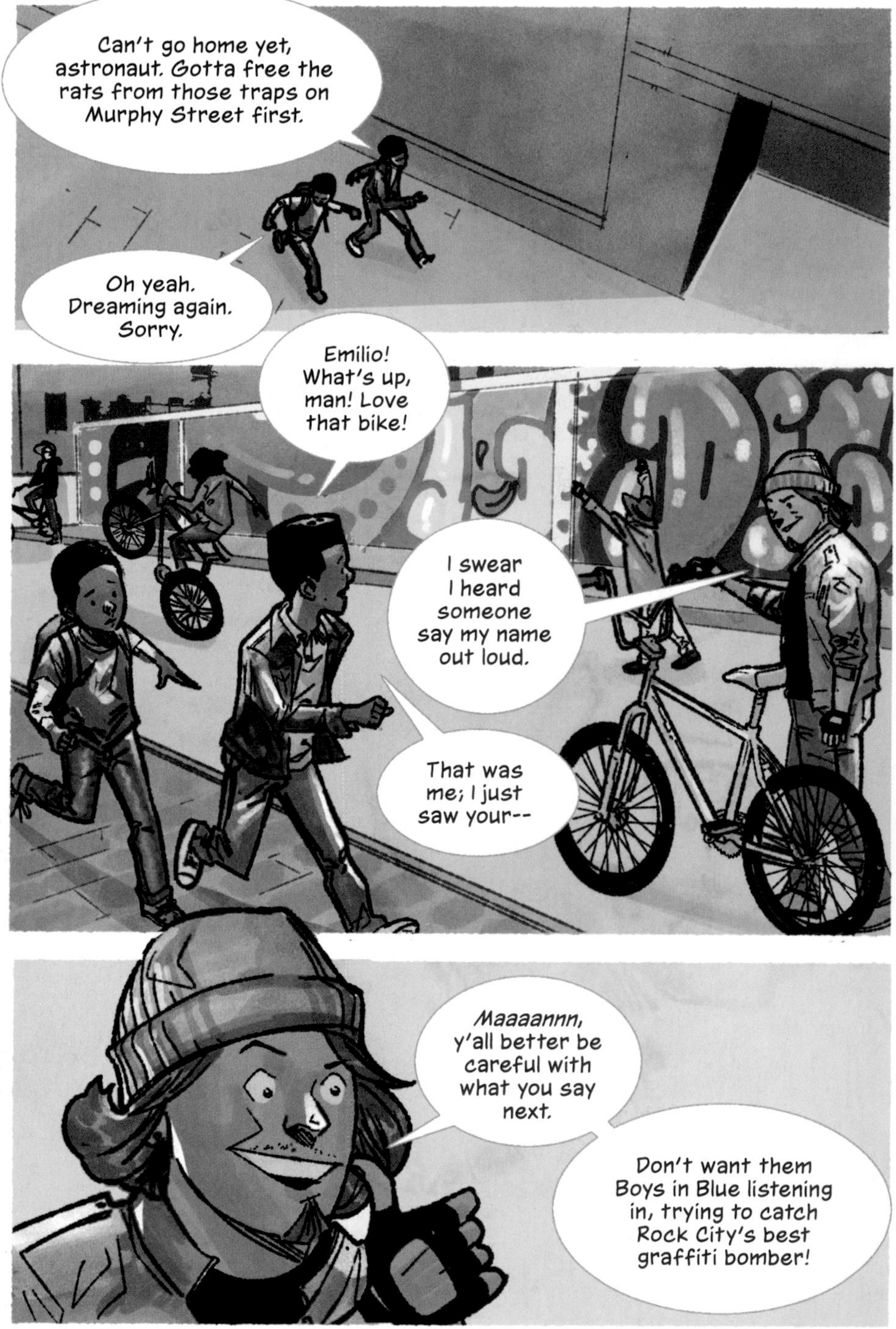
Can't go home yet, astronaut. Gotta free the rats from those traps on Murphy Street first.
Oh yeah. Dreaming again. Sorry.
Emilio! What's up, man! Love that bike!
I swear I heard someone say my name out loud.
That was me; I just saw your--
Maaaannn, y'all better be careful with what you say next.
Don't want them Boys in Blue listening in, trying to catch Rock City's best graffiti bomber!

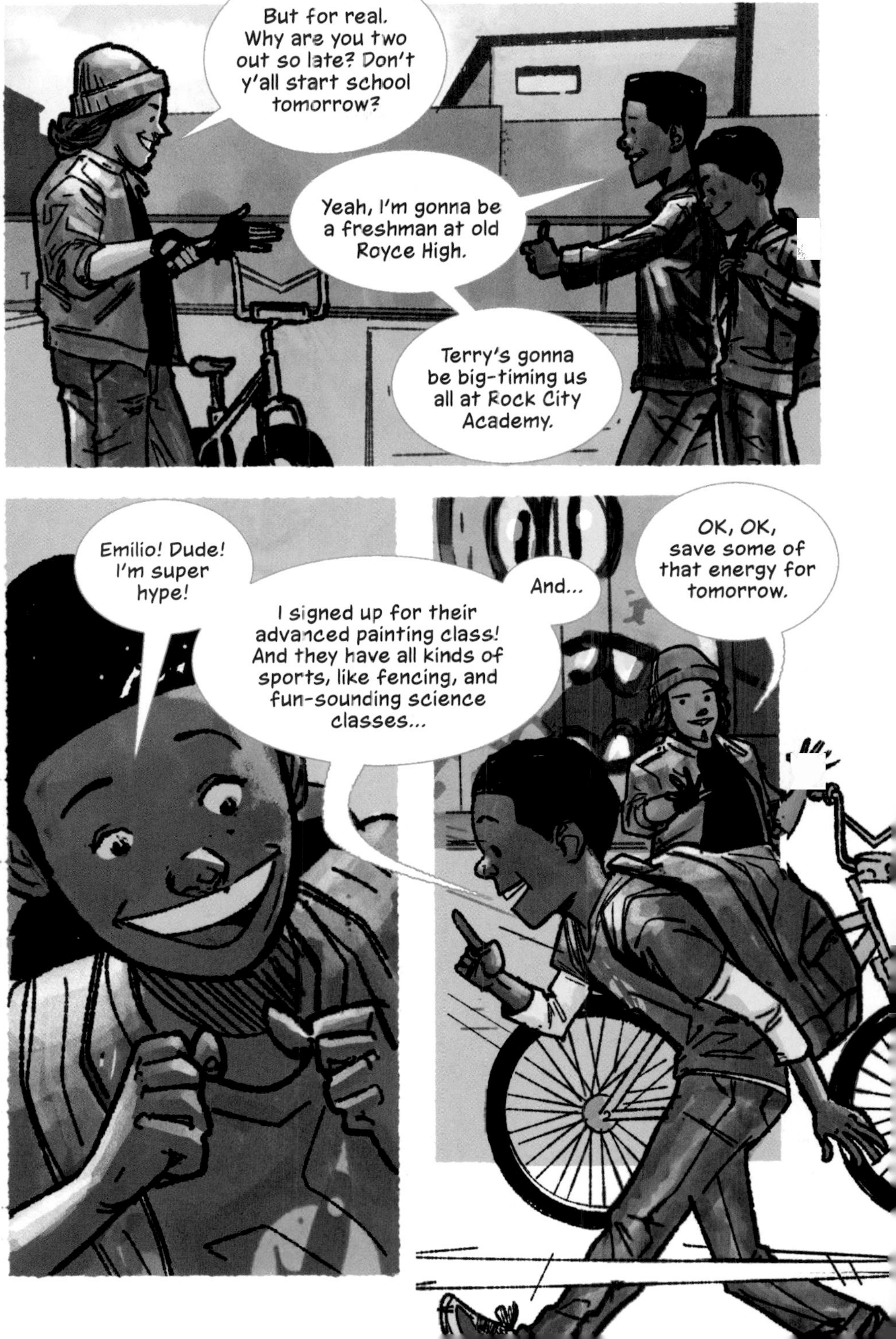
But for real. Why are you two out so late? Don't y'all start school tomorrow?
Yeah, I'm gonna be a freshman at old Royce High.
Terry's gonna be big-timing us all at Rock City Academy.
Emilio! Dude! I'm super hype!
I signed up for their advanced painting class! And they have all kinds of sports, like fencing, and fun-sounding science classes...
And...
OK, OK, save some of that energy for tomorrow.

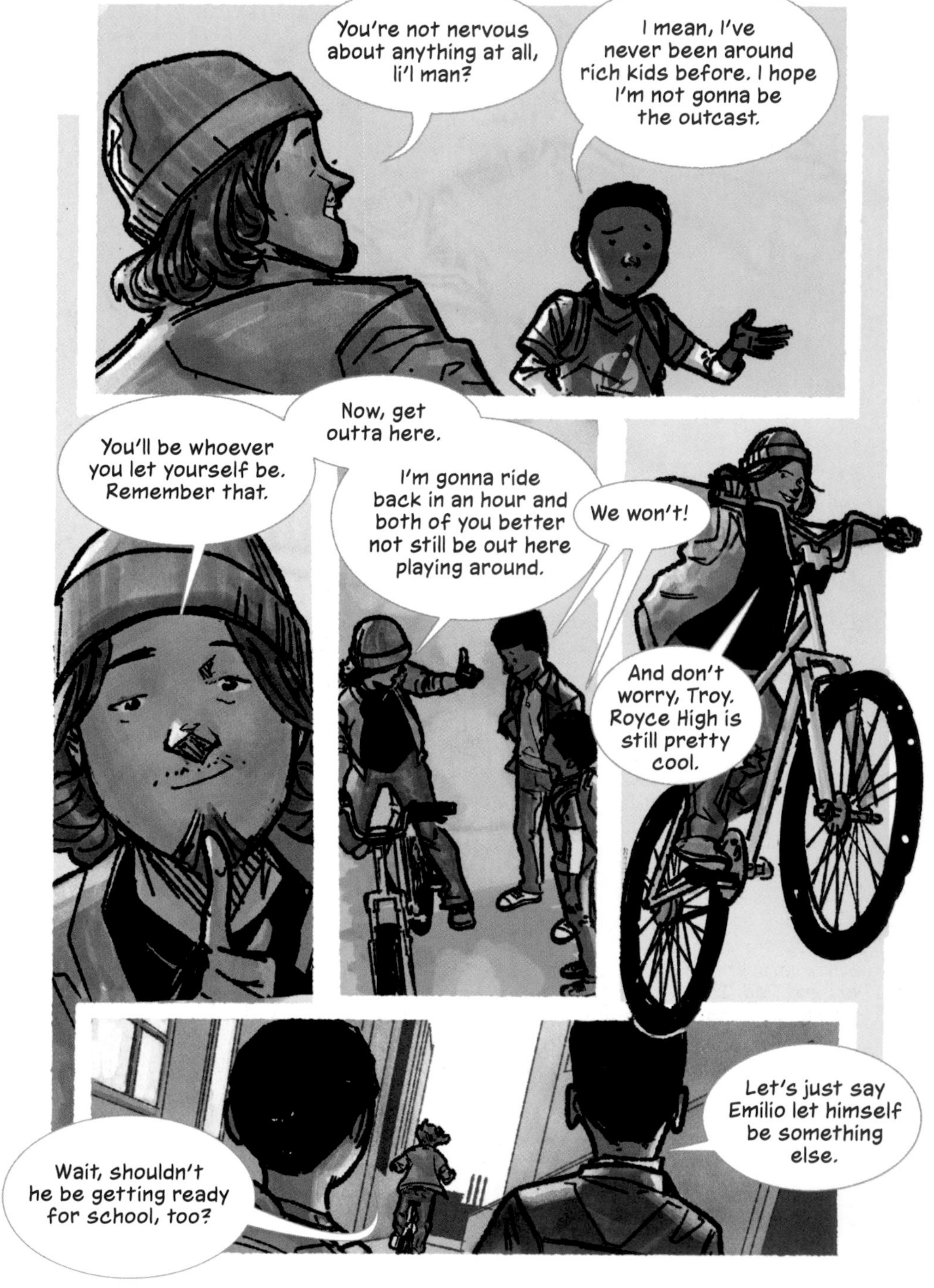
You're not nervous about anything at all, li'l man?
I mean, I've never been around rich kids before. I hope I'm not gonna be the outcast.
You'll be whoever you let yourself be. Remember that.
Now, get outta here.
I'm gonna ride back in an hour and both of you better not still be out here playing around.
We won't!
And don't worry, Troy. Royce High is still pretty cool.
Wait, shouldn't he be getting ready for school, too?
Let's just say Emilio let himself be something else.

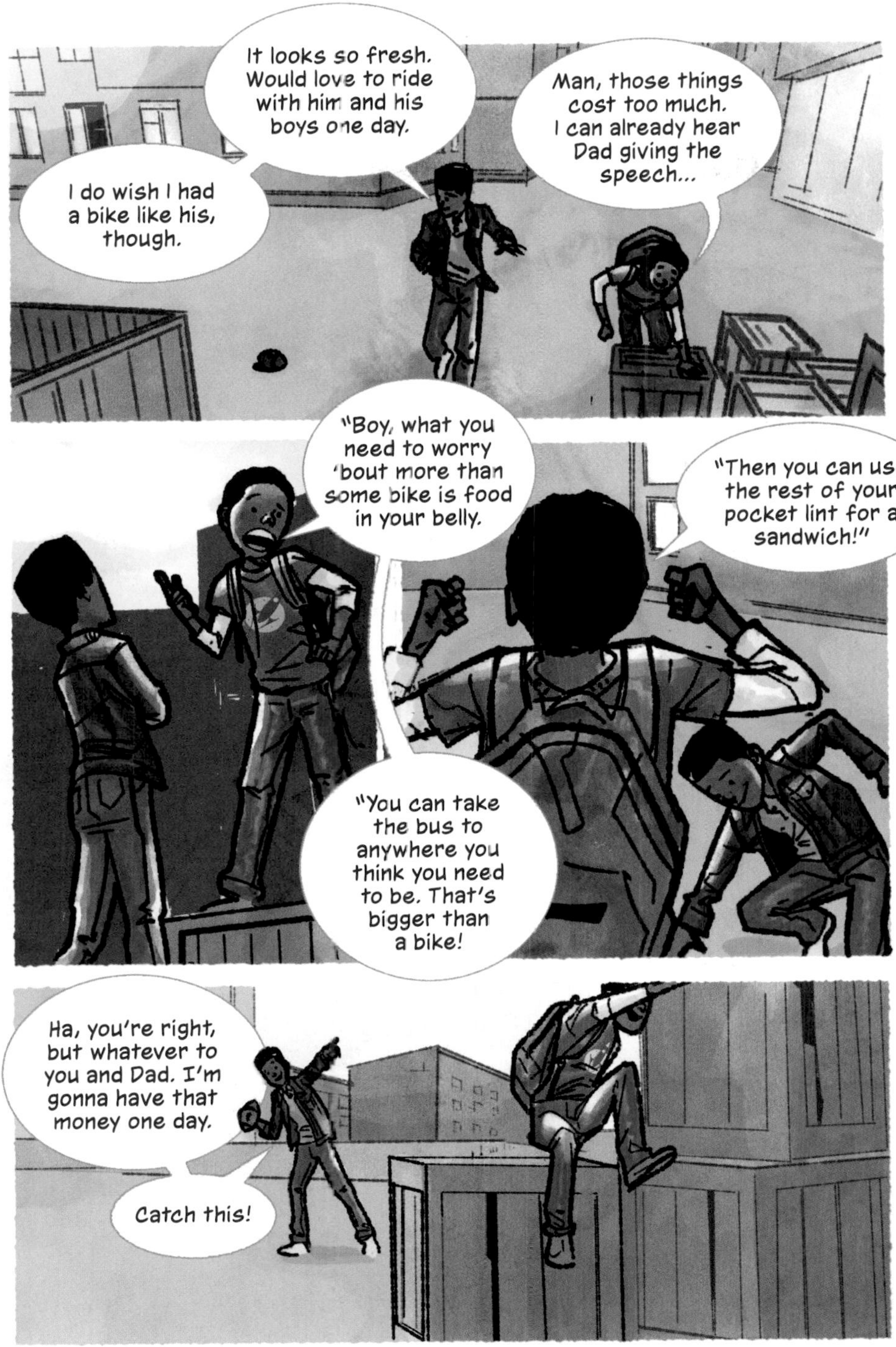
I do wish I had a bike like his, though.
It looks so fresh. Would love to ride with him and his boys one day.
Man, those things cost too much. I can already hear Dad giving the speech...
"Boy, what you need to worry 'bout more than some bike is food in your belly.
"Then you can use the rest of your pocket lint for a sandwich!"
"You can take the bus to anywhere you think you need to be. That's bigger than a bike!
Ha, you're right, but whatever to you and Dad. I'm gonna have that money one day.
Catch this!

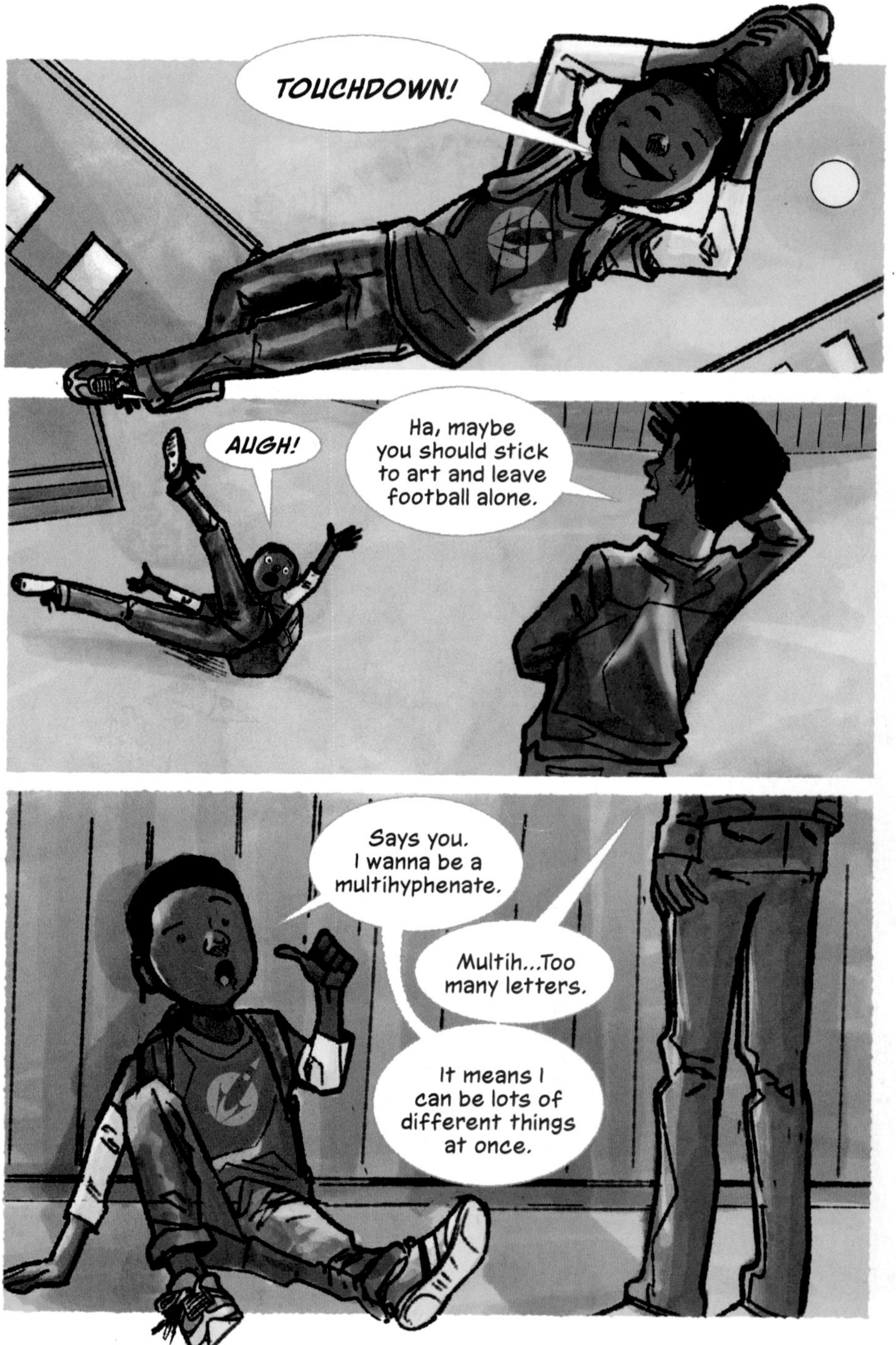
TOUCHDOWN!
AUGH!
Ha, maybe you should stick to art and leave football alone.
Says you. I wanna be a multihyphenate.
Multih...Too many letters.
It means I can be lots of different things at once.

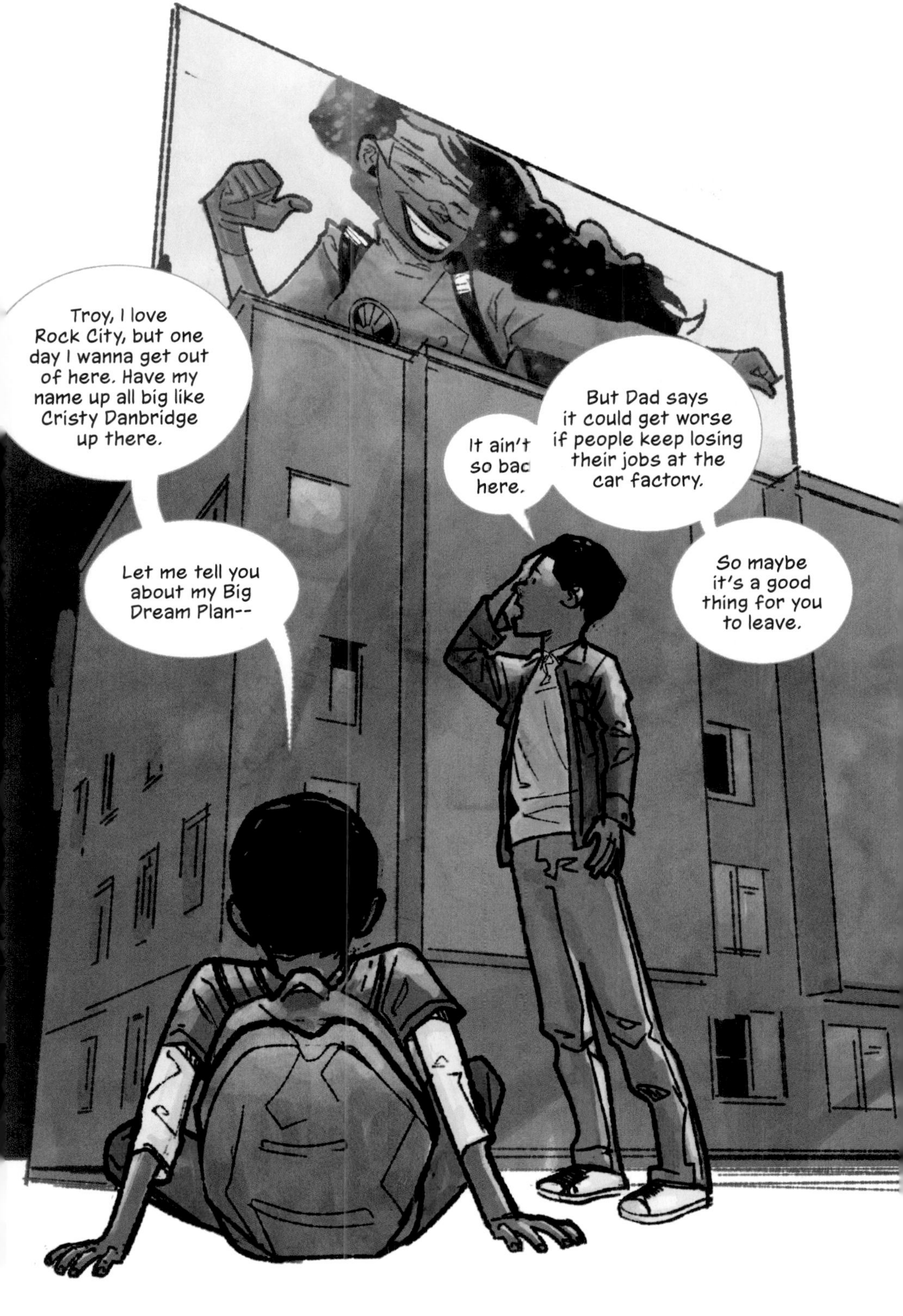
Troy, I love Rock City, but one day I wanna get out of here. Have my name up all big like Cristy Danbridge up there.
Let me tell you about my Big Dream Plan--
It ain't so bad here.
But Dad says it could get worse if people keep losing their jobs at the car factory.
So maybe it's a good thing for you to leave.

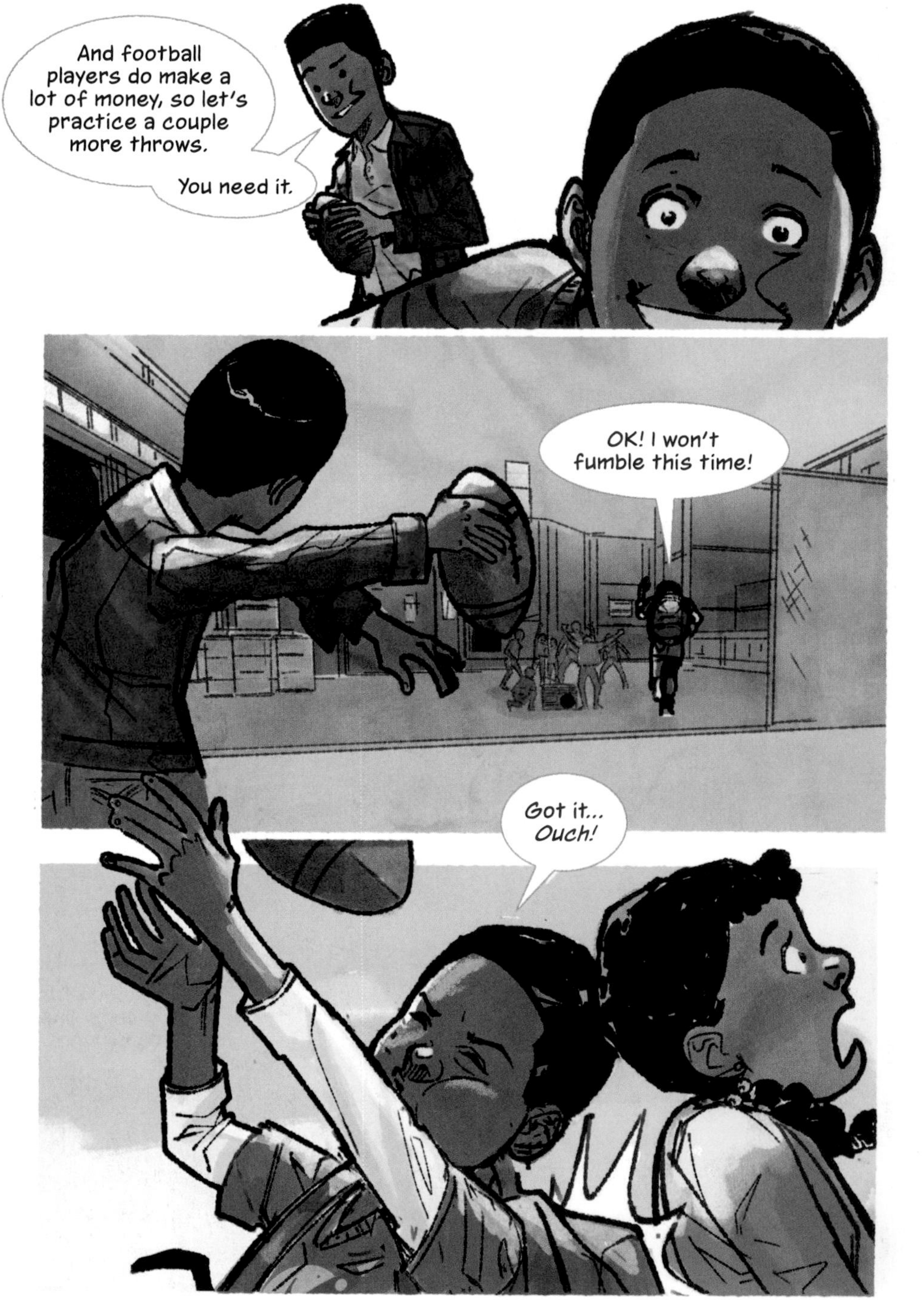
And football players do make a lot of money, so let's practice a couple more throws.
You need it.
OK! I won't fumble this time!
Got it... Ouch!

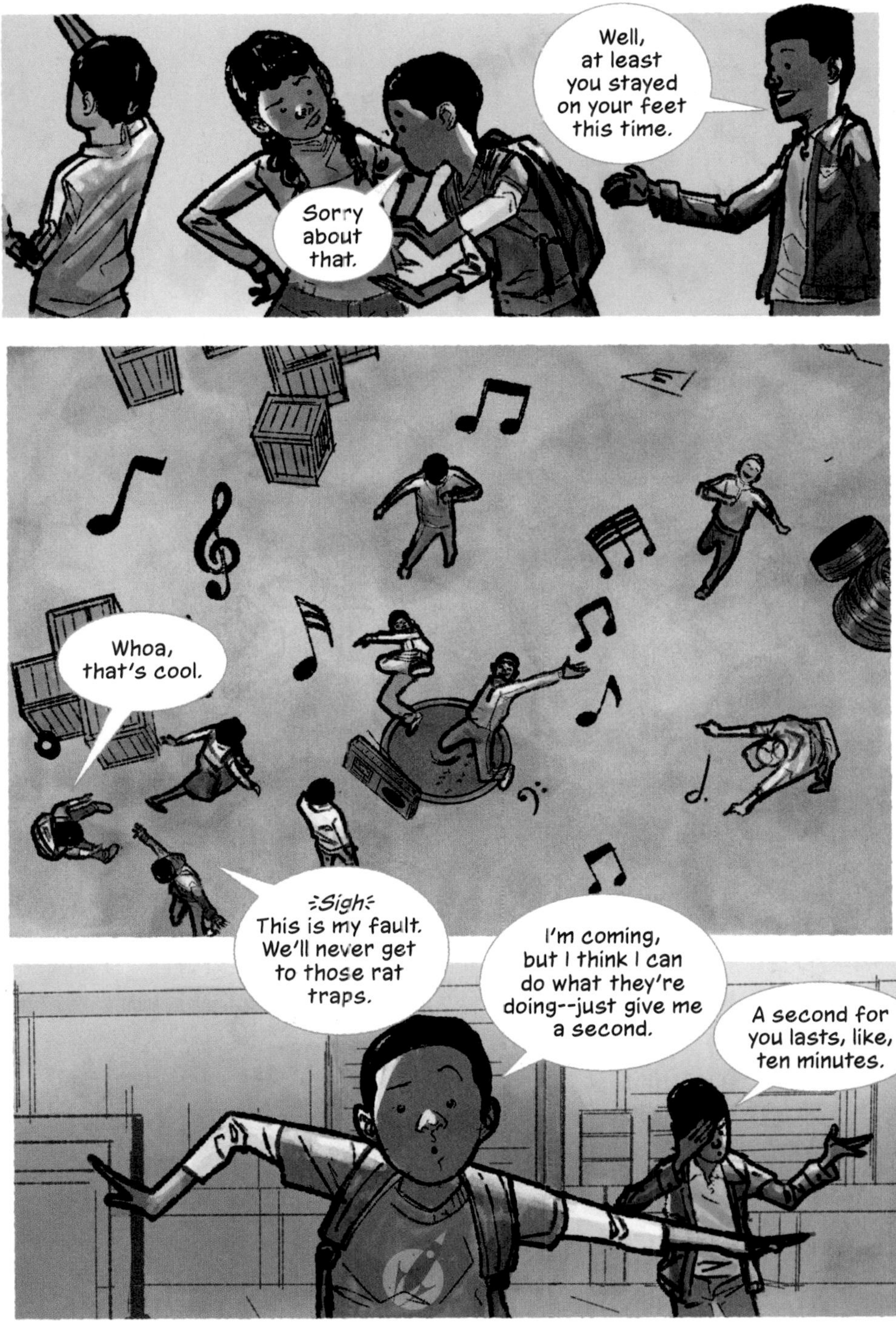
Sorry about that.
Well, at least you stayed on your feet this time.
Whoa, that's cool.
Sigh
This is my fault. We'll never get to those rat traps.
I'm coming, but I think I can do what they're doing--just give me a second.
A second for you lasts, like, ten minutes.

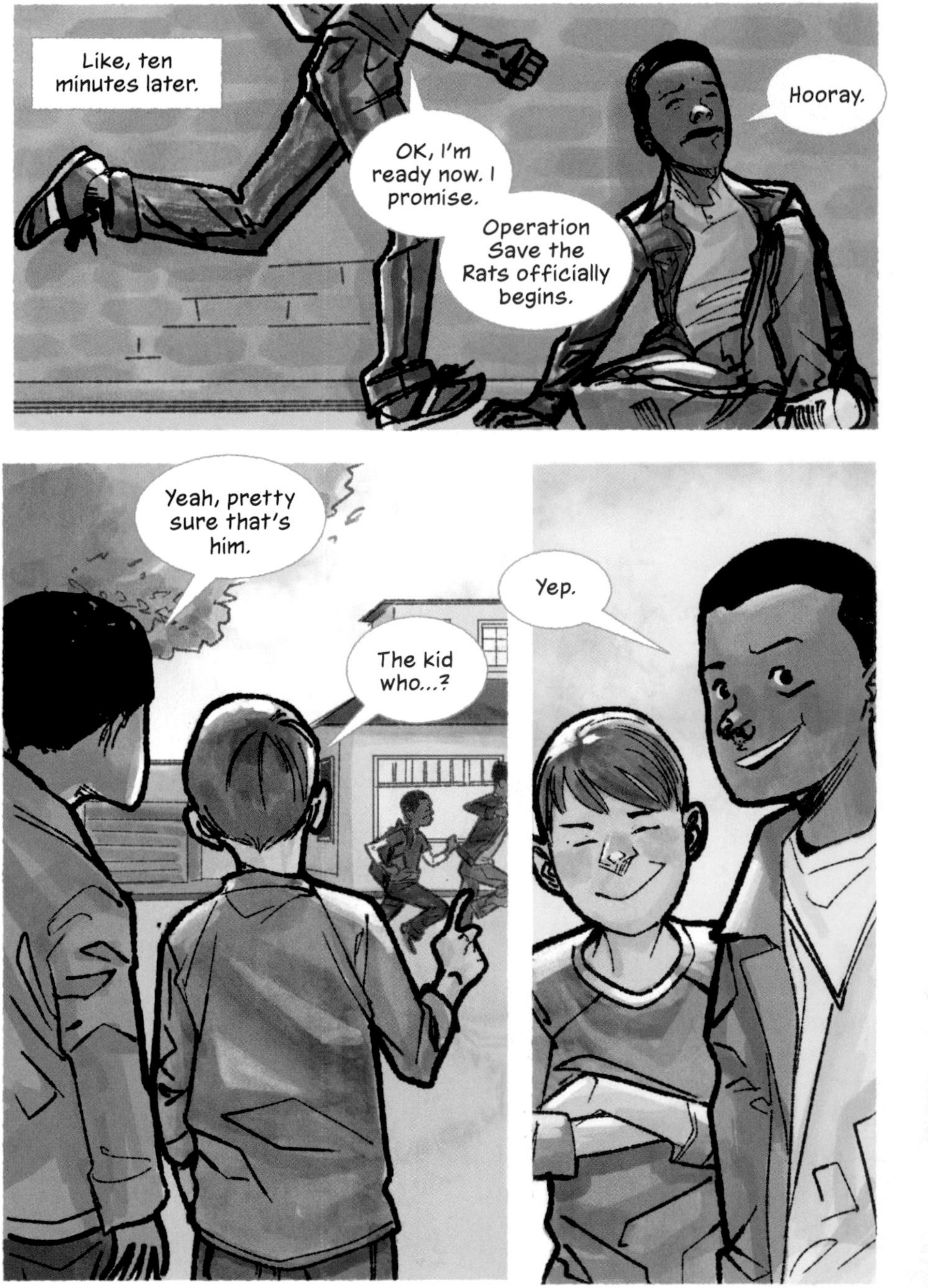
Like, ten minutes later.
OK, I'm ready now. I promise.
Operation Save the Rats officially begins.
Hooray.
Yeah, pretty sure that's him.
The kid who...?
Yep.

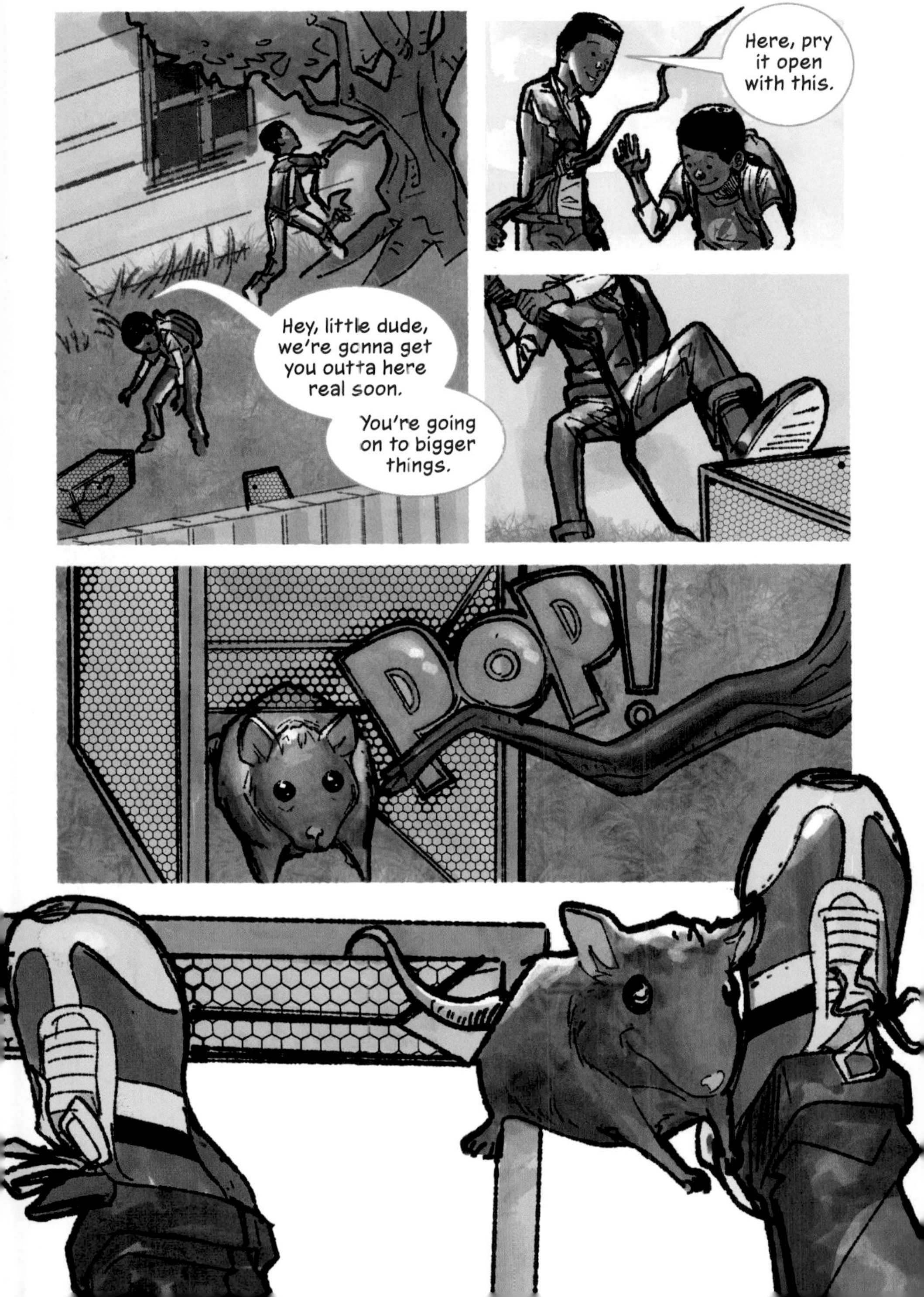
Hey, little dude, we're gonna get you outta here real soon.
You're going on to bigger things.
Here, pry it open with this.
POP!

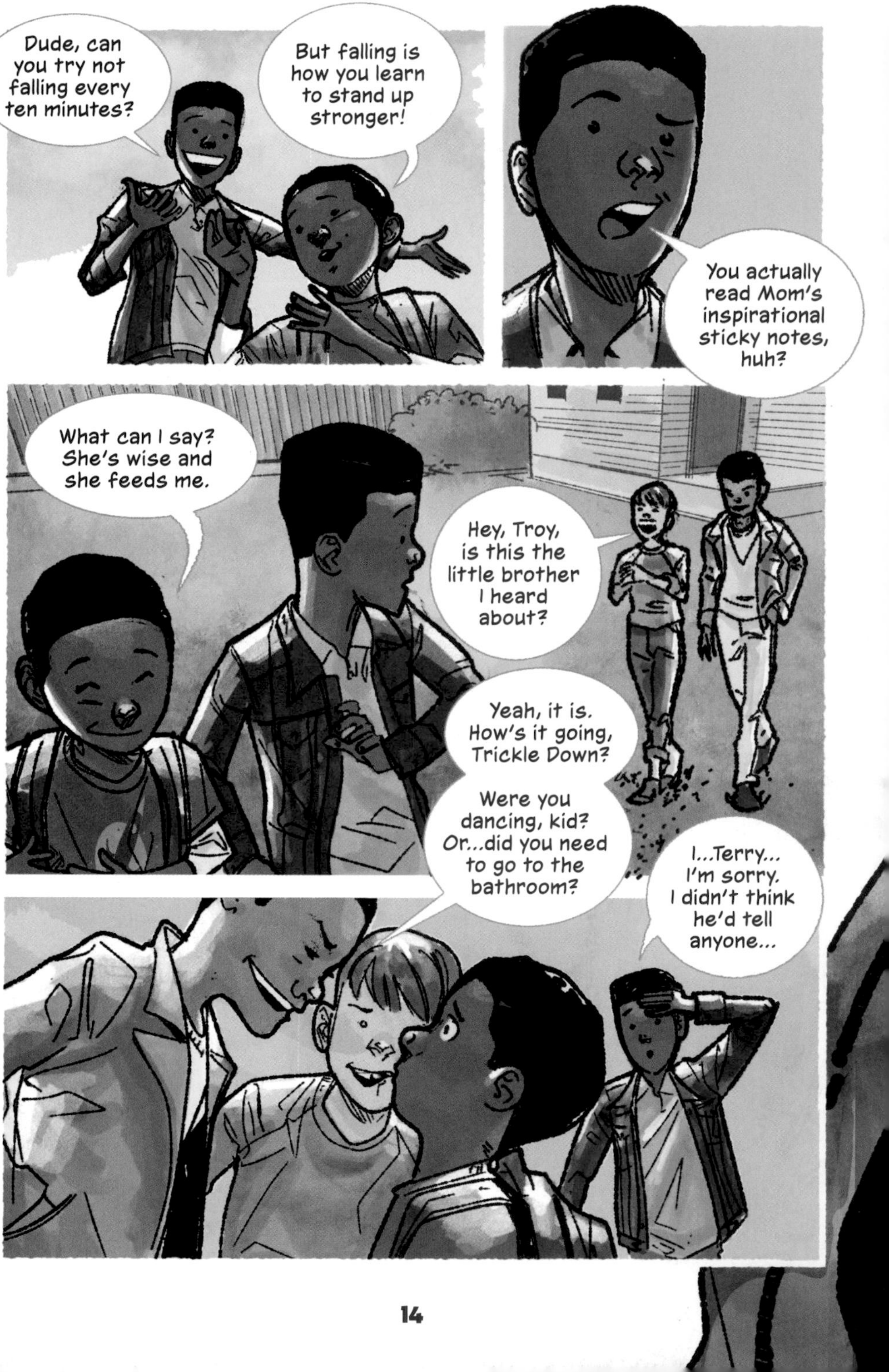
Dude, can you try not falling every ten minutes?
But falling is how you learn to stand up stronger!
You actually read Mom's inspirational sticky notes, huh?
What can I say? She's wise and she feeds me.
Hey, Troy, is this the little brother I heard about?
Yeah, it is. How's it going, Trickle Down?
Were you dancing, kid? Or...did you need to go to the bathroom?
I...Terry... I'm sorry. I didn't think he'd tell anyone...

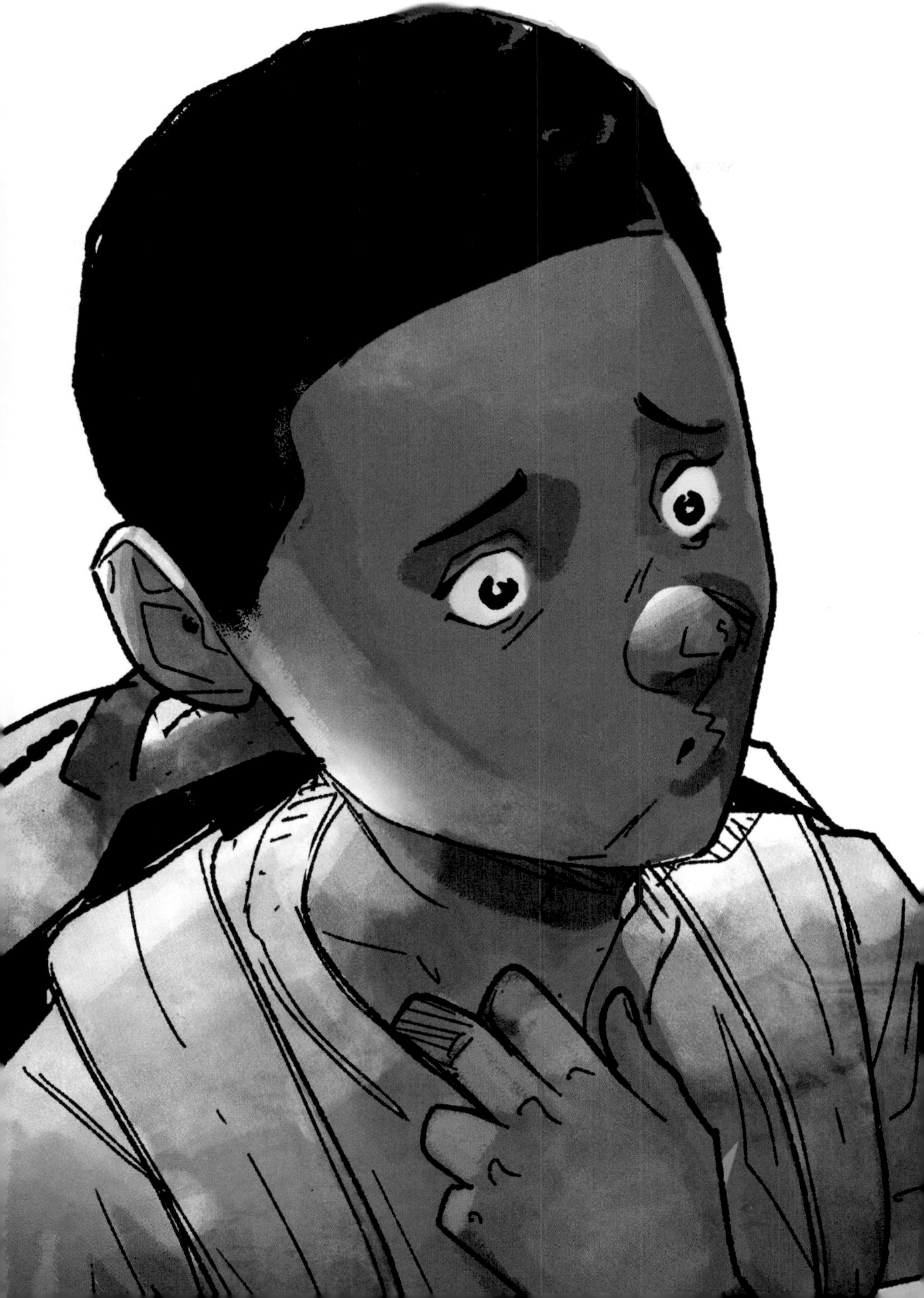

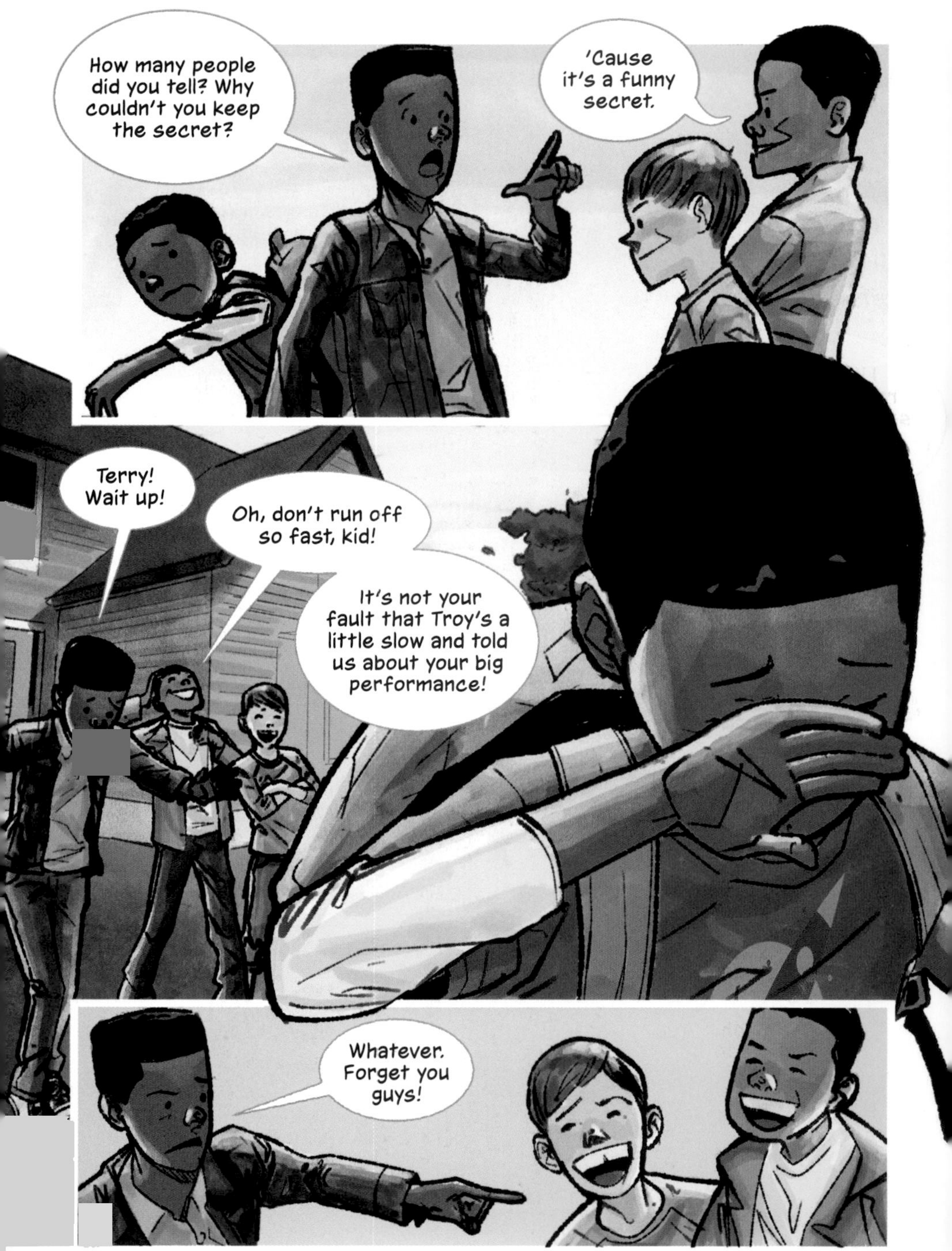
How many people did you tell? Why couldn't you keep the secret?
'Cause it's a funny secret.
Terry! Wait up!
Oh, don't run off so fast, kid!
It's not your fault that Troy's a little slow and told us about your big performance!
Whatever. Forget you guys!

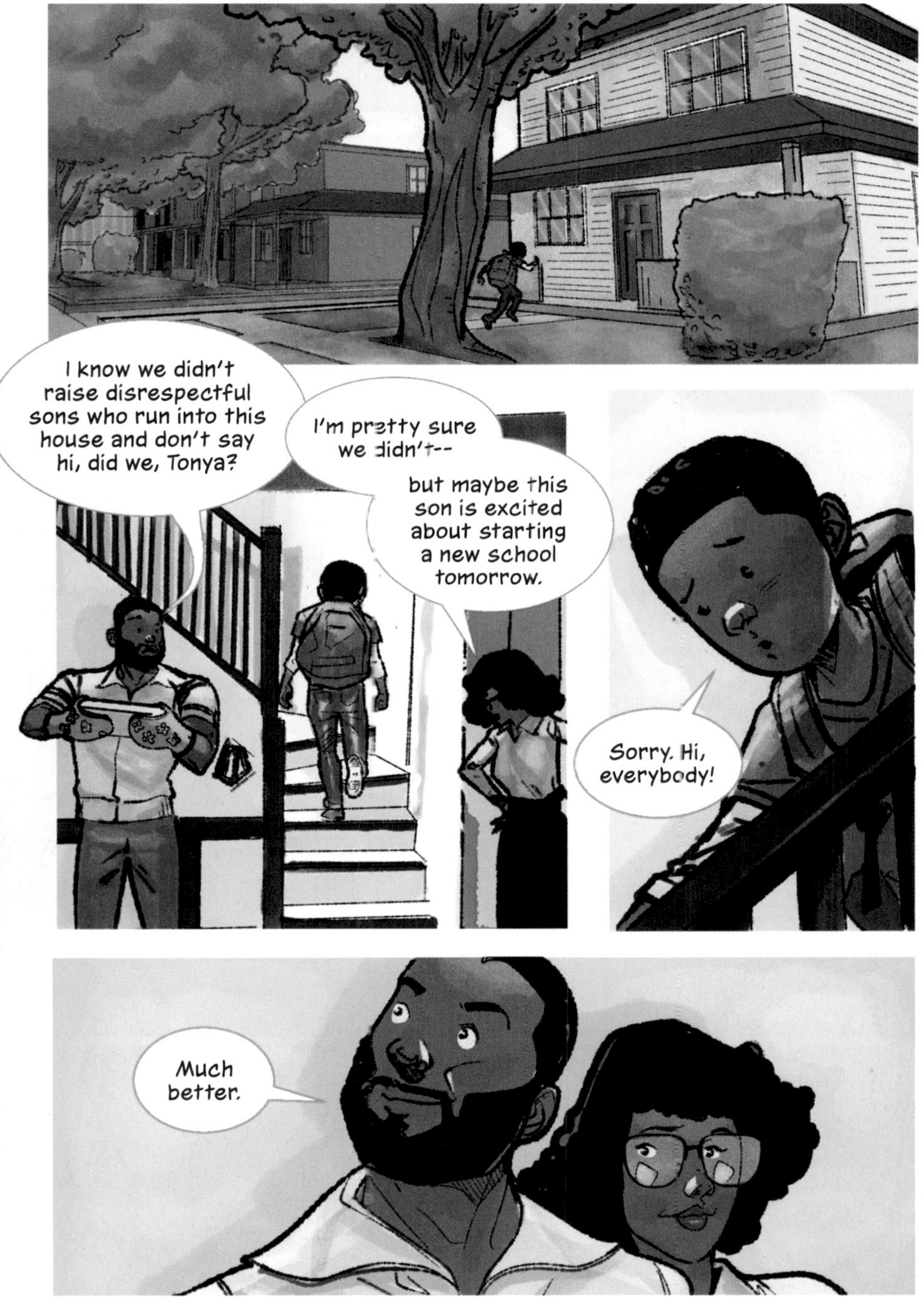

I know we didn't raise disrespectful sons who run into this house and don't say hi, did we, Tonya?
I'm pretty sure we didn't--
but maybe this son is excited about starting a new school tomorrow.
Sorry. Hi, everybody!
Much better.

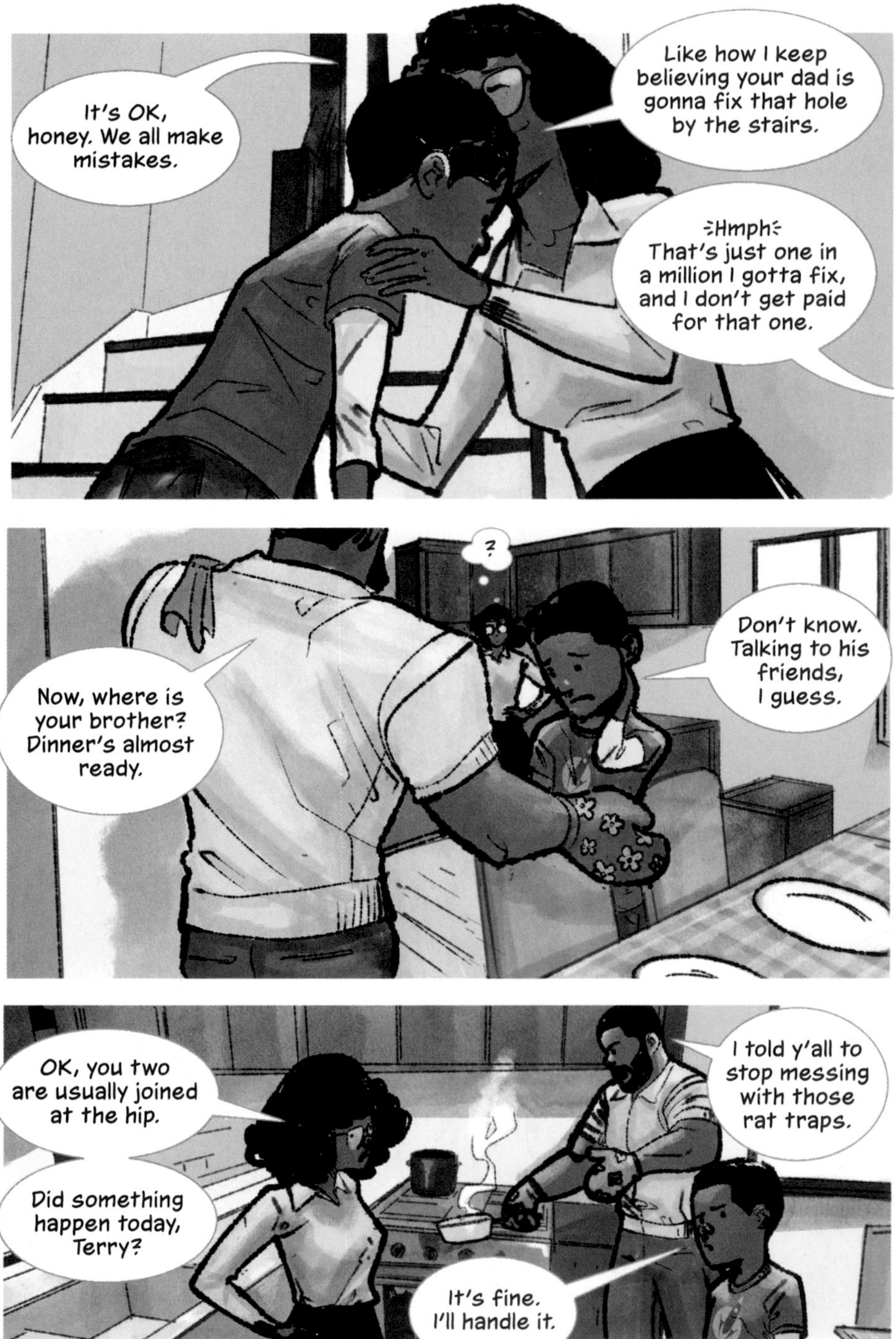
It's OK, honey. We all make mistakes.
Like how I keep believing your dad is gonna fix that hole by the stairs.
Hmph
That's just one in a million I gotta fix, and I don't get paid for that one.
?
Now, where is your brother? Dinner's almost ready.
Don't know. Talking to his friends, I guess.
OK, you two are usually joined at the hip.
Did something happen today, Terry?
I told y'all to stop messing with those rat traps.
It's fine. I'll handle it.

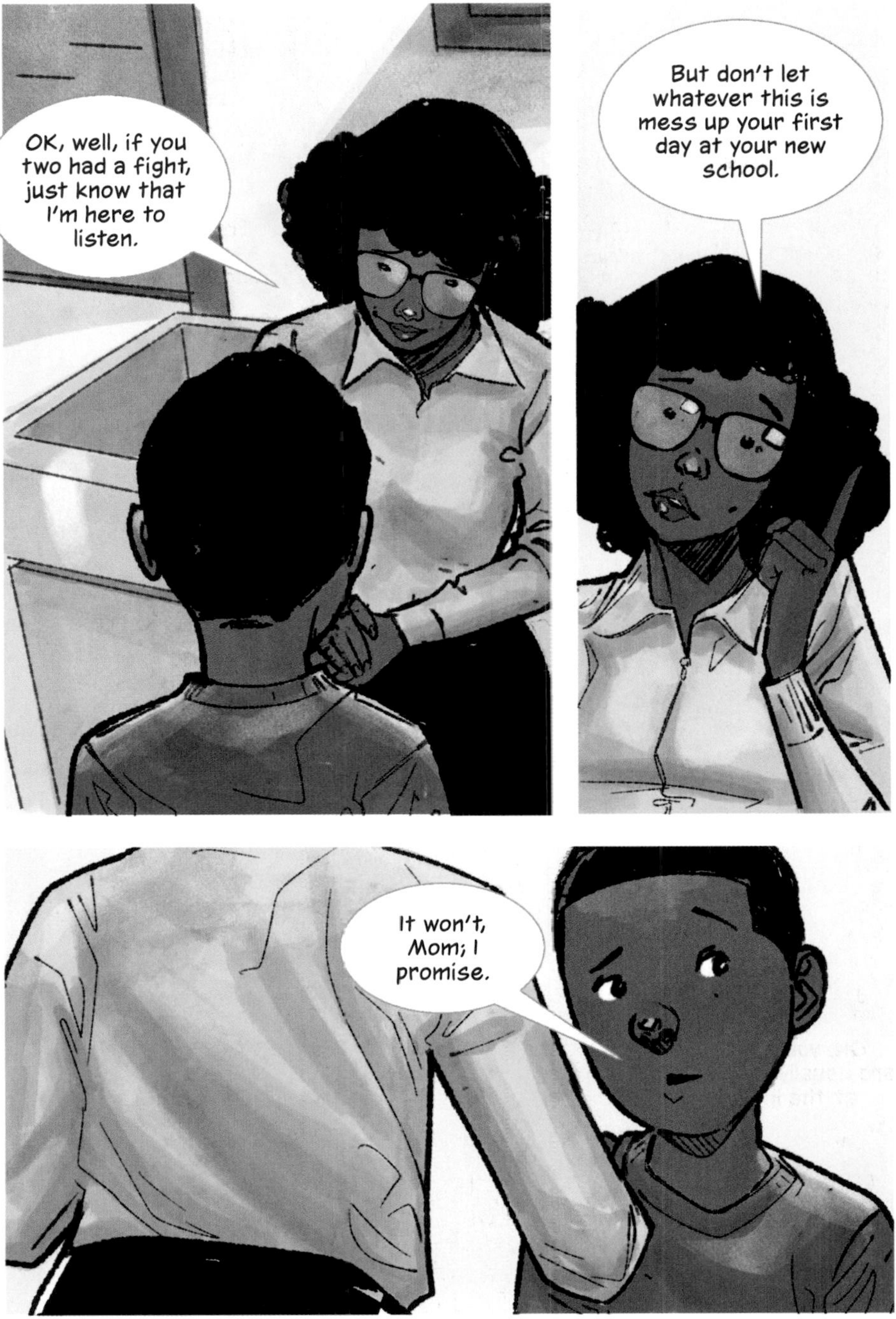
OK, well, if you two had a fight, just know that I'm here to listen.
But don't let whatever this is mess up your first day at your new school.
It won't, Mom; I promise.

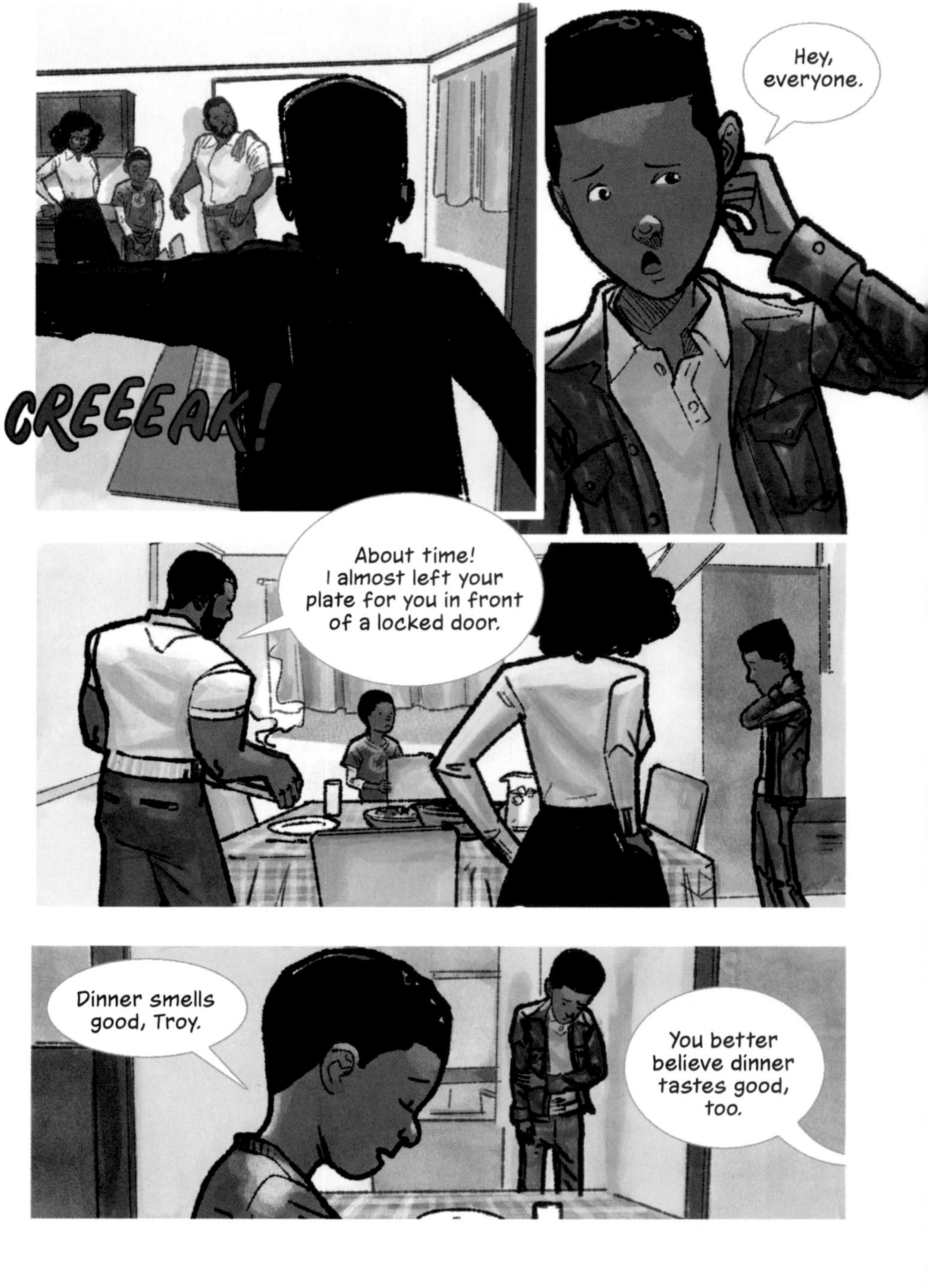
CREEEAK!
Hey, everyone.
About time! I almost left your plate for you in front of a locked door.
Dinner smells good, Troy.
You better believe dinner tastes good, too.

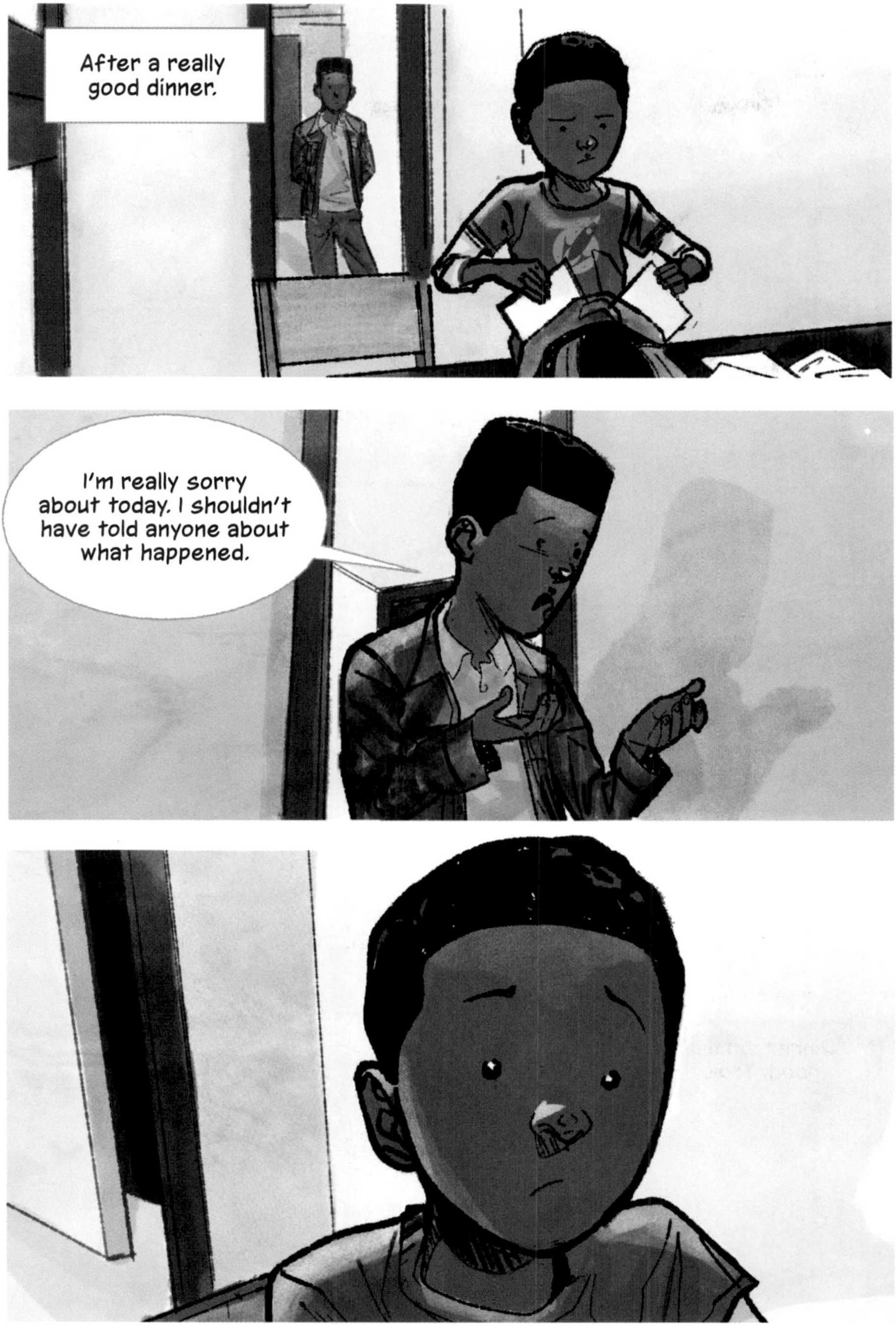
After a really good dinner.
I'm really sorry about today. I shouldn't have told anyone about what happened.

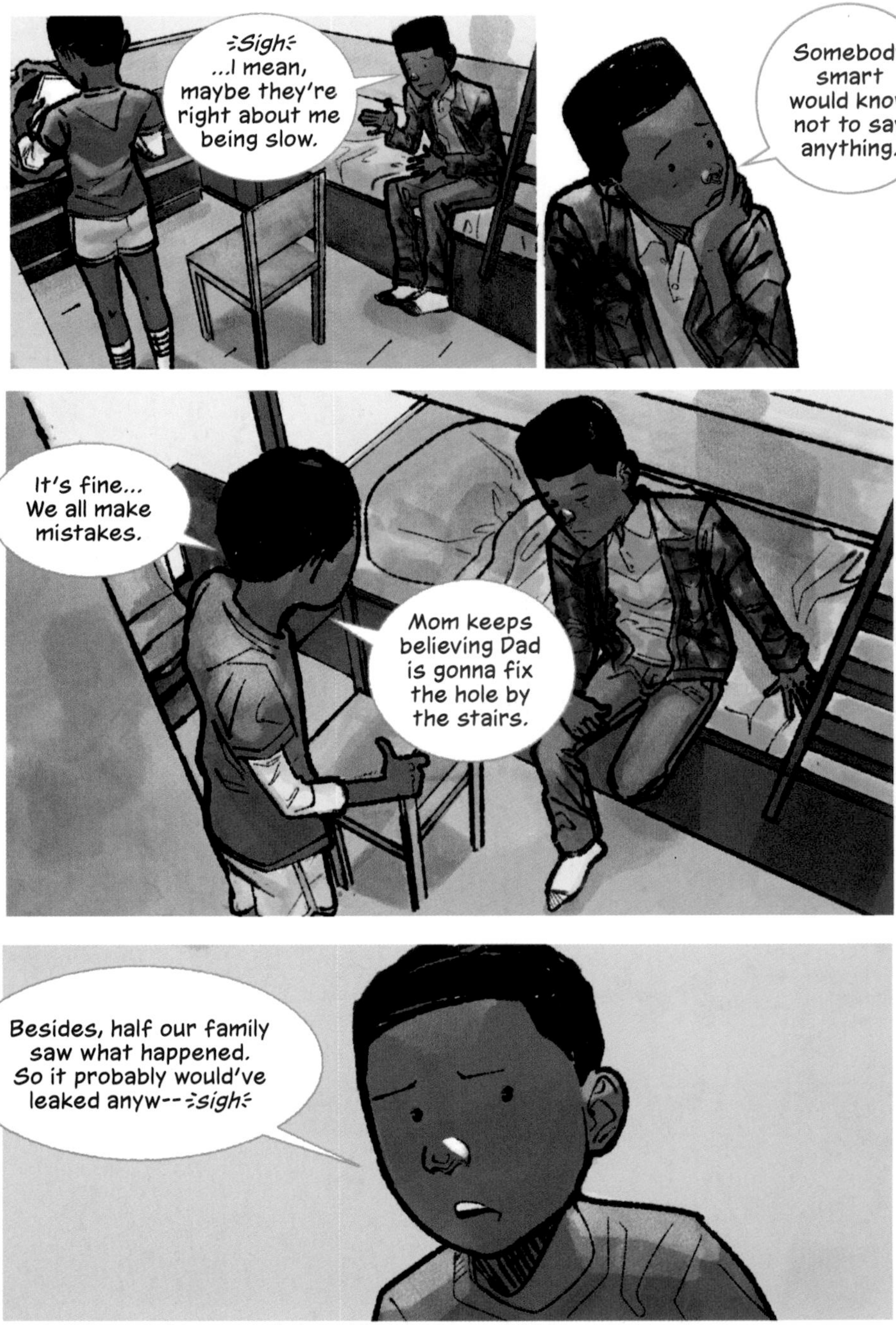

⁼Sigh⁼ ...I mean, maybe they're right about me being slow.
Somebody smart would know not to say anything.
It's fine... We all make mistakes.
Mom keeps believing Dad is gonna fix the hole by the stairs.
Besides, half our family saw what happened. So it probably would've leaked anyw-- ⁼sigh⁼

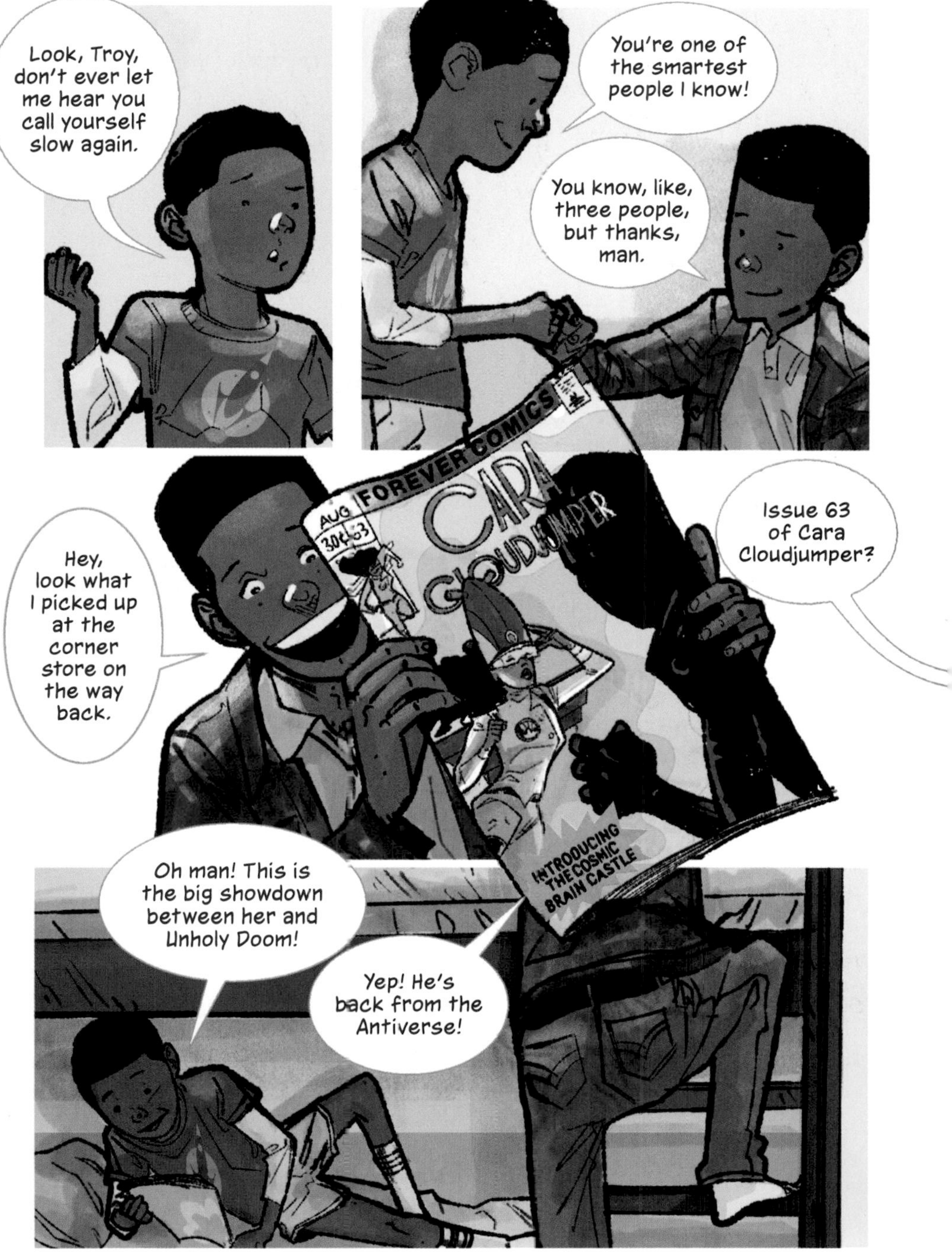
Look, Troy, don't ever let me hear you call yourself slow again.
You're one of the smartest people I know!
You know, like, three people, but thanks, man.
Hey, look what I picked up at the corner store on the way back.
FOREVER COMICS
AUG
CARA CLOUDJUMPER
INTRODUCING THE COSMIC BRAIN CASTLE
Issue 63 of Cara Cloudjumper?
Oh man! This is the big showdown between her and Unholy Doom!
Yep! He's back from the Antiverse!

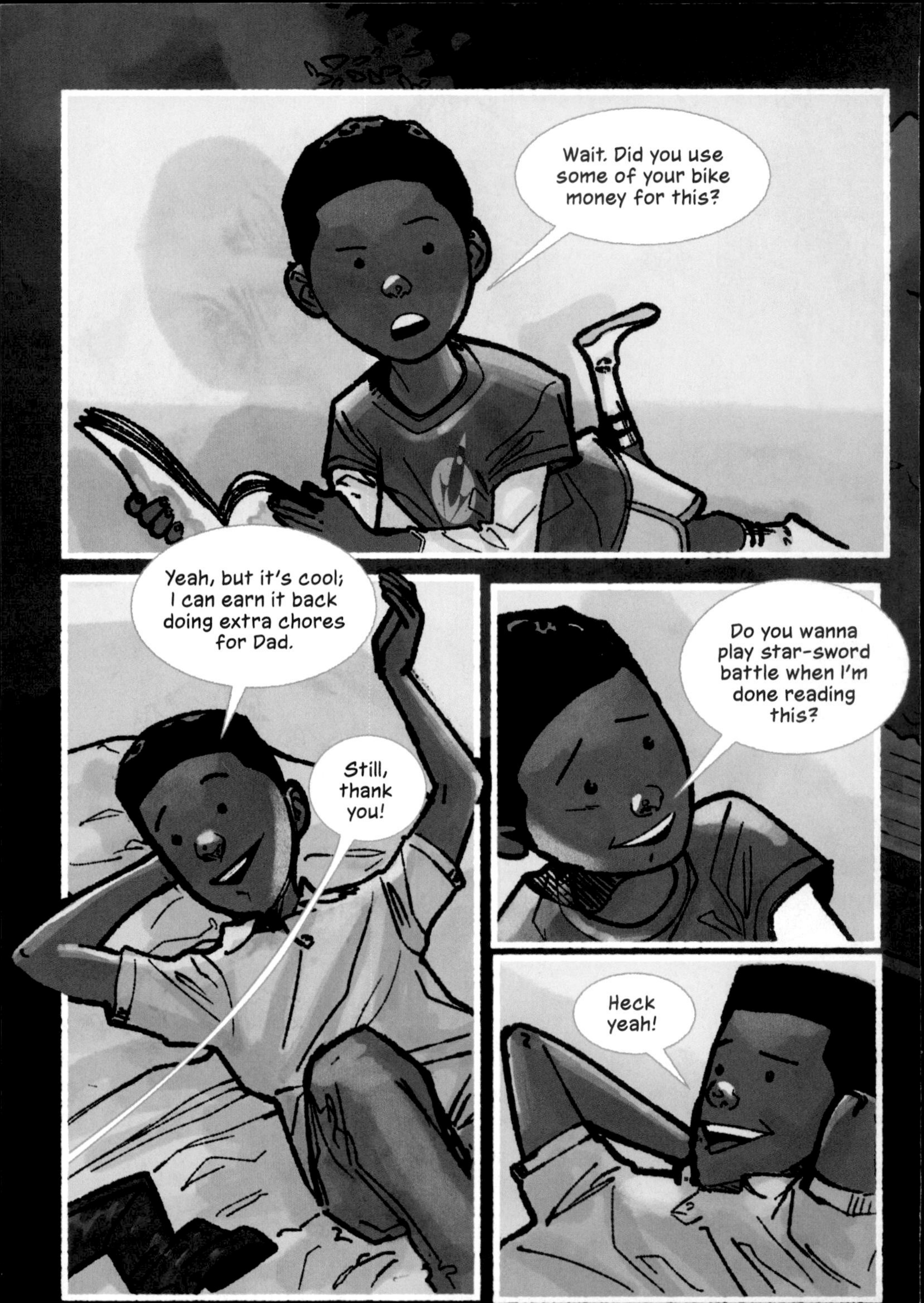
Wait. Did you use some of your bike money for this?
Yeah, but it's cool; I can earn it back doing extra chores for Dad.
Still, thank you!
Do you wanna play star-sword battle when I'm done reading this?
Heck yeah!

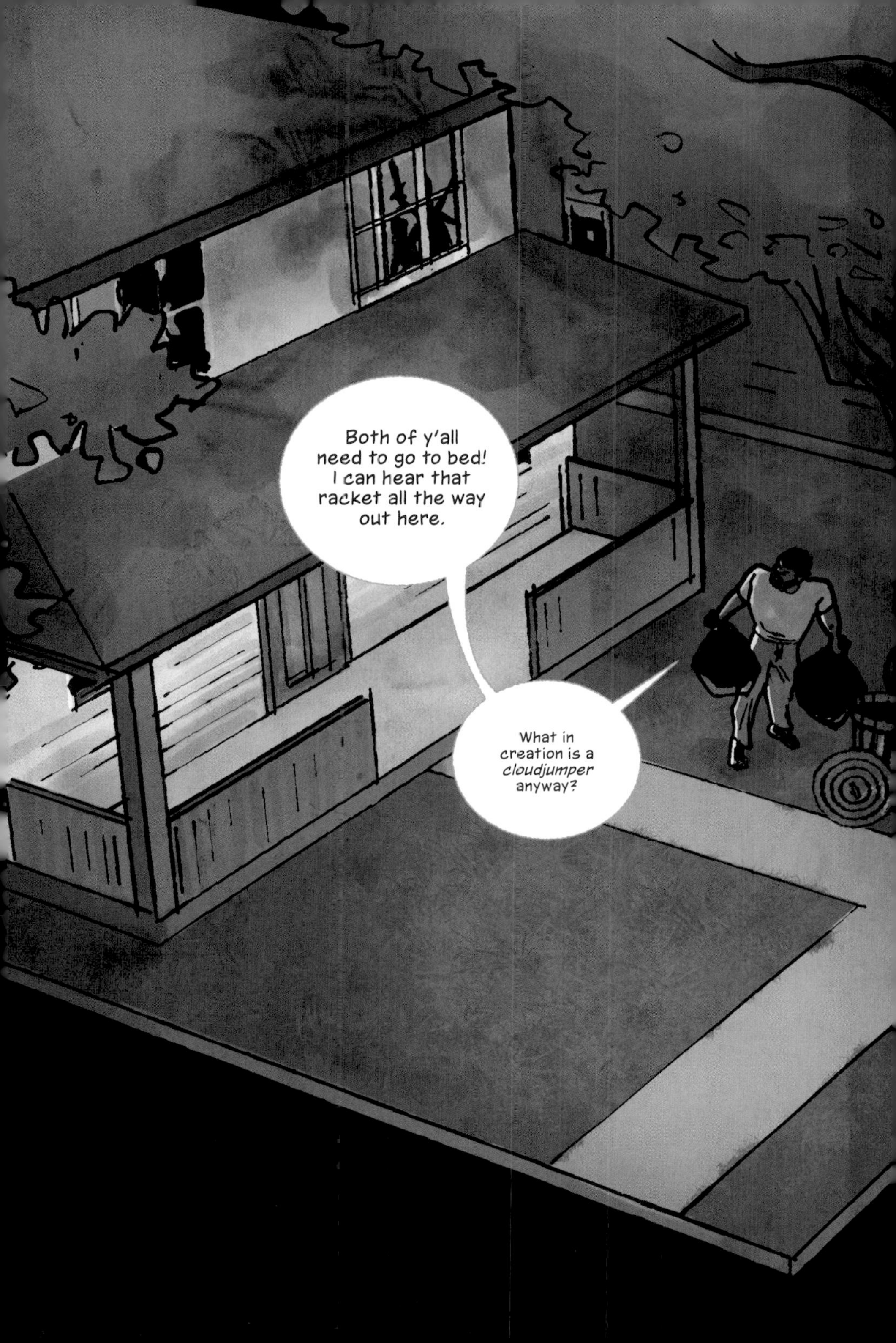
Both of y'all need to go to bed! I can hear that racket all the way out here.
What in creation is a *cloudjumper* anyway?

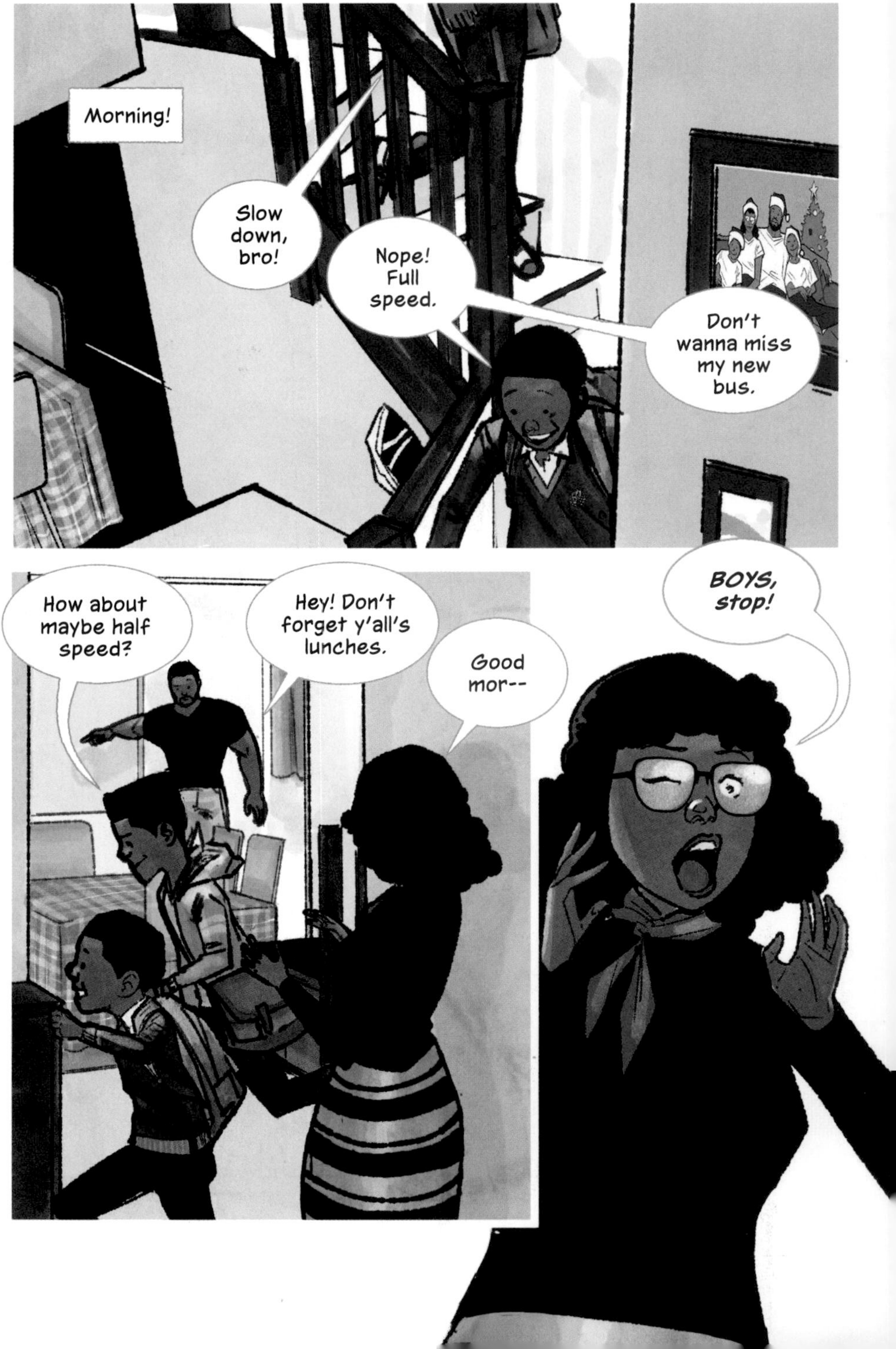
Morning!
Slow down, bro!
Nope! Full speed.
Don't wanna miss my new bus.
How about maybe half speed?
Hey! Don't forget y'all's lunches.
Good mor--
BOYS, stop!

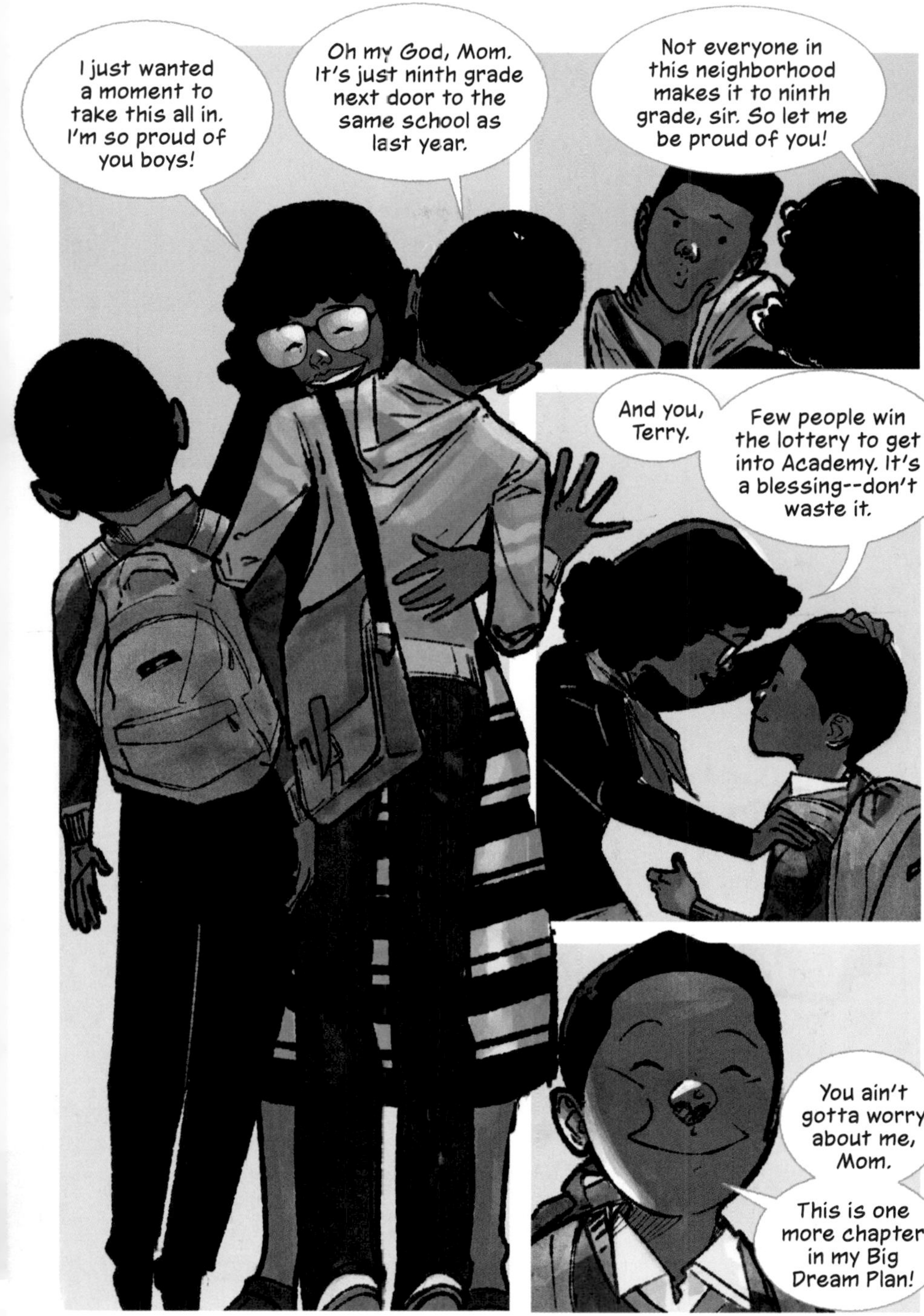

I just wanted a moment to take this all in. I'm so proud of you boys!
Oh my God, Mom. It's just ninth grade next door to the same school as last year.
Not everyone in this neighborhood makes it to ninth grade, sir. So let me be proud of you!
And you, Terry.
Few people win the lottery to get into Academy. It's a blessing--don't waste it.
You ain't gotta worry about me, Mom.
This is one more chapter in my Big Dream Plan!

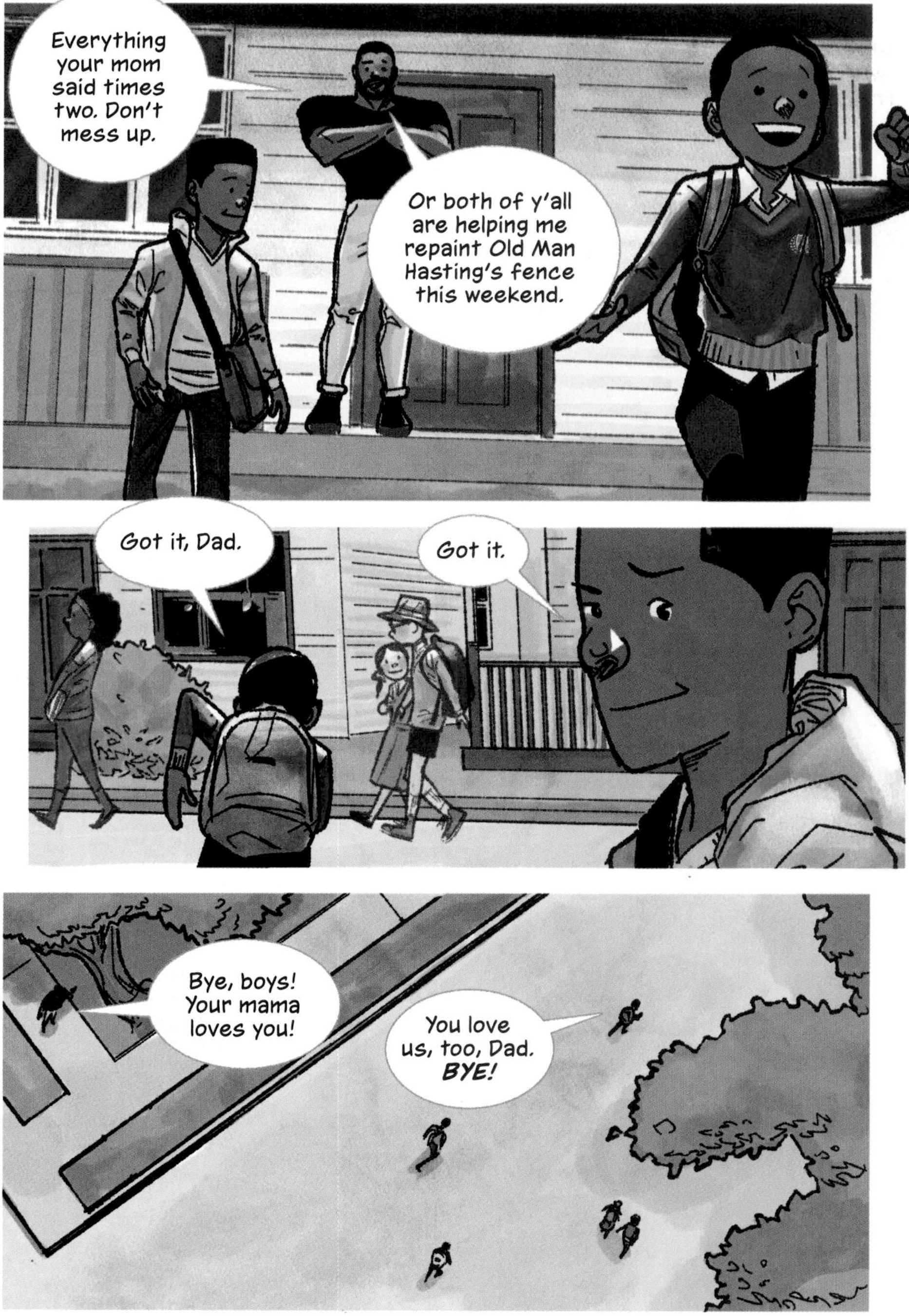
Everything your mom said times two. Don't mess up.
Or both of y'all are helping me repaint Old Man Hasting's fence this weekend.
Got it, Dad.
Got it.
Bye, boys! Your mama loves you!
You love us, too, Dad. *BYE!*

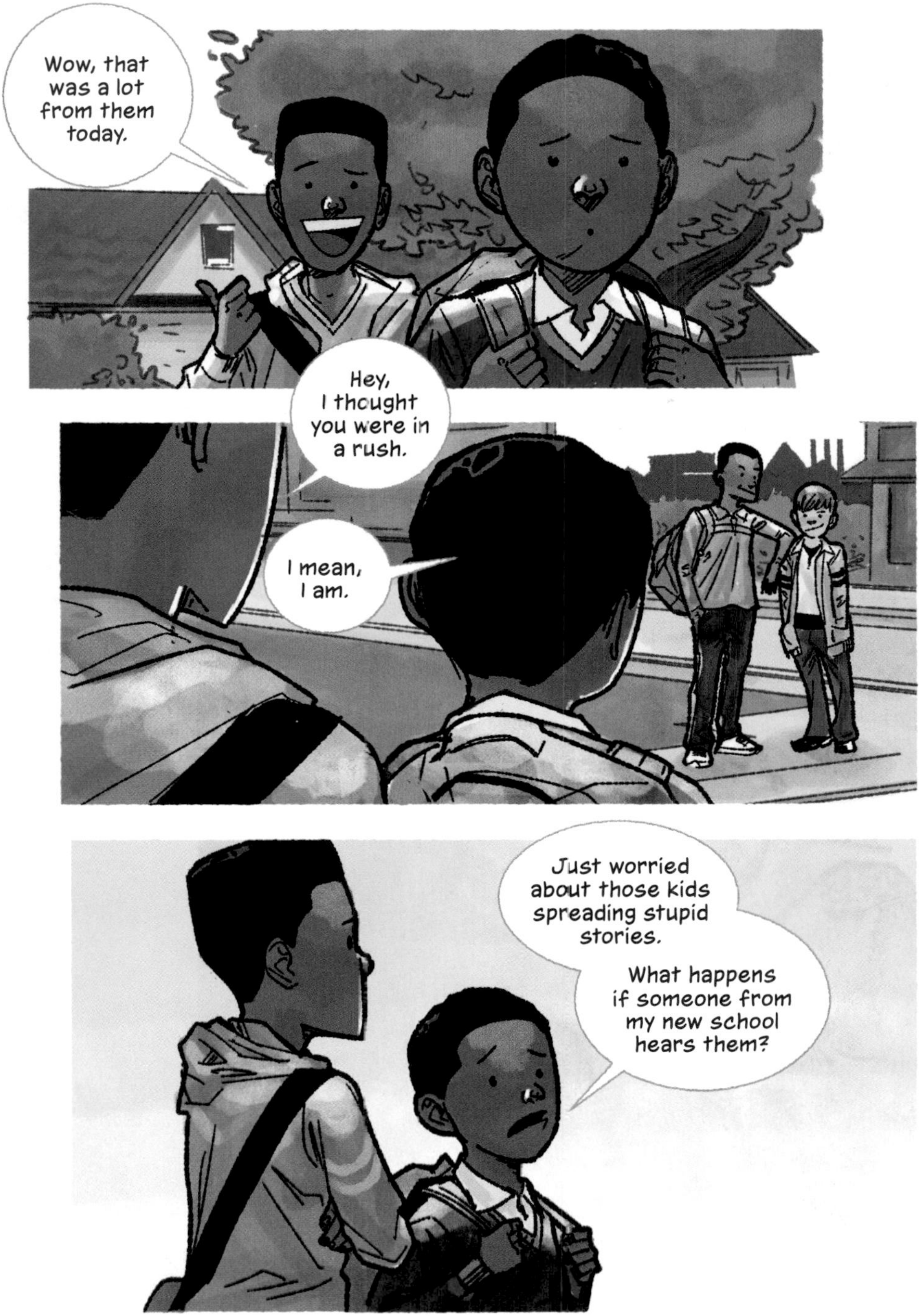
Wow, that was a lot from them today.
Hey, I thought you were in a rush.
I mean, I am.
Just worried about those kids spreading stupid stories.
What happens if someone from my new school hears them?

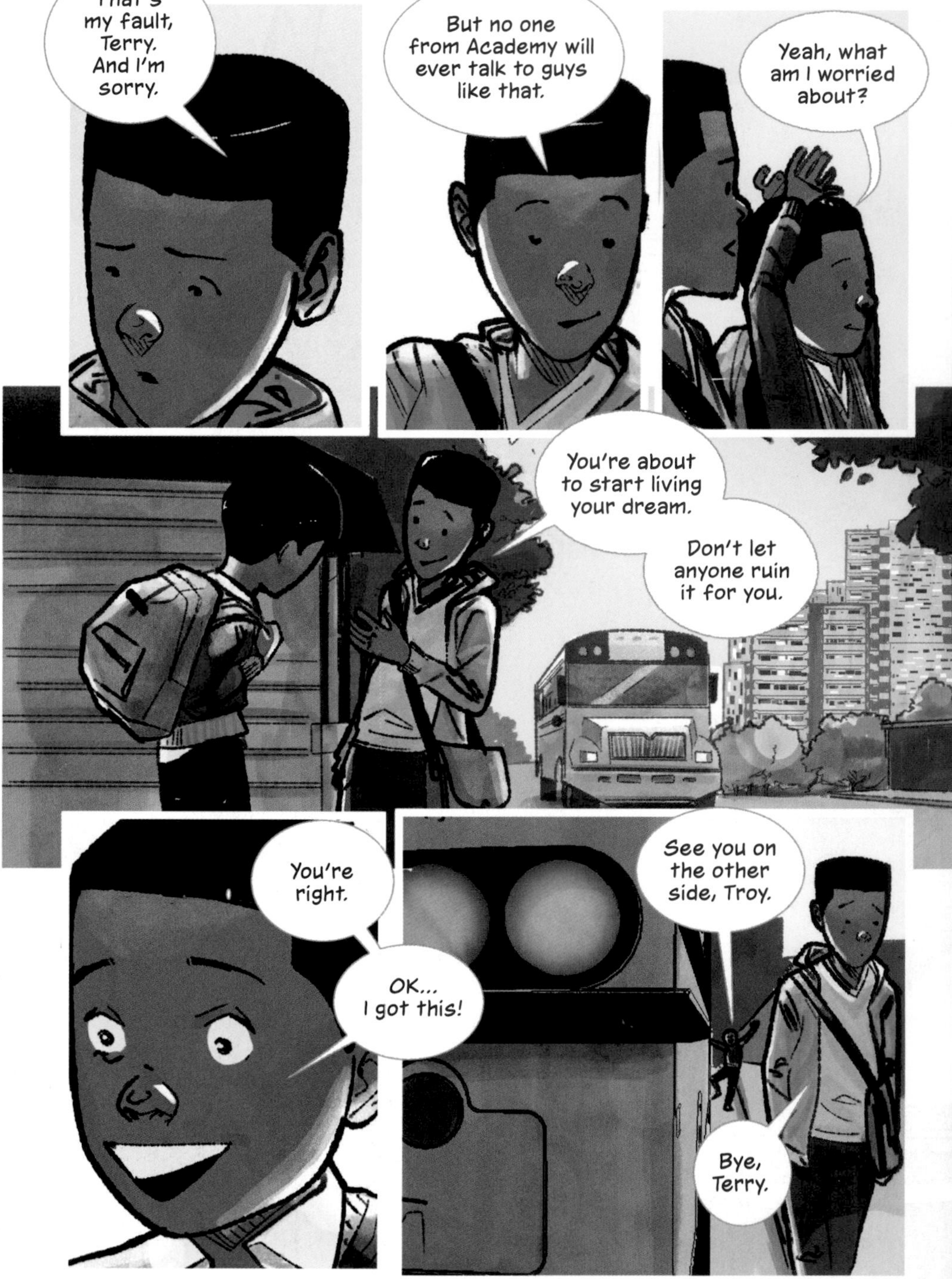
That's my fault, Terry. And I'm sorry.
But no one from Academy will ever talk to guys like that.
Yeah, what am I worried about?
You're about to start living your dream.
Don't let anyone ruin it for you.
You're right.
OK... I got this!
See you on the other side, Troy.
Bye, Terry.

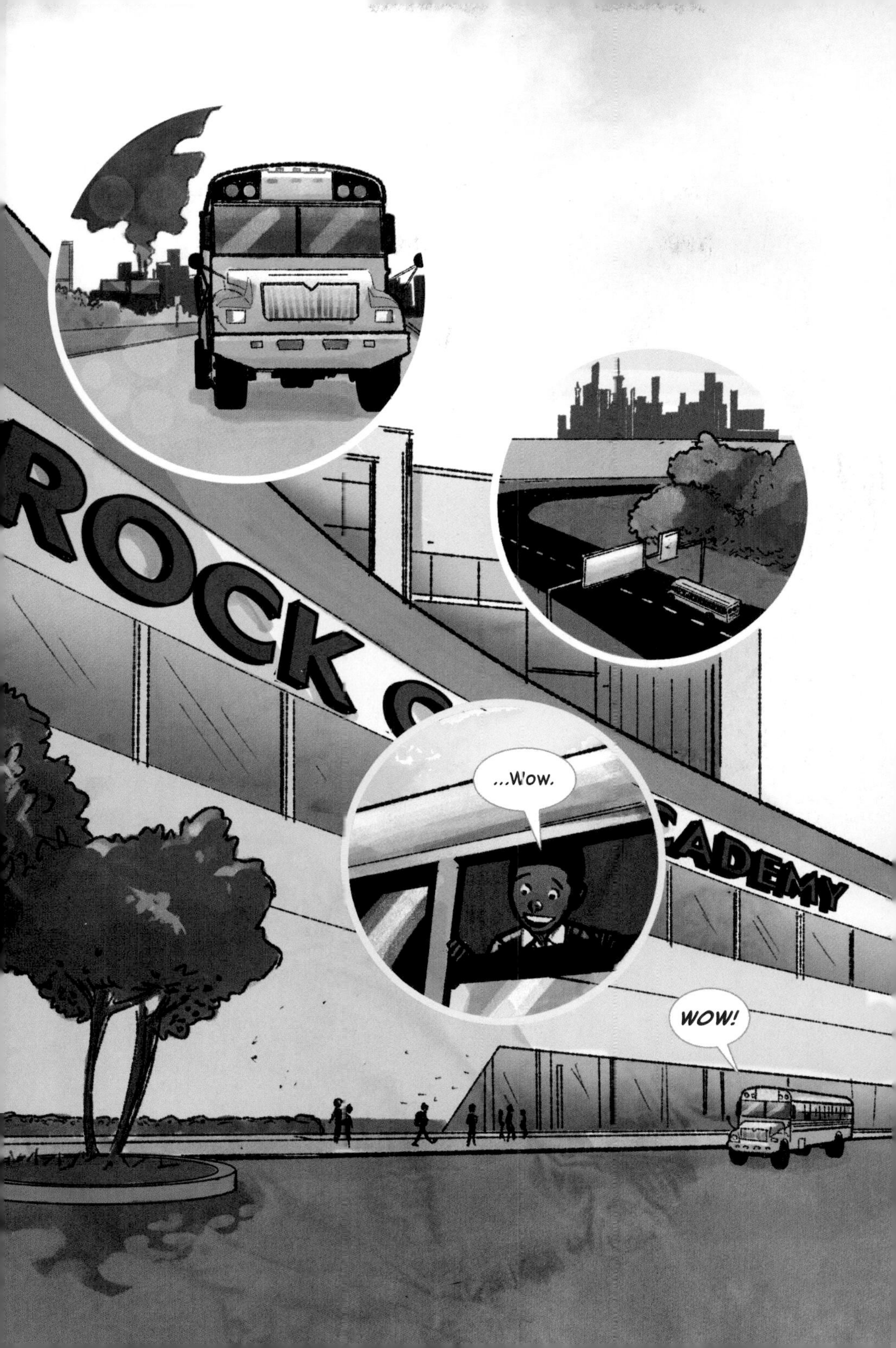
ROCK
...Wow.
WOW!

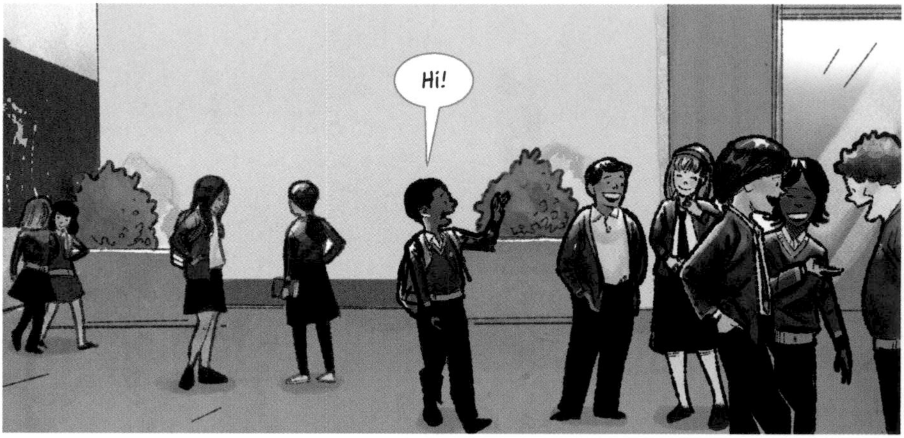
Hi!

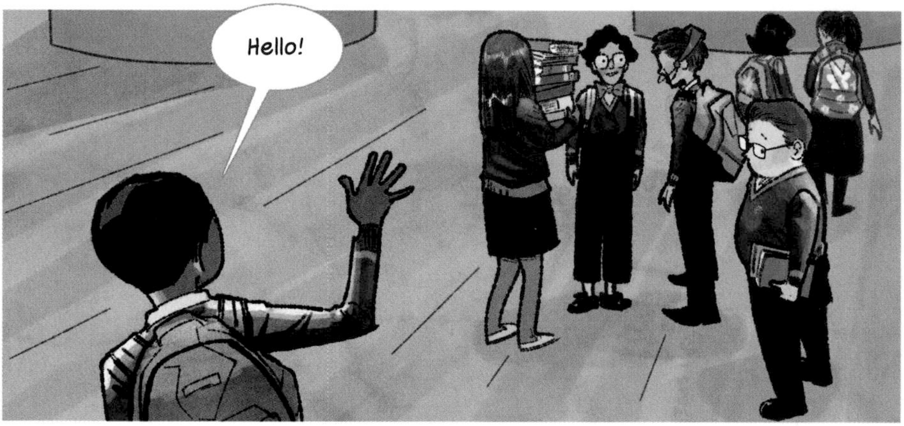
Hello!

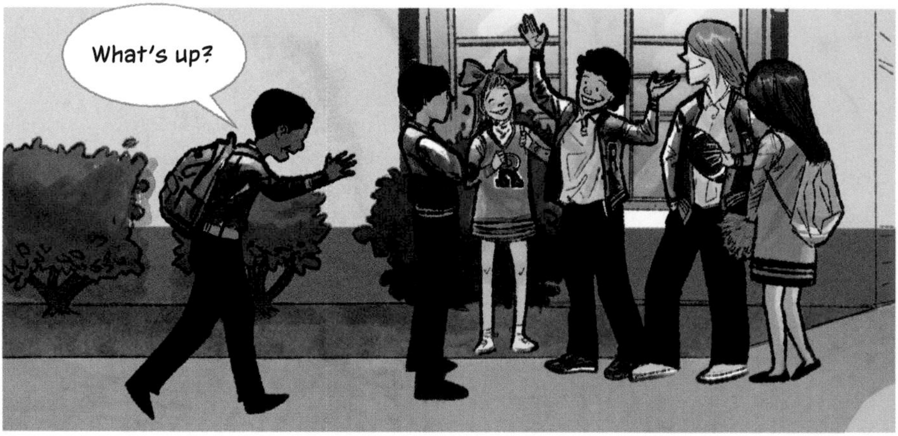
What's up?

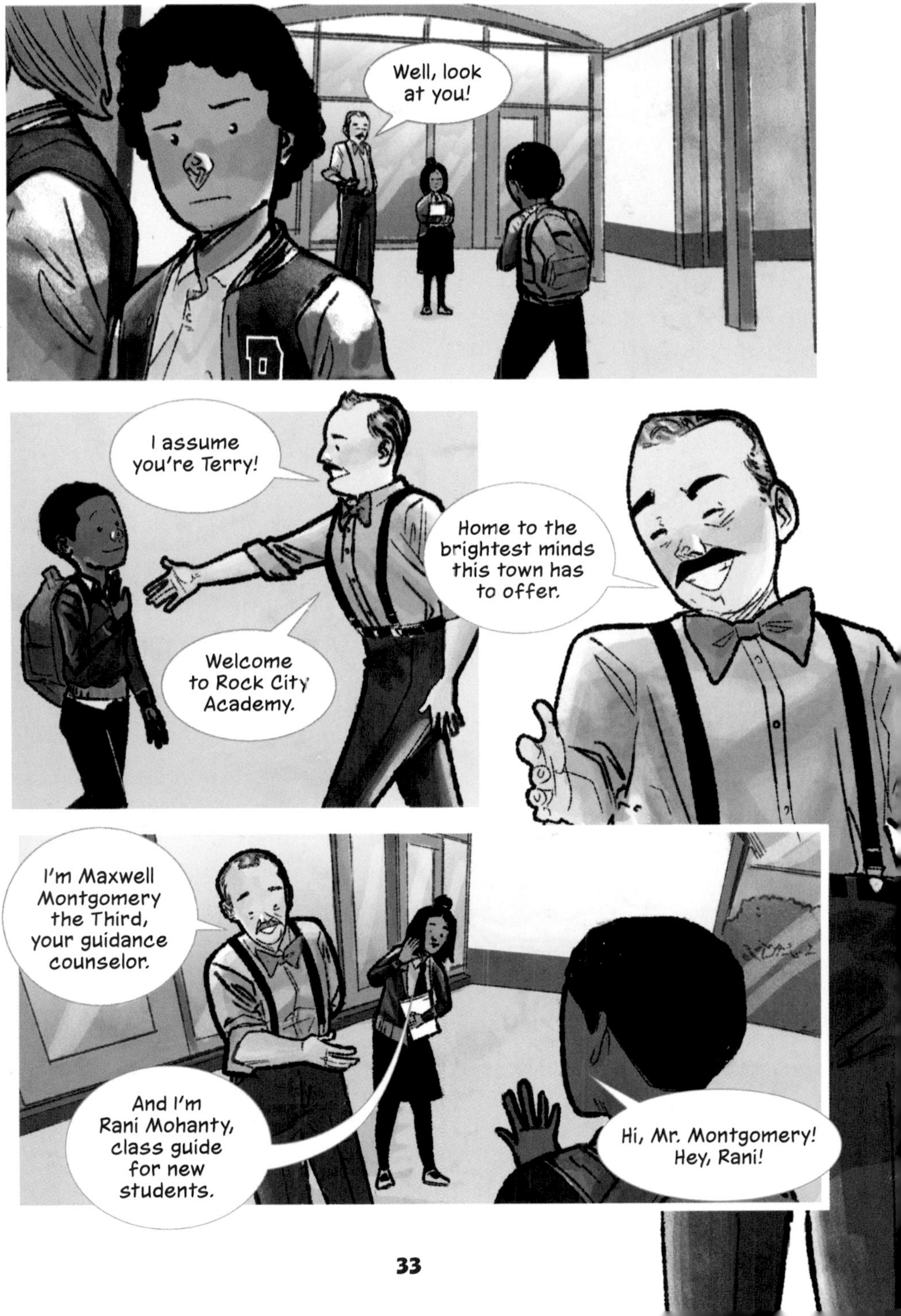

Well, look at you!
I assume you're Terry!
Welcome to Rock City Academy.
Home to the brightest minds this town has to offer.
I'm Maxwell Montgomery the Third, your guidance counselor.
And I'm Rani Mohanty, class guide for new students.
Hi, Mr. Montgomery! Hey, Rani!

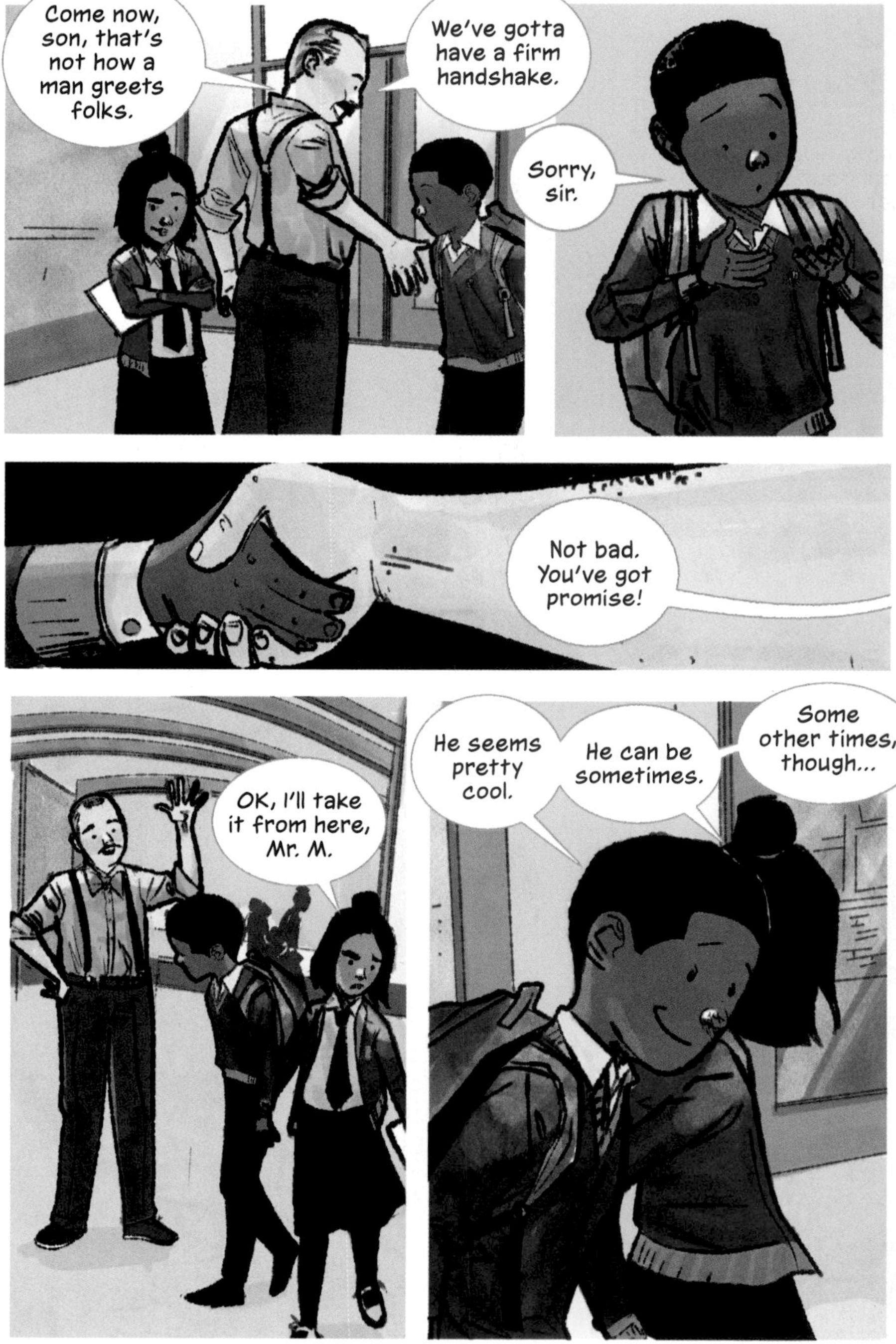
Come now, son, that's not how a man greets folks.
We've gotta have a firm handshake.
Sorry, sir.
Not bad. You've got promise!
OK, I'll take it from here, Mr. M.
He seems pretty cool.
He can be sometimes.
Some other times, though...

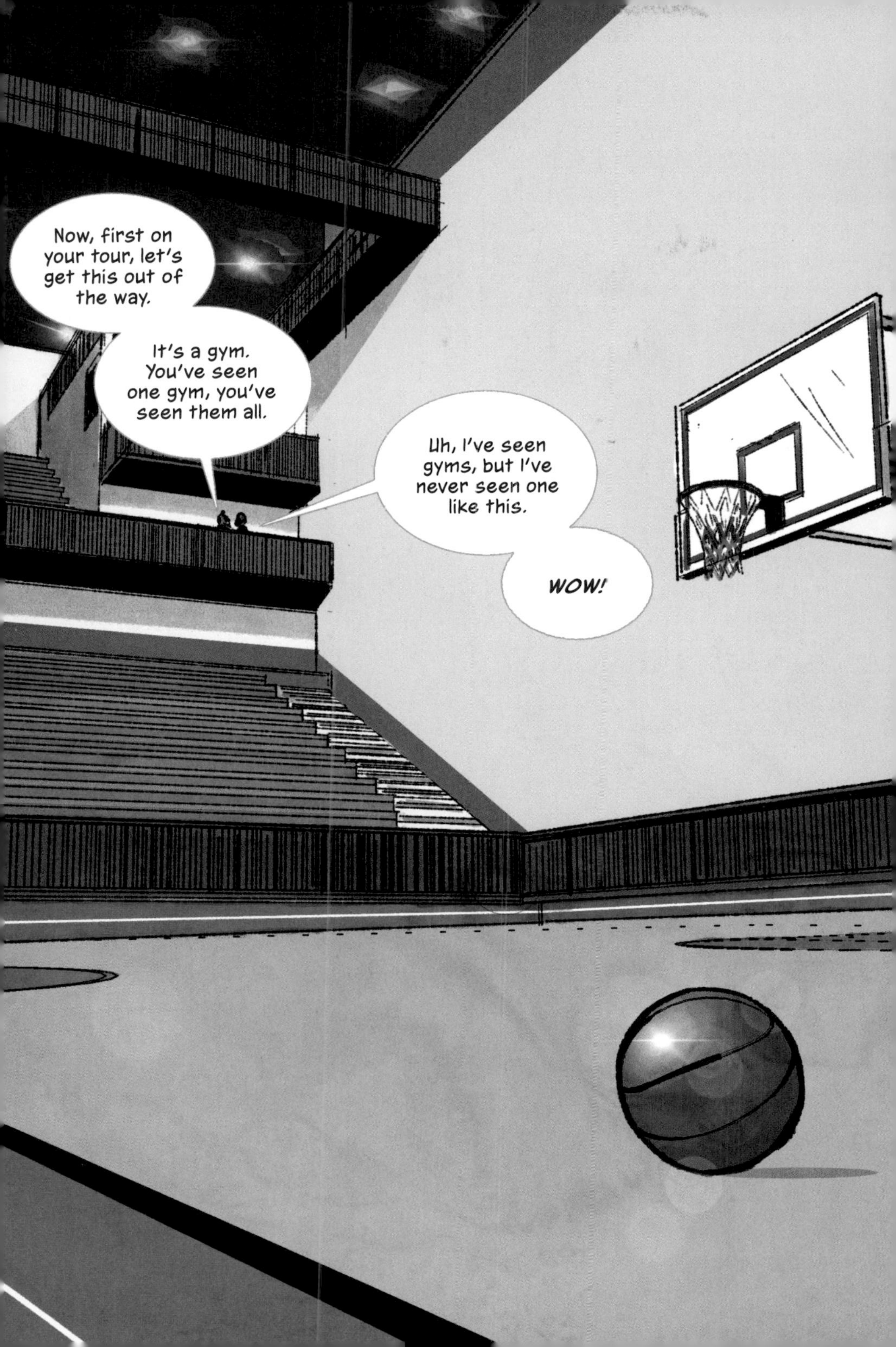
Now, first on your tour, let's get this out of the way.
It's a gym. You've seen one gym, you've seen them all.
Uh, I've seen gyms, but I've never seen one like this.
WOW!

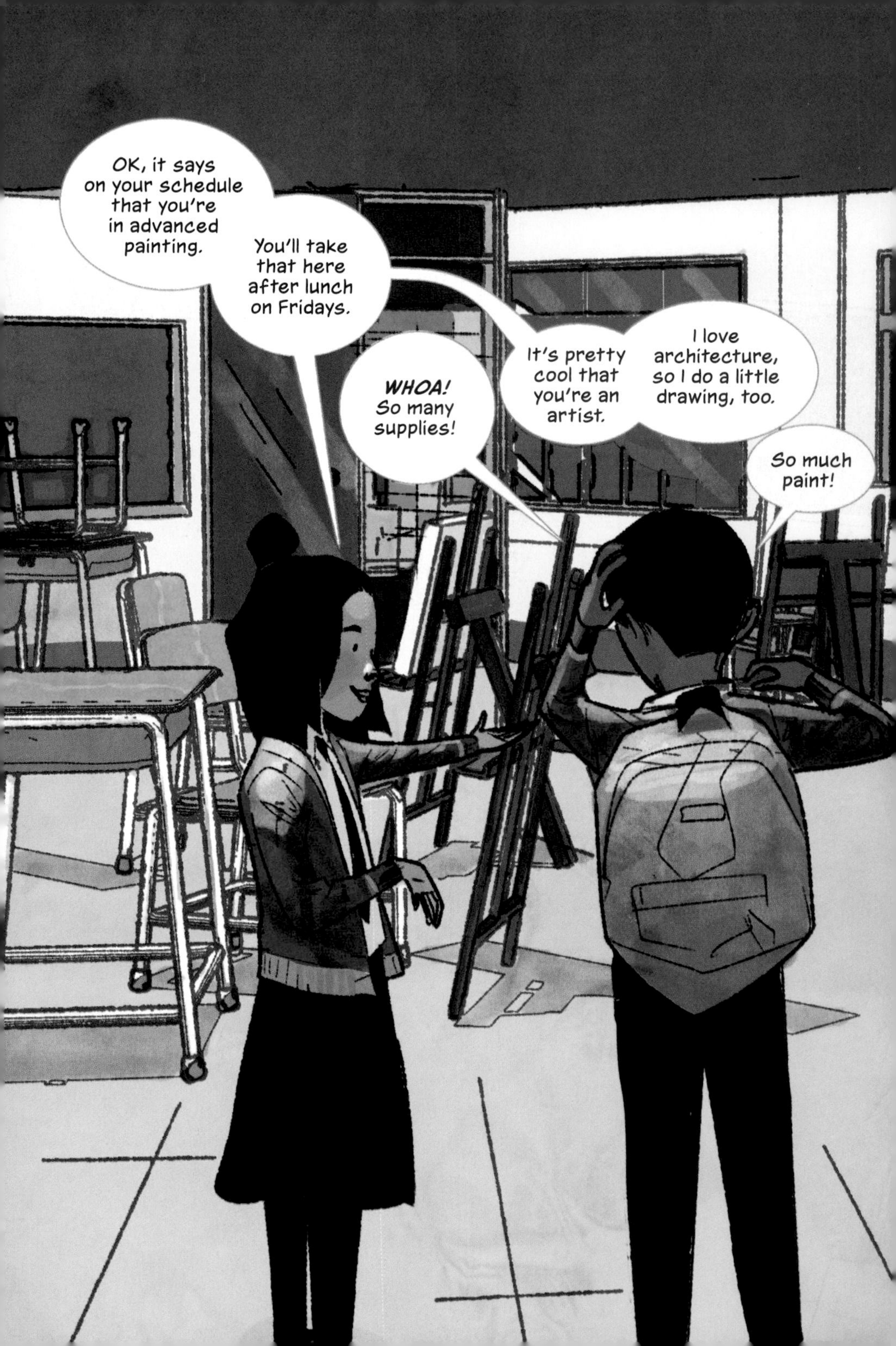
OK, it says on your schedule that you're in advanced painting.
You'll take that here after lunch on Fridays.
WHOA! So many supplies!
It's pretty cool that you're an artist.
I love architecture, so I do a little drawing, too.
So much paint!

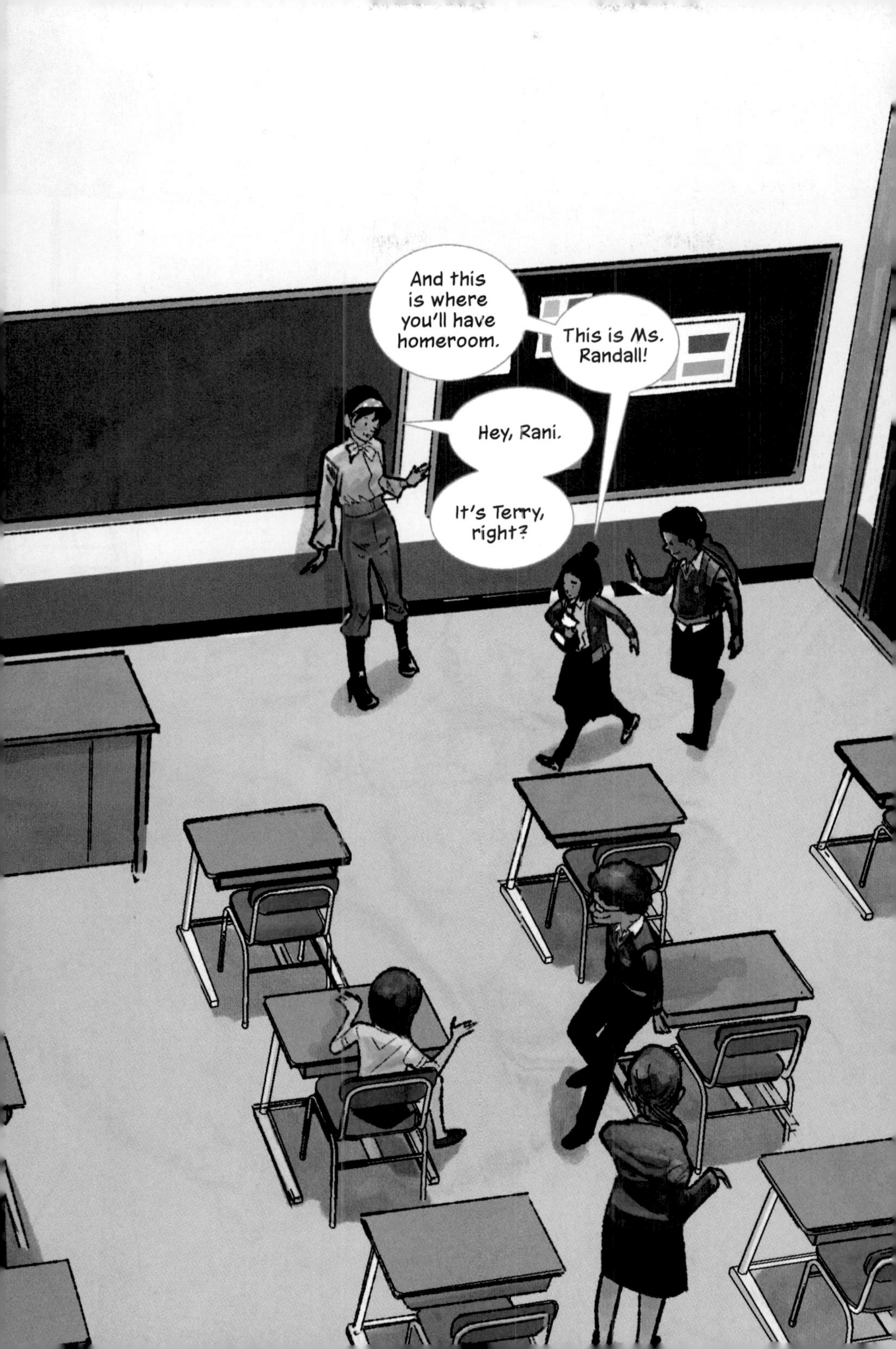
And this is where you'll have homeroom.
This is Ms. Randall!
Hey, Rani.
It's Terry, right?

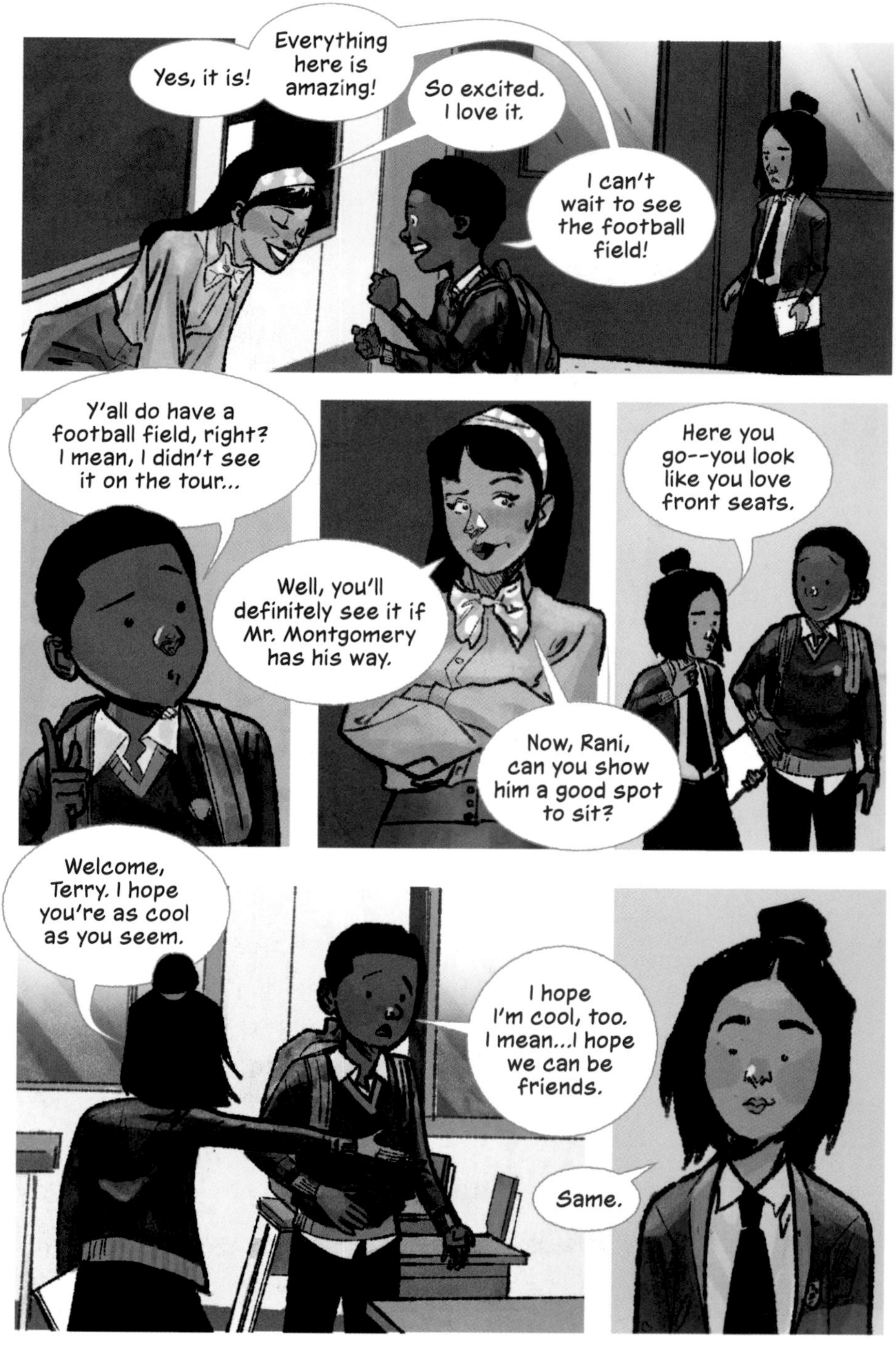
Yes, it is!
Everything here is amazing!
So excited. I love it.
I can't wait to see the football field!
Y'all do have a football field, right? I mean, I didn't see it on the tour...
Well, you'll definitely see it if Mr. Montgomery has his way.
Now, Rani, can you show him a good spot to sit?
Here you go--you look like you love front seats.
Welcome, Terry. I hope you're as cool as you seem.
I hope I'm cool, too. I mean...I hope we can be friends.
Same.

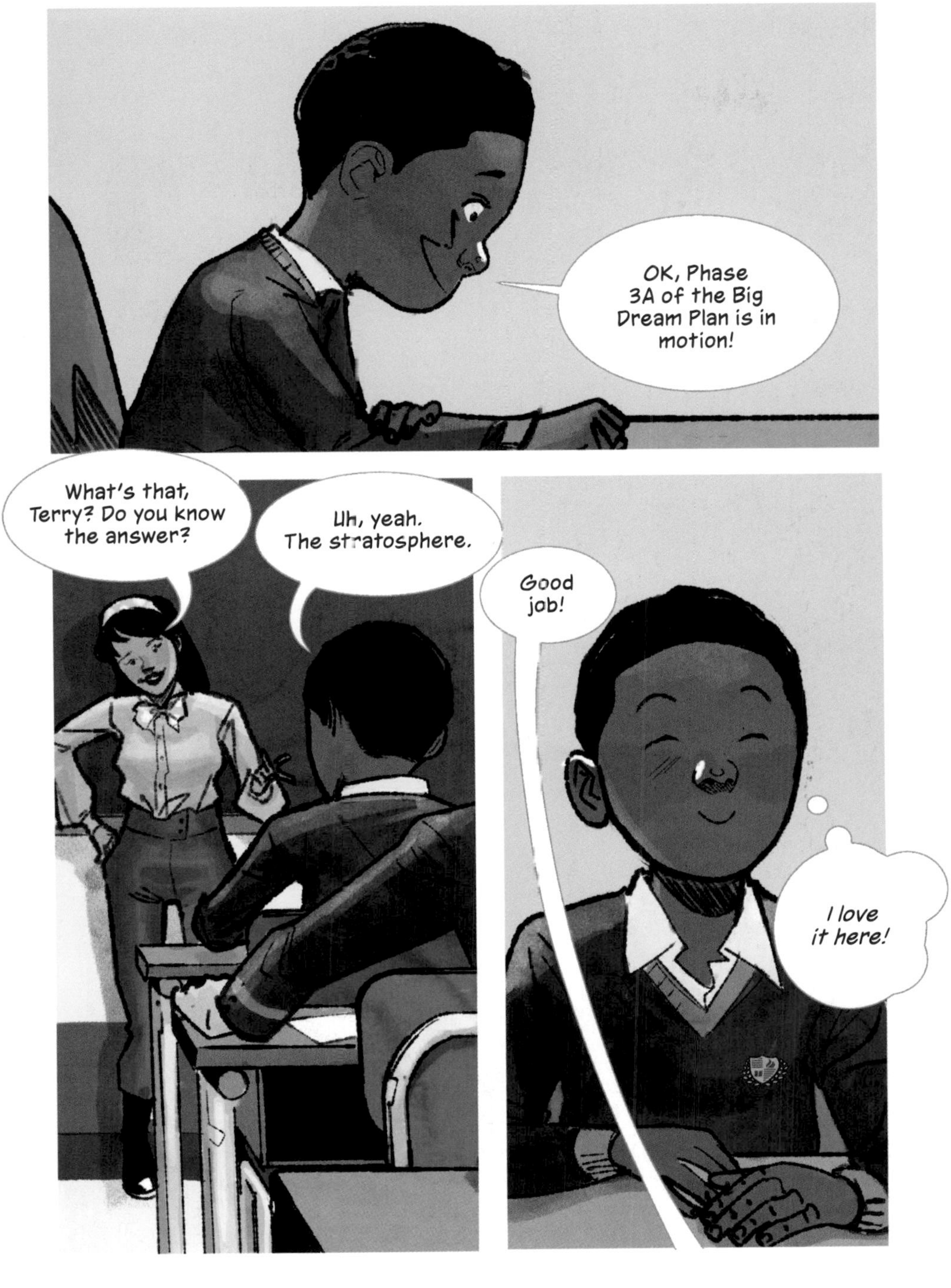
OK, Phase 3A of the Big Dream Plan is in motion!
What's that, Terry? Do you know the answer?
Uh, yeah. The stratosphere.
Good job!
I love it here!

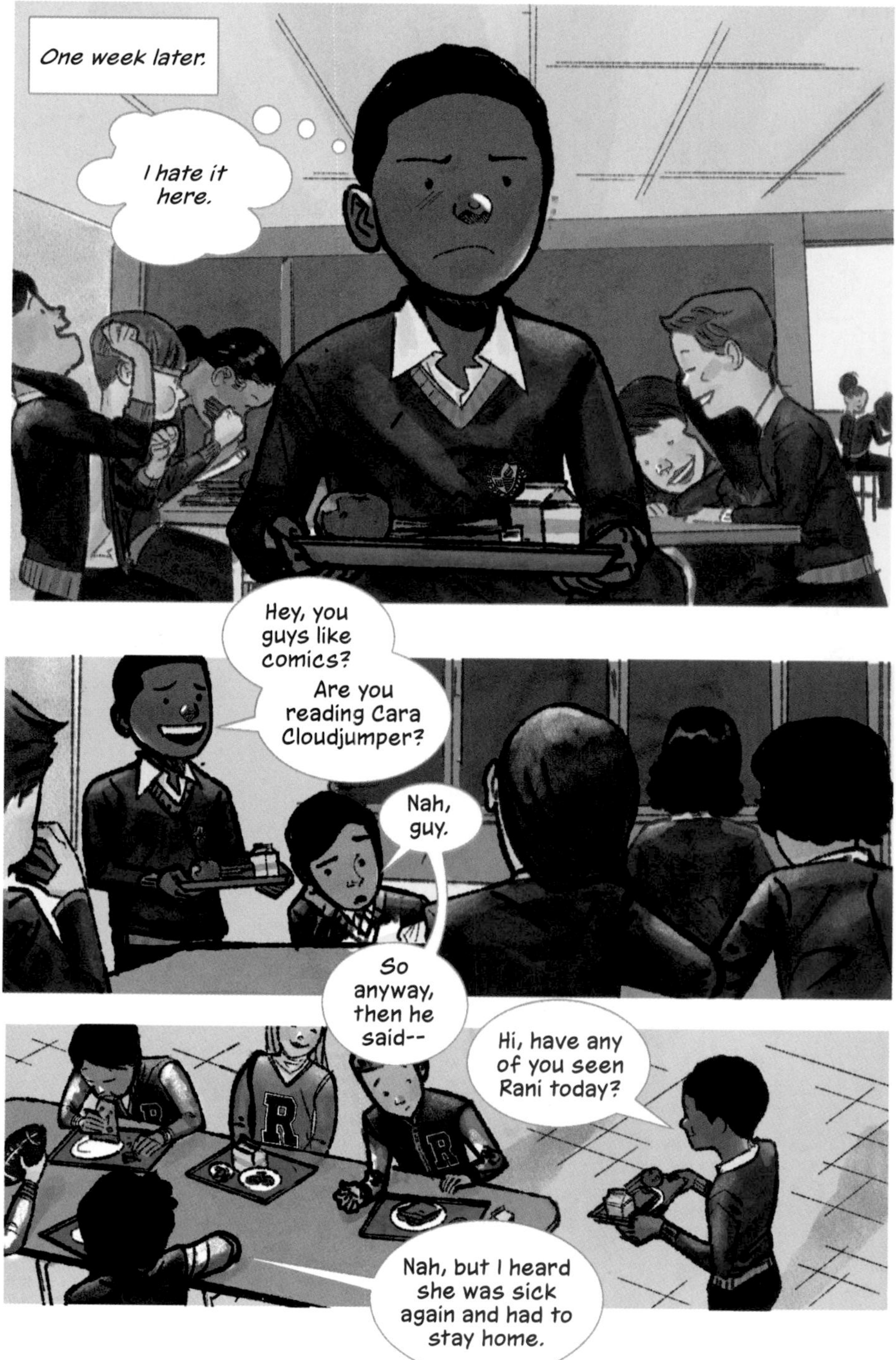
One week later.
I hate it here.
Hey, you guys like comics?
Are you reading Cara Cloudjumper?
Nah, guy.
So anyway, then he said--
Hi, have any of you seen Rani today?
Nah, but I heard she was sick again and had to stay home.

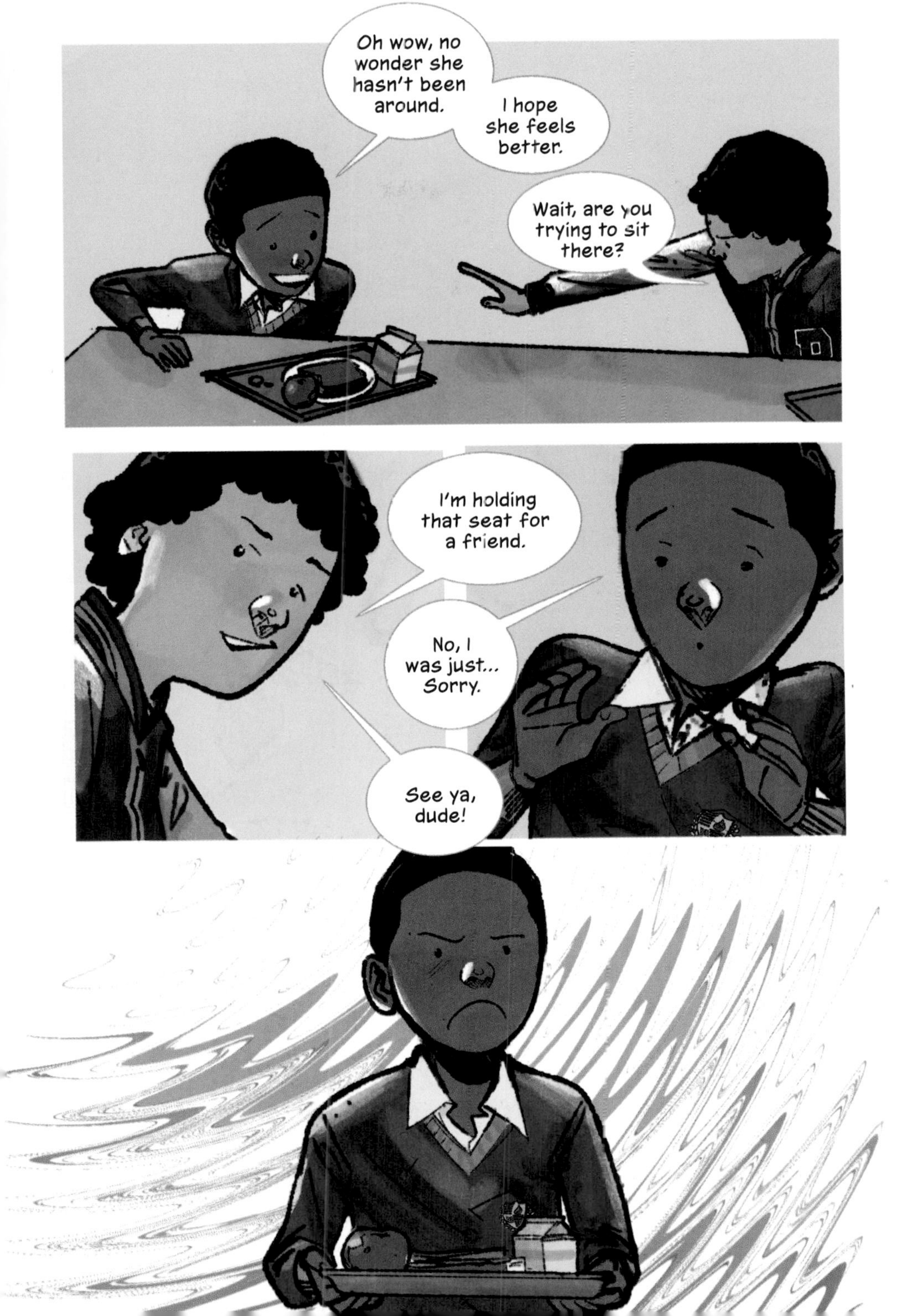
Oh wow, no wonder she hasn't been around.
I hope she feels better.
Wait, are you trying to sit there?
I'm holding that seat for a friend.
No, I was just... Sorry.
See ya, dude!

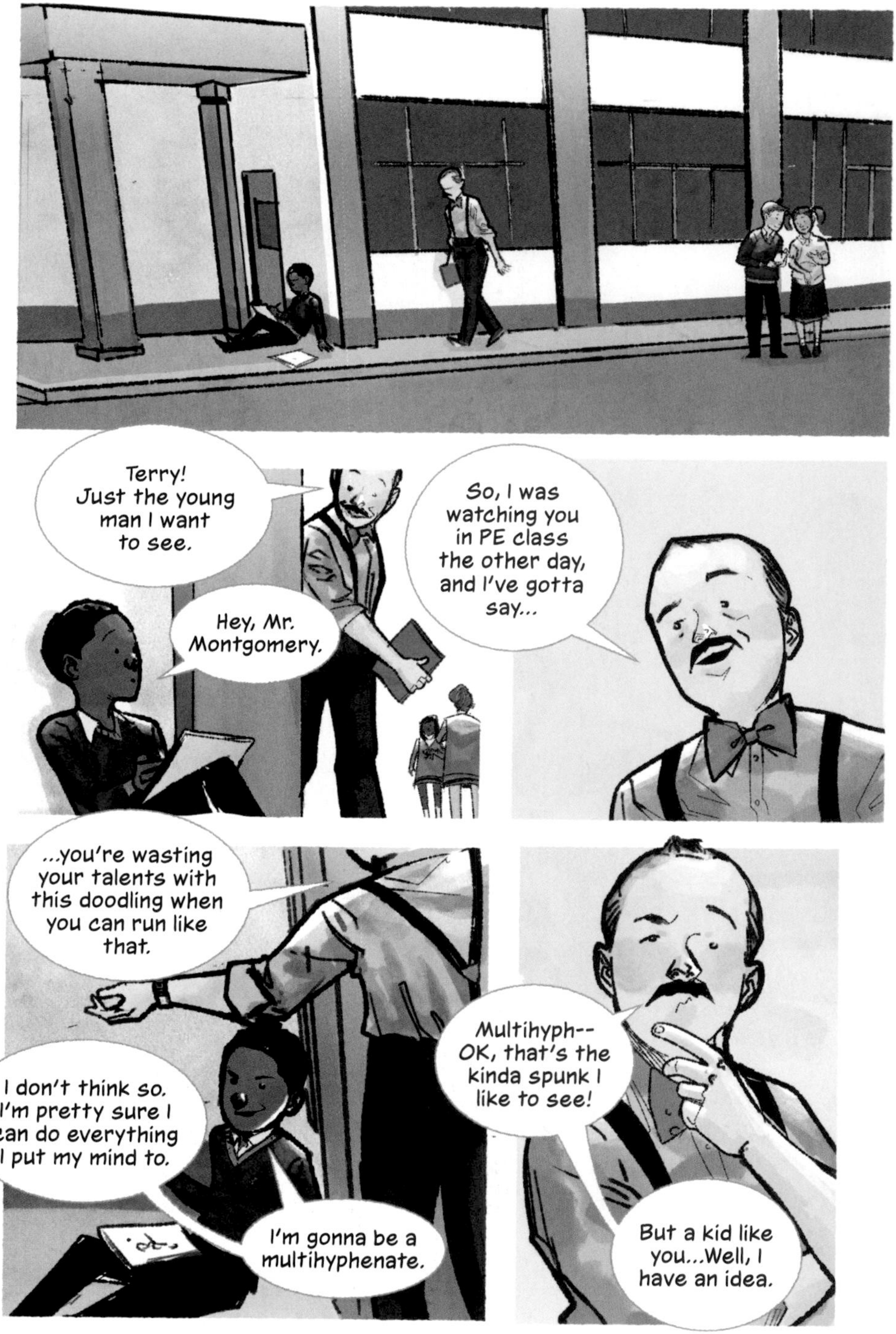

Terry! Just the young man I want to see.
Hey, Mr. Montgomery.
So, I was watching you in PE class the other day, and I've gotta say...
...you're wasting your talents with this doodling when you can run like that.
I don't think so. I'm pretty sure I can do everything I put my mind to.
I'm gonna be a multihyphenate.
Multihyph-- OK, that's the kinda spunk I like to see!
But a kid like you...Well, I have an idea.

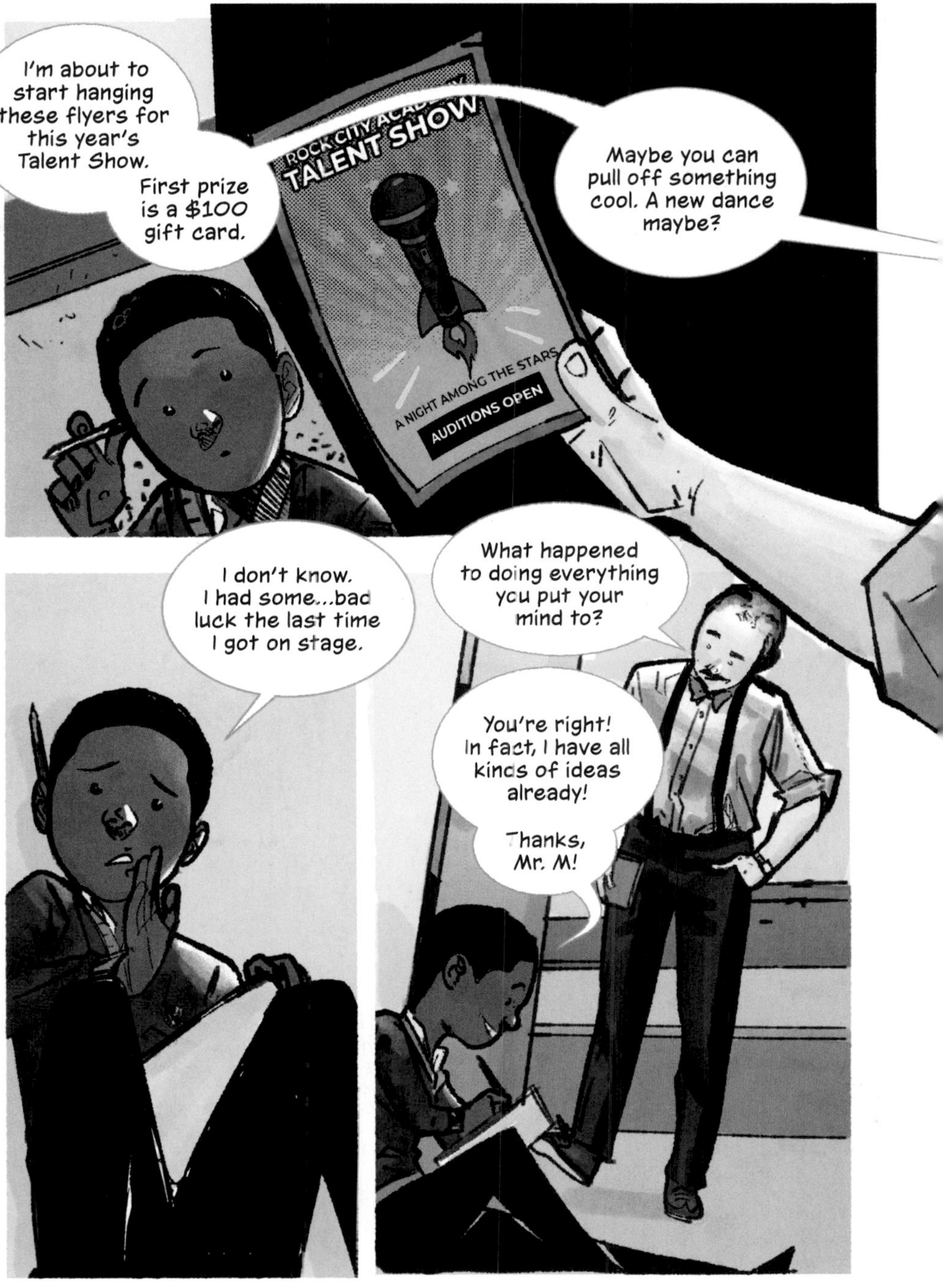
I'm about to start hanging these flyers for this year's Talent Show.
First prize is a $100 gift card.
ROCK CITY ACADEMY TALENT SHOW
A NIGHT AMONG THE STARS
AUDITIONS OPEN
Maybe you can pull off something cool. A new dance maybe?
I don't know. I had some...bad luck the last time I got on stage.
What happened to doing everything you put your mind to?
You're right! In fact, I have all kinds of ideas already!
Thanks, Mr. M!

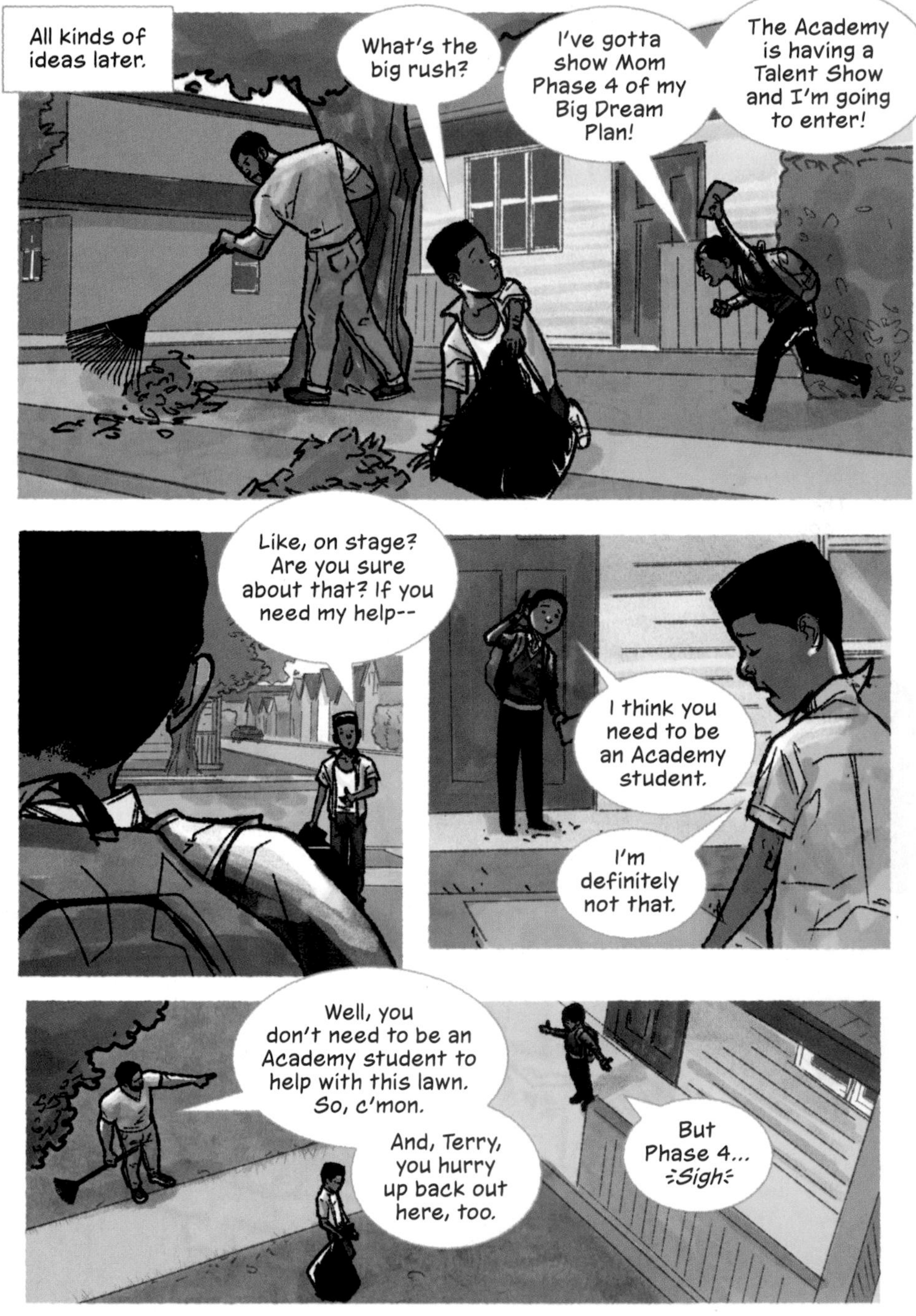
All kinds of ideas later.
What's the big rush?
I've gotta show Mom Phase 4 of my Big Dream Plan!
The Academy is having a Talent Show and I'm going to enter!
Like, on stage? Are you sure about that? If you need my help--
I think you need to be an Academy student.
I'm definitely not that.
Well, you don't need to be an Academy student to help with this lawn. So, c'mon.
And, Terry, you hurry up back out here, too.
But Phase 4...
Sigh

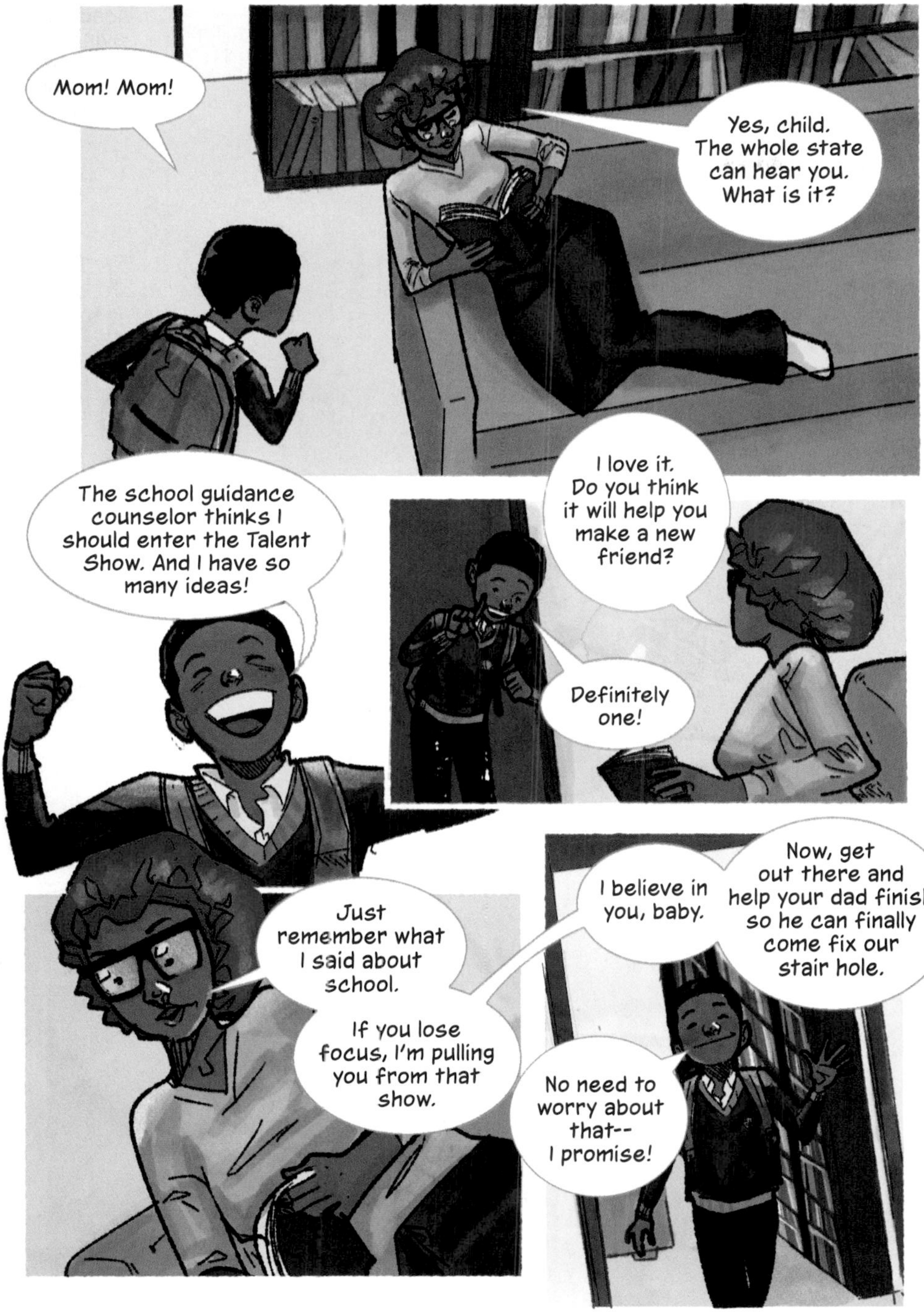

Mom! Mom!
Yes, child. The whole state can hear you. What is it?
The school guidance counselor thinks I should enter the Talent Show. And I have so many ideas!
I love it. Do you think it will help you make a new friend?
Definitely one!
Just remember what I said about school.
If you lose focus, I'm pulling you from that show.
I believe in you, baby.
Now, get out there and help your dad finish so he can finally come fix our stair hole.
No need to worry about that-- I promise!

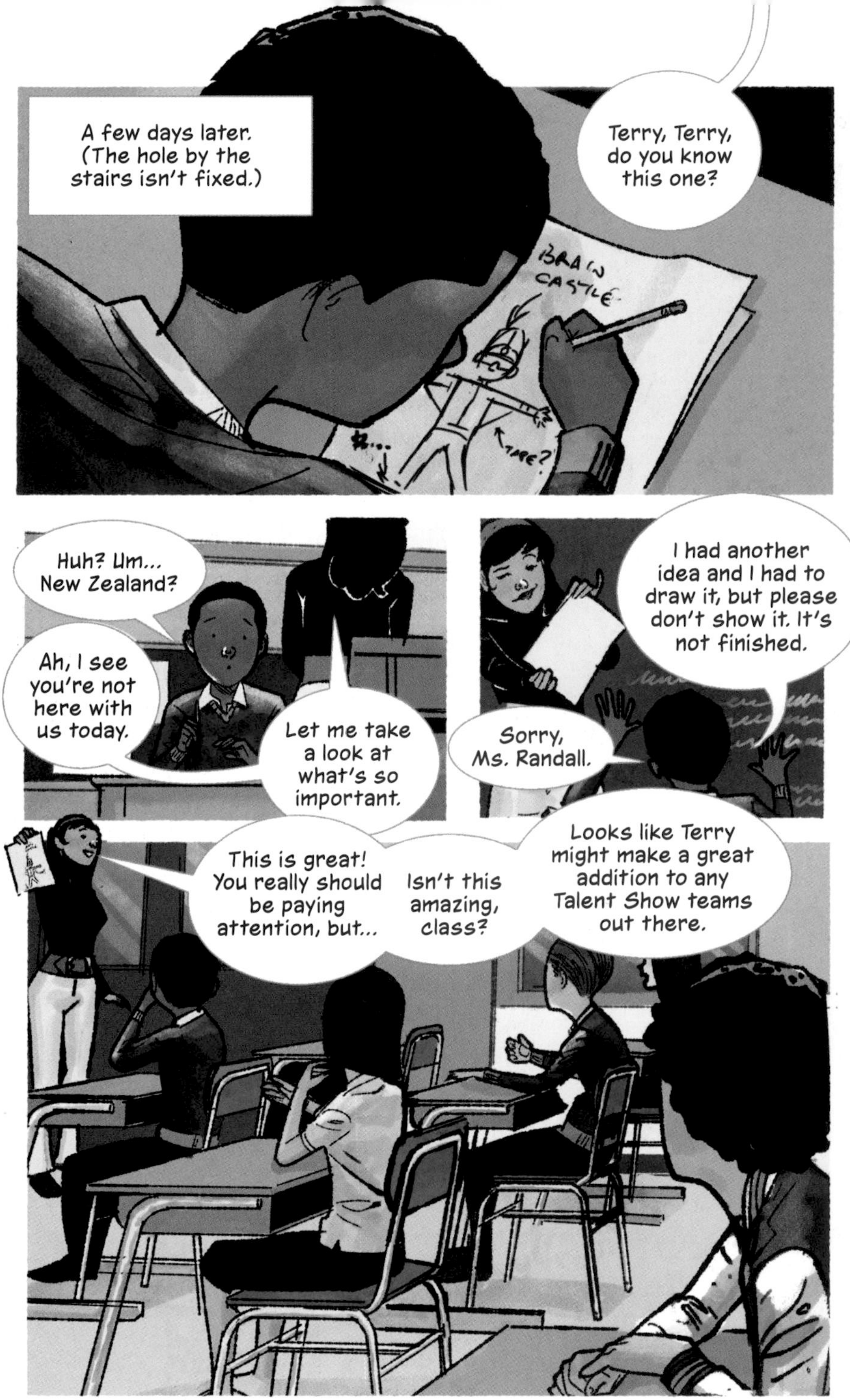
A few days later. (The hole by the stairs isn't fixed.)
Terry, Terry, do you know this one?
BRAIN CASTLE
TAPE?
Huh? Um... New Zealand?
Ah, I see you're not here with us today.
Let me take a look at what's so important.
I had another idea and I had to draw it, but please don't show it. It's not finished.
Sorry, Ms. Randall.
This is great! You really should be paying attention, but...
Isn't this amazing, class?
Looks like Terry might make a great addition to any Talent Show teams out there.

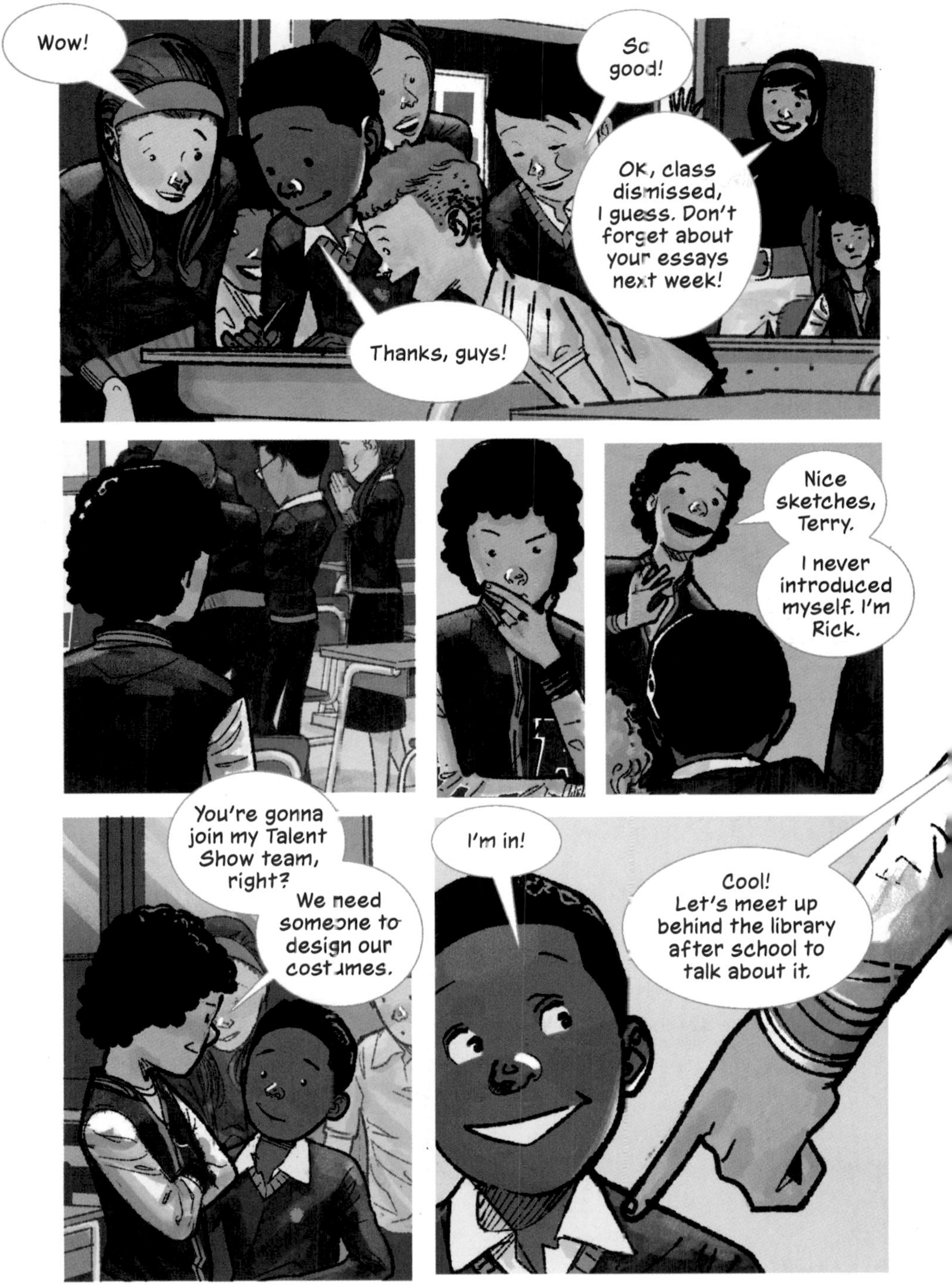
Wow!
So good!
OK, class dismissed, I guess. Don't forget about your essays next week!
Thanks, guys!
Nice sketches, Terry.
I never introduced myself. I'm Rick.
You're gonna join my Talent Show team, right?
We need someone to design our costumes.
I'm in!
Cool! Let's meet up behind the library after school to talk about it.

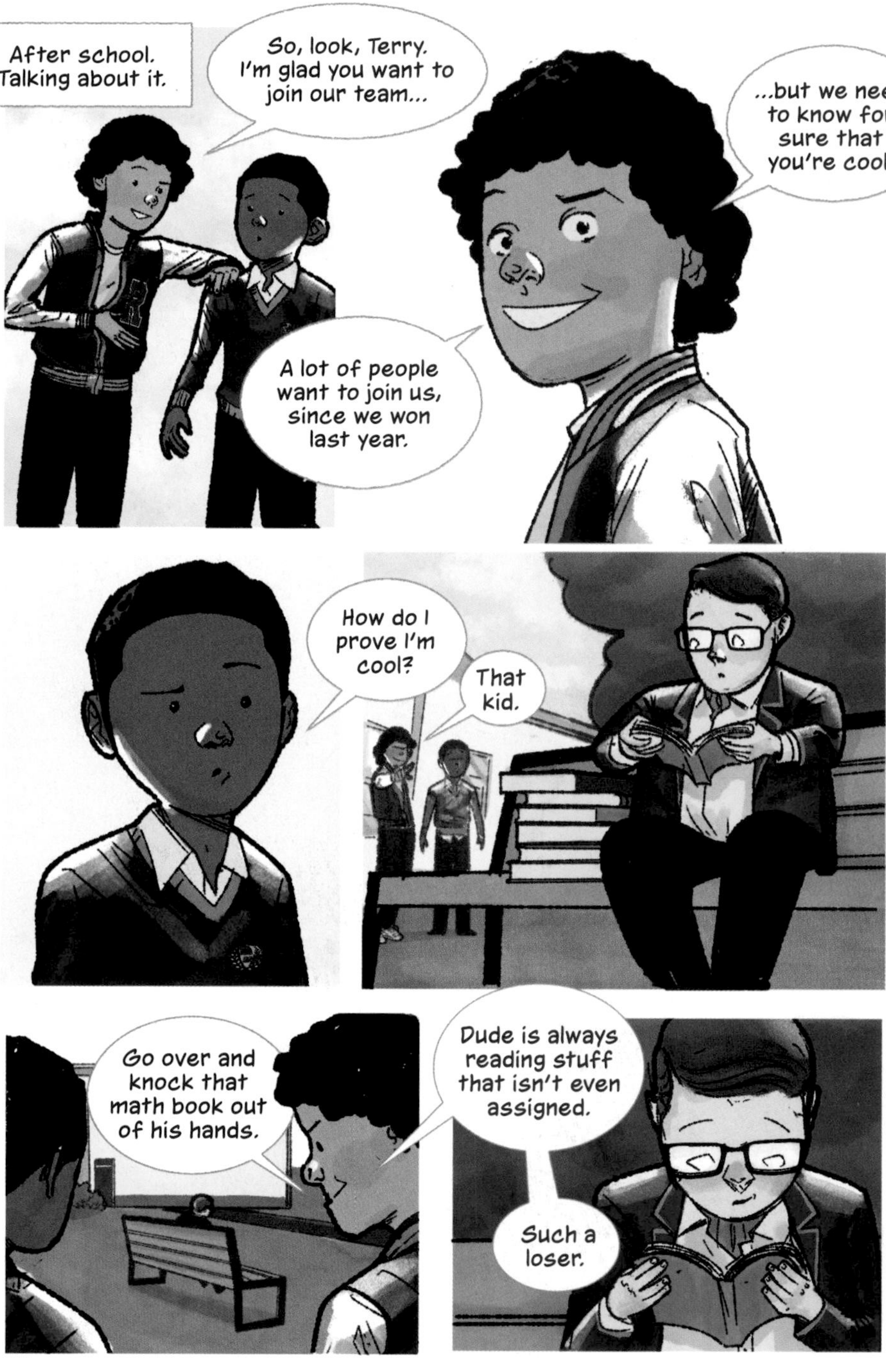
After school. Talking about it.
So, look, Terry. I'm glad you want to join our team...
...but we need to know for sure that you're cool.
A lot of people want to join us, since we won last year.
How do I prove I'm cool?
That kid.
Go over and knock that math book out of his hands.
Dude is always reading stuff that isn't even assigned.
Such a loser.

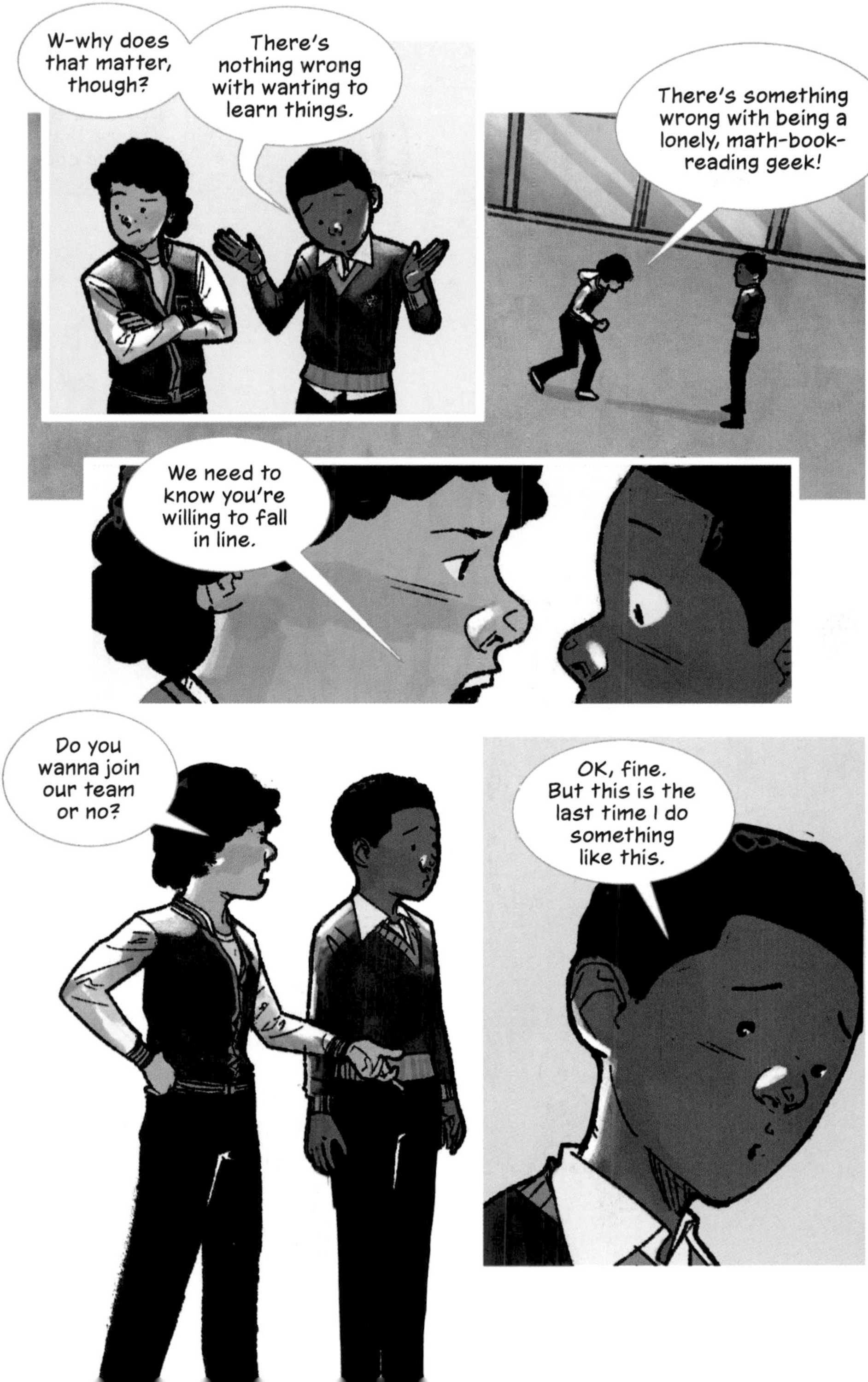
W-why does that matter, though?
There's nothing wrong with wanting to learn things.
There's something wrong with being a lonely, math-book-reading geek!
We need to know you're willing to fall in line.
Do you wanna join our team or no?
OK, fine. But this is the last time I do something like this.

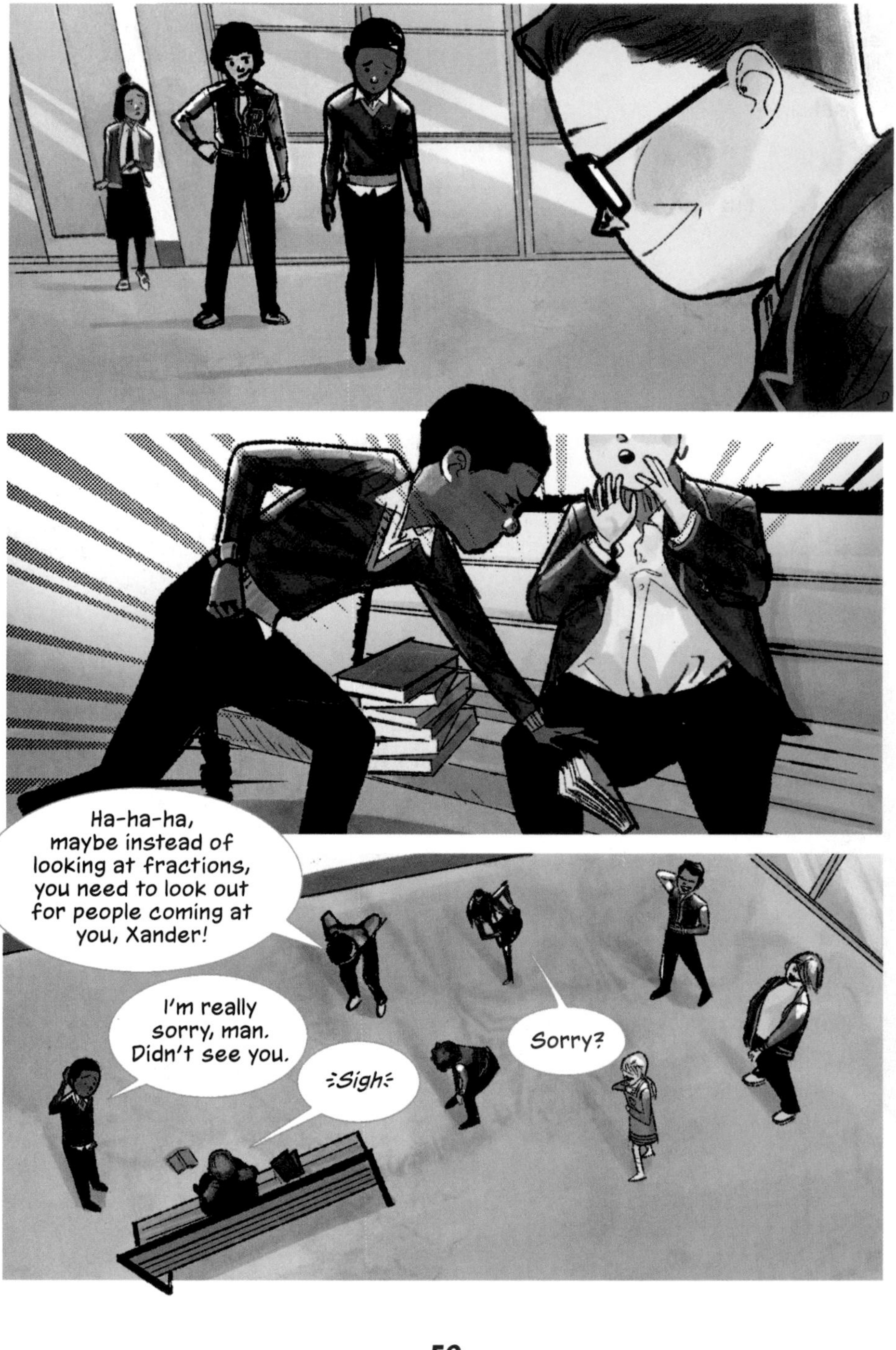
Ha-ha-ha, maybe instead of looking at fractions, you need to look out for people coming at you, Xander!
I'm really sorry, man. Didn't see you.
Sigh
Sorry?

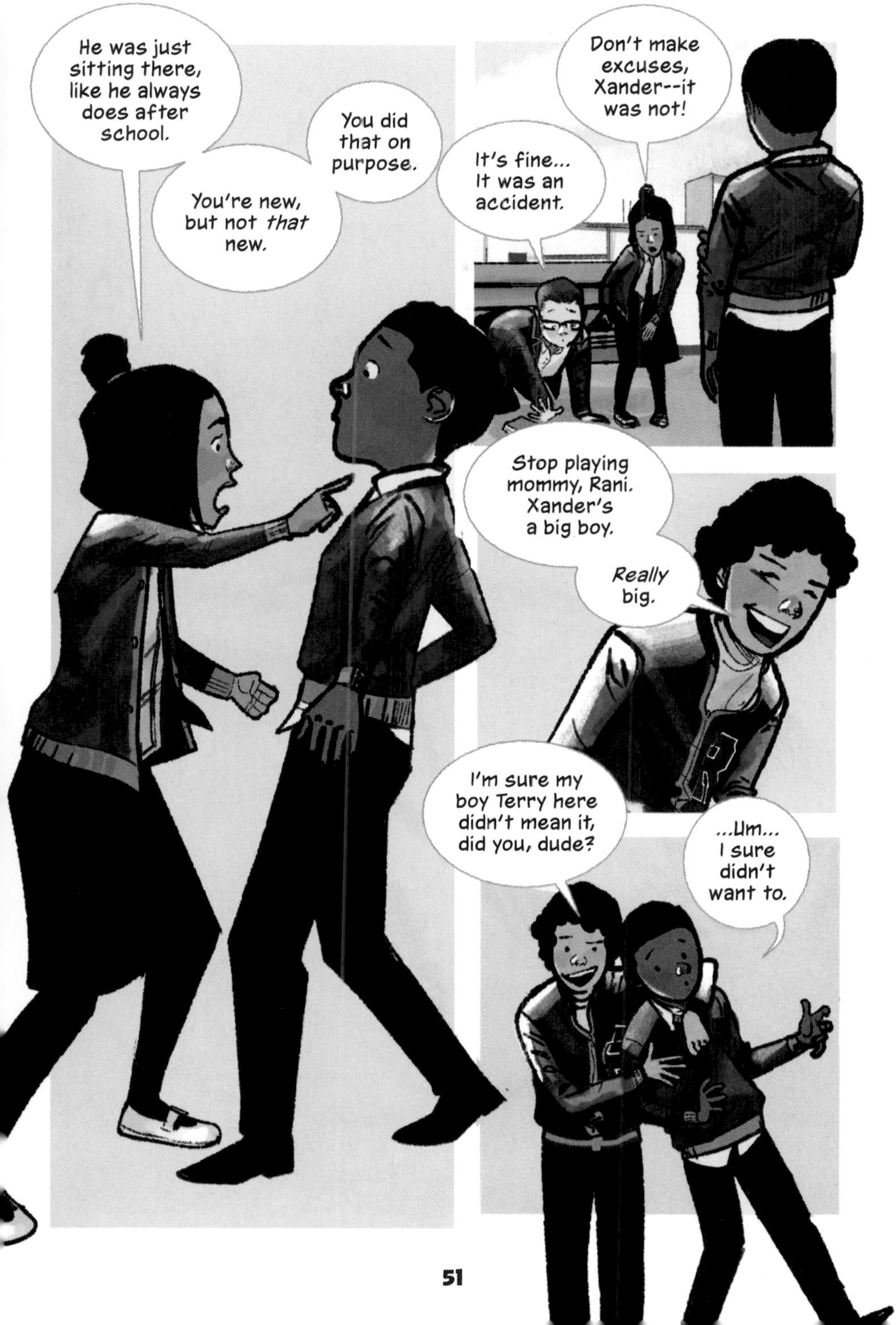
He was just sitting there, like he always does after school.
You're new, but not *that* new.
You did that on purpose.
It's fine... It was an accident.
Don't make excuses, Xander--it was not!
Stop playing mommy, Rani. Xander's a big boy.
Really big.
I'm sure my boy Terry here didn't mean it, did you, dude?
...Um... I sure didn't want to.

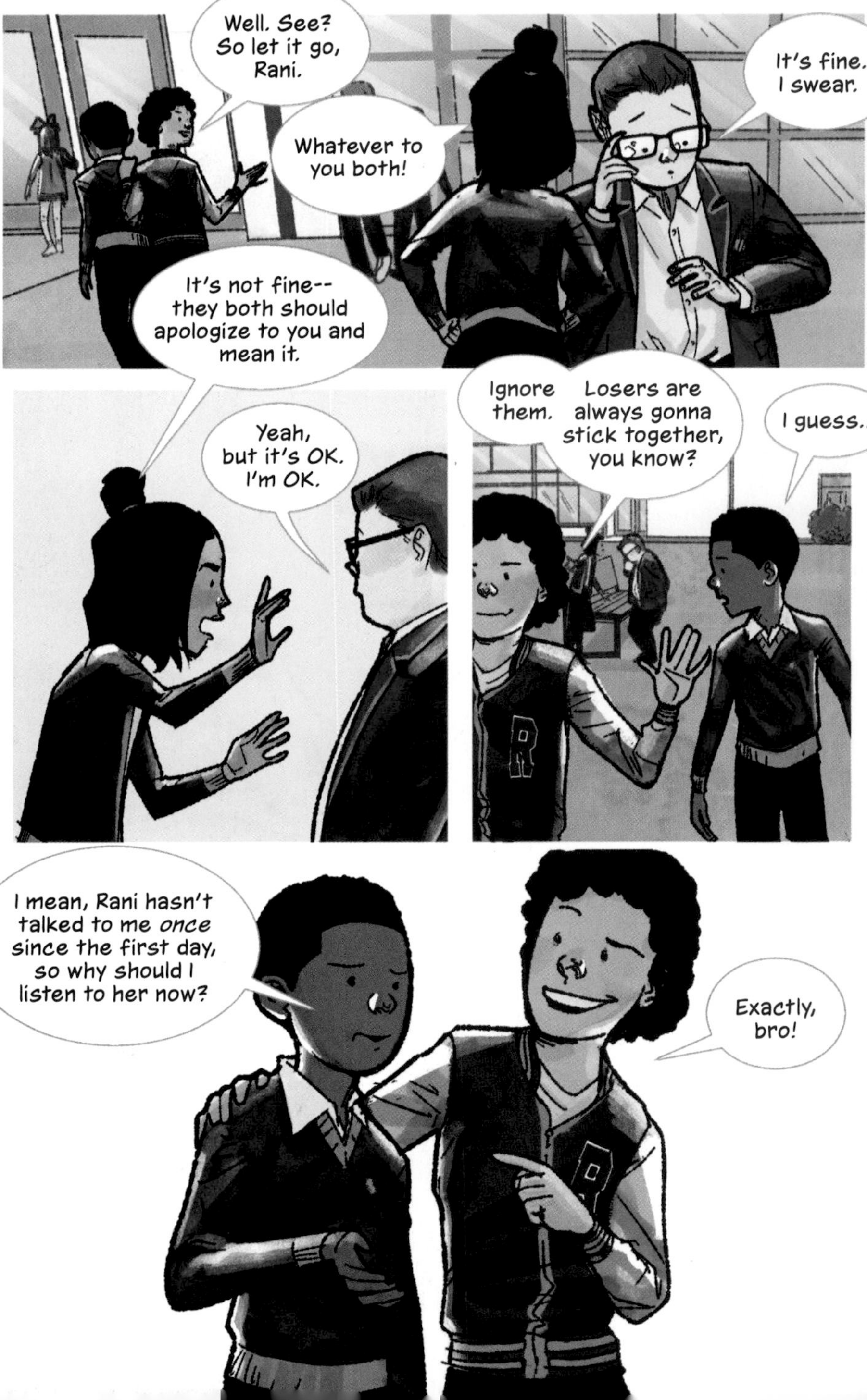
Well. See? So let it go, Rani.
Whatever to you both!
It's fine. I swear.
It's not fine--they both should apologize to you and mean it.
Yeah, but it's OK. I'm OK.
Ignore them.
Losers are always gonna stick together, you know?
I guess...
I mean, Rani hasn't talked to me *once* since the first day, so why should I listen to her now?
Exactly, bro!

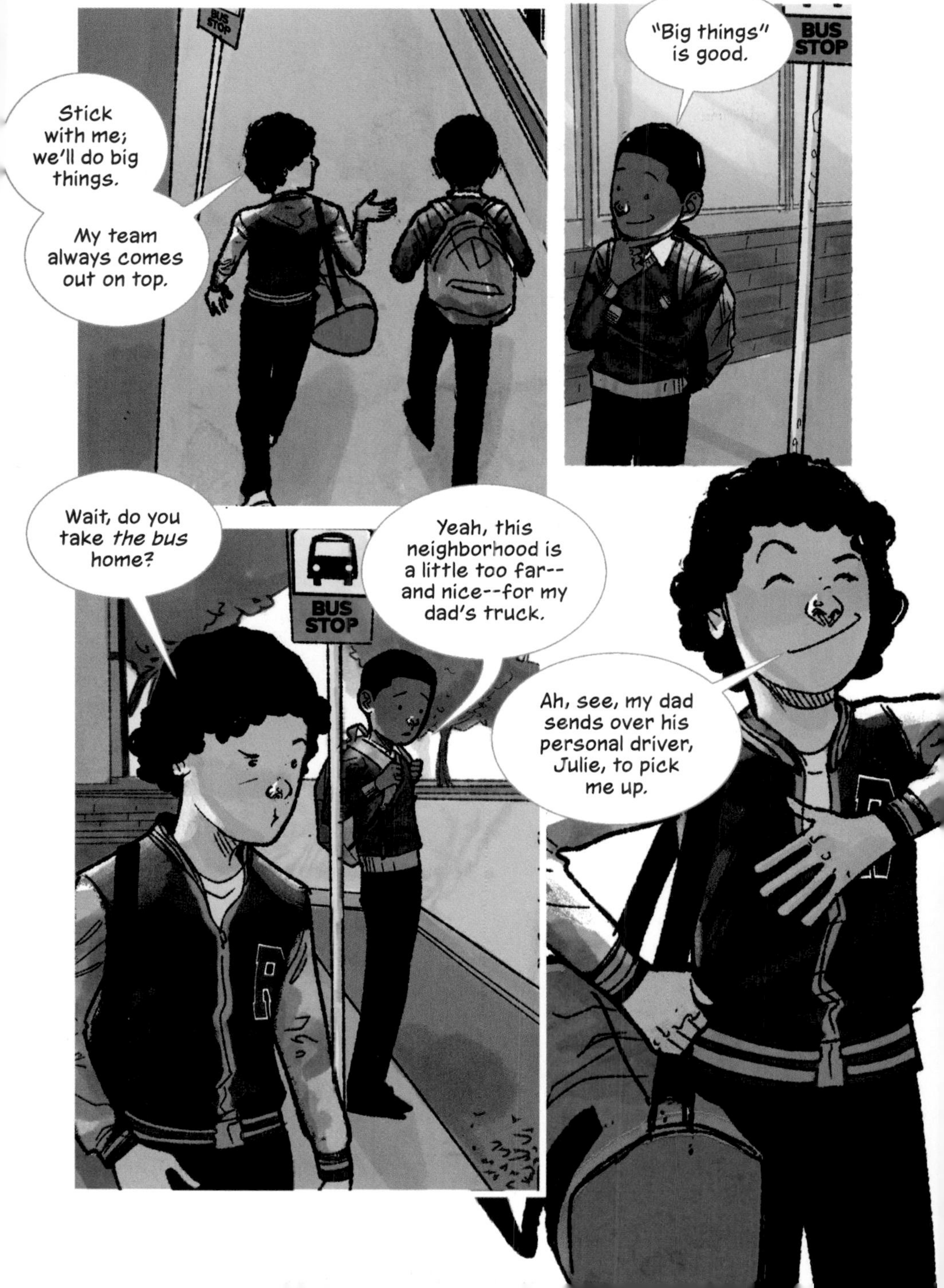

BUS STOP
Stick with me; we'll do big things.
My team always comes out on top.
"Big things" is good.
BUS STOP
Wait, do you take *the bus* home?
BUS STOP
Yeah, this neighborhood is a little too far--and nice--for my dad's truck.
Ah, see, my dad sends over his personal driver, Julie, to pick me up.

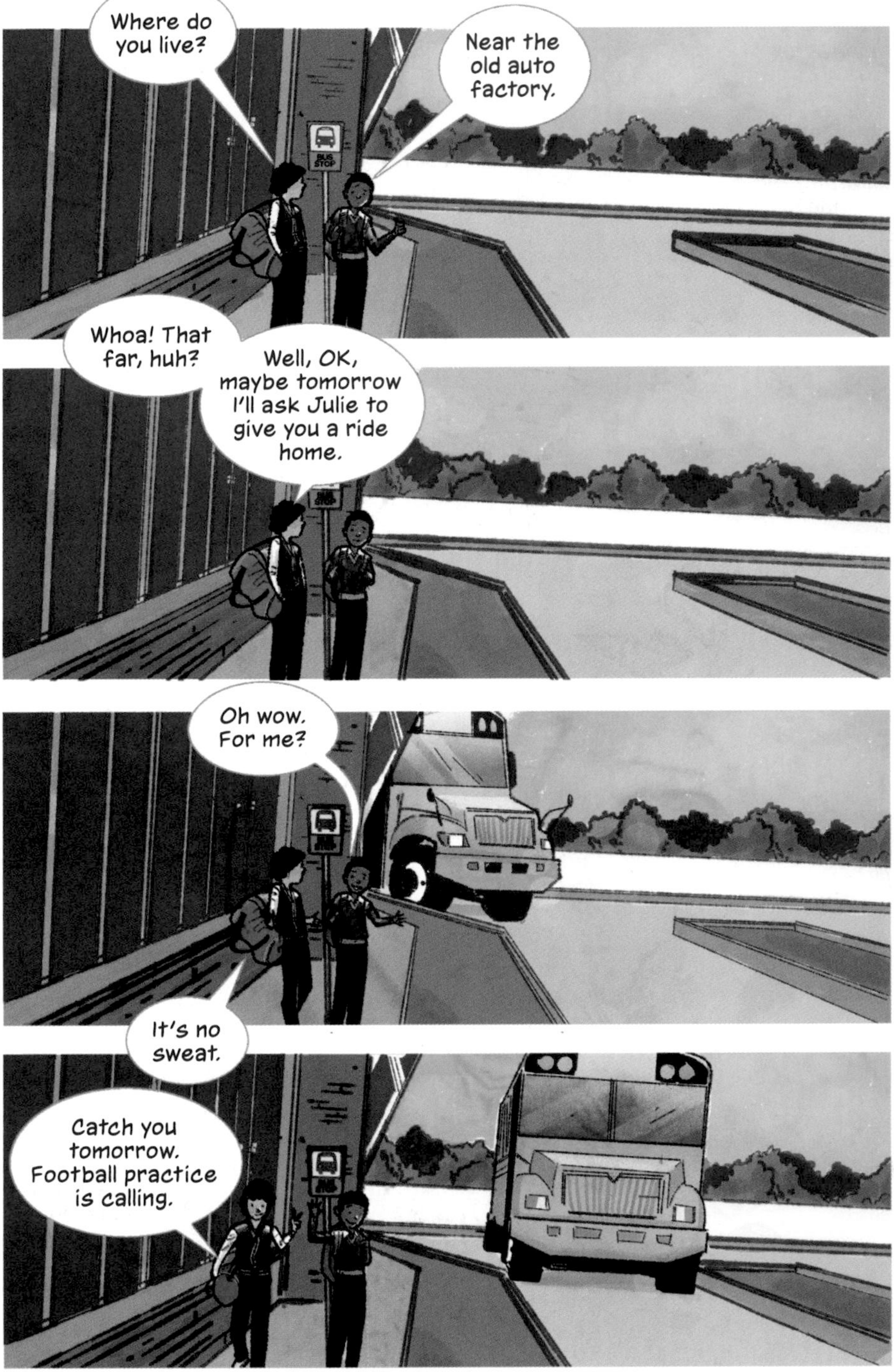

Where do you live?
Near the old auto factory.
Whoa! That far, huh?
Well, OK, maybe tomorrow I'll ask Julie to give you a ride home.
BUS STOP
Oh wow. For me?
It's no sweat.
Catch you tomorrow. Football practice is calling.

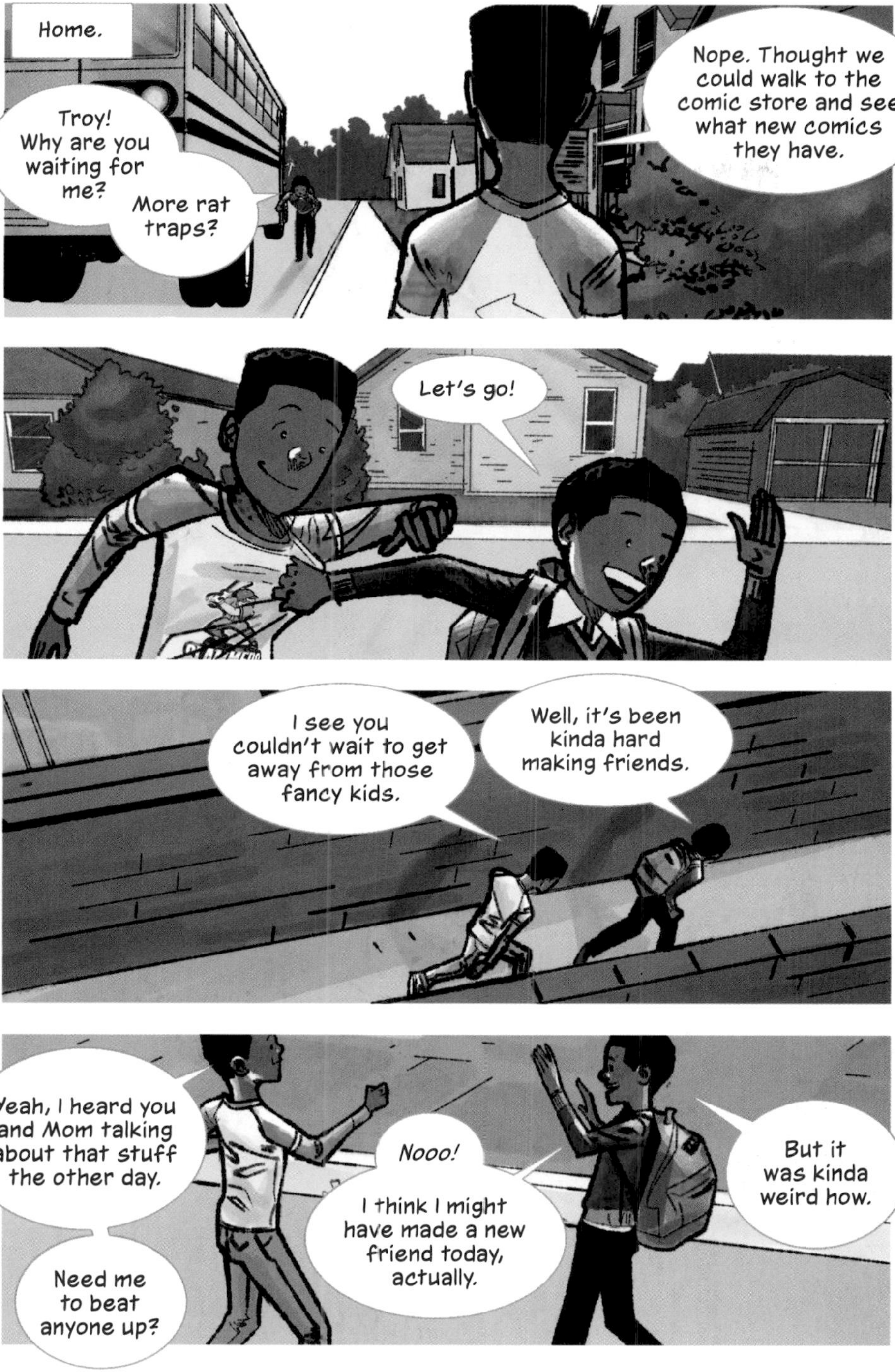
Home.
Troy! Why are you waiting for me?
More rat traps?
Nope. Thought we could walk to the comic store and see what new comics they have.
Let's go!
I see you couldn't wait to get away from those fancy kids.
Well, it's been kinda hard making friends.
Yeah, I heard you and Mom talking about that stuff the other day.
Need me to beat anyone up?
Nooo!
I think I might have made a new friend today, actually.
But it was kinda weird how.

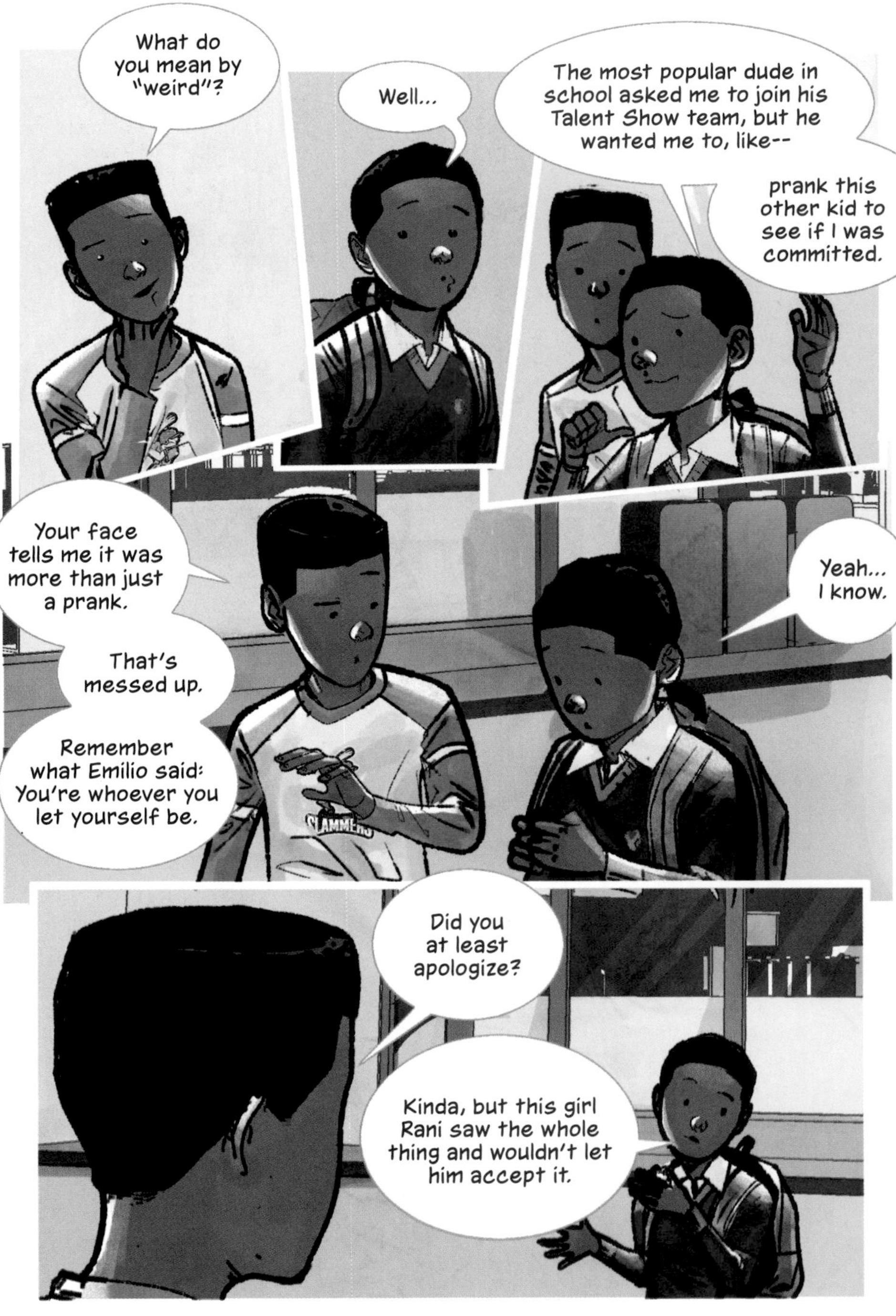
What do you mean by "weird"?
Well...
The most popular dude in school asked me to join his Talent Show team, but he wanted me to, like--
prank this other kid to see if I was committed.
Your face tells me it was more than just a prank.
That's messed up.
Remember what Emilio said: You're whoever you let yourself be.
Yeah... I know.
SLAMMERS
Did you at least apologize?
Kinda, but this girl Rani saw the whole thing and wouldn't let him accept it.

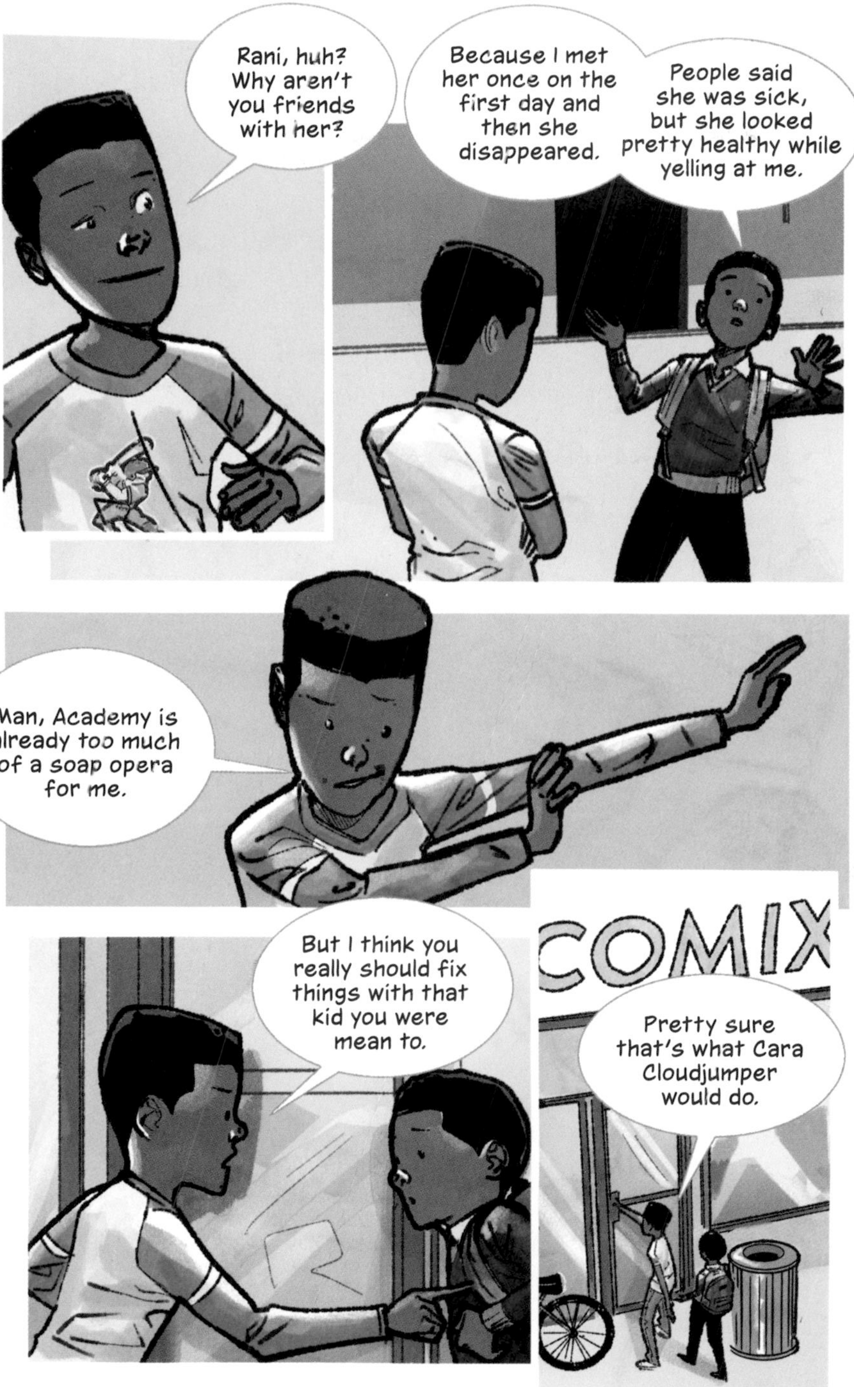
Rani, huh? Why aren't you friends with her?
Because I met her once on the first day and then she disappeared.
People said she was sick, but she looked pretty healthy while yelling at me.
Man, Academy is already too much of a soap opera for me.
But I think you really should fix things with that kid you were mean to.
COMIX
Pretty sure that's what Cara Cloudjumper would do.

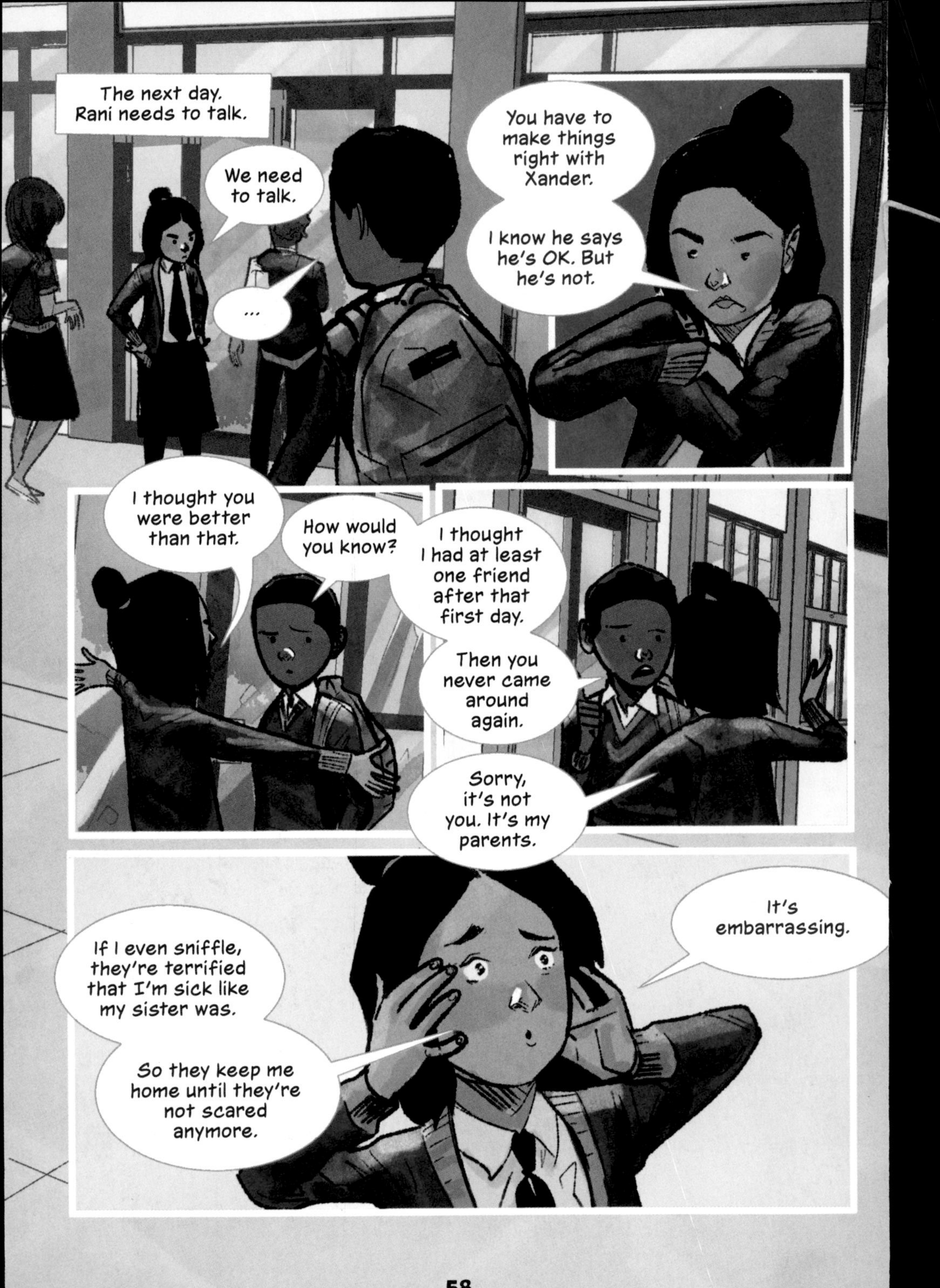

The next day. Rani needs to talk.
We need to talk.
...
You have to make things right with Xander.
I know he says he's OK. But he's not.
I thought you were better than that.
How would you know?
I thought I had at least one friend after that first day.
Then you never came around again.
Sorry, it's not you. It's my parents.
If I even sniffle, they're terrified that I'm sick like my sister was.
So they keep me home until they're not scared anymore.
It's embarrassing.

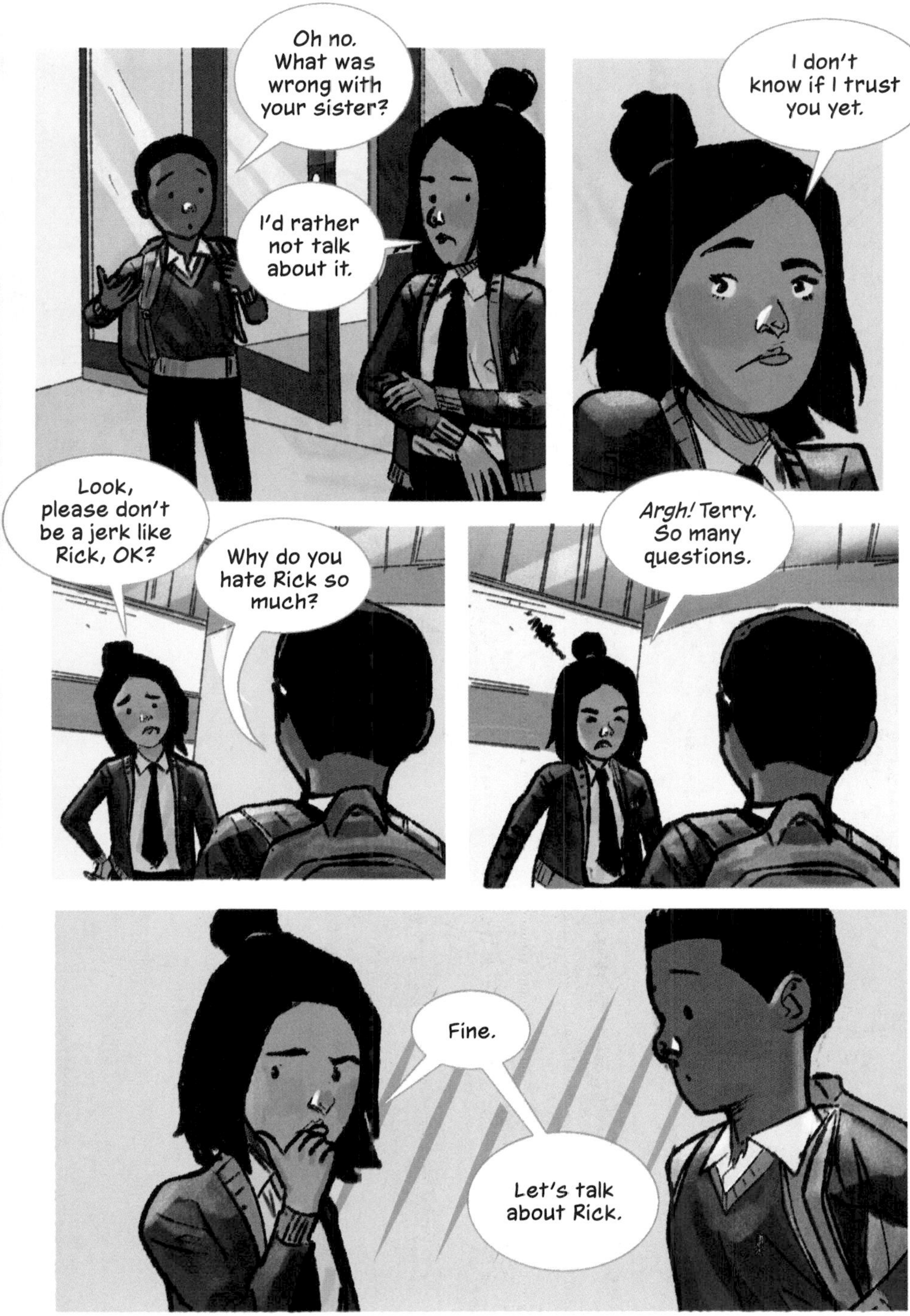
Oh no. What was wrong with your sister?
I'd rather not talk about it.
I don't know if I trust you yet.
Look, please don't be a jerk like Rick, OK?
Why do you hate Rick so much?
Argh! Terry. So many questions.
Fine.
Let's talk about Rick.

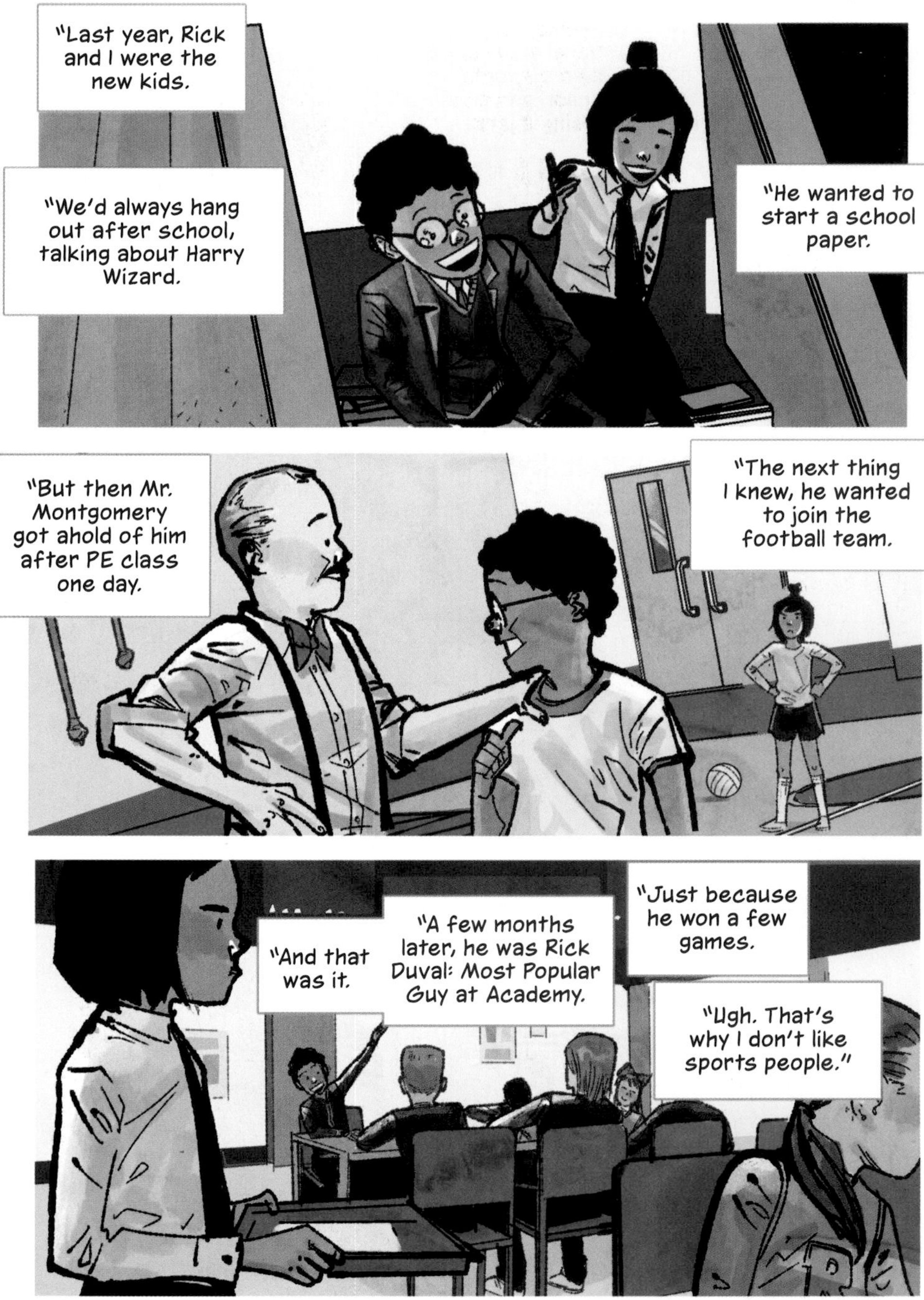
"Last year, Rick and I were the new kids.
"We'd always hang out after school, talking about Harry Wizard.
"He wanted to start a school paper.
"But then Mr. Montgomery got ahold of him after PE class one day.
"The next thing I knew, he wanted to join the football team.
"And that was it.
"A few months later, he was Rick Duval: Most Popular Guy at Academy.
"Just because he won a few games.
"Ugh. That's why I don't like sports people."

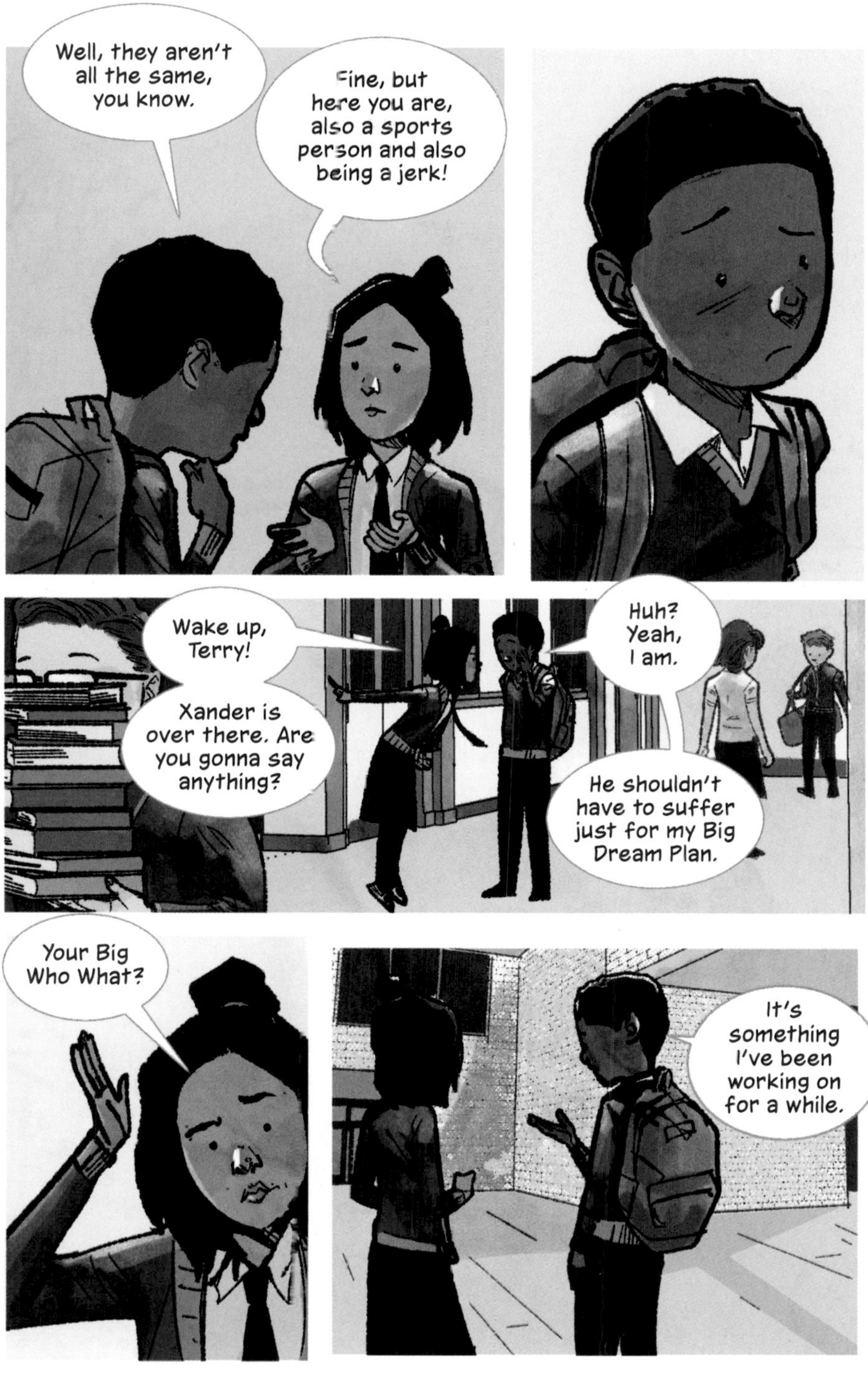

Well, they aren't all the same, you know.
Fine, but here you are, also a sports person and also being a jerk!
Wake up, Terry!
Xander is over there. Are you gonna say anything?
Huh? Yeah, I am.
He shouldn't have to suffer just for my Big Dream Plan.
Your Big Who What?
It's something I've been working on for a while.

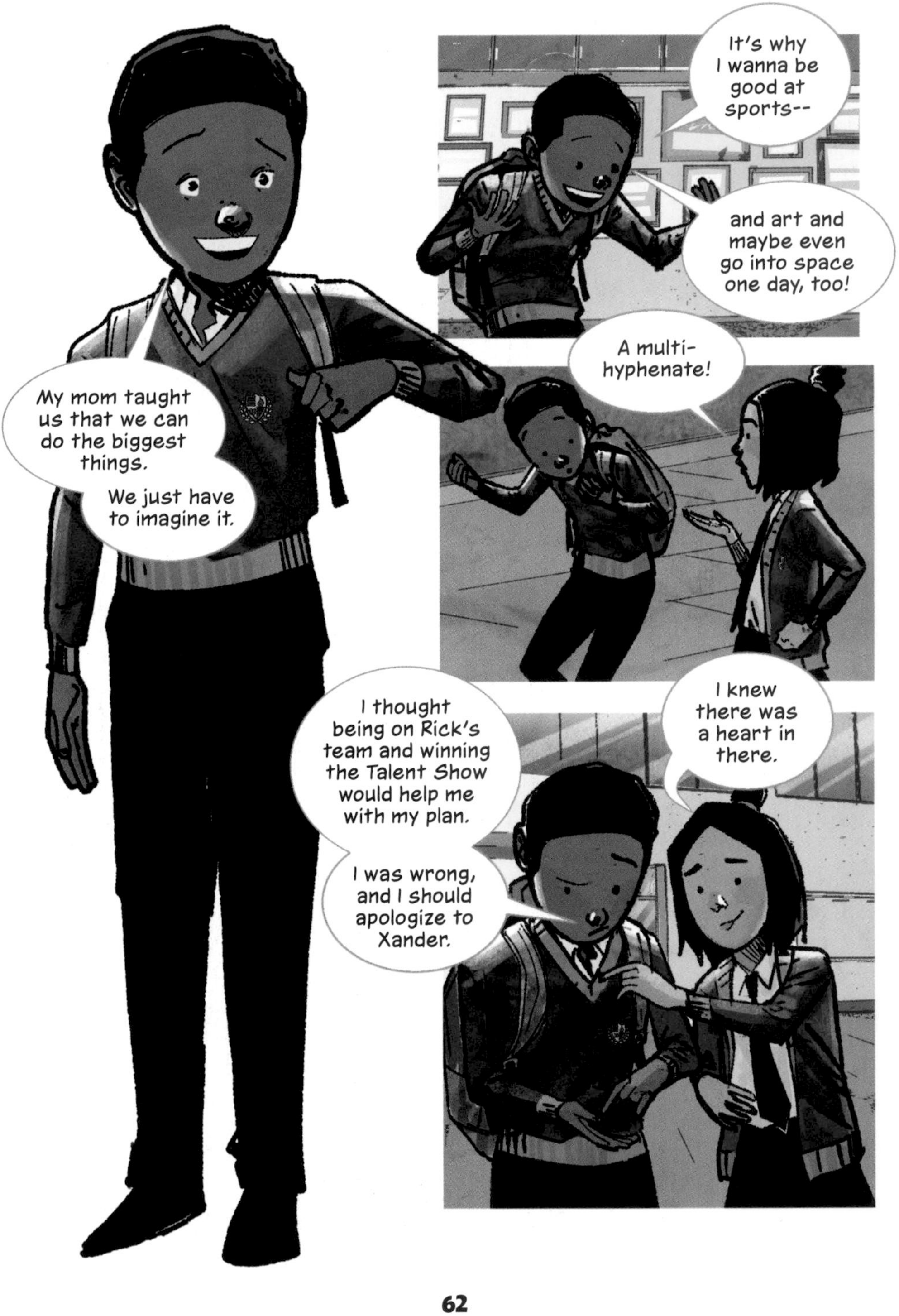
My mom taught us that we can do the biggest things.
We just have to imagine it.
It's why I wanna be good at sports--
and art and maybe even go into space one day, too!
A multi-hyphenate!
I thought being on Rick's team and winning the Talent Show would help me with my plan.
I was wrong, and I should apologize to Xander.
I knew there was a heart in there.

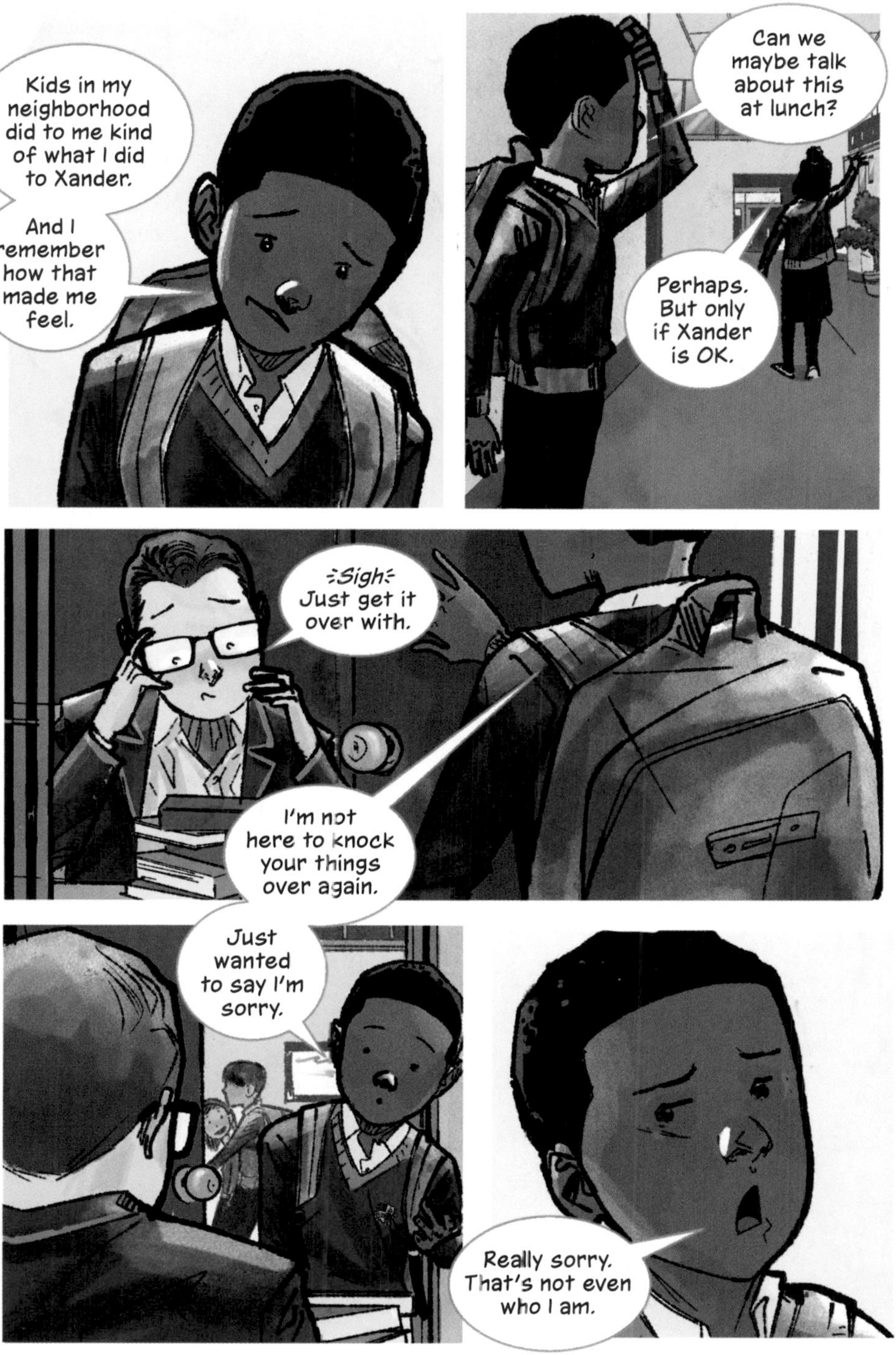
Kids in my neighborhood did to me kind of what I did to Xander.
And I remember how that made me feel.
Can we maybe talk about this at lunch?
Perhaps. But only if Xander is OK.
Sigh
Just get it over with.
I'm not here to knock your things over again.
Just wanted to say I'm sorry.
Really sorry. That's not even who I am.

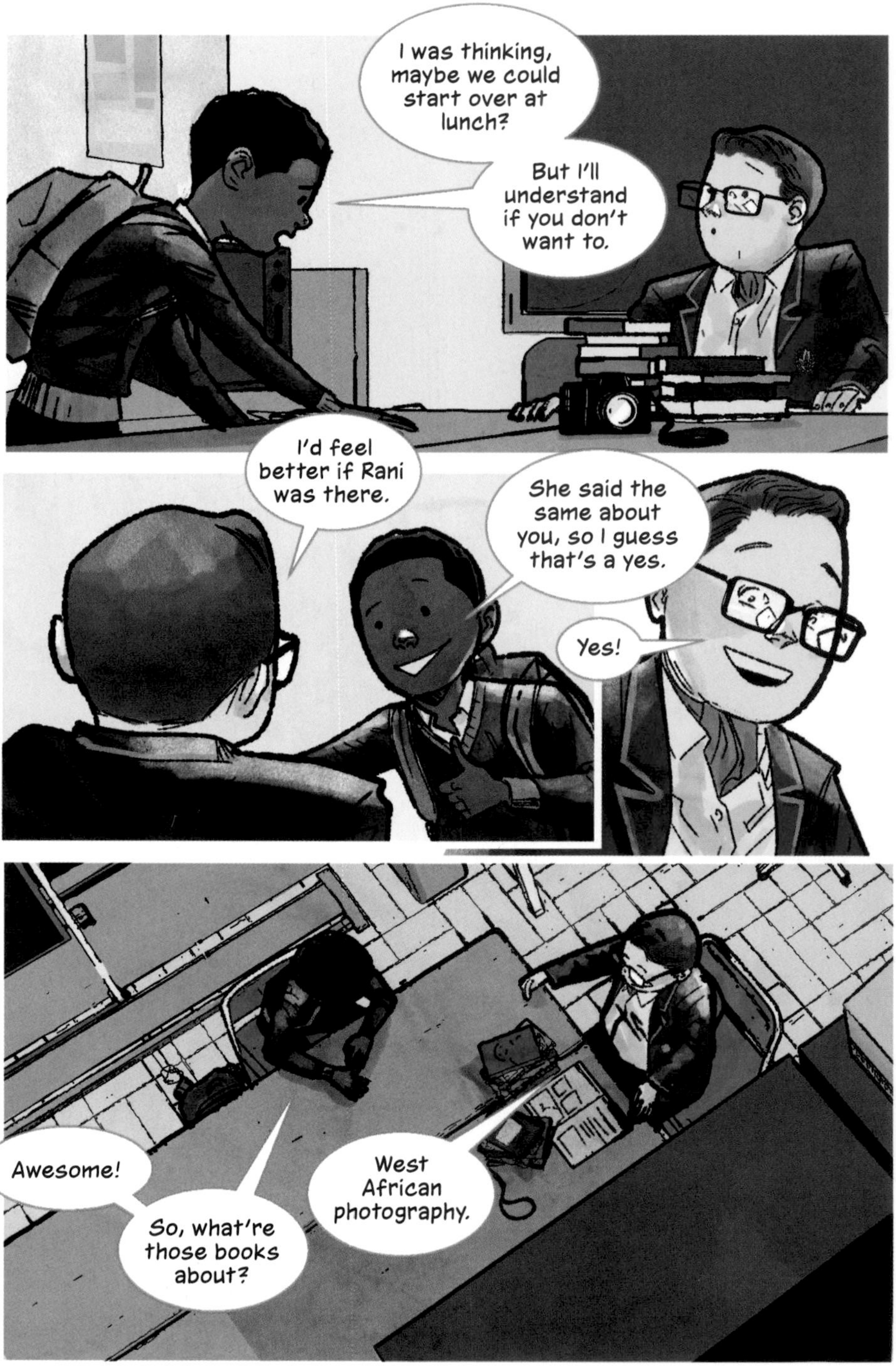
I was thinking, maybe we could start over at lunch?
But I'll understand if you don't want to.
I'd feel better if Rani was there.
She said the same about you, so I guess that's a yes.
Yes!
Awesome!
So, what're those books about?
West African photography.

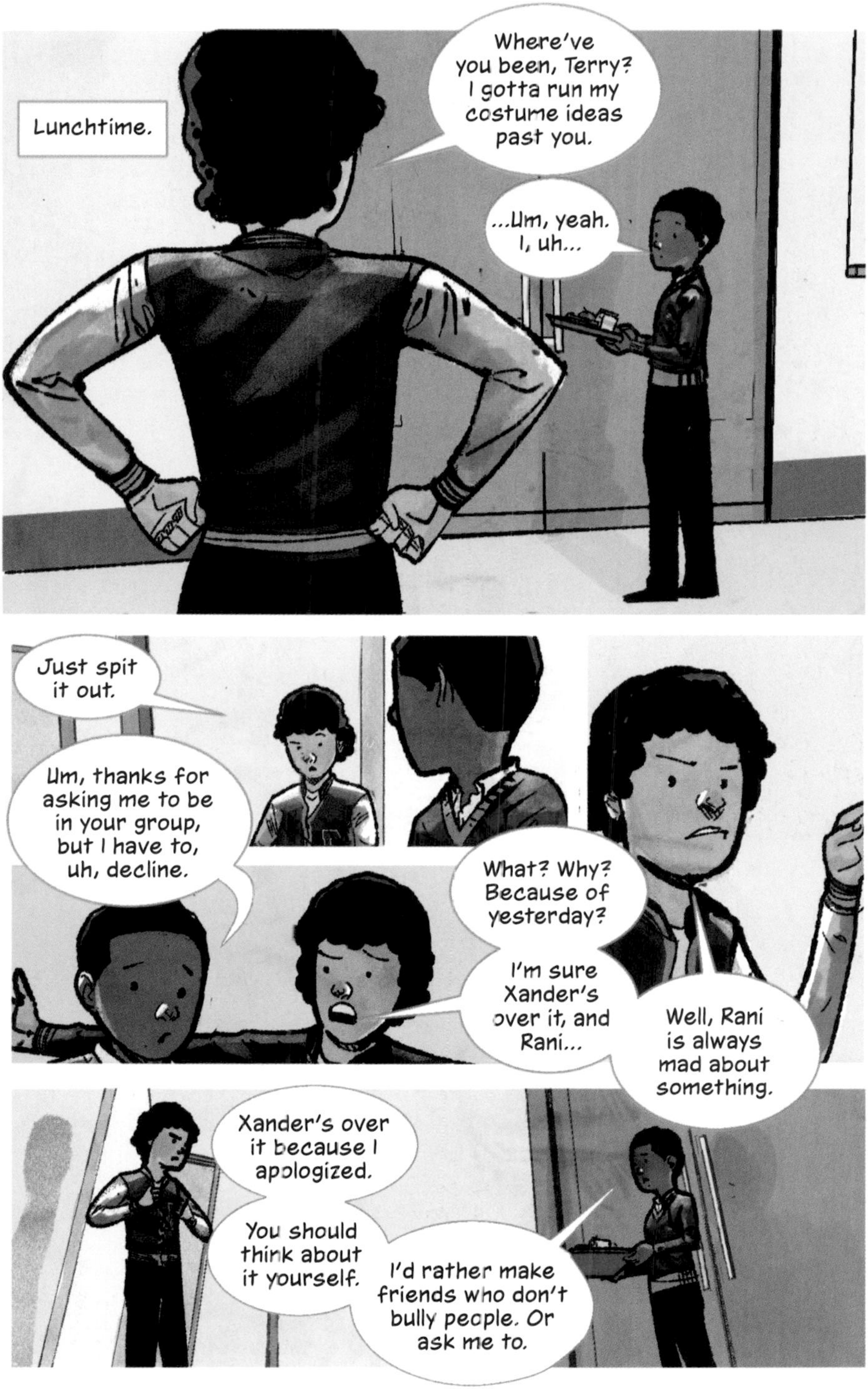
Lunchtime.
Where've you been, Terry? I gotta run my costume ideas past you.
...Um, yeah. I, uh...
Just spit it out.
Um, thanks for asking me to be in your group, but I have to, uh, decline.
What? Why? Because of yesterday?
I'm sure Xander's over it, and Rani...
Well, Rani is always mad about something.
Xander's over it because I apologized.
You should think about it yourself.
I'd rather make friends who don't bully people. Or ask me to.

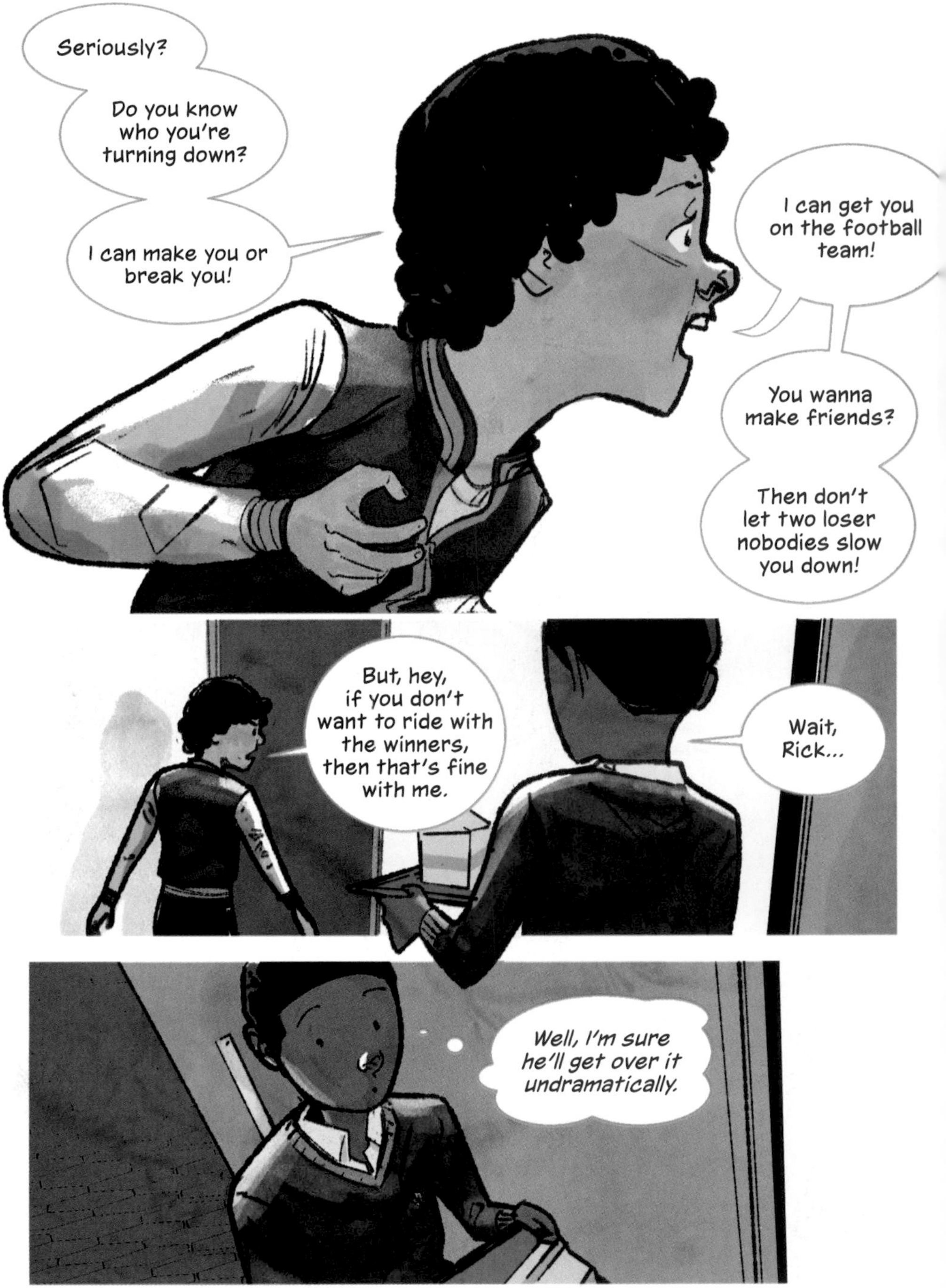
Seriously?
Do you know who you're turning down?
I can make you or break you!
I can get you on the football team!
You wanna make friends?
Then don't let two loser nobodies slow you down!
But, hey, if you don't want to ride with the winners, then that's fine with me.
Wait, Rick...
Well, I'm sure he'll get over it undramatically.

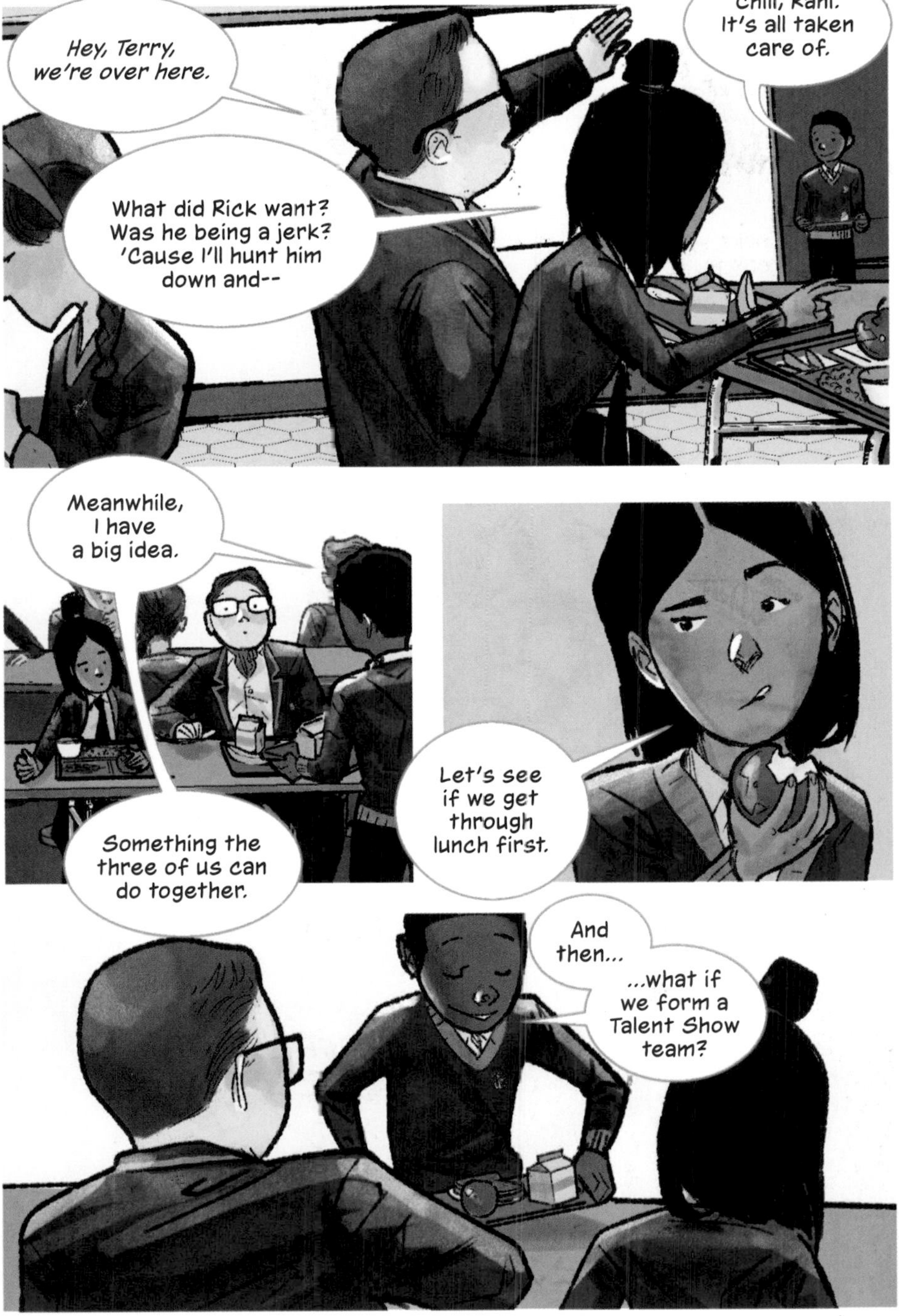
Hey, Terry, we're over here.
Chill, Rani. It's all taken care of.
What did Rick want? Was he being a jerk? 'Cause I'll hunt him down and--
Meanwhile, I have a big idea.
Something the three of us can do together.
Let's see if we get through lunch first.
And then...
...what if we form a Talent Show team?

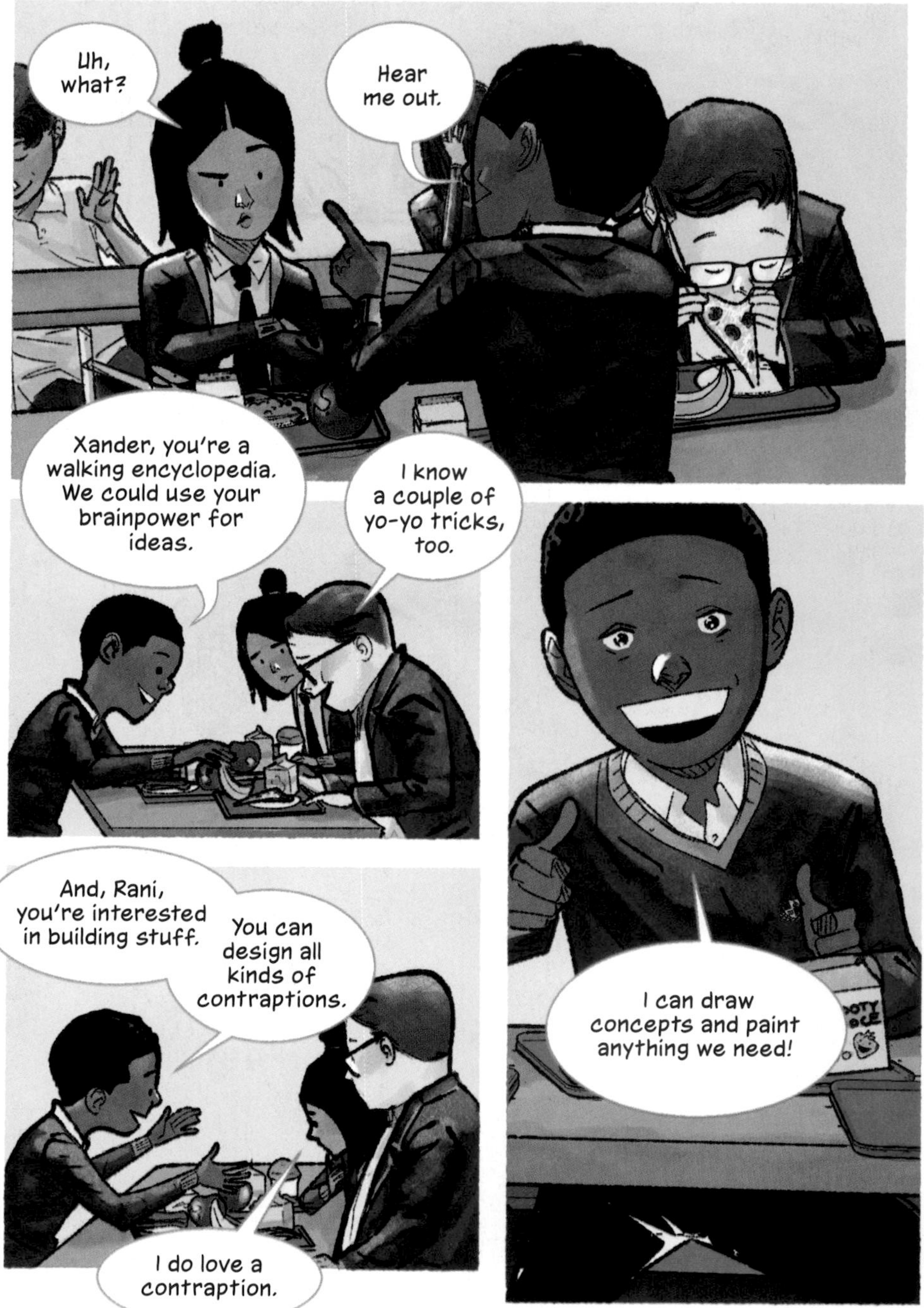

Uh, what?
Hear me out.
Xander, you're a walking encyclopedia. We could use your brainpower for ideas.
I know a couple of yo-yo tricks, too.
I can draw concepts and paint anything we need!
And, Rani, you're interested in building stuff.
You can design all kinds of contraptions.
I do love a contraption.

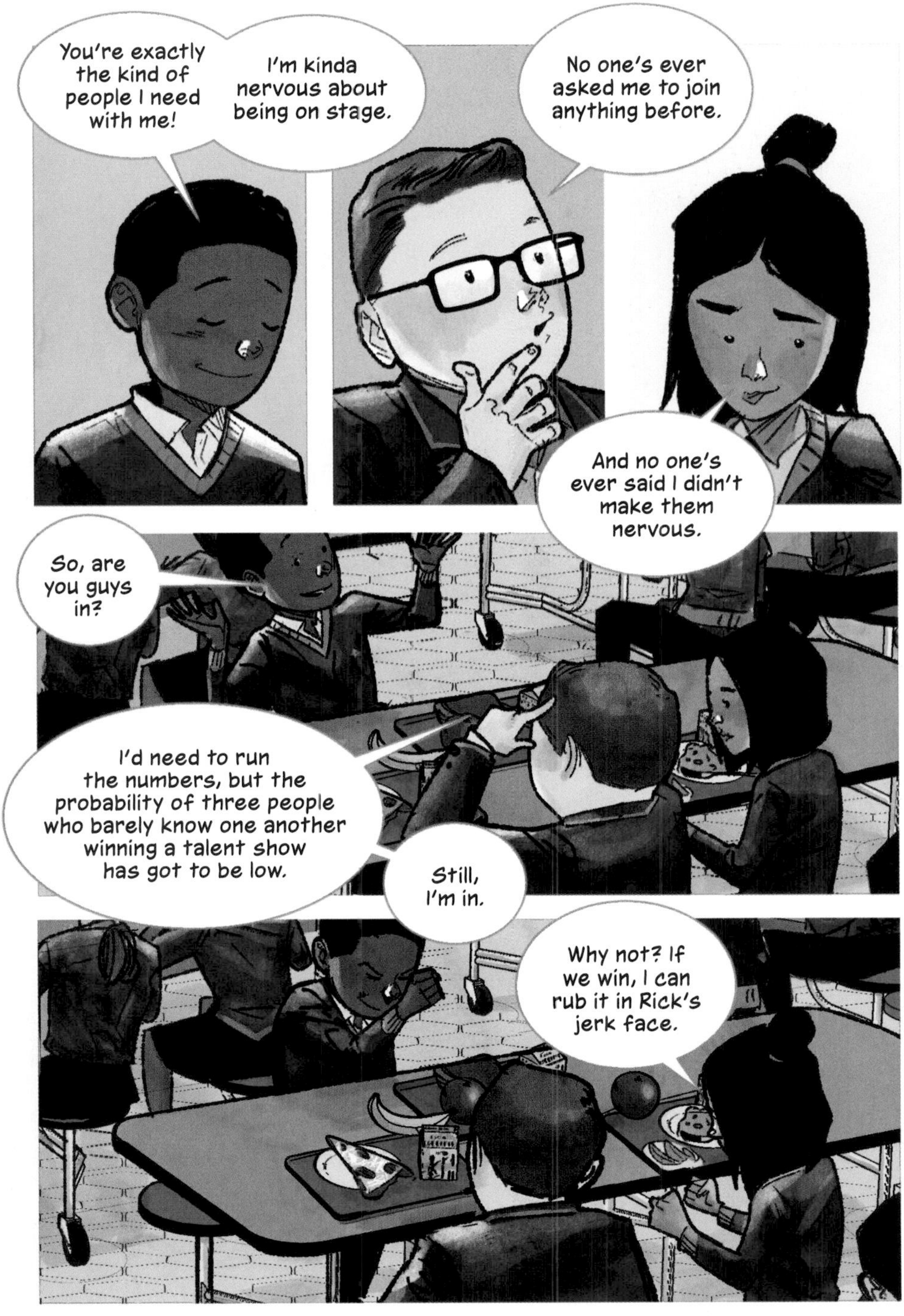
You're exactly the kind of people I need with me!
I'm kinda nervous about being on stage.
No one's ever asked me to join anything before.
And no one's ever said I didn't make them nervous.
So, are you guys in?
I'd need to run the numbers, but the probability of three people who barely know one another winning a talent show has got to be low.
Still, I'm in.
Why not? If we win, I can rub it in Rick's jerk face.

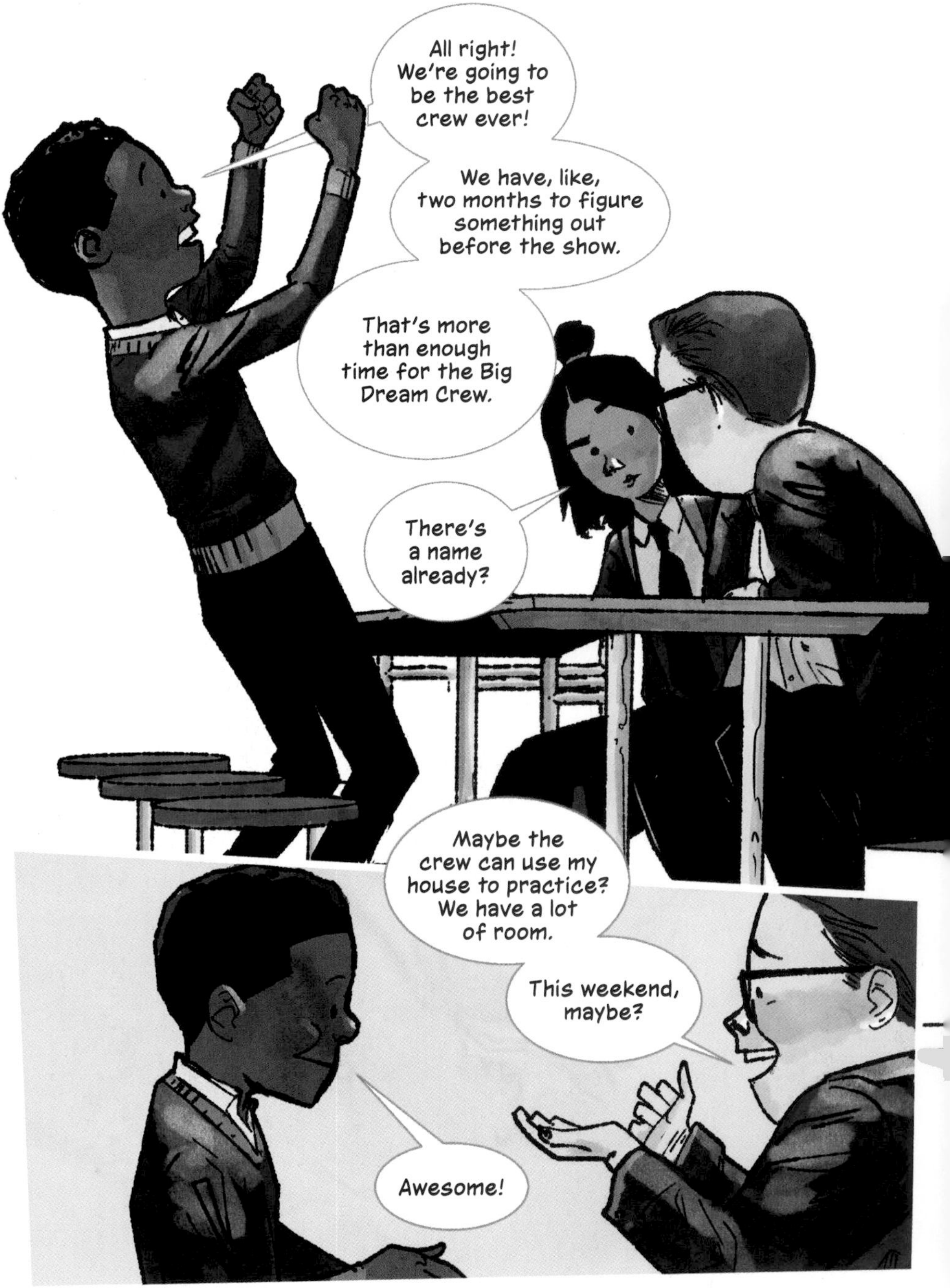
All right! We're going to be the best crew ever!
We have, like, two months to figure something out before the show.
That's more than enough time for the Big Dream Crew.
There's a name already?
Maybe the crew can use my house to practice? We have a lot of room.
This weekend, maybe?
Awesome!

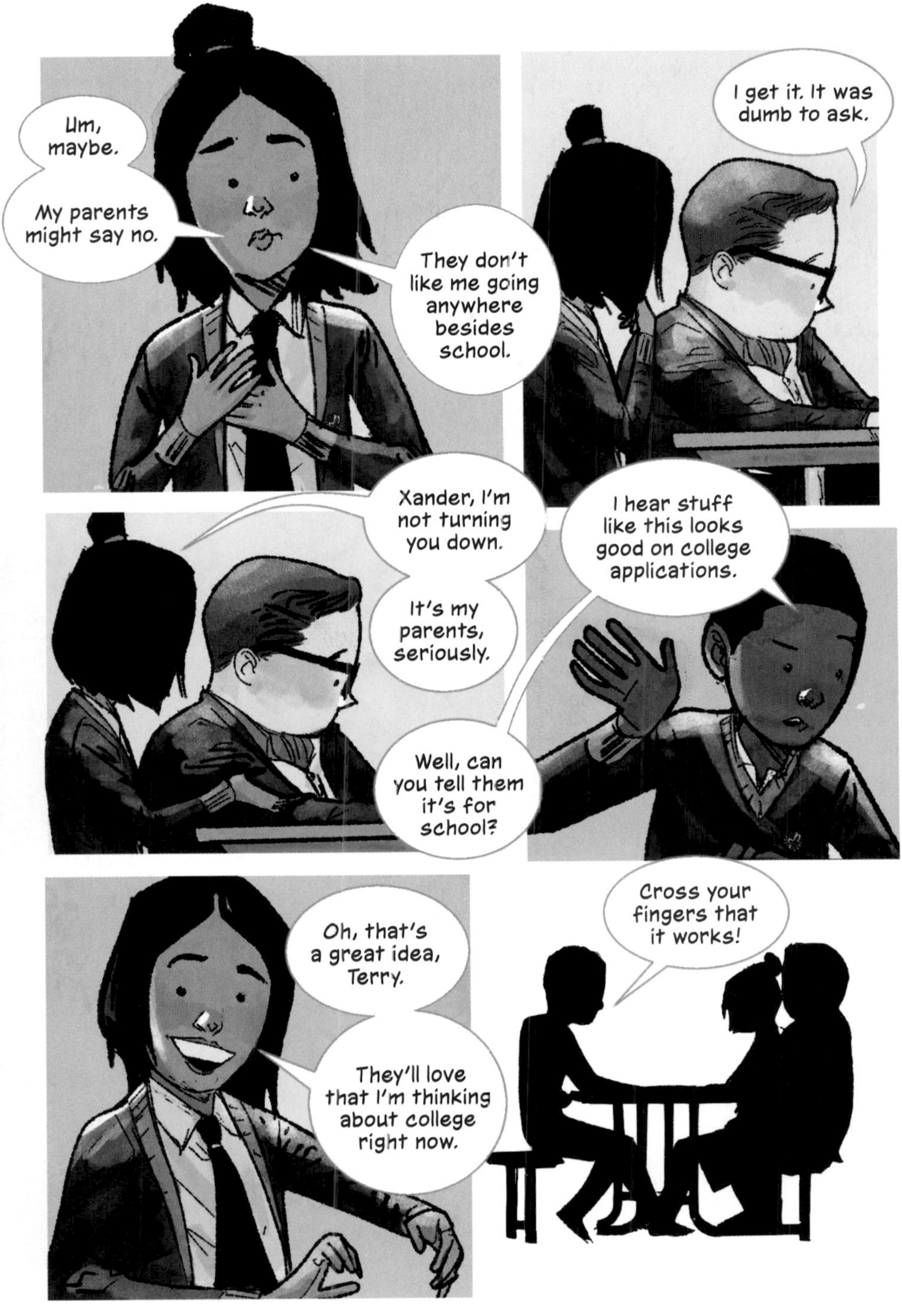
Um, maybe.
My parents might say no.
They don't like me going anywhere besides school.
I get it. It was dumb to ask.
Xander, I'm not turning you down.
It's my parents, seriously.
I hear stuff like this looks good on college applications.
Well, can you tell them it's for school?
Oh, that's a great idea, Terry.
They'll love that I'm thinking about college right now.
Cross your fingers that it works!

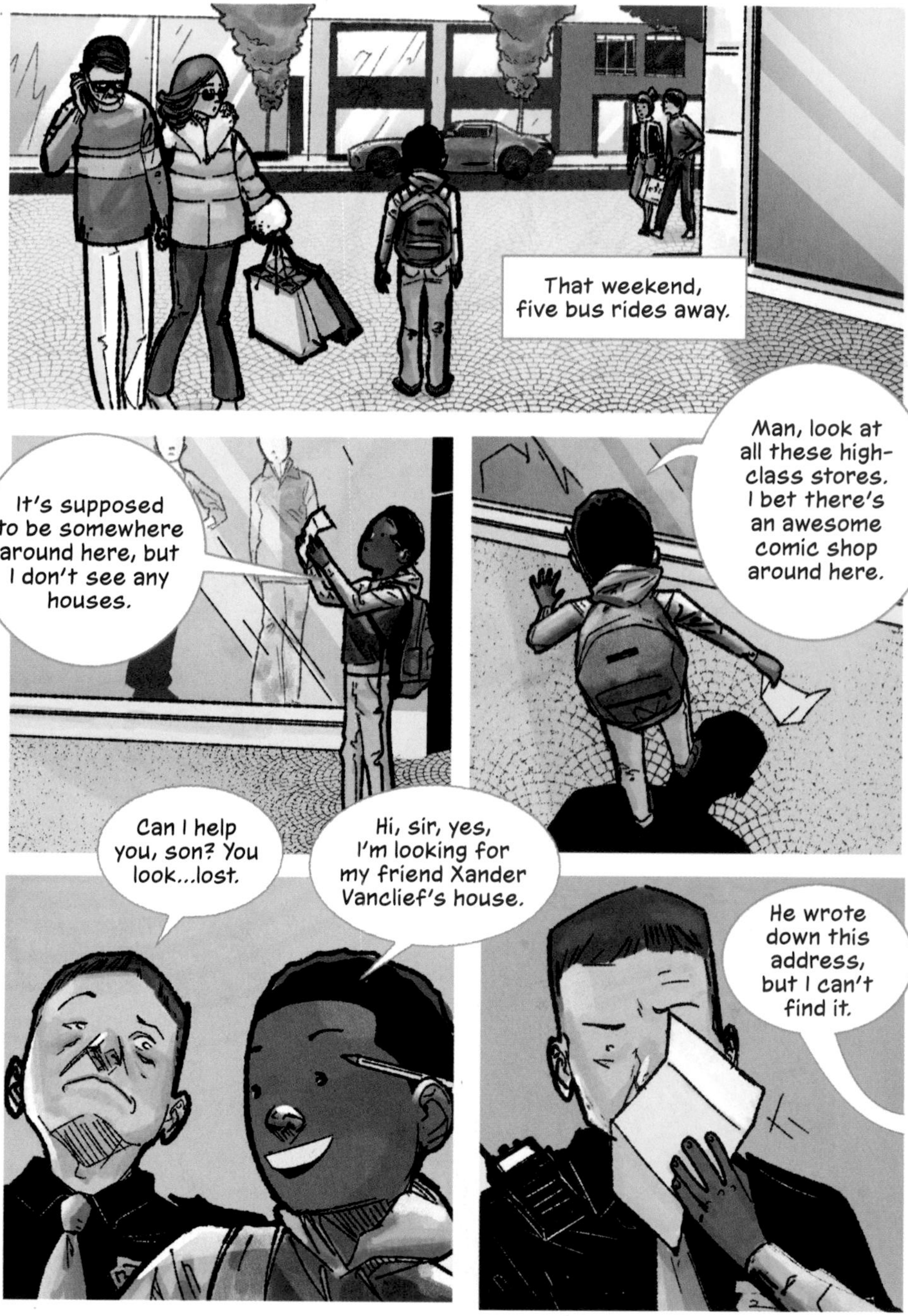
That weekend, five bus rides away.
It's supposed to be somewhere around here, but I don't see any houses.
Man, look at all these high-class stores. I bet there's an awesome comic shop around here.
Can I help you, son? You look...lost.
Hi, sir, yes, I'm looking for my friend Xander Vanclief's house.
He wrote down this address, but I can't find it.

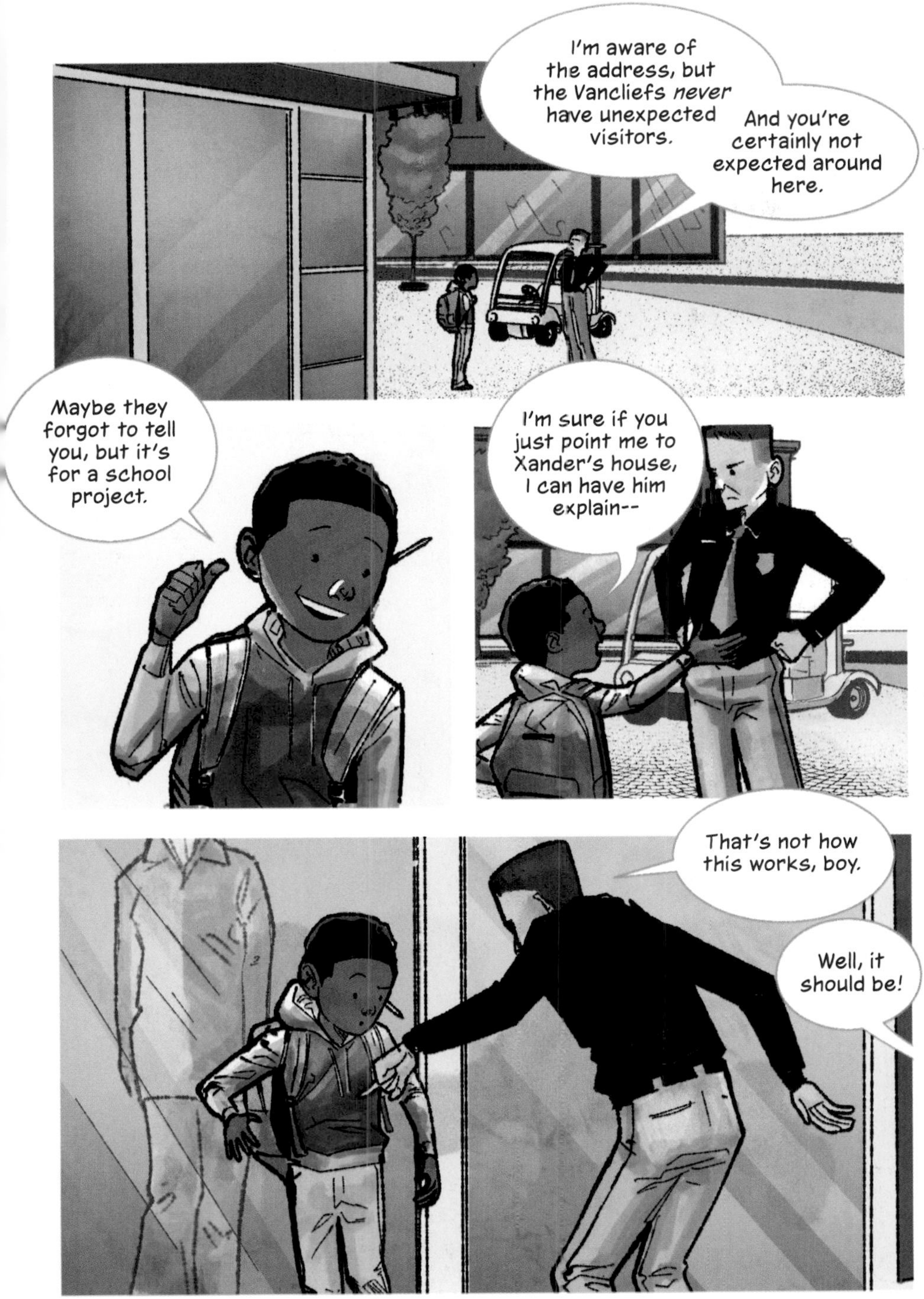
I'm aware of the address, but the Vancliefs *never* have unexpected visitors.
And you're certainly not expected around here.
Maybe they forgot to tell you, but it's for a school project.
I'm sure if you just point me to Xander's house, I can have him explain--
That's not how this works, boy.
Well, it should be!

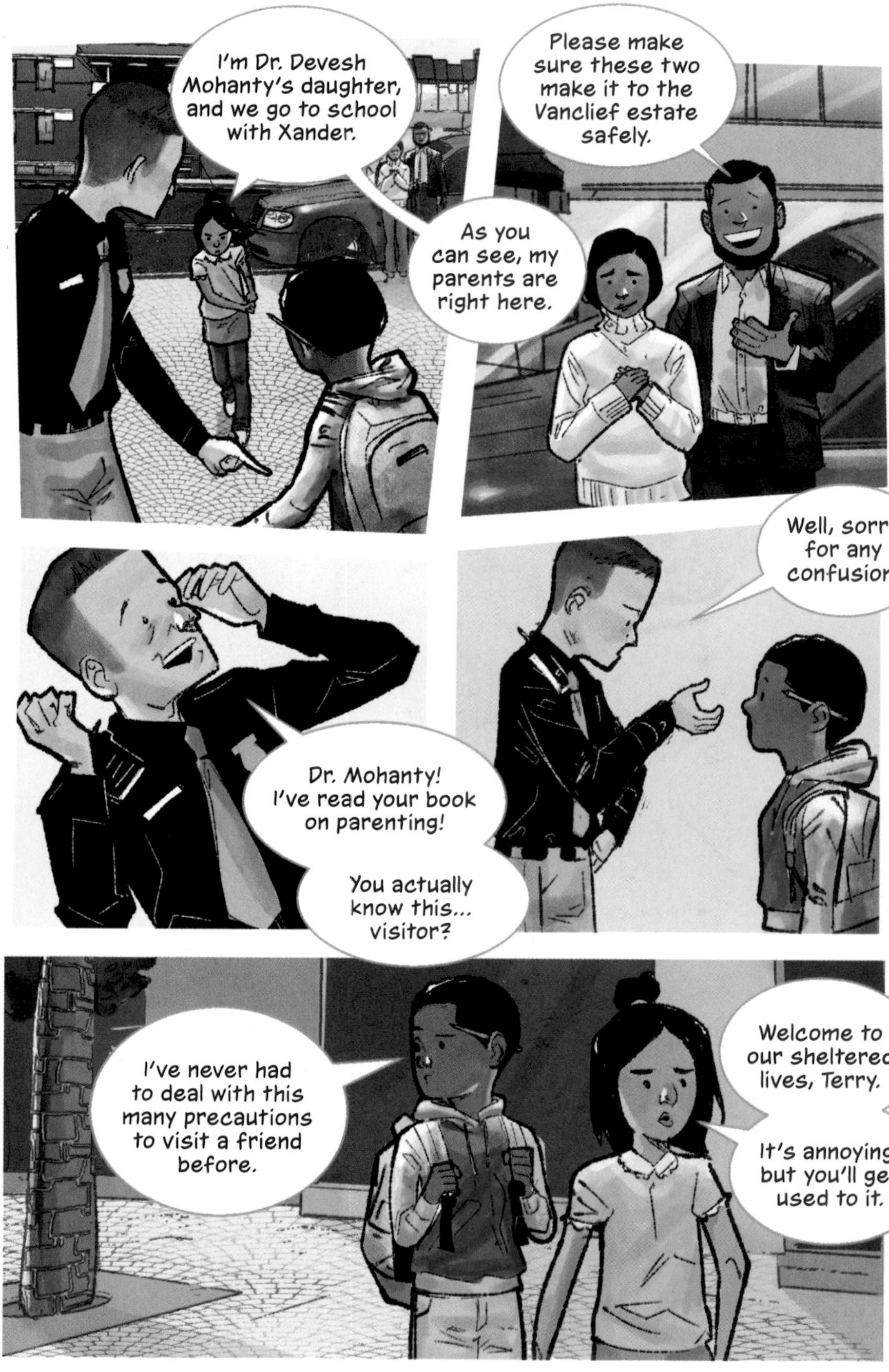
I'm Dr. Devesh Mohanty's daughter, and we go to school with Xander.
As you can see, my parents are right here.
Please make sure these two make it to the Vanclief estate safely.
Dr. Mohanty! I've read your book on parenting!
You actually know this... visitor?
Well, sorry for any confusion.
I've never had to deal with this many precautions to visit a friend before.
Welcome to our sheltered lives, Terry.
It's annoying, but you'll get used to it.

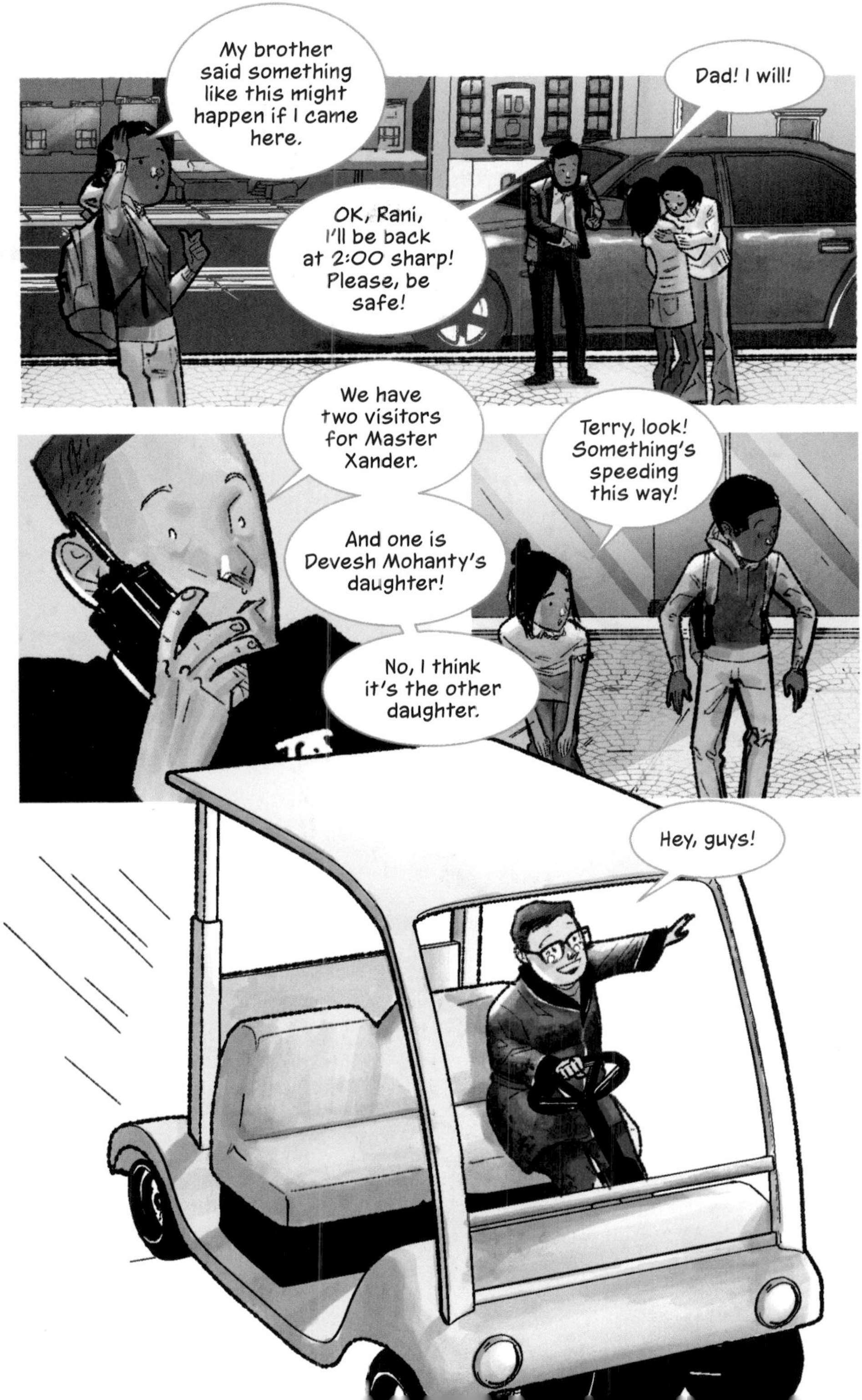
My brother said something like this might happen if I came here.
OK, Rani, I'll be back at 2:00 sharp! Please, be safe!
Dad! I will!
We have two visitors for Master Xander.
And one is Devesh Mohanty's daughter!
No, I think it's the other daughter.
Terry, look! Something's speeding this way!
Hey, guys!

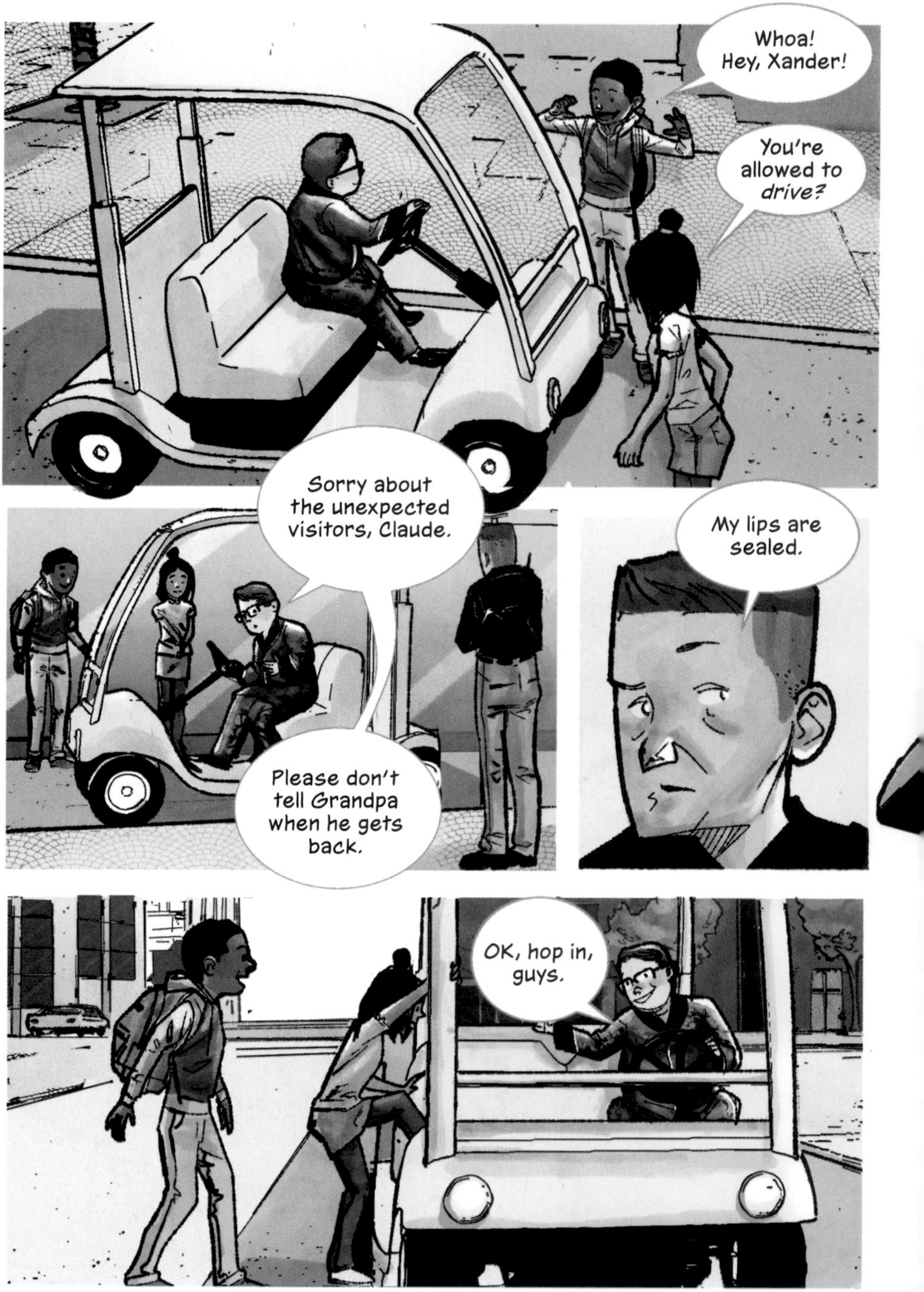
Whoa! Hey, Xander!
You're allowed to *drive?*
Sorry about the unexpected visitors, Claude.
Please don't tell Grandpa when he gets back.
My lips are sealed.
OK, hop in, guys.

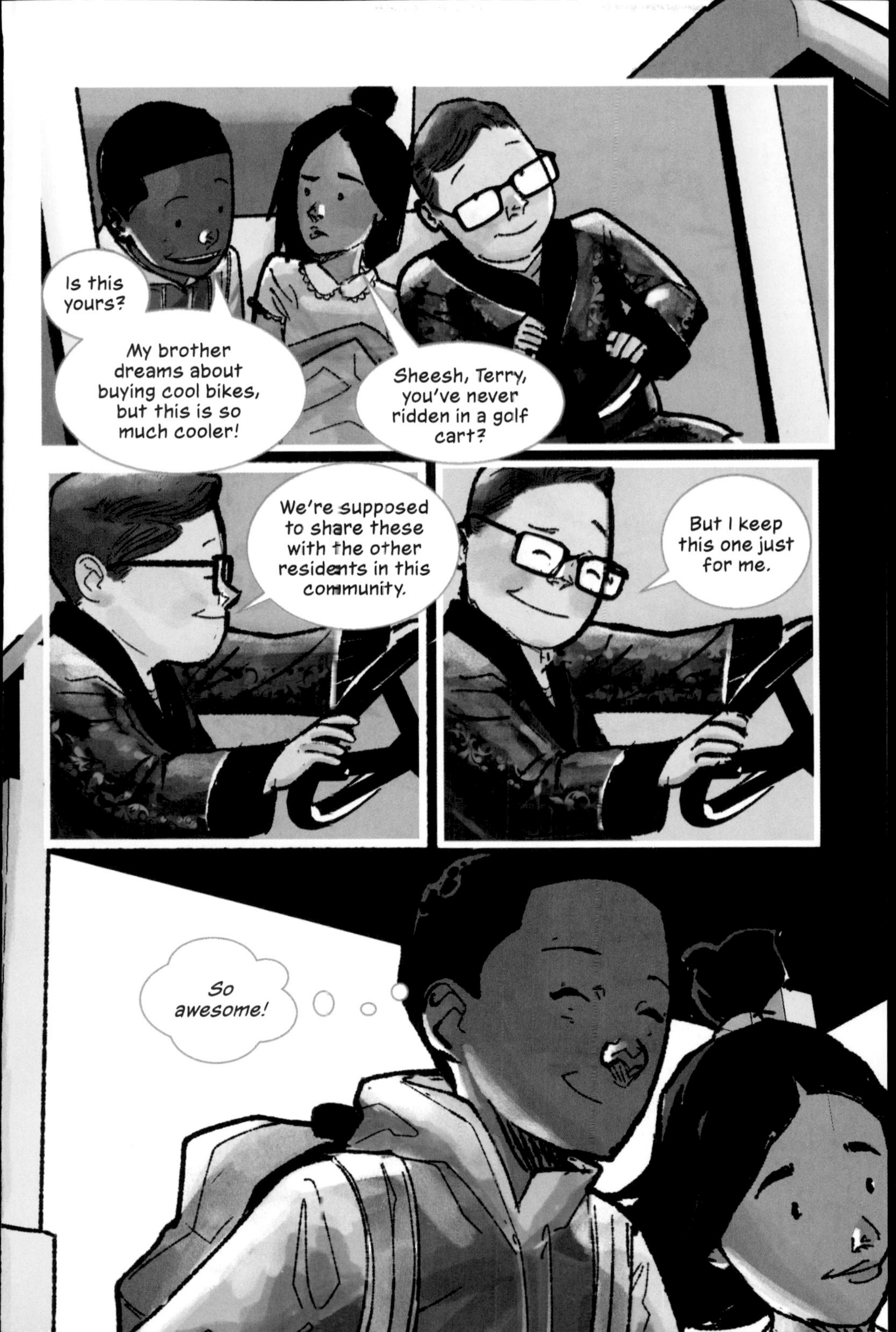
Is this yours?
My brother dreams about buying cool bikes, but this is so much cooler!
Sheesh, Terry, you've never ridden in a golf cart?
We're supposed to share these with the other residents in this community.
But I keep this one just for me.
So awesome!

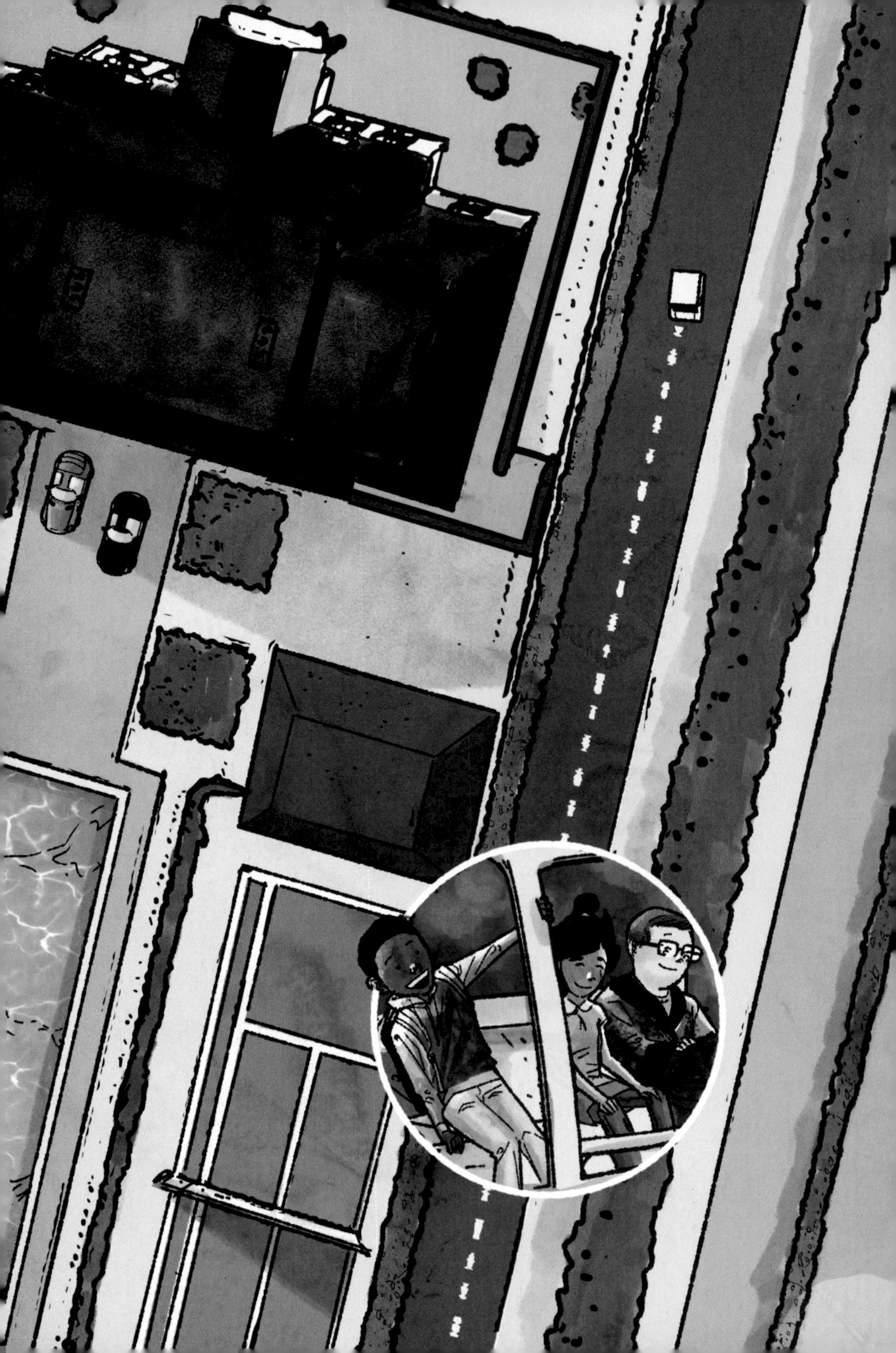

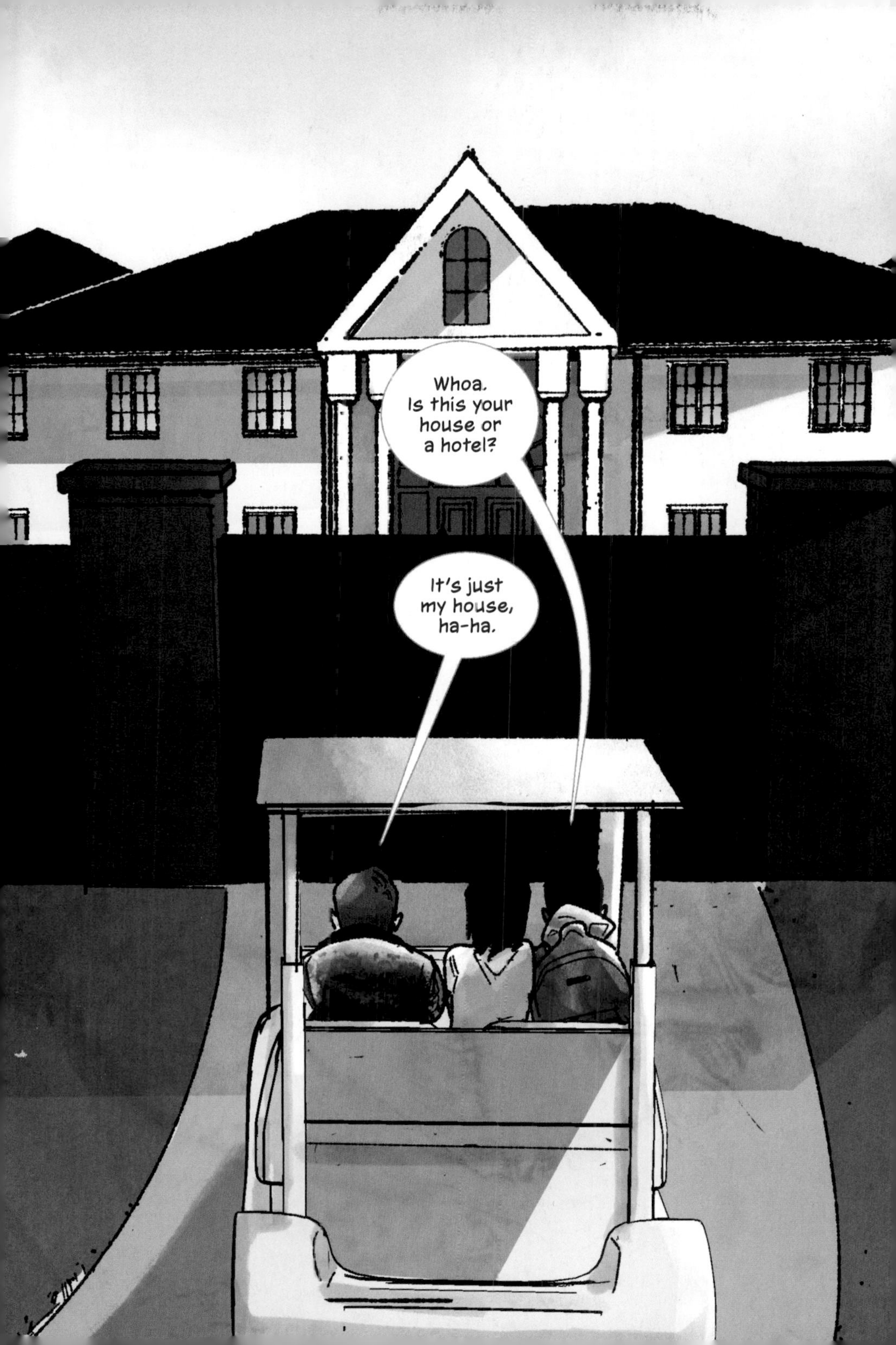
Whoa. Is this your house or a hotel?
It's just my house, ha-ha.

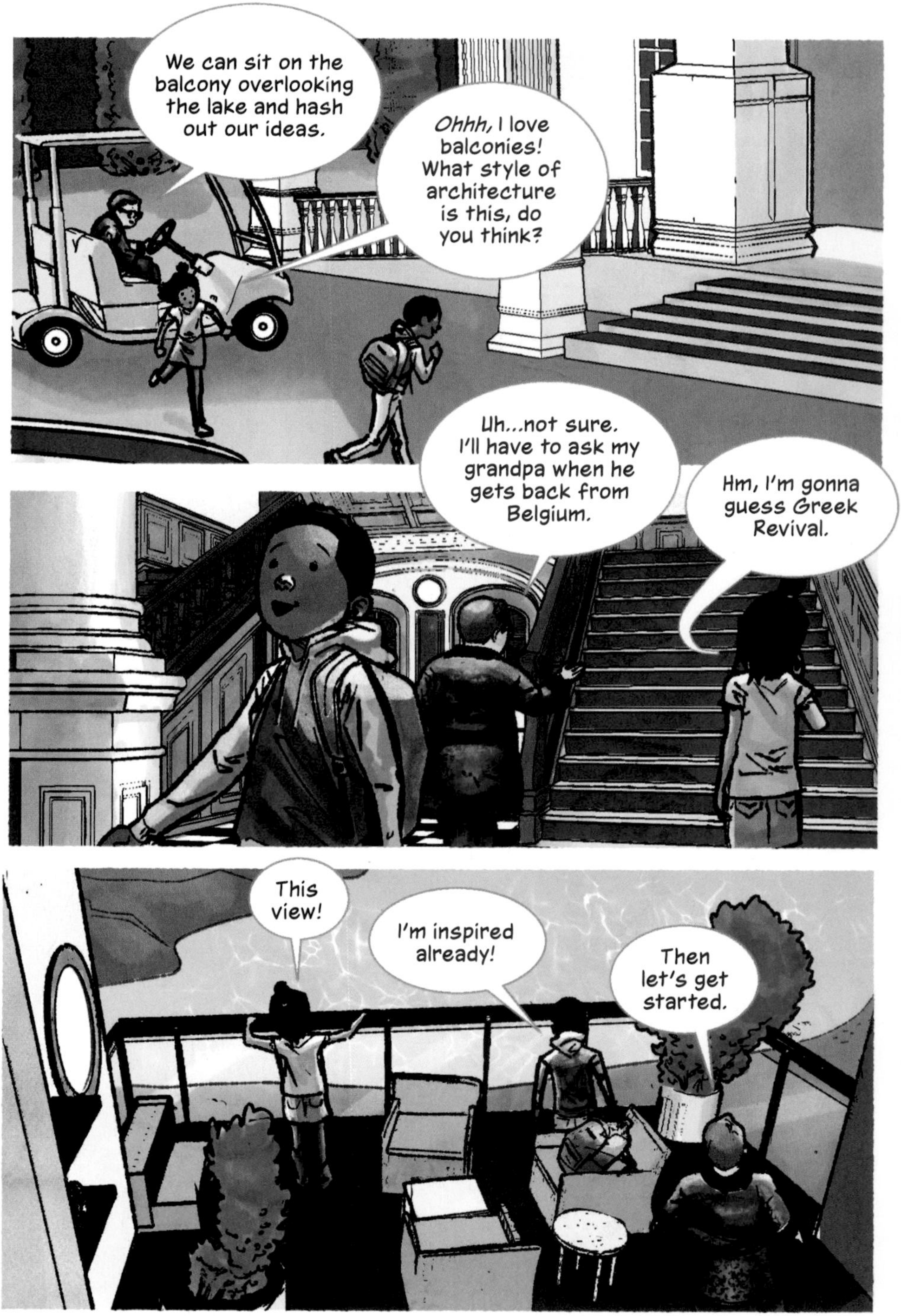
We can sit on the balcony overlooking the lake and hash out our ideas.
Ohhh, I love balconies! What style of architecture is this, do you think?
Uh...not sure. I'll have to ask my grandpa when he gets back from Belgium.
Hm, I'm gonna guess Greek Revival.
This view!
I'm inspired already!
Then let's get started.

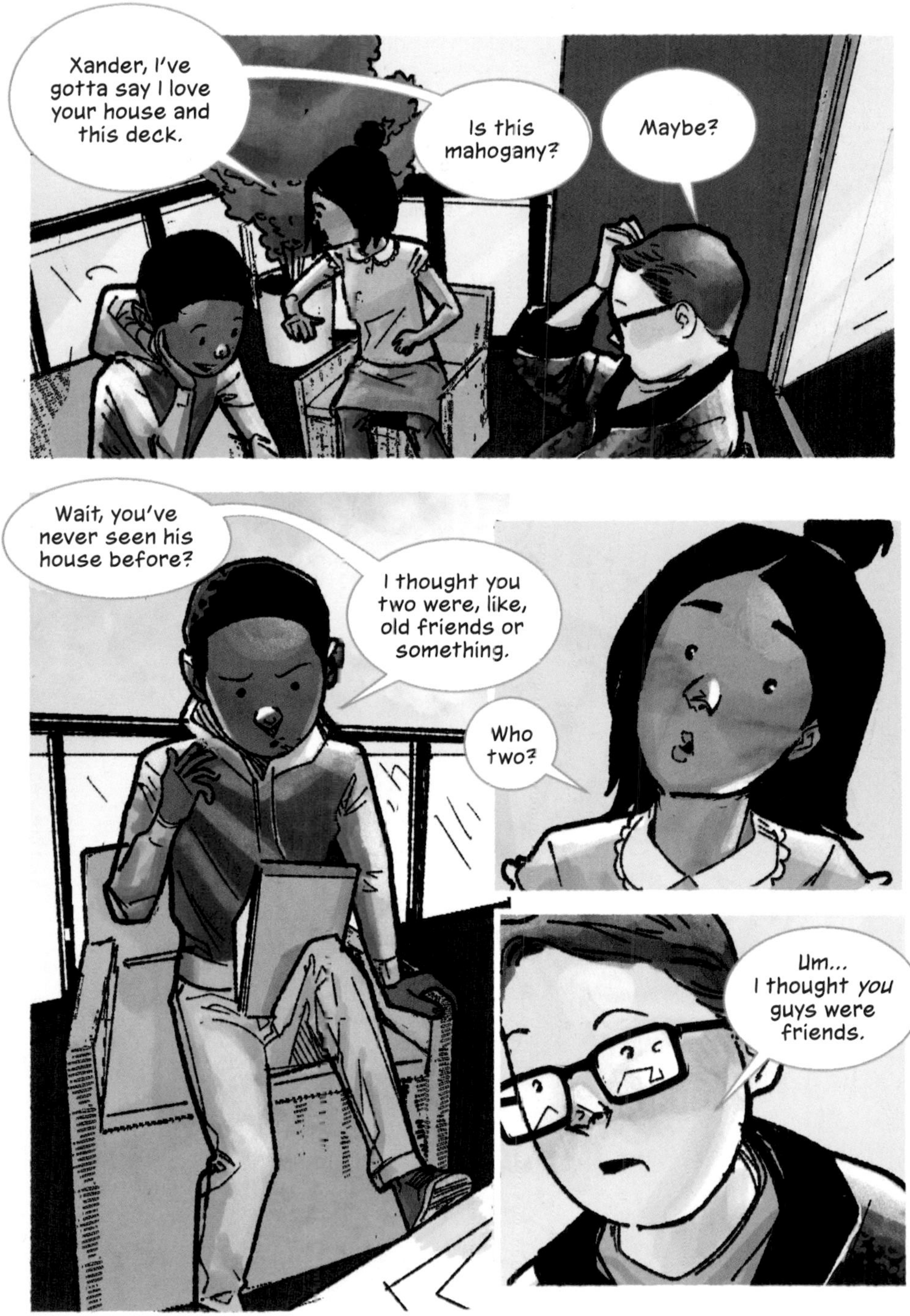
Xander, I've gotta say I love your house and this deck.
Is this mahogany?
Maybe?
Wait, you've never seen his house before?
I thought you two were, like, old friends or something.
Who two?
Um... I thought *you* guys were friends.

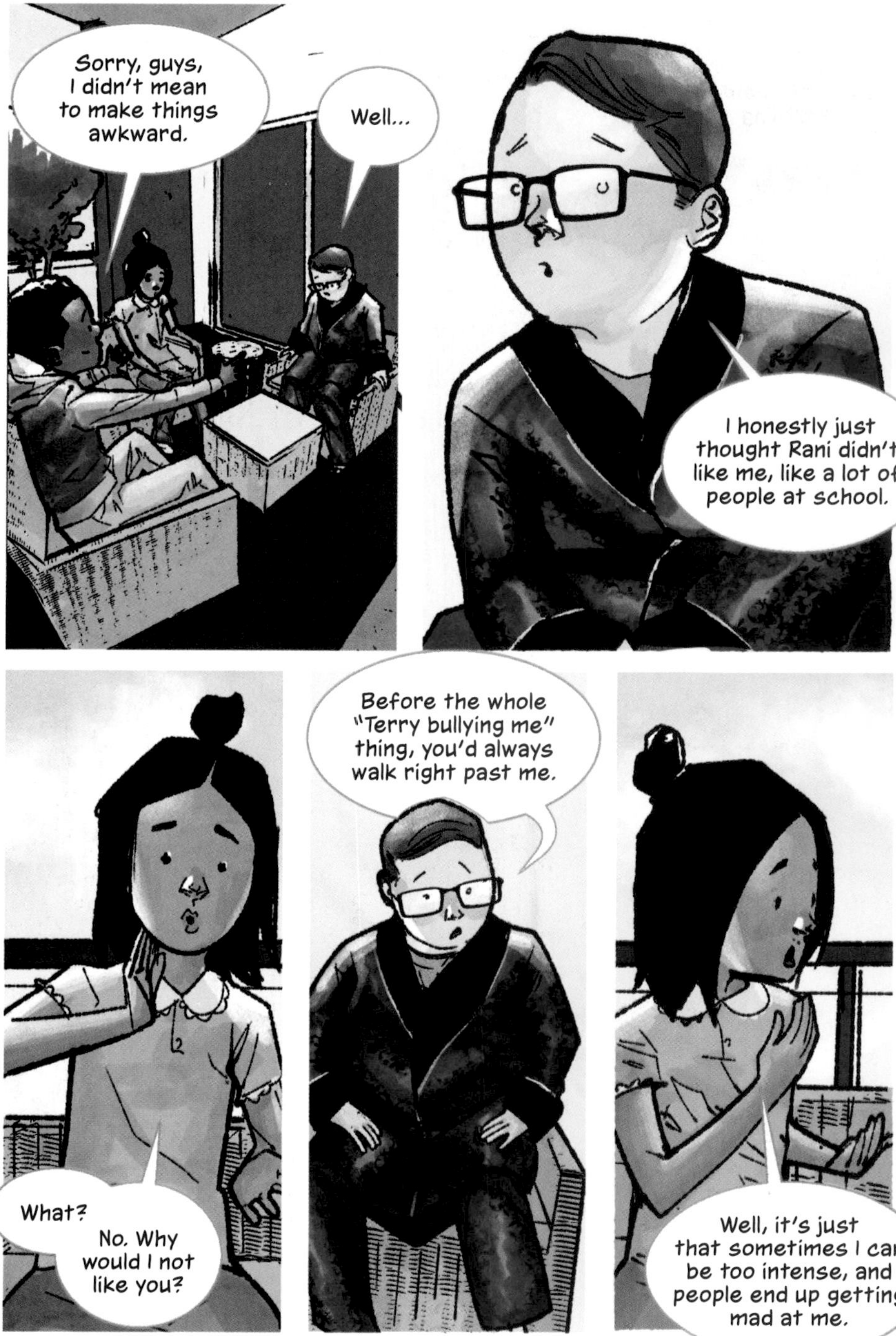

Sorry, guys, I didn't mean to make things awkward.
Well...
I honestly just thought Rani didn't like me, like a lot of people at school.
Before the whole "Terry bullying me" thing, you'd always walk right past me.
What?
No. Why would I not like you?
Well, it's just that sometimes I can be too intense, and people end up getting mad at me.

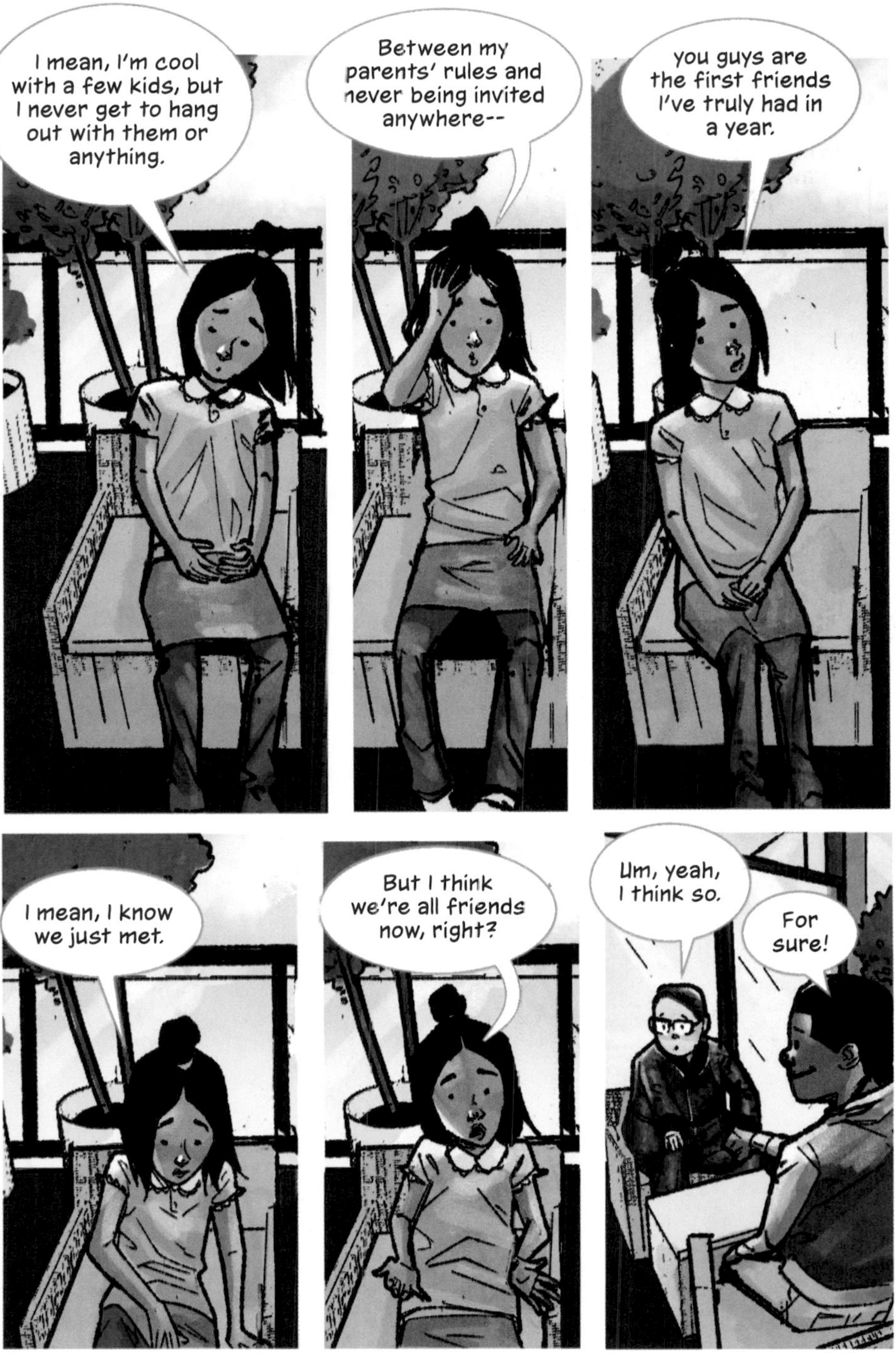
I mean, I'm cool with a few kids, but I never get to hang out with them or anything.
Between my parents' rules and never being invited anywhere--
you guys are the first friends I've truly had in a year.
I mean, I know we just met.
But I think we're all friends now, right?
Um, yeah, I think so.
For sure!

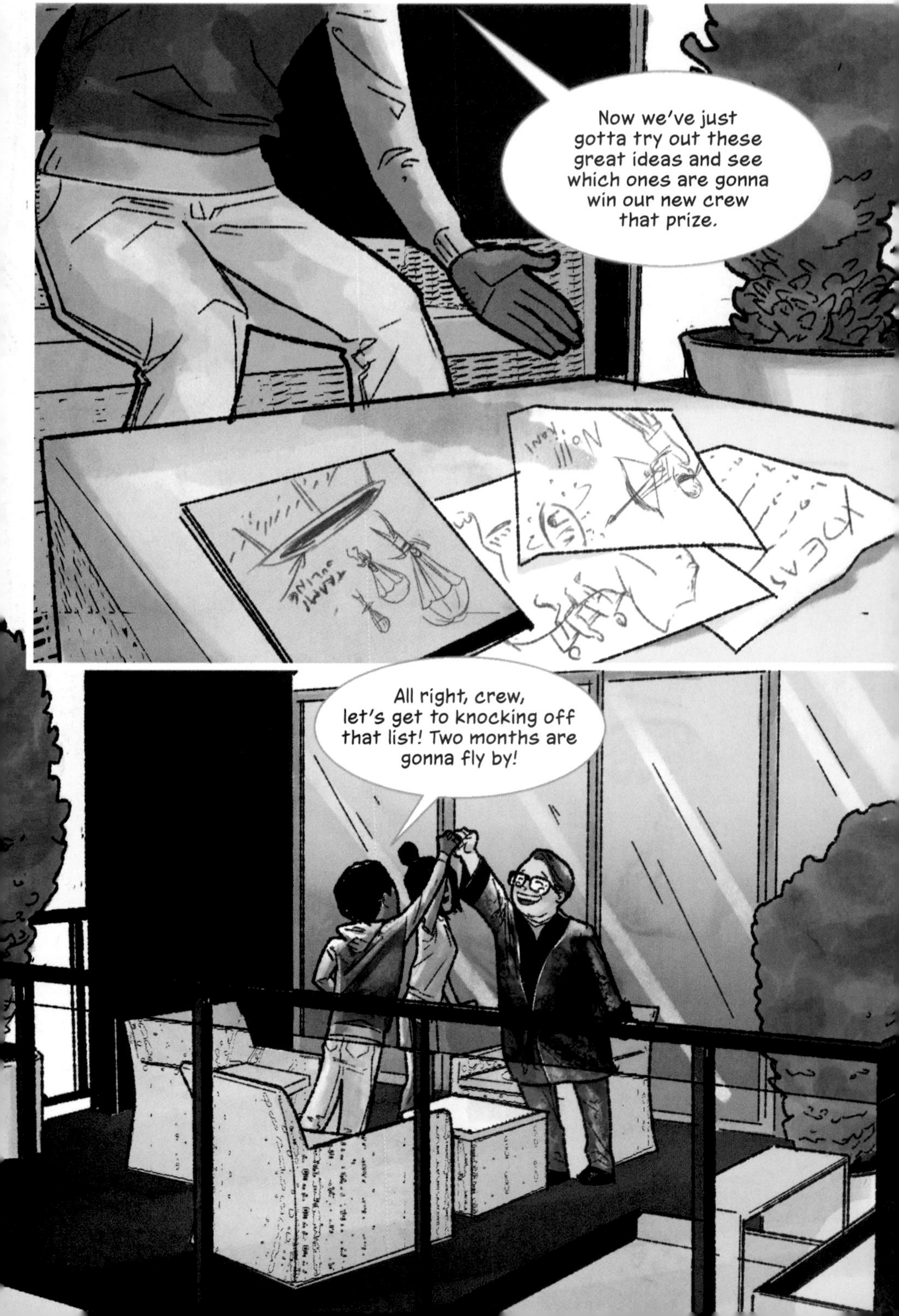
Now we've just gotta try out these great ideas and see which ones are gonna win our new crew that prize.
All right, crew, let's get to knocking off that list! Two months are gonna fly by!

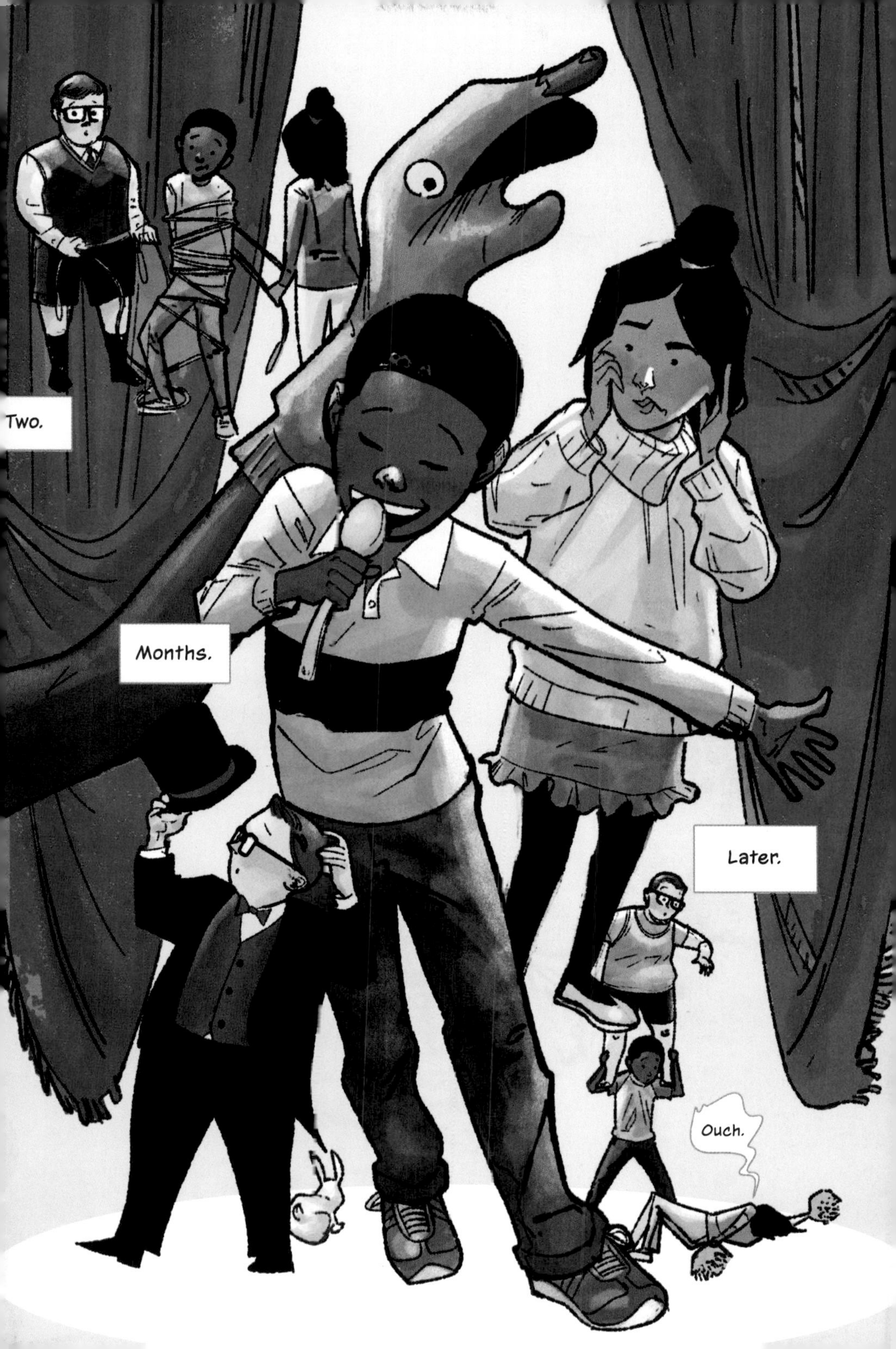
Two.
Months.
Later.
Ouch.

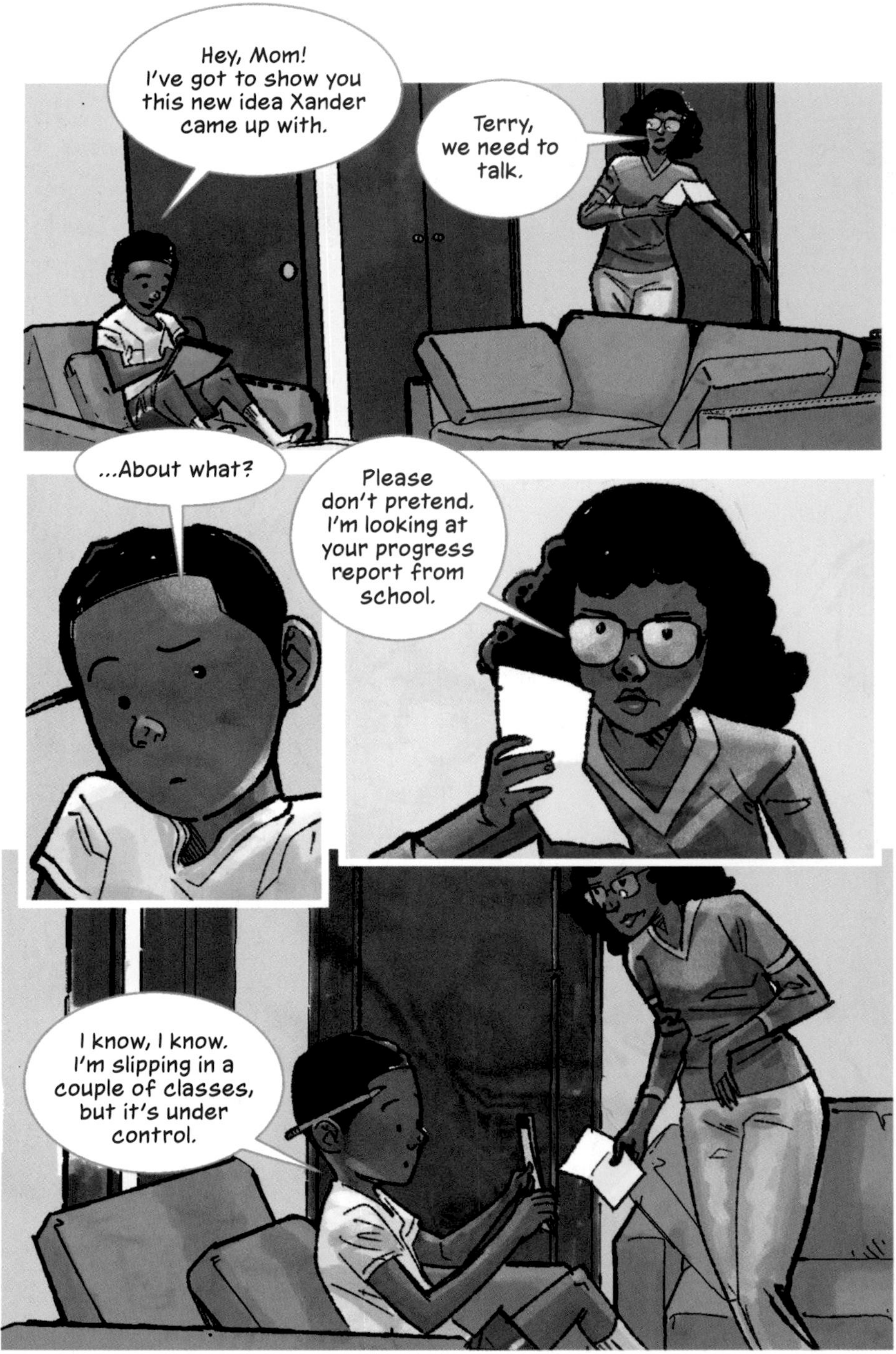

Hey, Mom! I've got to show you this new idea Xander came up with.
Terry, we need to talk.
...About what?
Please don't pretend. I'm looking at your progress report from school.
I know, I know. I'm slipping in a couple of classes, but it's under control.

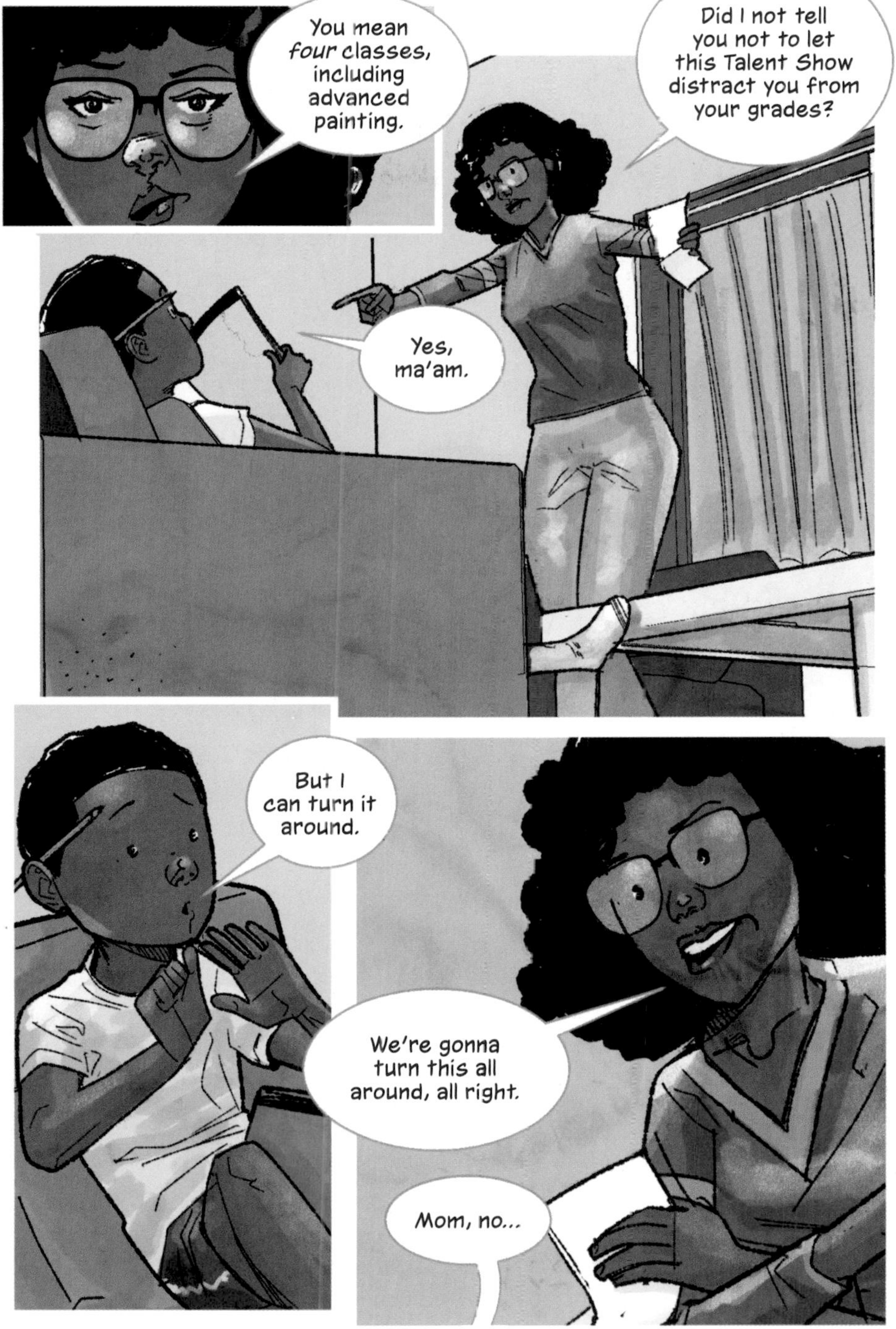
You mean *four* classes, including advanced painting.
Did I not tell you not to let this Talent Show distract you from your grades?
Yes, ma'am.
But I can turn it around.
We're gonna turn this all around, all right.
Mom, no...

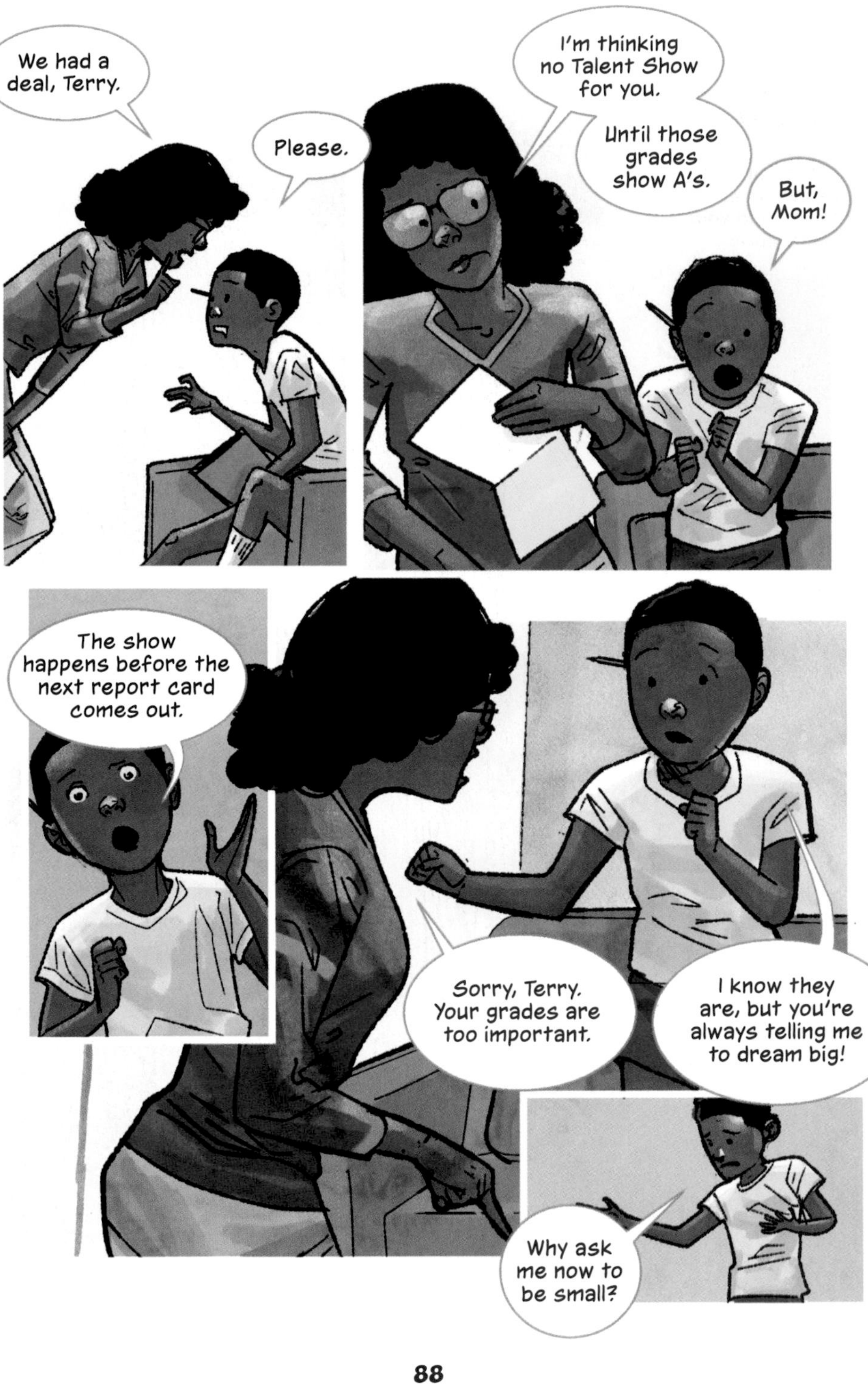
We had a deal, Terry.
Please.
I'm thinking no Talent Show for you.
Until those grades show A's.
But, Mom!
The show happens before the next report card comes out.
Sorry, Terry. Your grades are too important.
I know they are, but you're always telling me to dream big!
Why ask me now to be small?

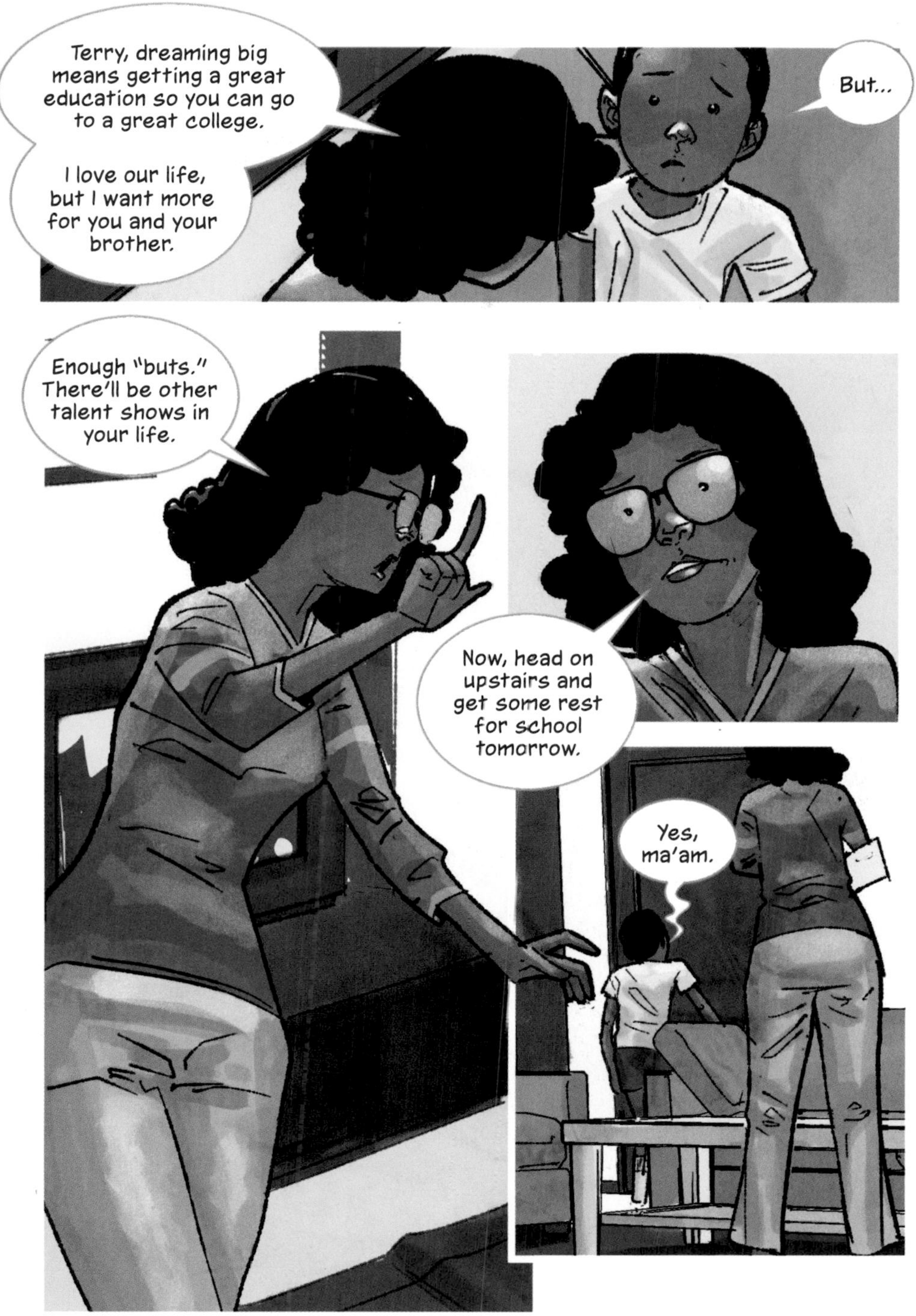
Terry, dreaming big means getting a great education so you can go to a great college.
I love our life, but I want more for you and your brother.
But...
Enough "buts." There'll be other talent shows in your life.
Now, head on upstairs and get some rest for school tomorrow.
Yes, ma'am.

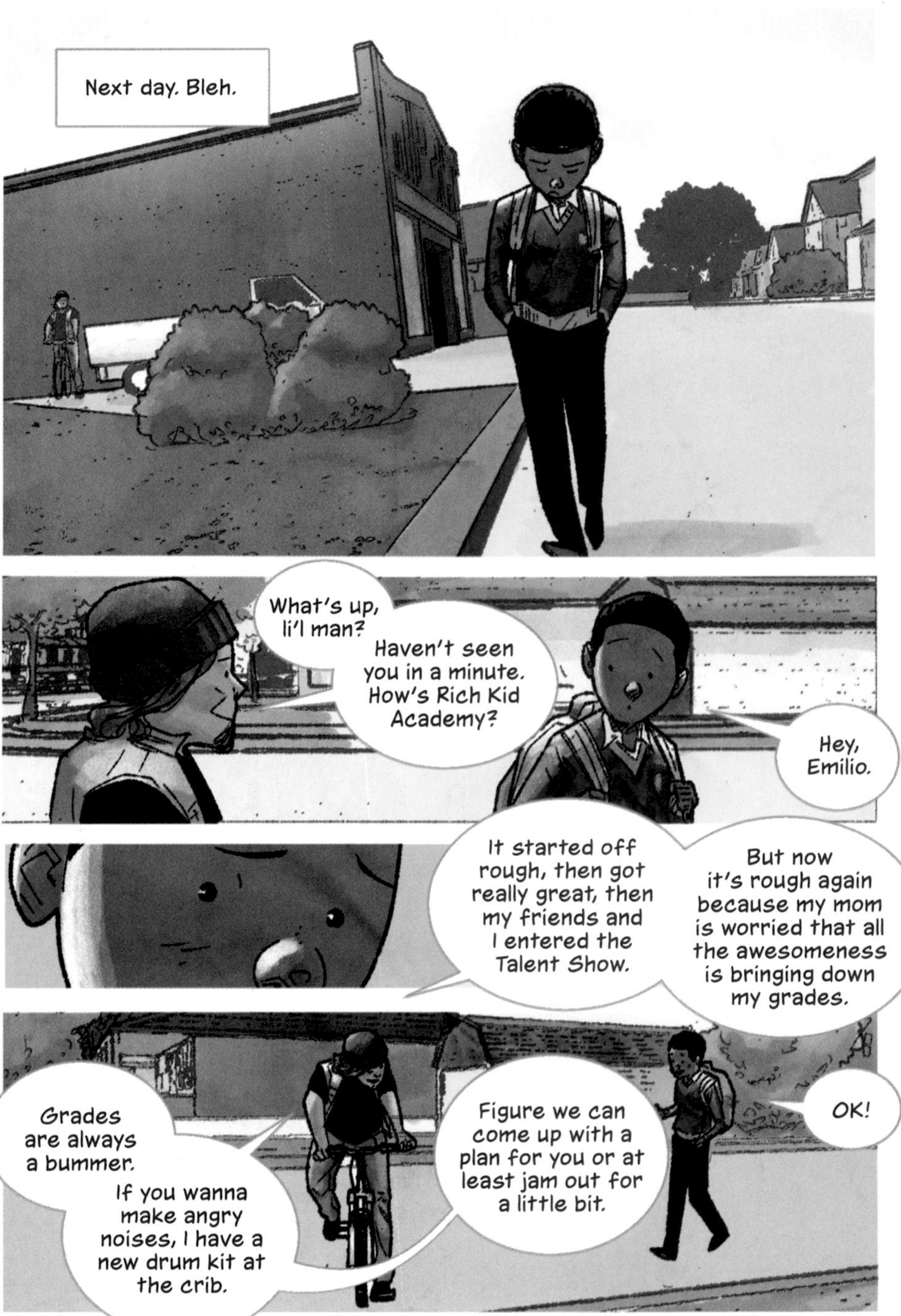
Next day. Bleh.
What's up, li'l man?
Haven't seen you in a minute. How's Rich Kid Academy?
Hey, Emilio.
It started off rough, then got really great, then my friends and I entered the Talent Show.
But now it's rough again because my mom is worried that all the awesomeness is bringing down my grades.
Grades are always a bummer.
If you wanna make angry noises, I have a new drum kit at the crib.
Figure we can come up with a plan for you or at least jam out for a little bit.
OK!

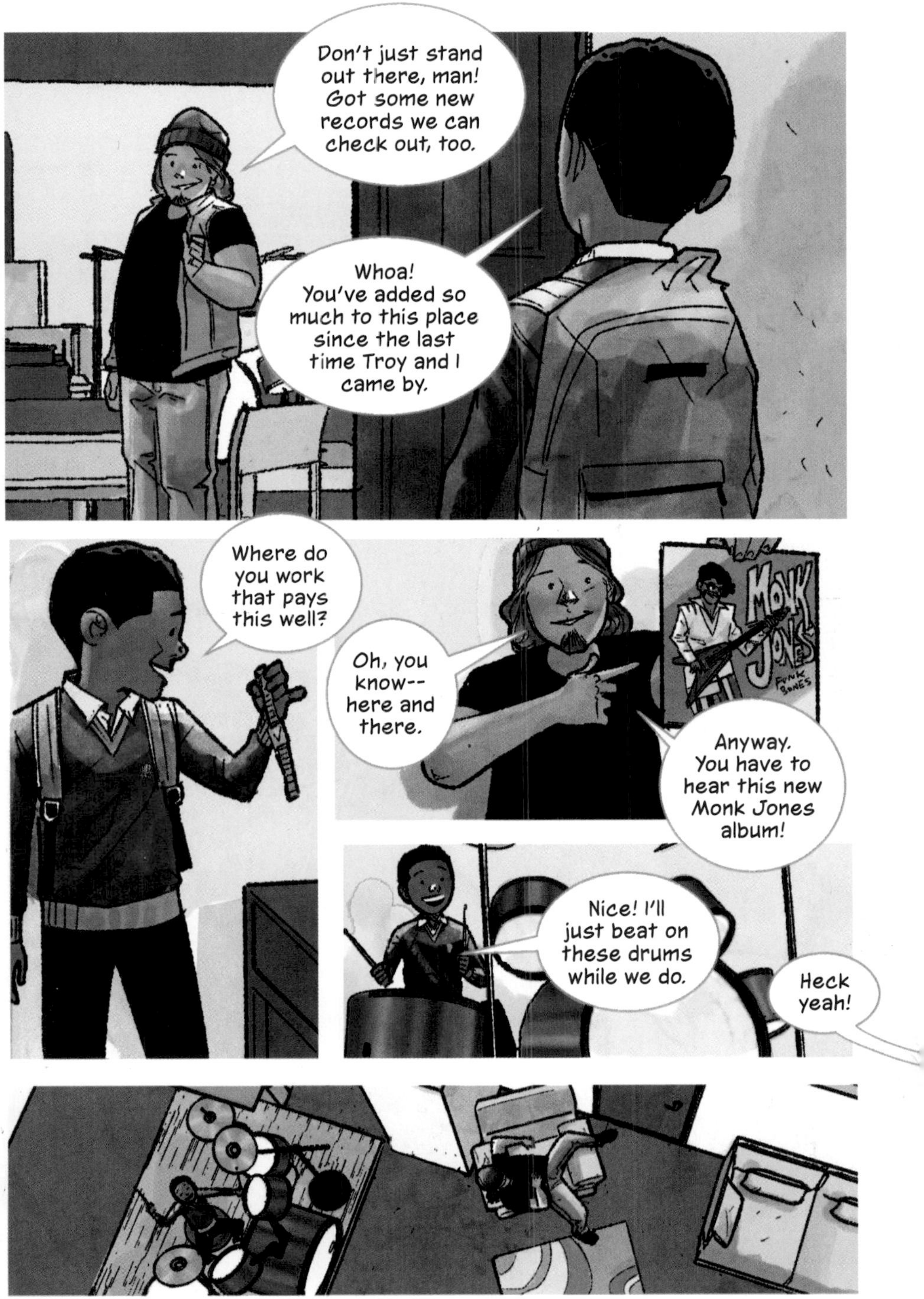
Don't just stand out there, man! Got some new records we can check out, too.
Whoa! You've added so much to this place since the last time Troy and I came by.
Where do you work that pays this well?
Oh, you know-- here and there.
MONK JONES
FUNK BONES
Anyway. You have to hear this new Monk Jones album!
Nice! I'll just beat on these drums while we do.
Heck yeah!

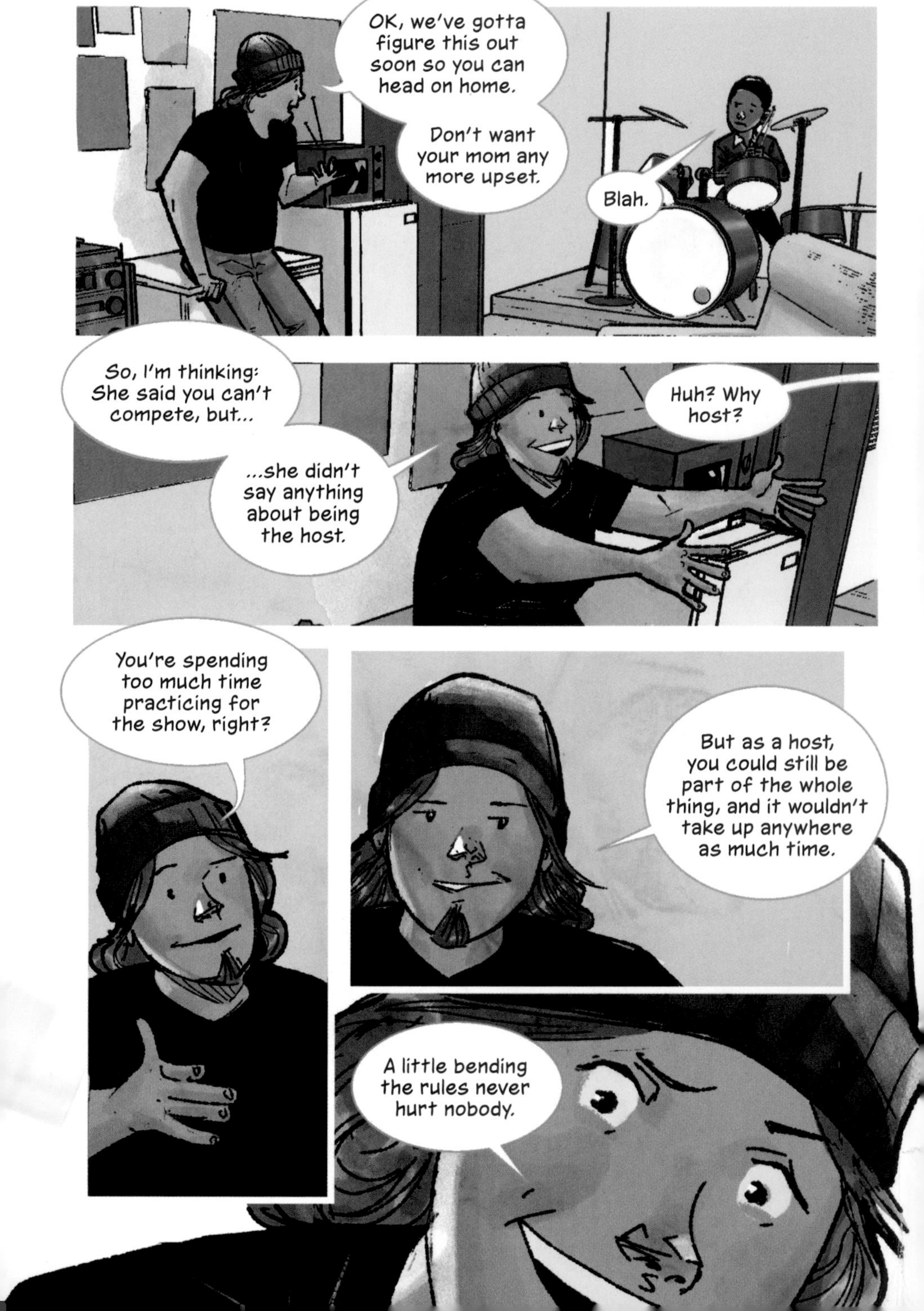
OK, we've gotta figure this out soon so you can head on home.
Don't want your mom any more upset.
Blah.
So, I'm thinking: She said you can't compete, but...
...she didn't say anything about being the host.
Huh? Why host?
You're spending too much time practicing for the show, right?
But as a host, you could still be part of the whole thing, and it wouldn't take up anywhere as much time.
A little bending the rules never hurt nobody.

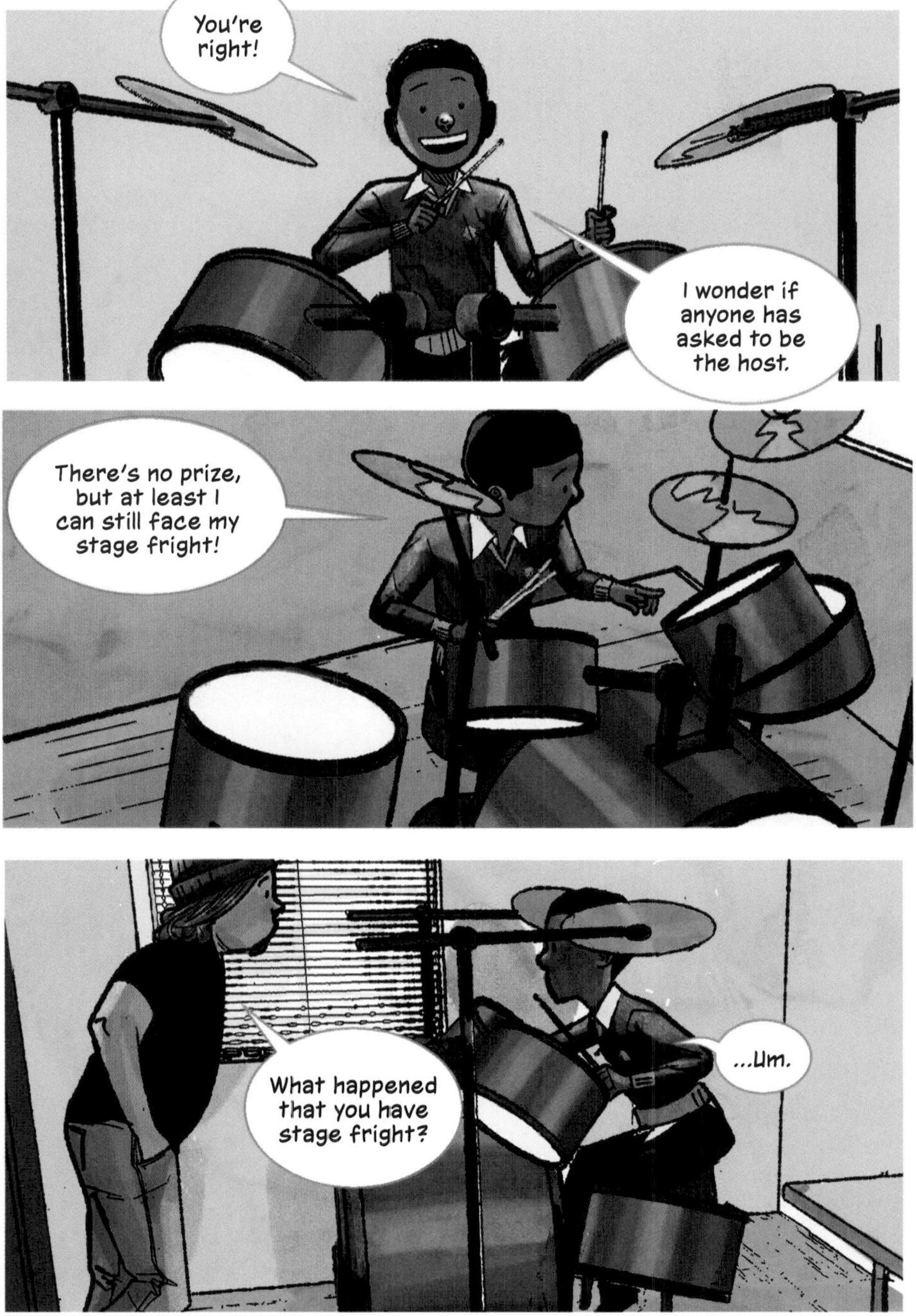
You're right!
I wonder if anyone has asked to be the host.
There's no prize, but at least I can still face my stage fright!
What happened that you have stage fright?
...Um.

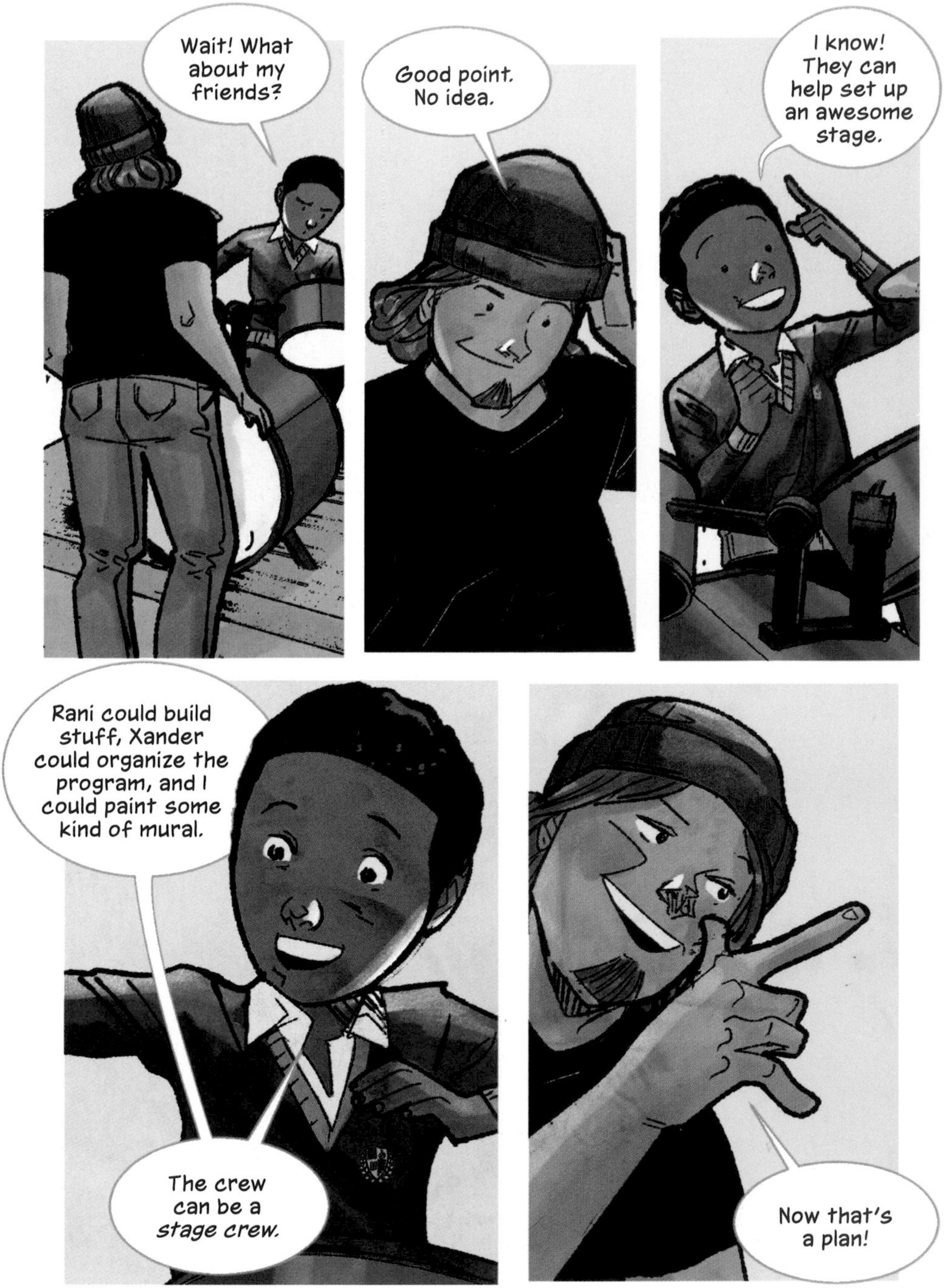
Wait! What about my friends?
Good point. No idea.
I know! They can help set up an awesome stage.
Rani could build stuff, Xander could organize the program, and I could paint some kind of mural.
The crew can be a *stage crew.*
Now that's a plan!

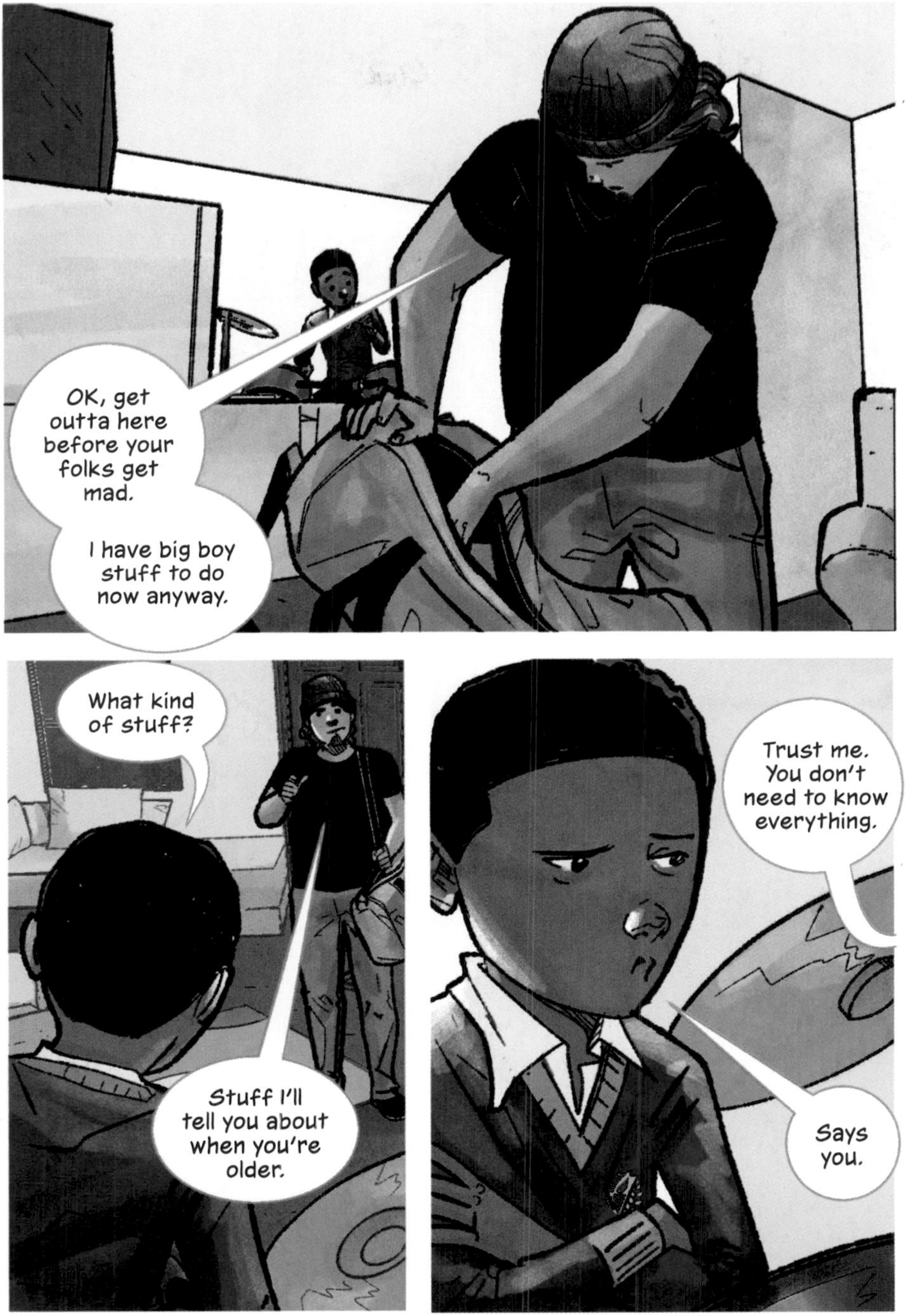
OK, get outta here before your folks get mad.
I have big boy stuff to do now anyway.
What kind of stuff?
Stuff I'll tell you about when you're older.
Trust me. You don't need to know everything.
Says you.

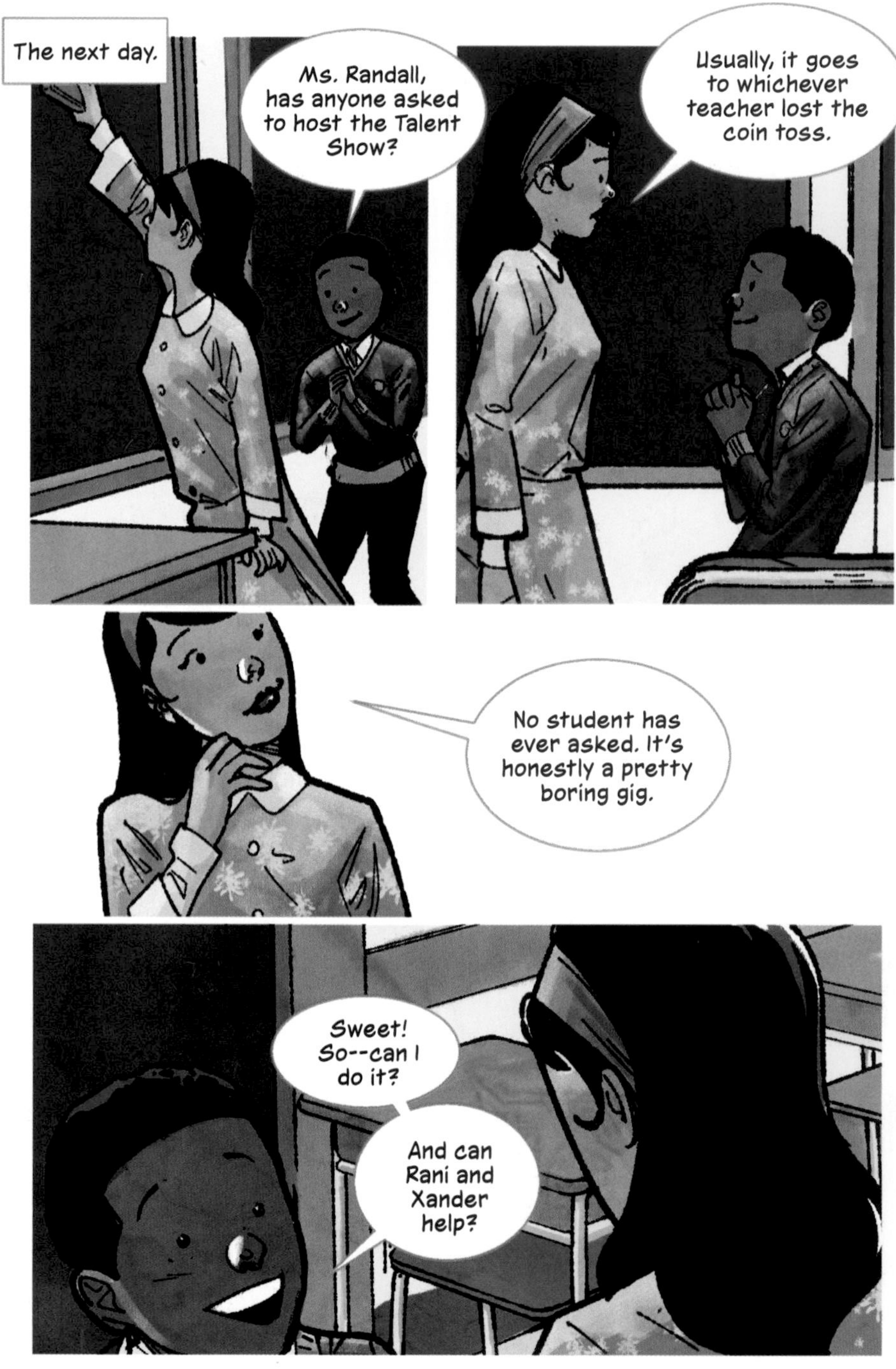
The next day.
Ms. Randall, has anyone asked to host the Talent Show?
Usually, it goes to whichever teacher lost the coin toss.
No student has ever asked. It's honestly a pretty boring gig.
Sweet! So--can I do it?
And can Rani and Xander help?

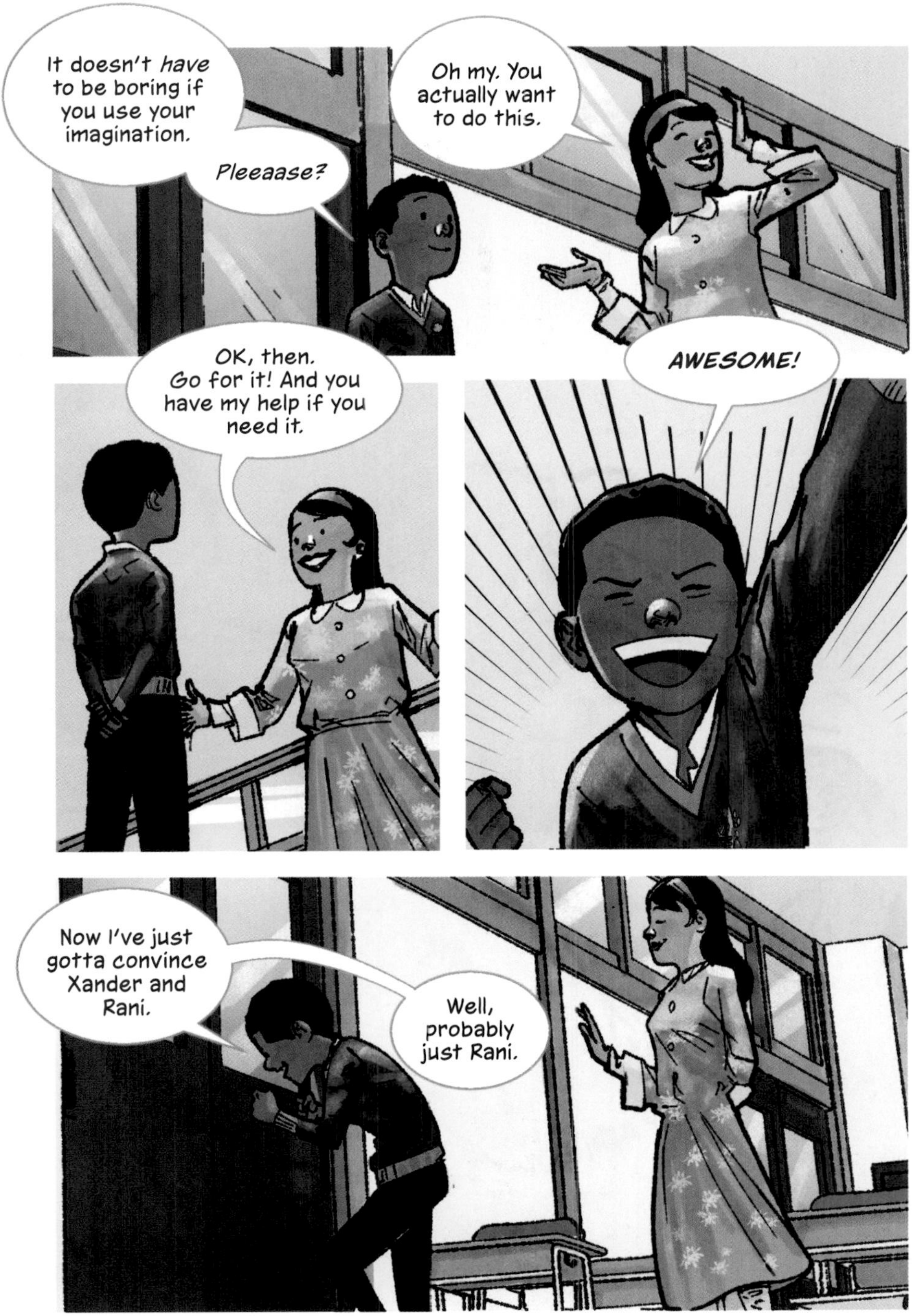
It doesn't *have* to be boring if you use your imagination.
Pleeaase?
Oh my. You actually want to do this.
OK, then. Go for it! And you have my help if you need it.
AWESOME!
Now I've just gotta convince Xander and Rani.
Well, probably just Rani.

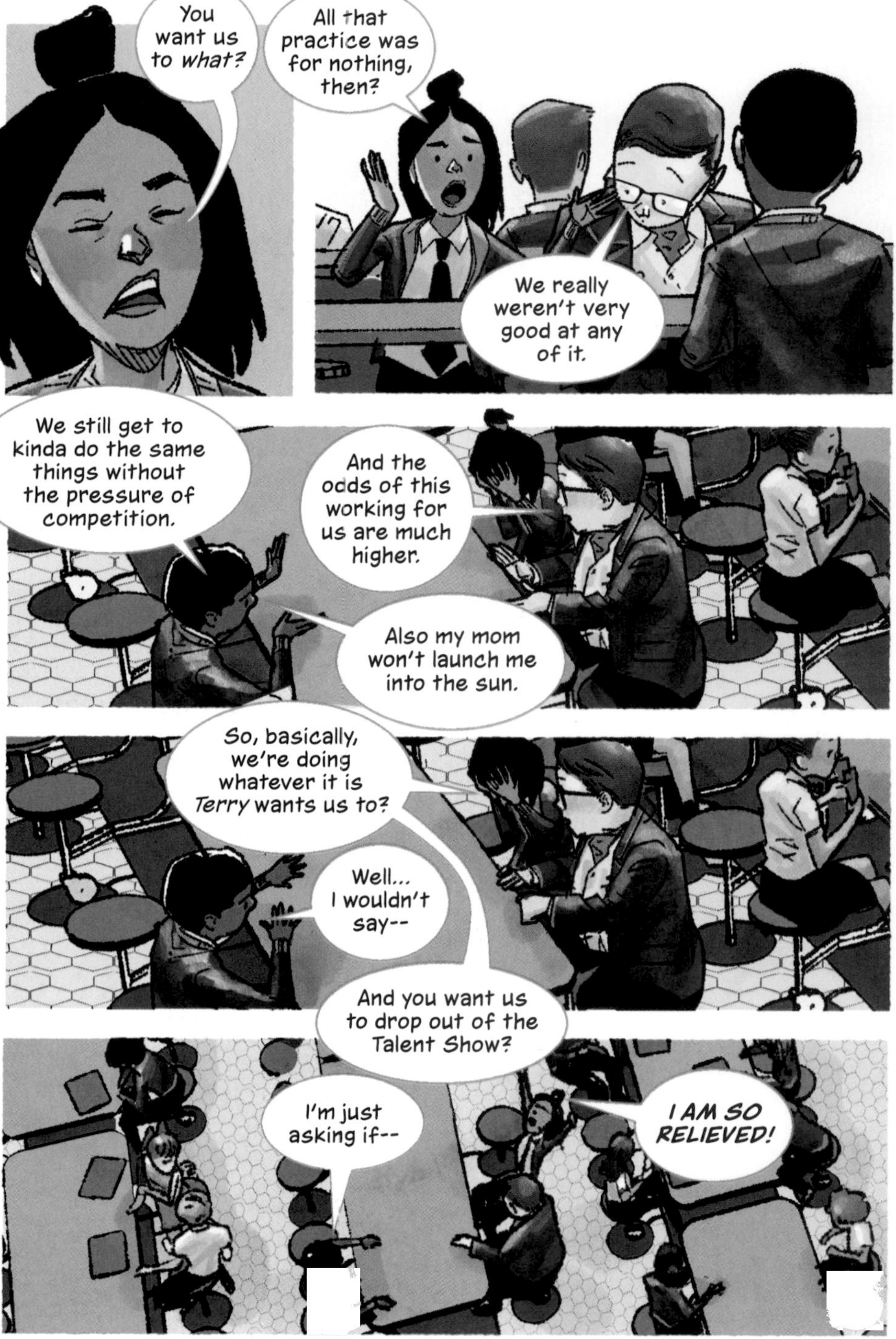
You want us to *what?*
All that practice was for nothing, then?
We really weren't very good at any of it.
We still get to kinda do the same things without the pressure of competition.
And the odds of this working for us are much higher.
Also my mom won't launch me into the sun.
So, basically, we're doing whatever it is *Terry* wants us to?
Well... I wouldn't say--
And you want us to drop out of the Talent Show?
I'm just asking if--
I AM SO RELIEVED!

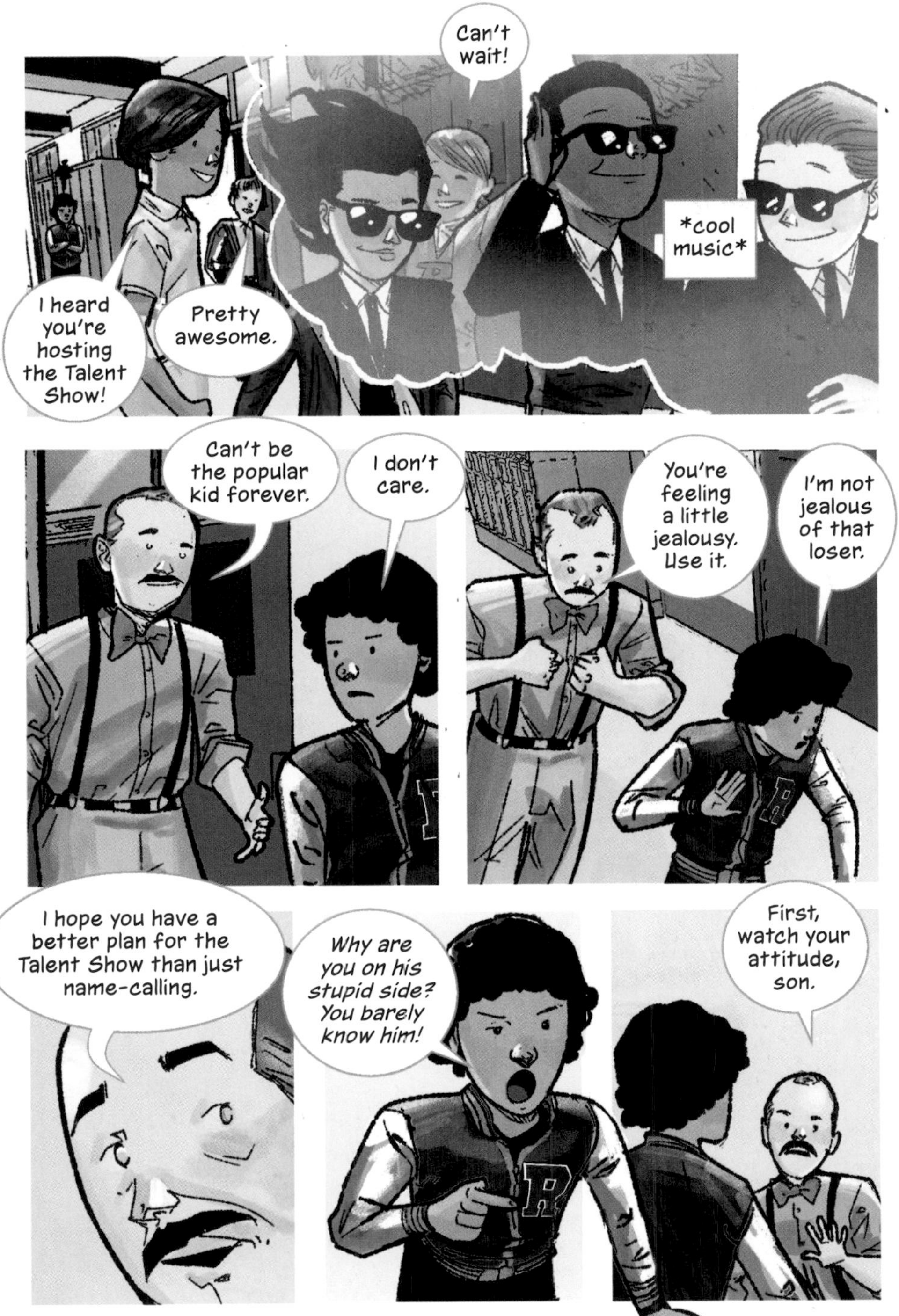
I heard you're hosting the Talent Show!
Pretty awesome.
Can't wait!
cool music
Can't be the popular kid forever.
I don't care.
You're feeling a little jealousy. Use it.
I'm not jealous of that loser.
I hope you have a better plan for the Talent Show than just name-calling.
Why are you on his stupid side? You barely know him!
First, watch your attitude, son.

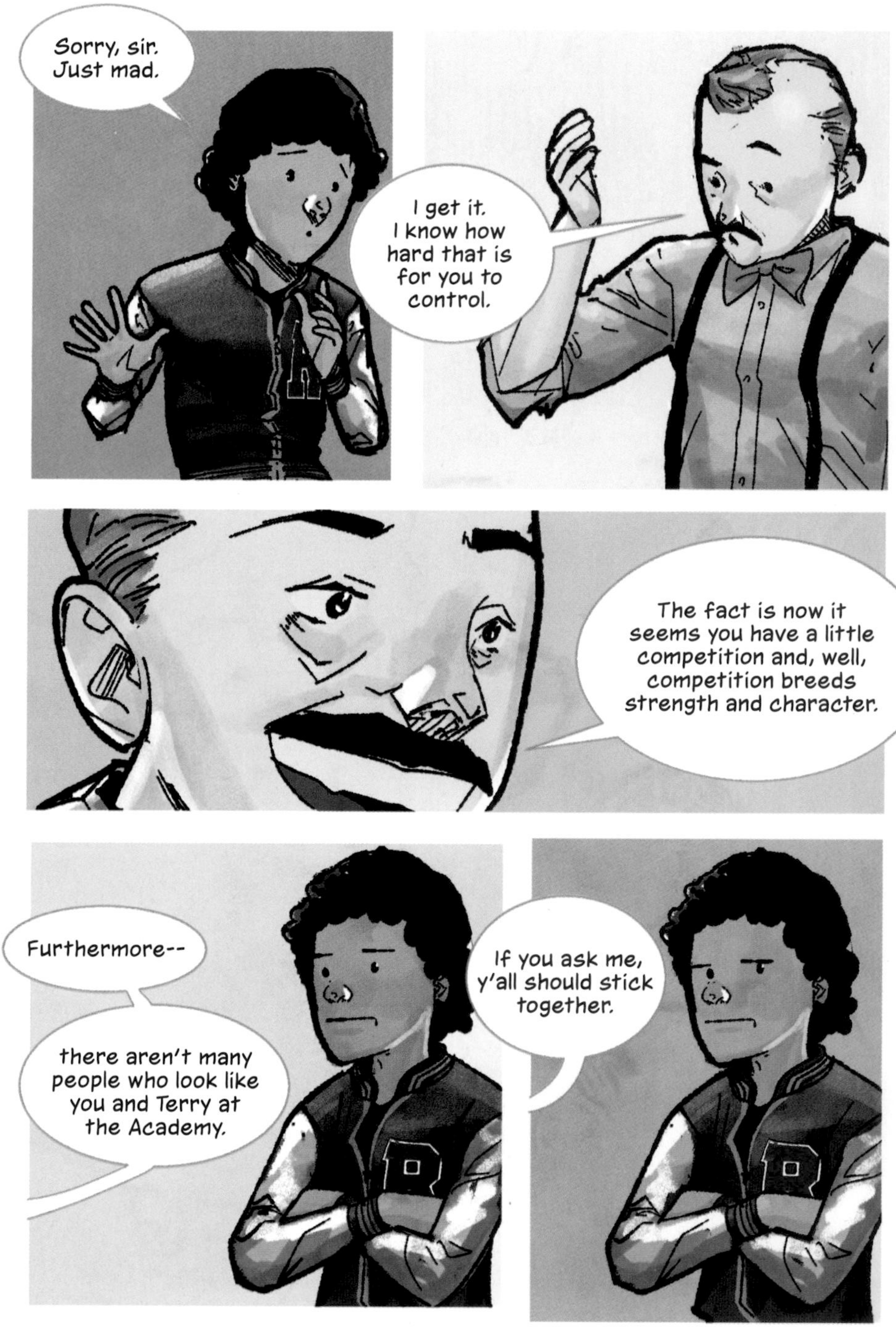
Sorry, sir.
Just mad.
I get it.
I know how
hard that is
for you to
control.
The fact is now it
seems you have a little
competition and, well,
competition breeds
strength and character.
Furthermore--
there aren't many
people who look like
you and Terry at
the Academy.
If you ask me,
y'all should stick
together.

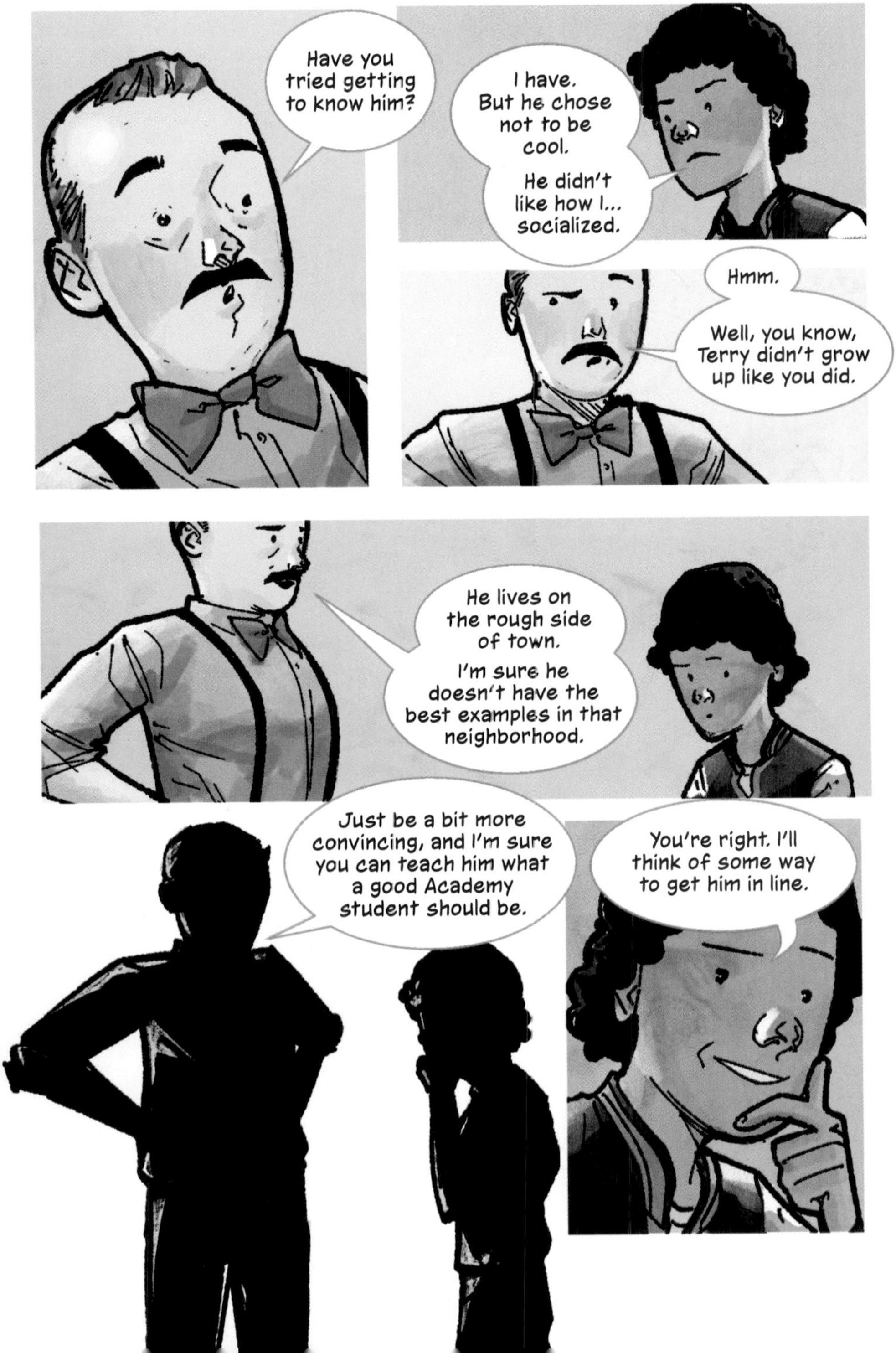
Have you tried getting to know him?
I have. But he chose not to be cool.
He didn't like how I... socialized.
Hmm.
Well, you know, Terry didn't grow up like you did.
He lives on the rough side of town.
I'm sure he doesn't have the best examples in that neighborhood.
Just be a bit more convincing, and I'm sure you can teach him what a good Academy student should be.
You're right. I'll think of some way to get him in line.

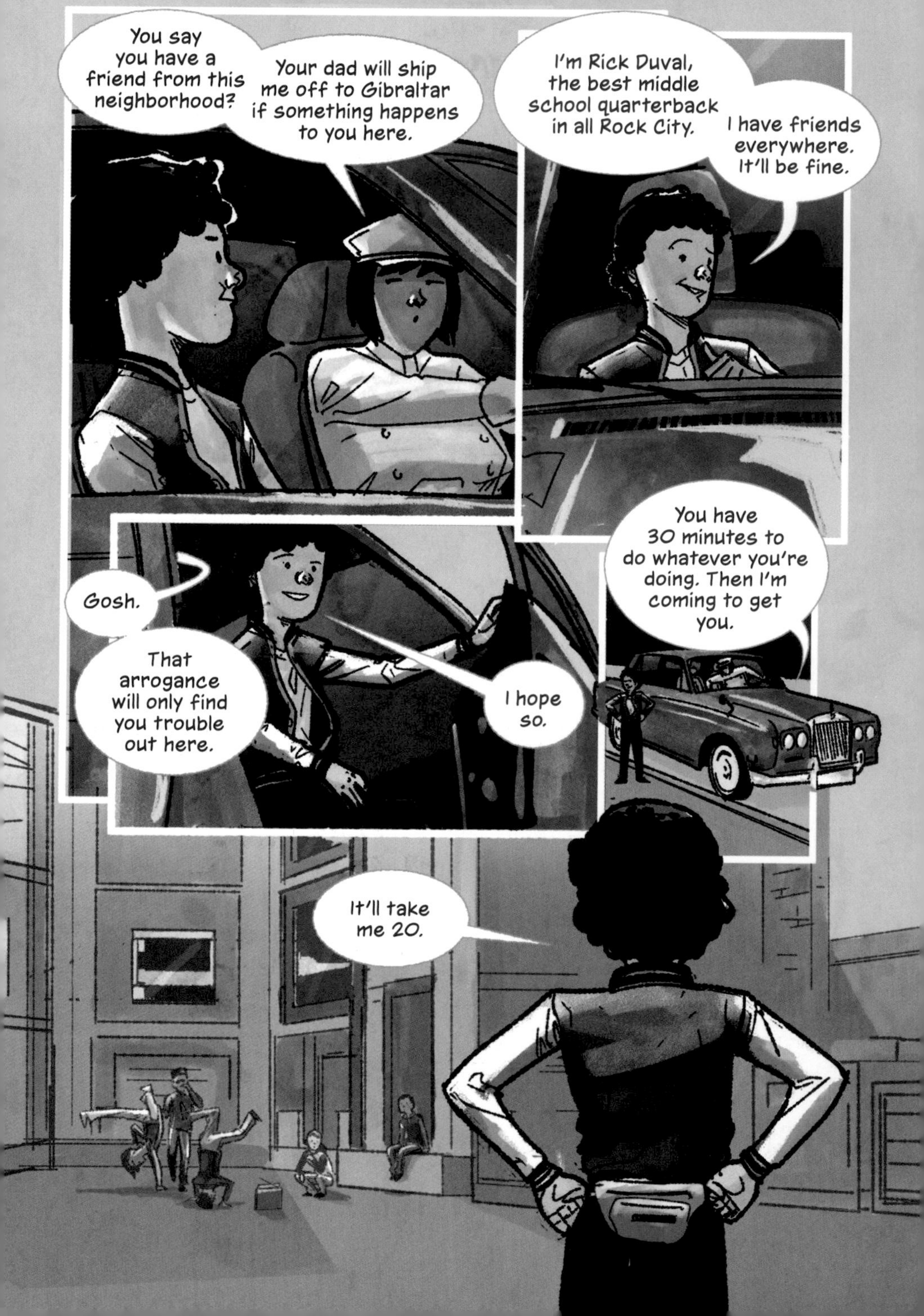
You say you have a friend from this neighborhood?
Your dad will ship me off to Gibraltar if something happens to you here.
I'm Rick Duval, the best middle school quarterback in all Rock City.
I have friends everywhere. It'll be fine.
Gosh.
That arrogance will only find you trouble out here.
I hope so.
You have 30 minutes to do whatever you're doing. Then I'm coming to get you.
It'll take me 20.

Yo! Are you Rick Duval?

Can't be. Why's an all-star athlete hanging out here?

Yeah, you all must have seen me in the newspaper. Or maybe one of you has a TV?

Man, when you threw that Hail Mary and won the state championship, my whole family was cheering.

Yeah, man, you repping Rock City well. What brings you here?

You looking for Emilio?

Well, there's this new kid at my school who lives around here.

He may be trying out for the team soon.

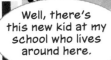

I wanted to find out more about Terry before making any real decisions.

Ha, oh man. You mean Trickle Down?! That dude can barely walk without tripping.

Among *other things* he can't control.

What other things?

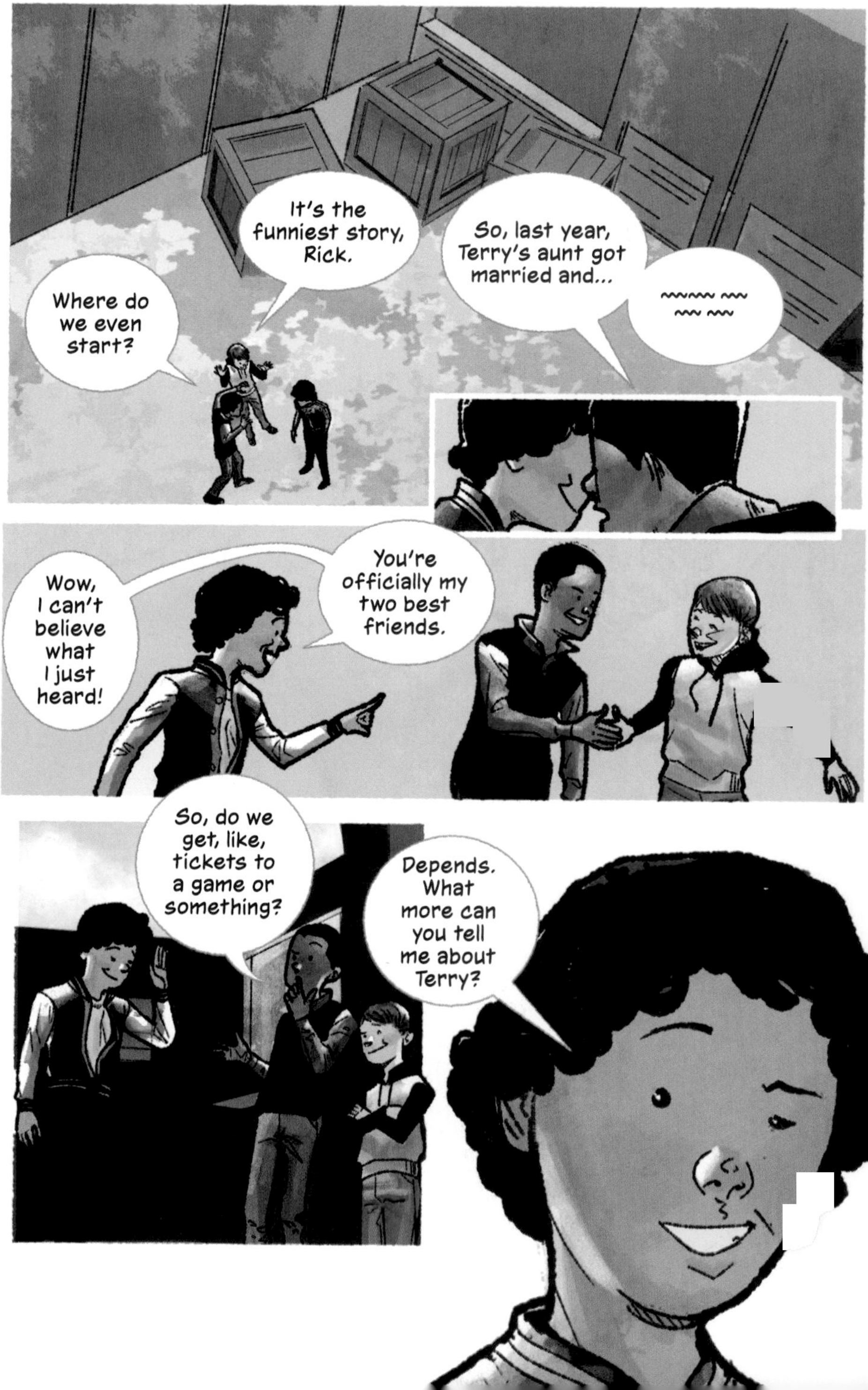
Where do we even start?
It's the funniest story, Rick.
So, last year, Terry's aunt got married and...
Wow, I can't believe what I just heard!
You're officially my two best friends.
So, do we get, like, tickets to a game or something?
Depends. What more can you tell me about Terry?

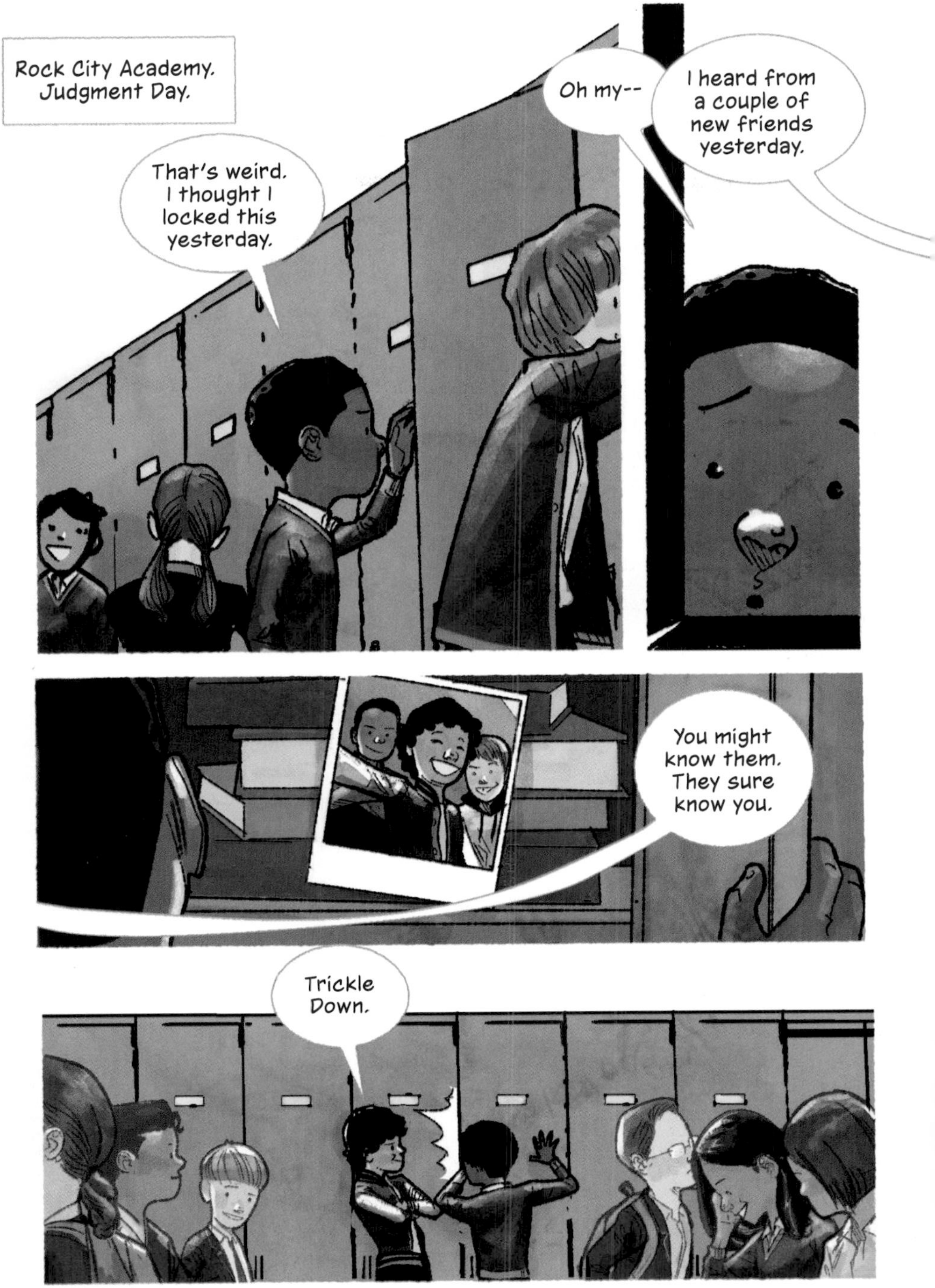
Rock City Academy. Judgment Day.
That's weird. I thought I locked this yesterday.
Oh my--
I heard from a couple of new friends yesterday.
You might know them. They sure know you.
Trickle Down.

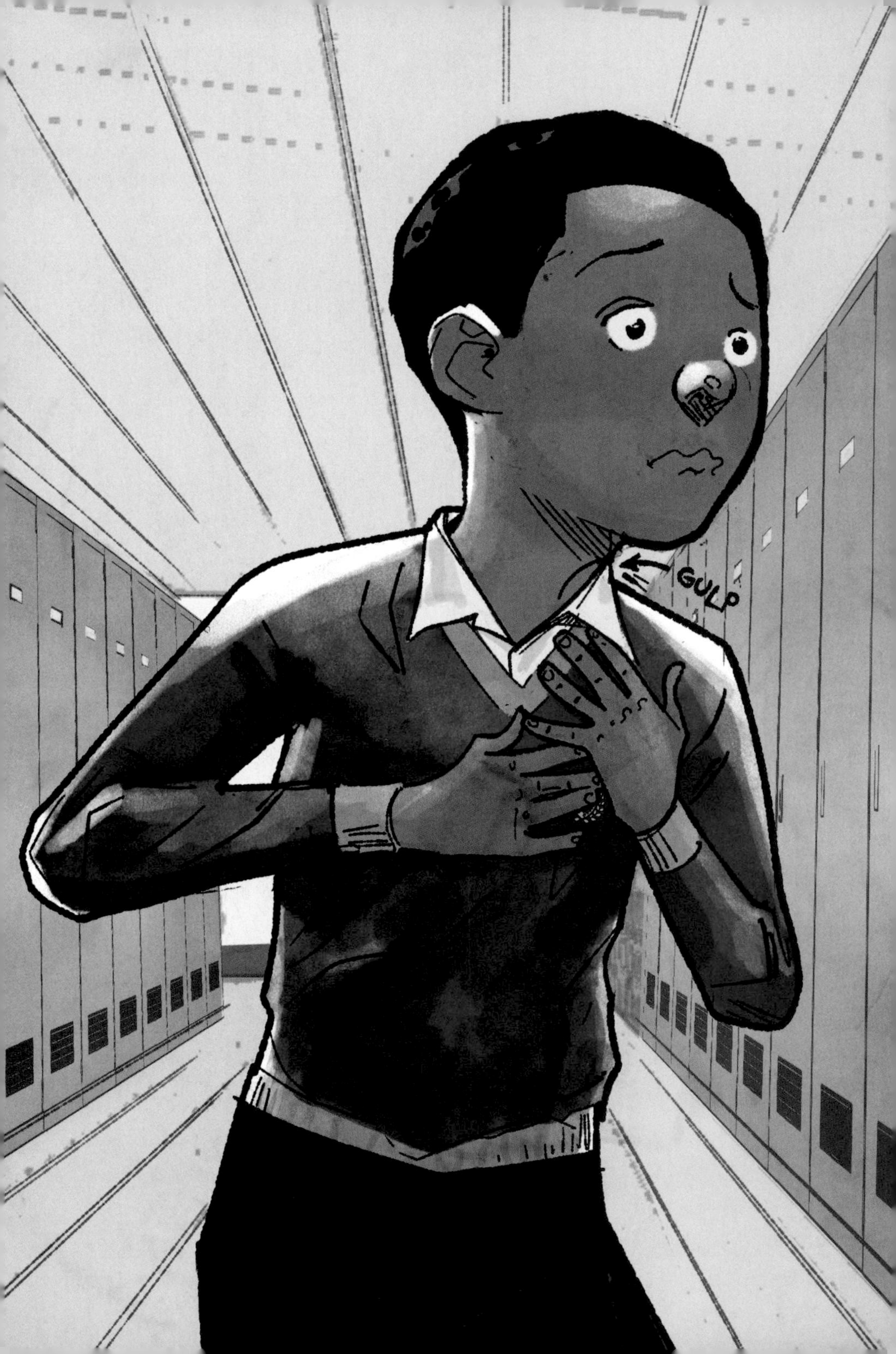
GULP

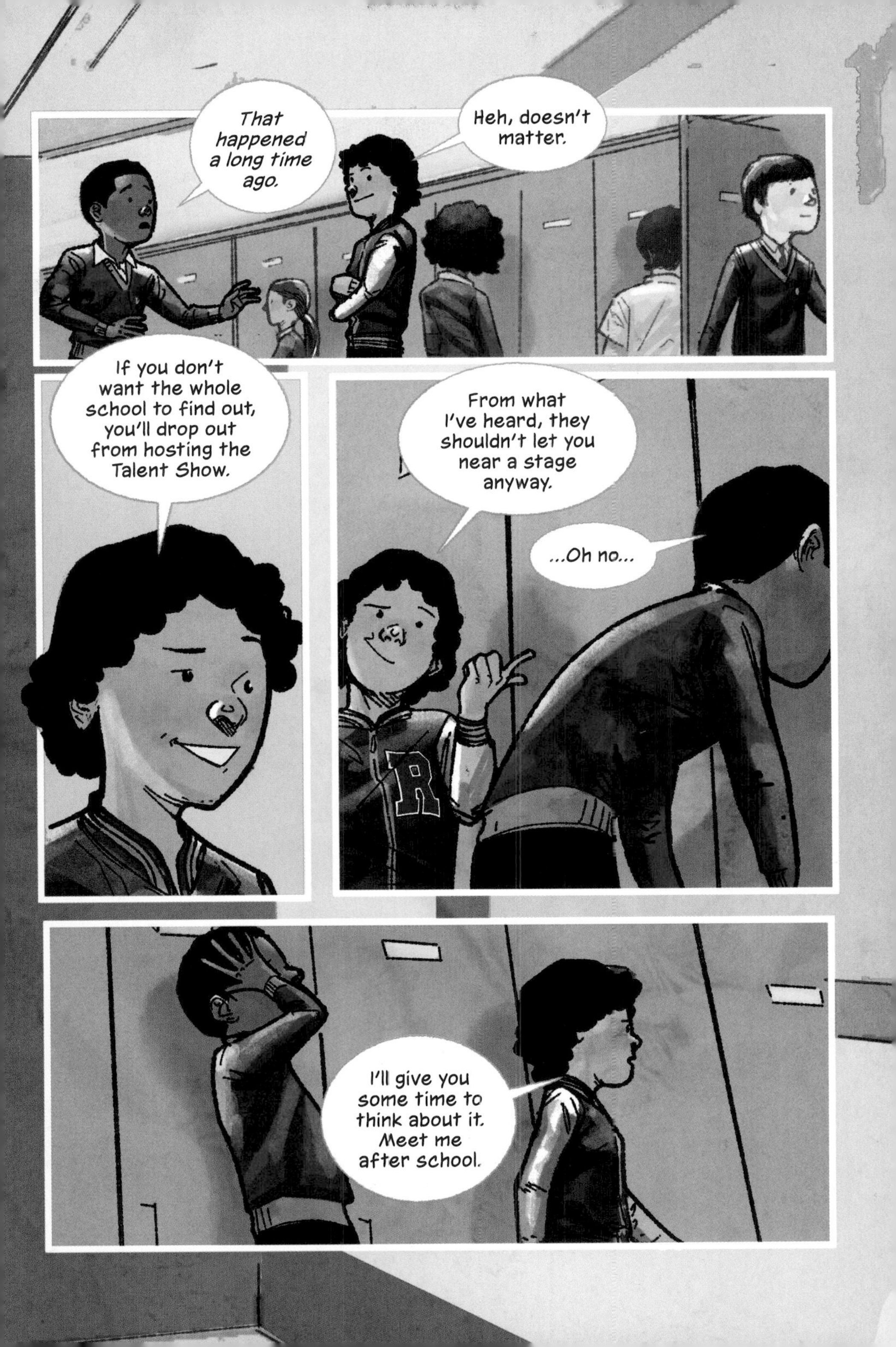
That happened a long time ago.
Heh, doesn't matter.
If you don't want the whole school to find out, you'll drop out from hosting the Talent Show.
From what I've heard, they shouldn't let you near a stage anyway.
...Oh no...
I'll give you some time to think about it. Meet me after school.

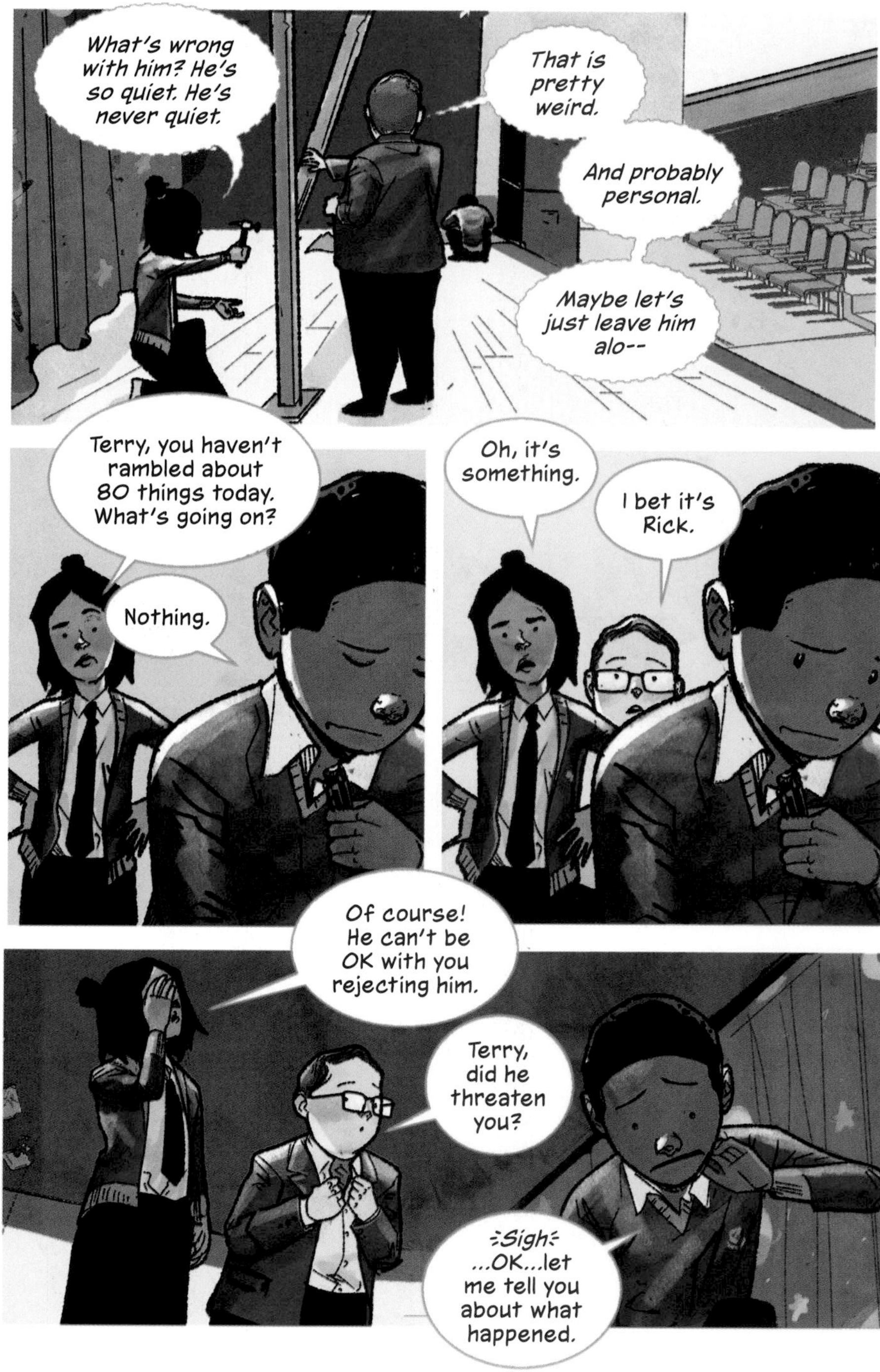
What's wrong with him? He's so quiet. He's never quiet.
That is pretty weird.
And probably personal.
Maybe let's just leave him alo--
Terry, you haven't rambled about 80 things today. What's going on?
Nothing.
Oh, it's something.
I bet it's Rick.
Of course! He can't be OK with you rejecting him.
Terry, did he threaten you?
=Sigh= ...OK...let me tell you about what happened.

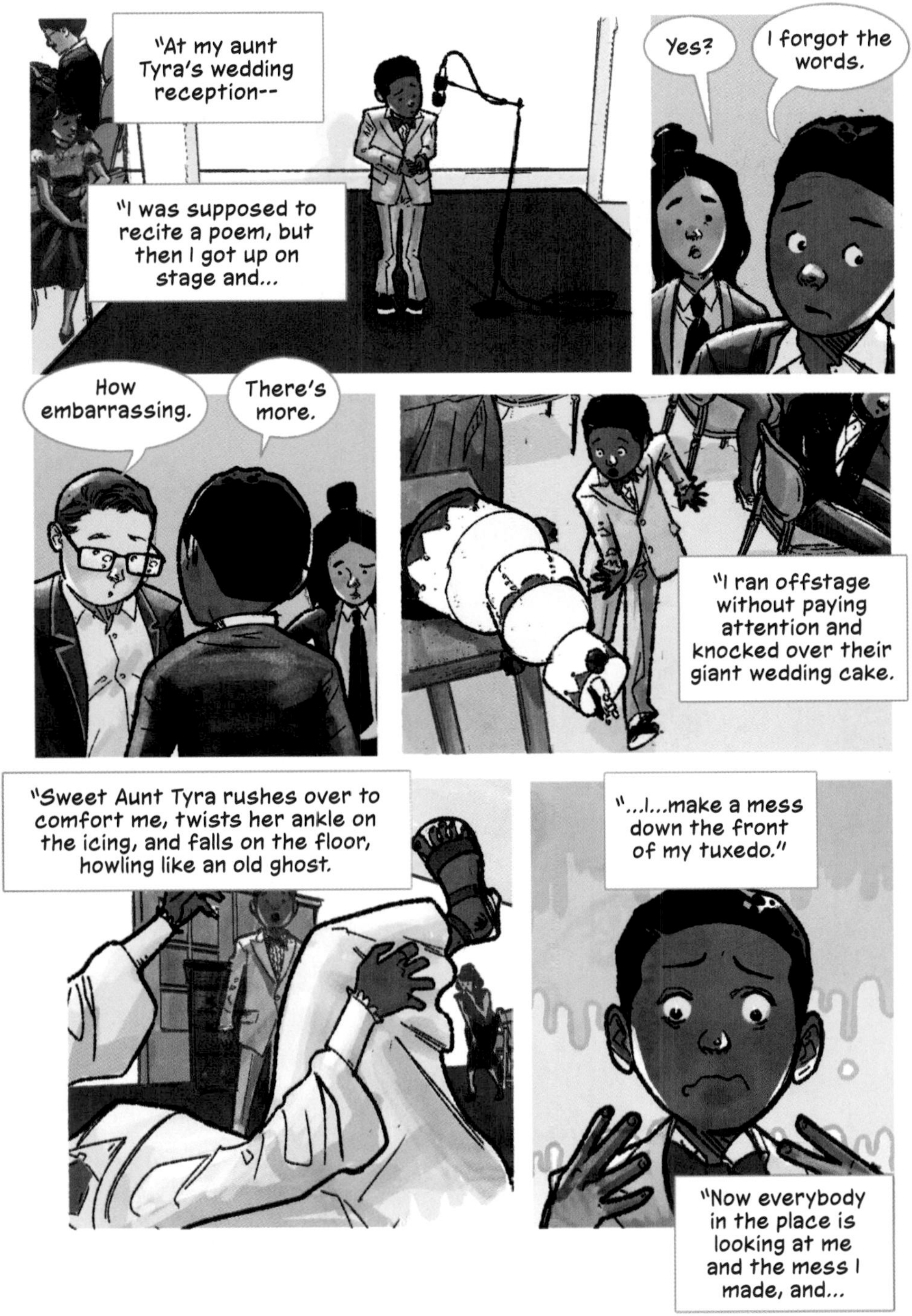
"At my aunt Tyra's wedding reception--
"I was supposed to recite a poem, but then I got up on stage and...
Yes?
I forgot the words.
How embarrassing.
There's more.
"I ran offstage without paying attention and knocked over their giant wedding cake.
"Sweet Aunt Tyra rushes over to comfort me, twists her ankle on the icing, and falls on the floor, howling like an old ghost.
"...I...make a mess down the front of my tuxedo."
"Now everybody in the place is looking at me and the mess I made, and...

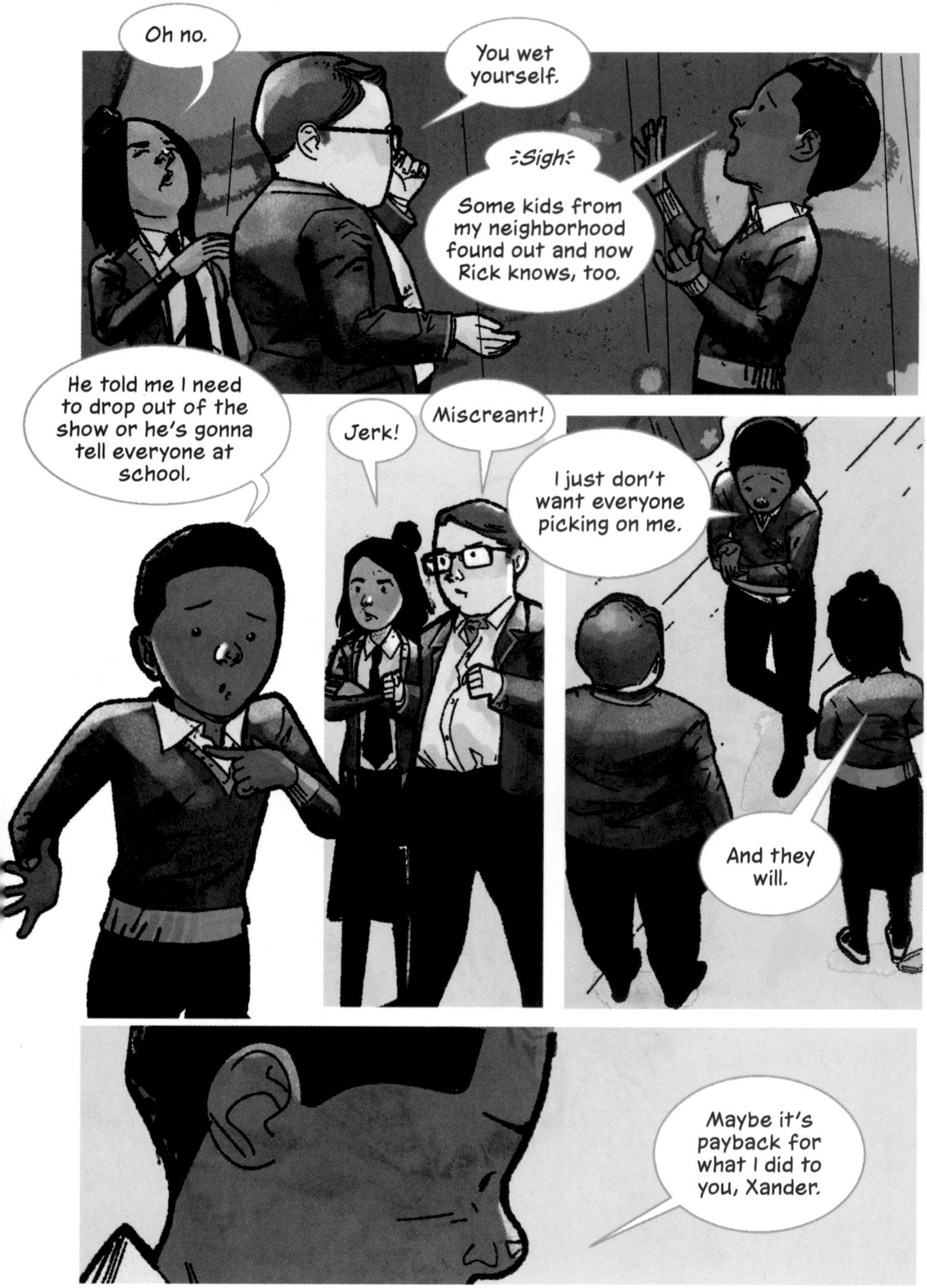

Oh no.
You wet yourself.
-Sigh-
Some kids from my neighborhood found out and now Rick knows, too.
He told me I need to drop out of the show or he's gonna tell everyone at school.
Jerk!
Miscreant!
I just don't want everyone picking on me.
And they will.
Maybe it's payback for what I did to you, Xander.

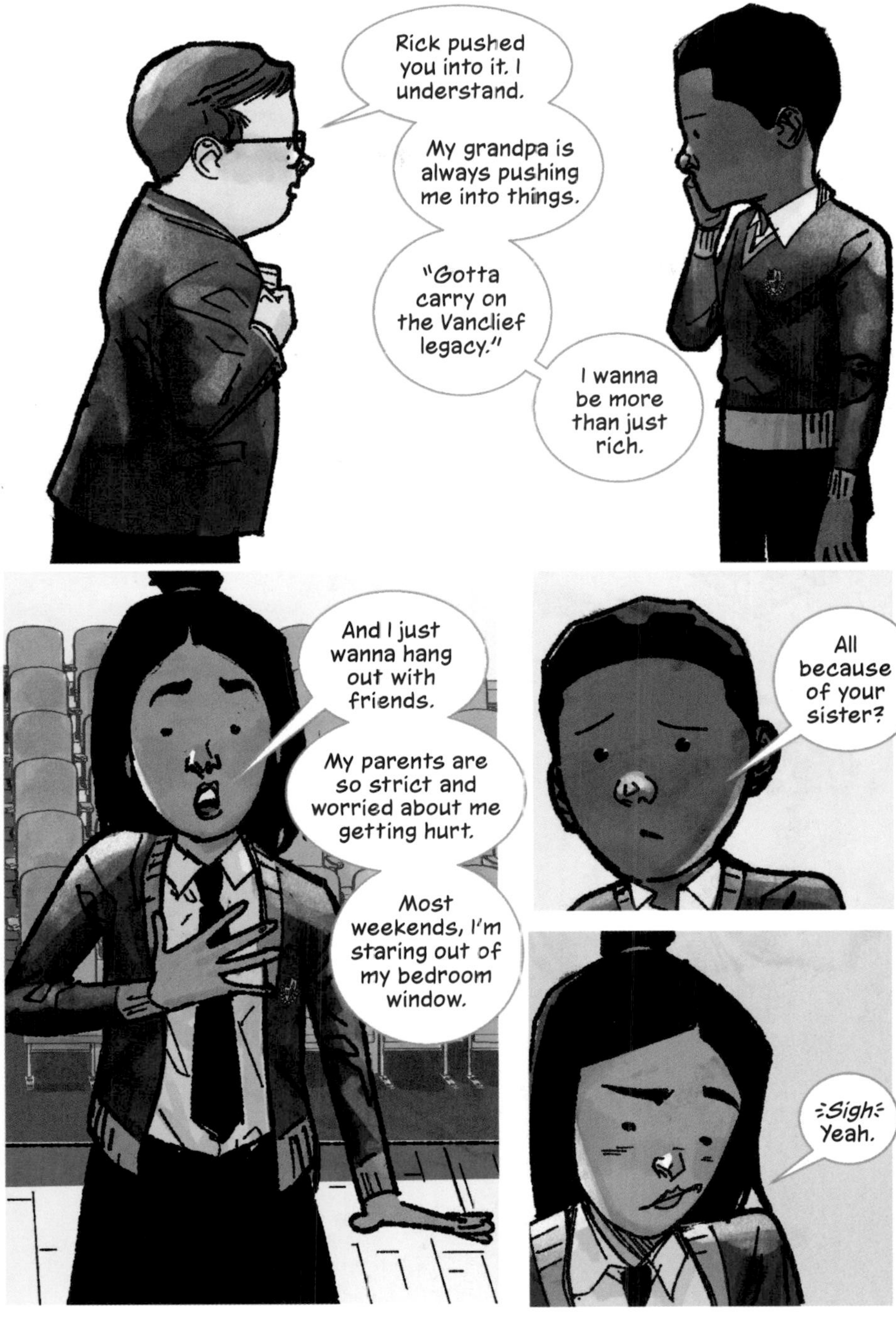
Rick pushed you into it. I understand.
My grandpa is always pushing me into things.
"Gotta carry on the Vanclief legacy."
I wanna be more than just rich.
And I just wanna hang out with friends.
My parents are so strict and worried about me getting hurt.
Most weekends, I'm staring out of my bedroom window.
All because of your sister?
Sigh
Yeah.

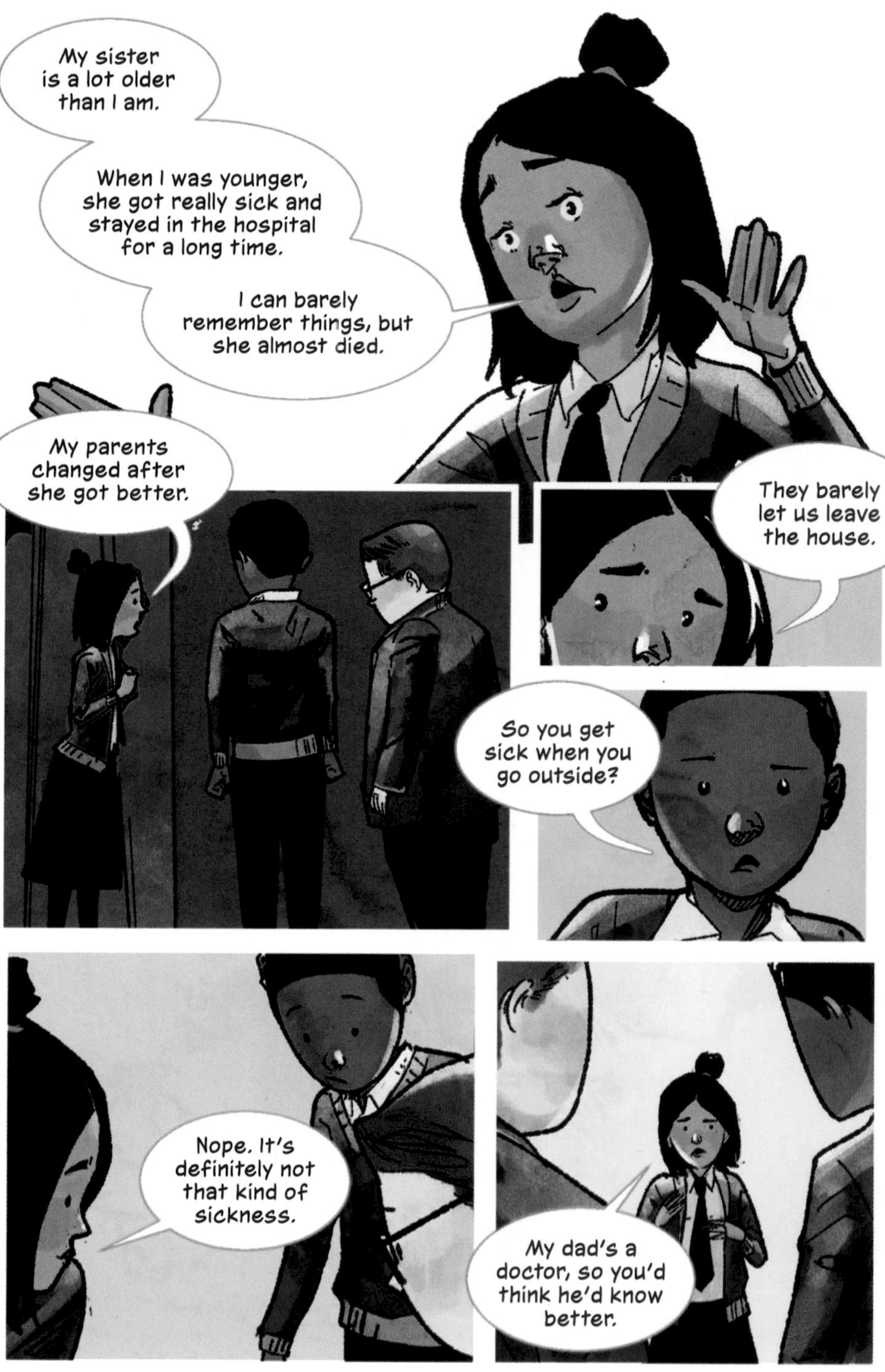
My sister is a lot older than I am.
When I was younger, she got really sick and stayed in the hospital for a long time.
I can barely remember things, but she almost died.
My parents changed after she got better.
They barely let us leave the house.
So you get sick when you go outside?
Nope. It's definitely not that kind of sickness.
My dad's a doctor, so you'd think he'd know better.

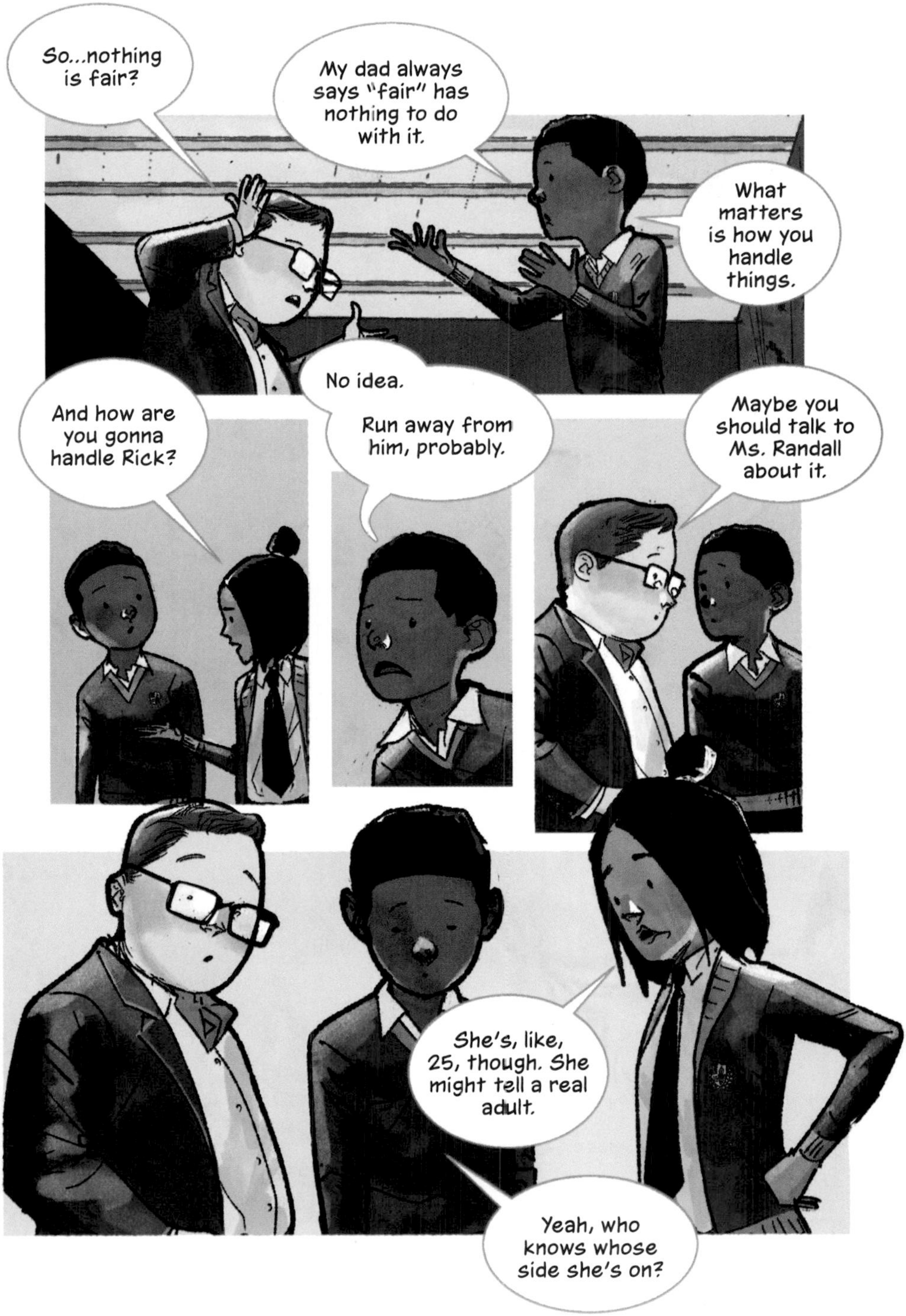
So...nothing is fair?
My dad always says "fair" has nothing to do with it.
What matters is how you handle things.
And how are you gonna handle Rick?
No idea.
Run away from him, probably.
Maybe you should talk to Ms. Randall about it.
She's, like, 25, though. She might tell a real adult.
Yeah, who knows whose side she's on?

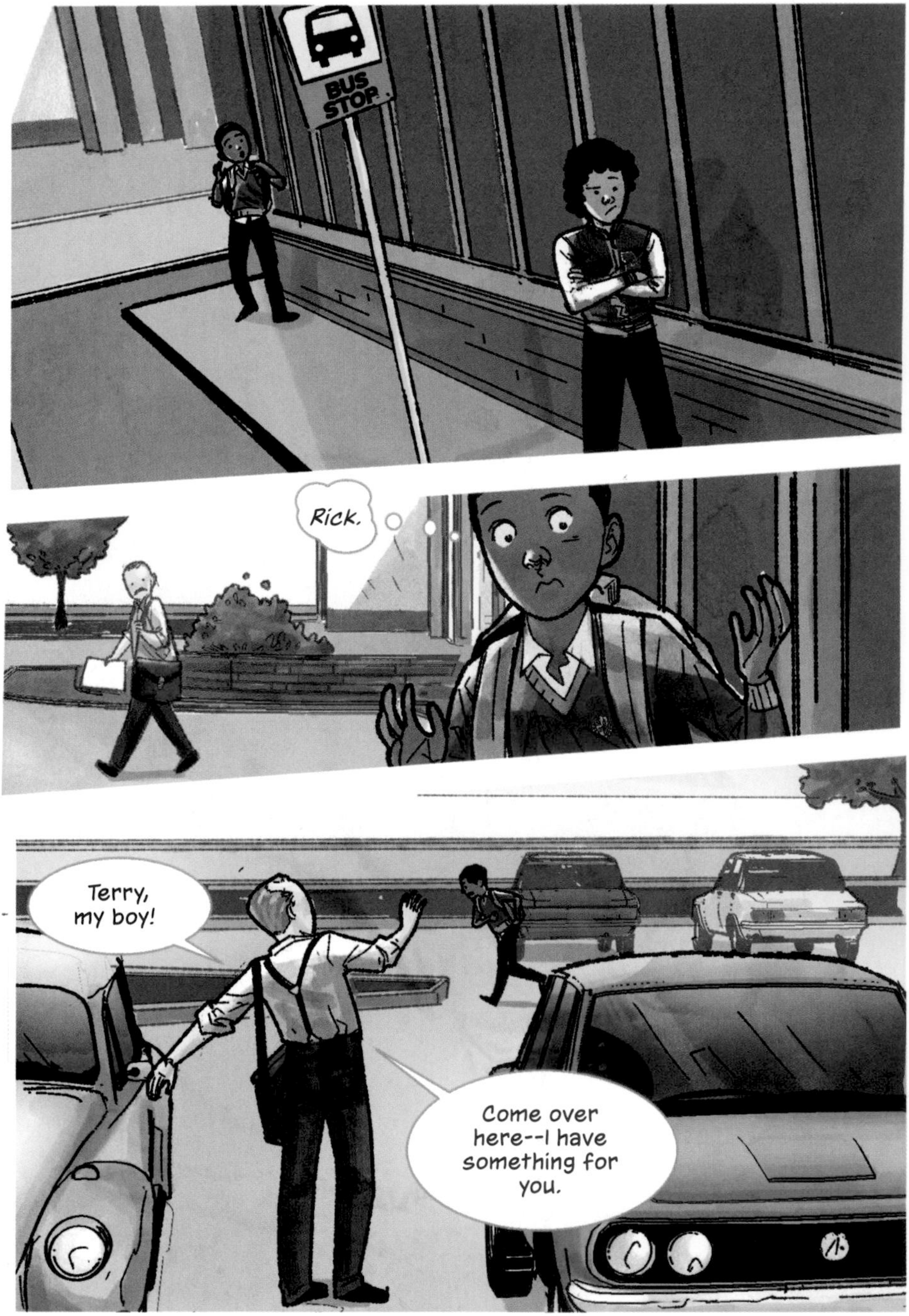
BUS STOP
Rick.
Terry, my boy!
Come over here--I have something for you.

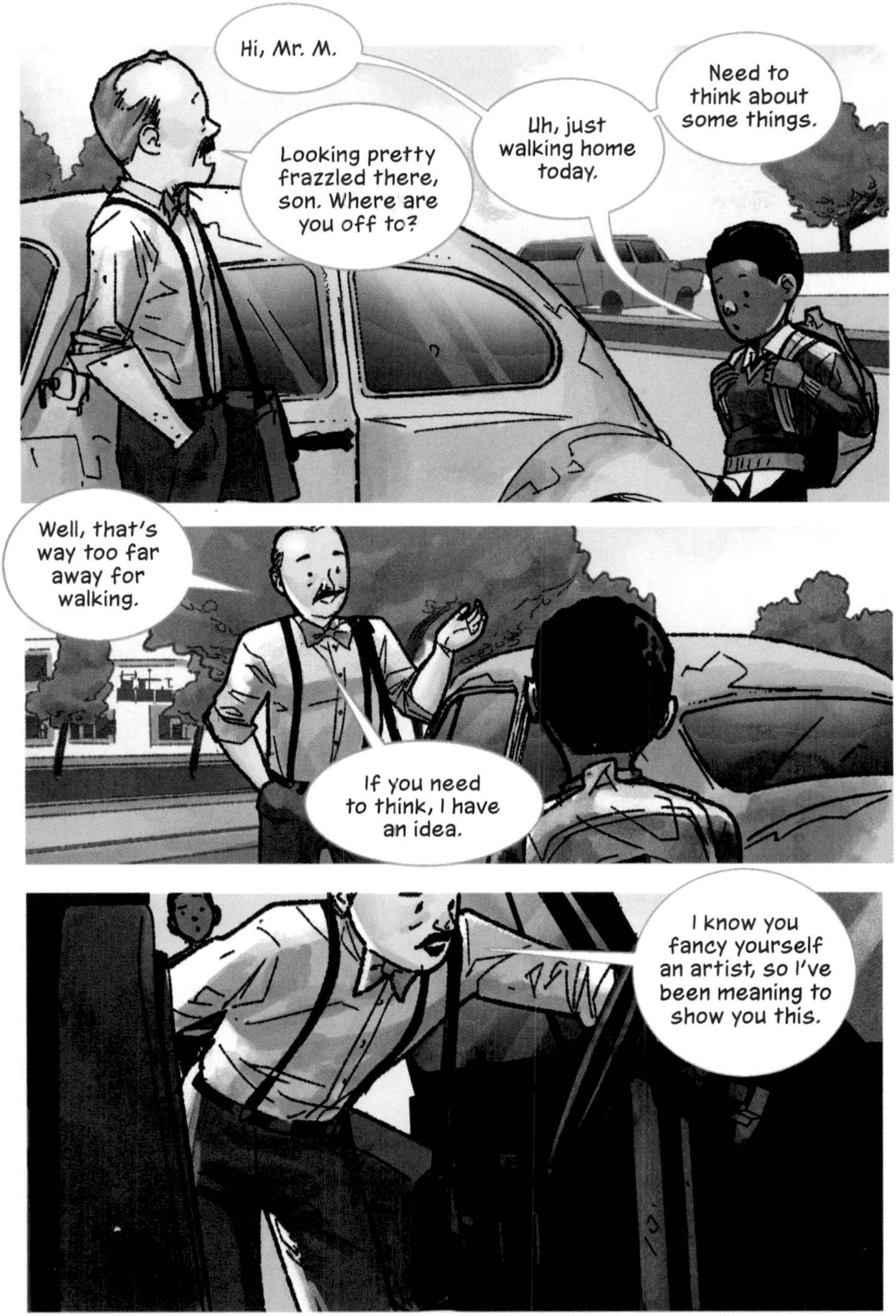
Hi, Mr. M.
Looking pretty frazzled there, son. Where are you off to?
Uh, just walking home today.
Need to think about some things.
Well, that's way too far away for walking.
If you need to think, I have an idea.
I know you fancy yourself an artist, so I've been meaning to show you this.

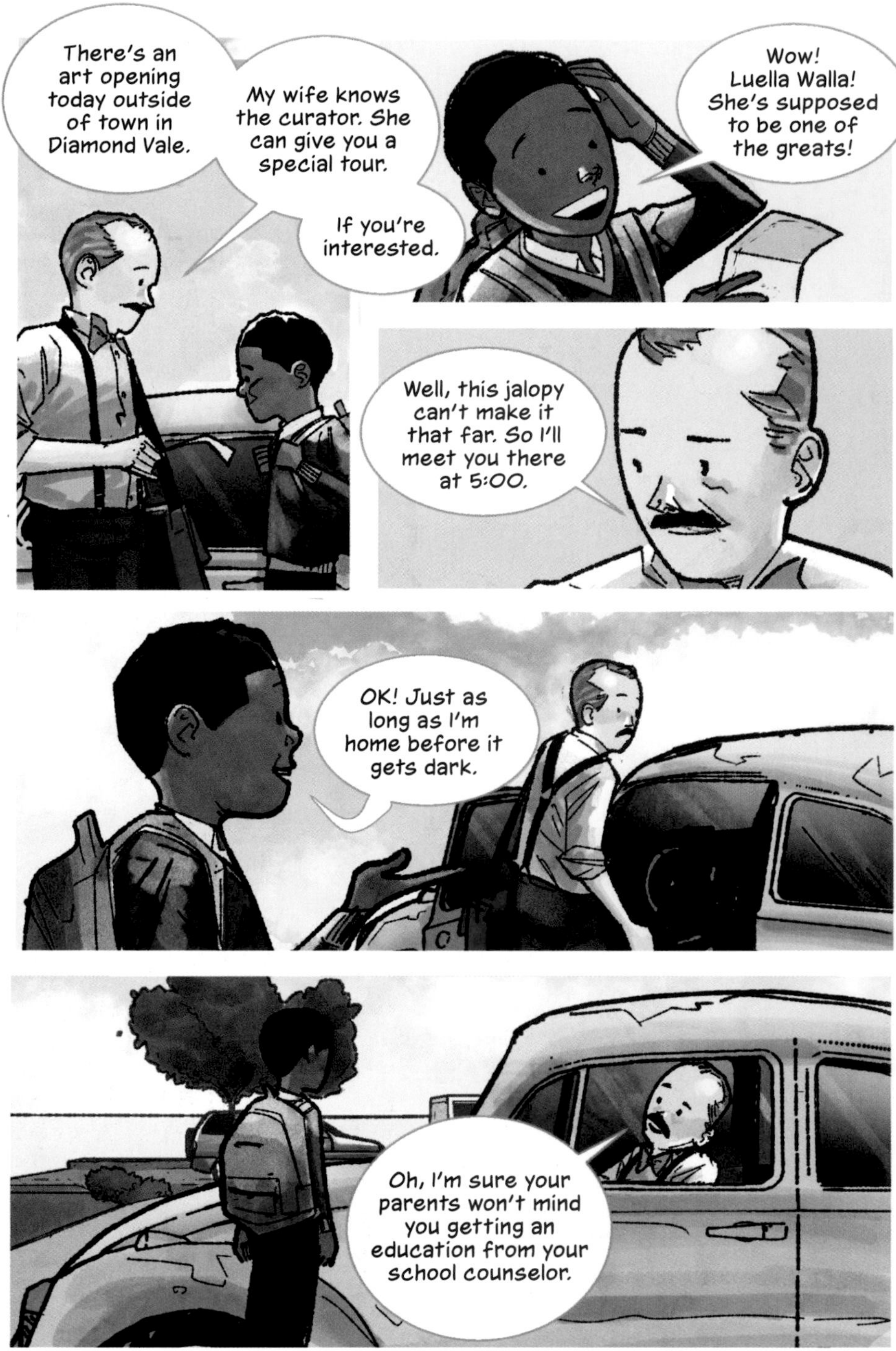
There's an art opening today outside of town in Diamond Vale.
My wife knows the curator. She can give you a special tour.
If you're interested.
Wow! Luella Walla! She's supposed to be one of the greats!
Well, this jalopy can't make it that far. So I'll meet you there at 5:00.
OK! Just as long as I'm home before it gets dark.
Oh, I'm sure your parents won't mind you getting an education from your school counselor.

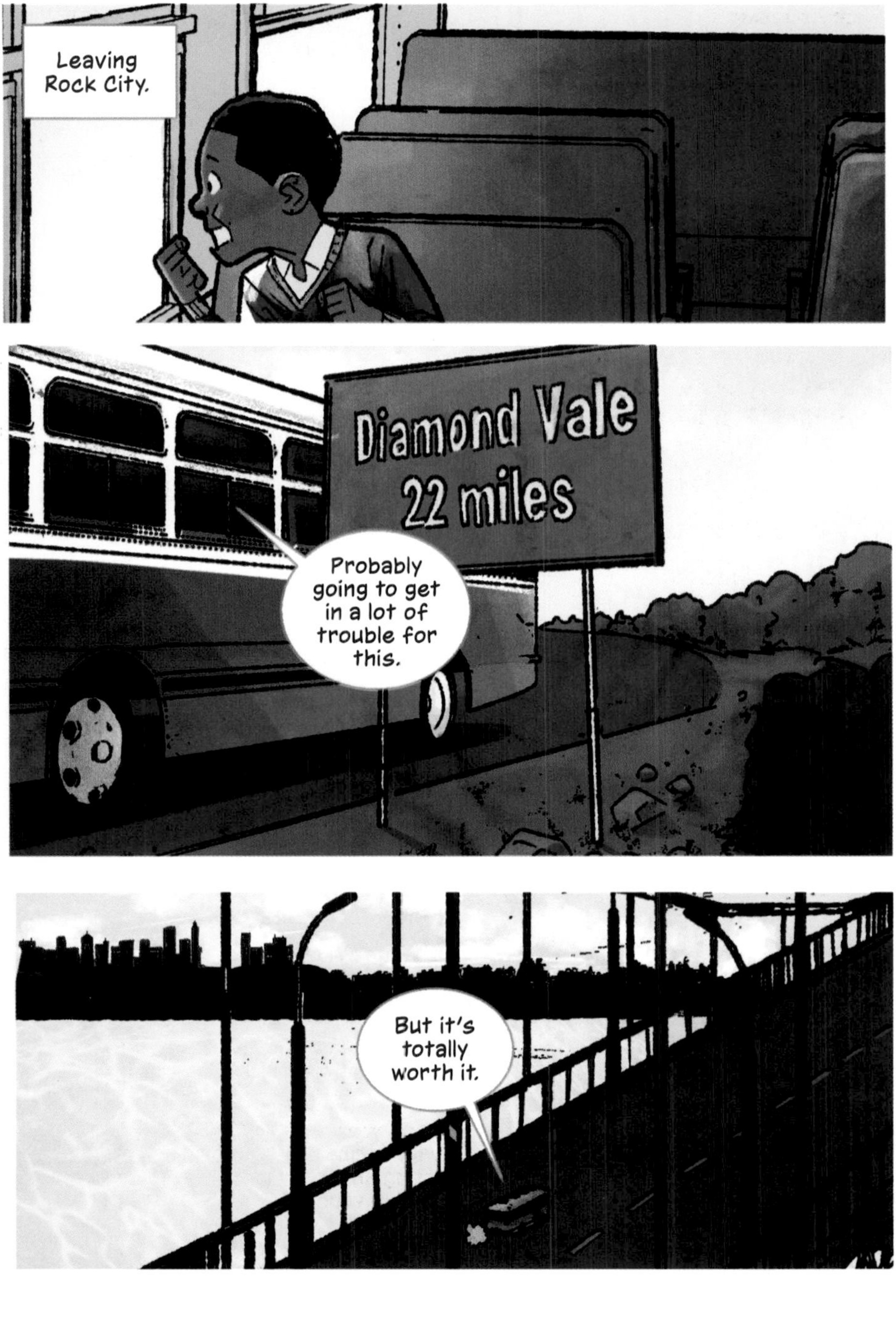
Leaving
Rock City.
Diamond Vale
22 miles
Probably going to get in a lot of trouble for this.
But it's totally worth it.

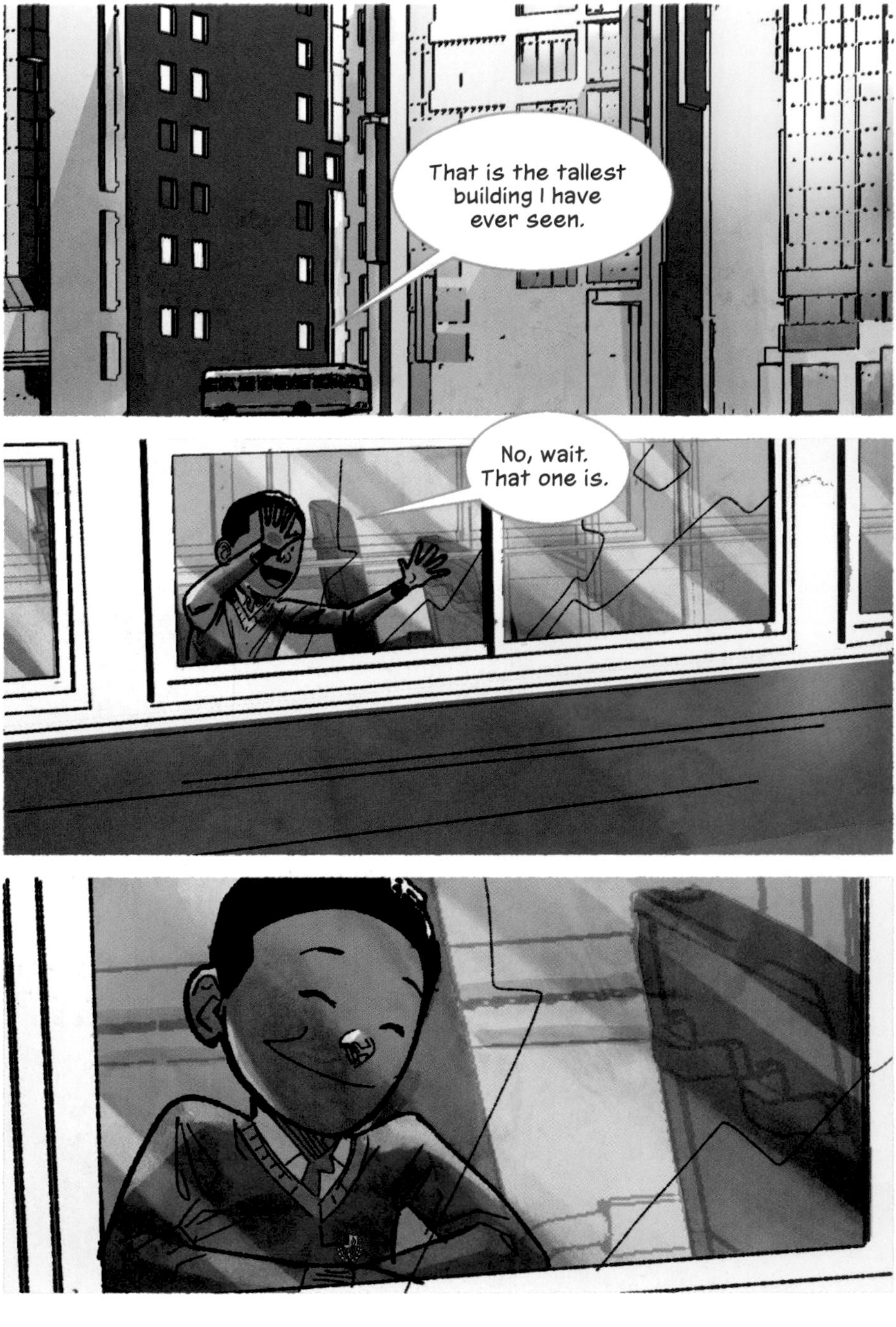
That is the tallest building I have ever seen.
No, wait. That one is.

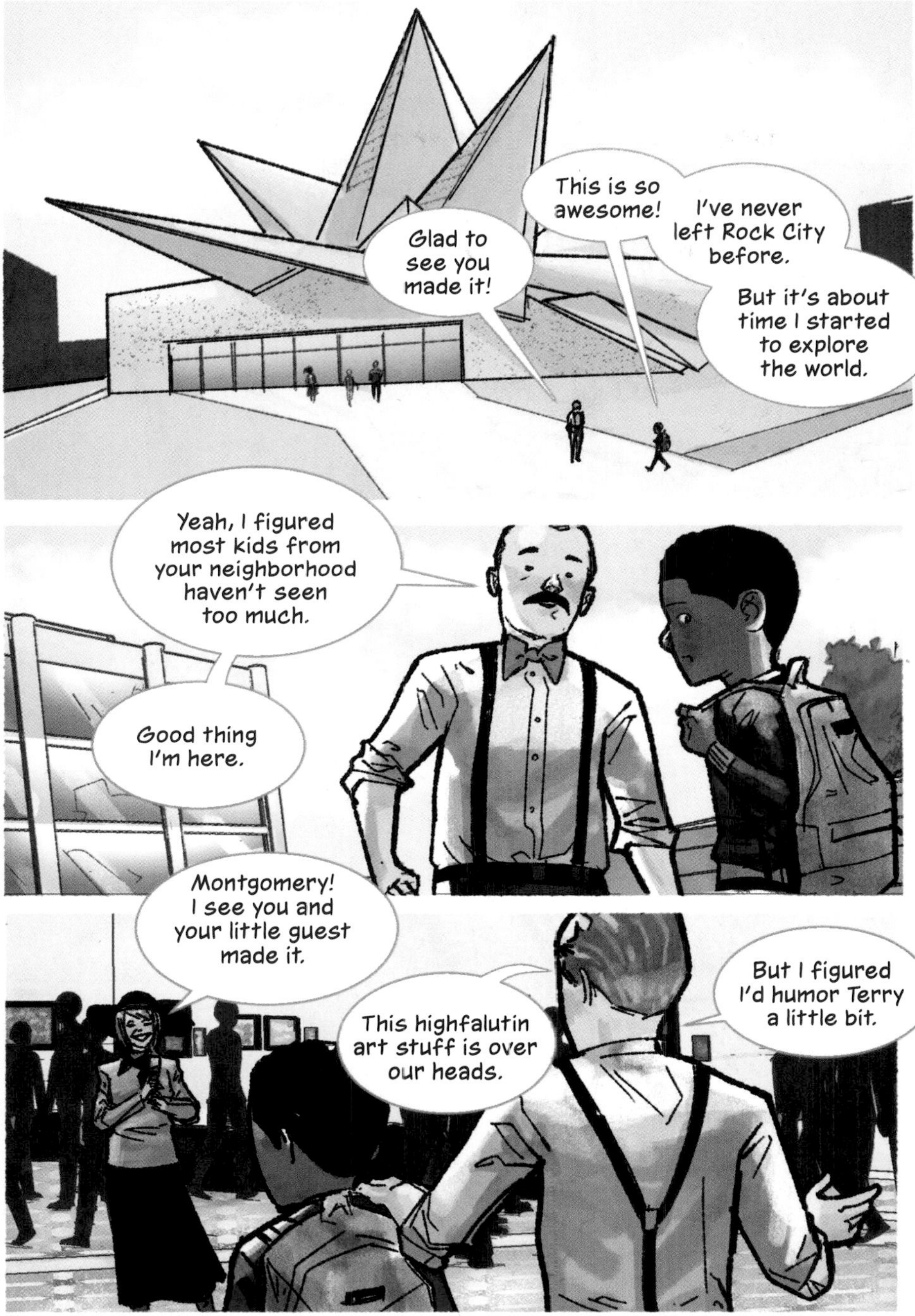
Glad to see you made it!
This is so awesome!
I've never left Rock City before.
But it's about time I started to explore the world.
Yeah, I figured most kids from your neighborhood haven't seen too much.
Good thing I'm here.
Montgomery! I see you and your little guest made it.
This highfalutin art stuff is over our heads.
But I figured I'd humor Terry a little bit.

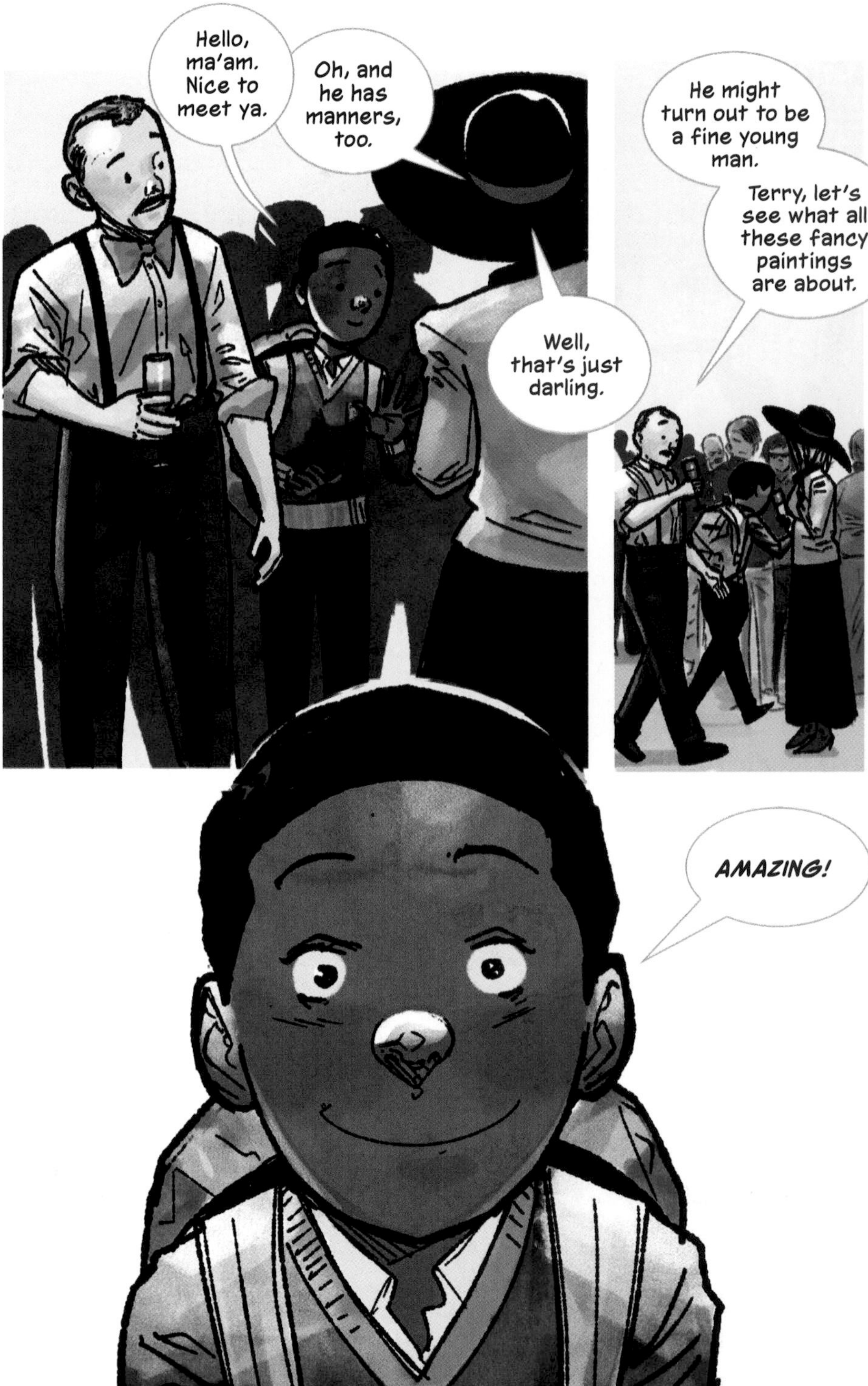
Hello, ma'am. Nice to meet ya.
Oh, and he has manners, too.
Well, that's just darling.
He might turn out to be a fine young man.
Terry, let's see what all these fancy paintings are about.
AMAZING!

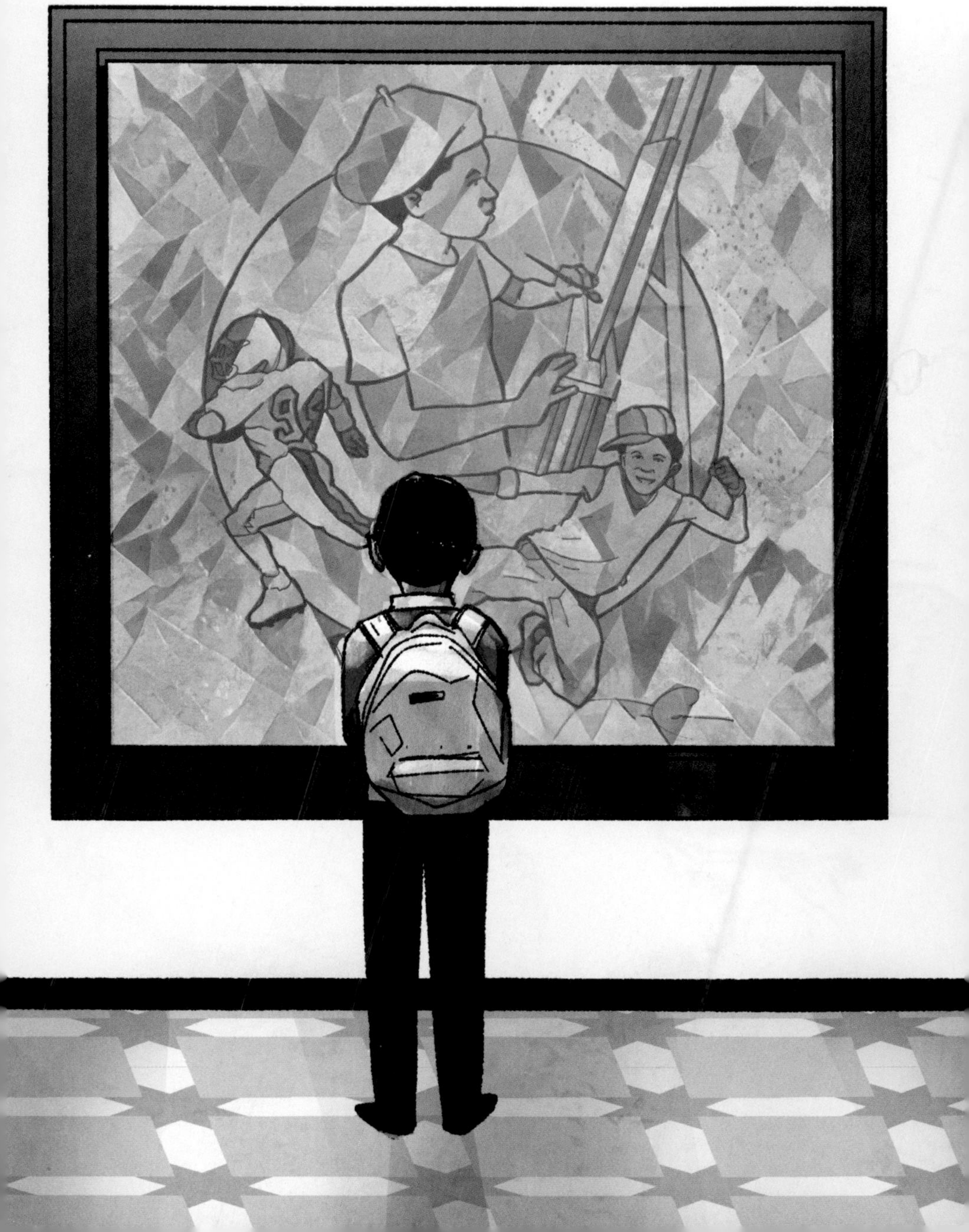

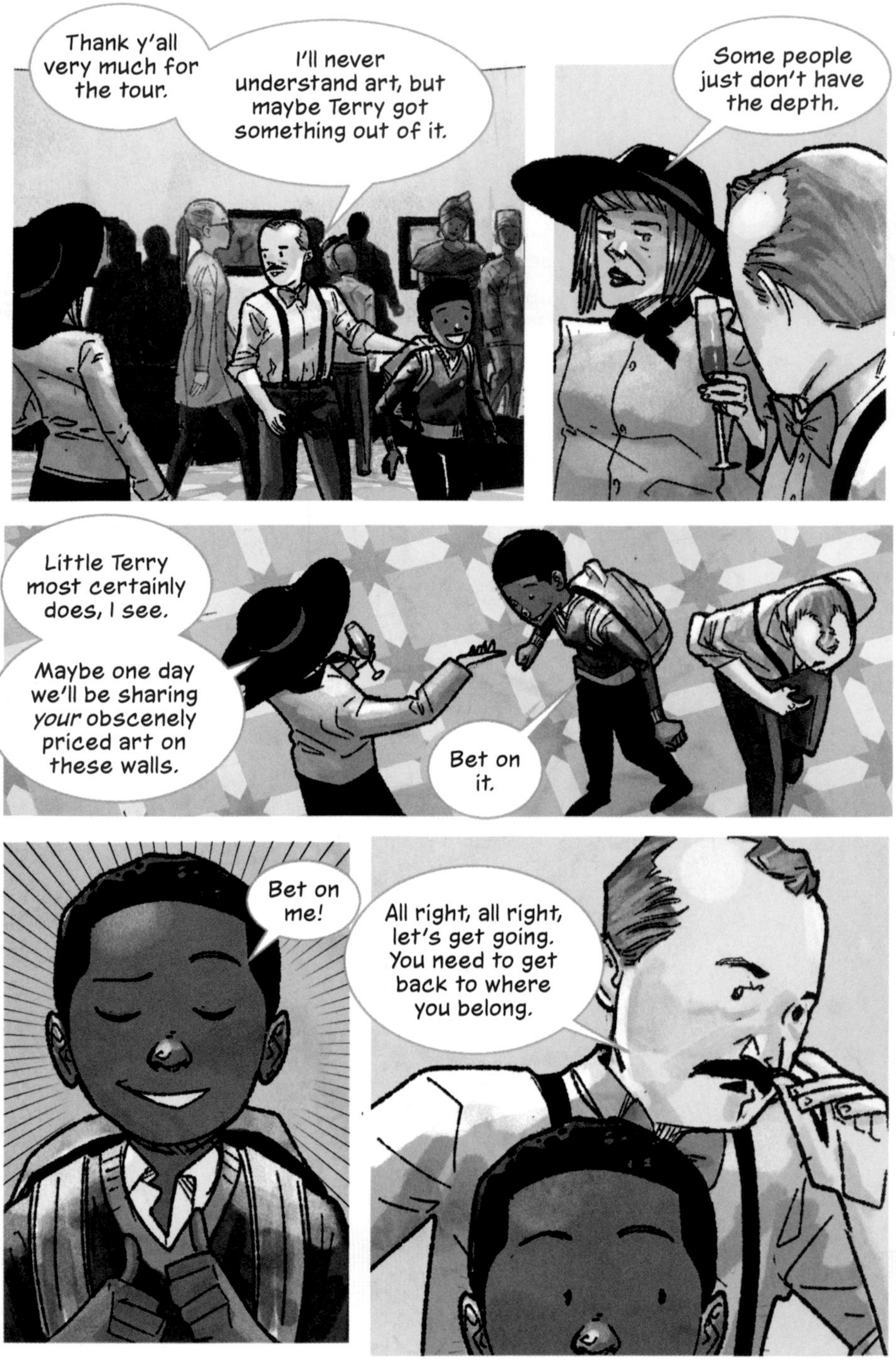
Thank y'all very much for the tour.
I'll never understand art, but maybe Terry got something out of it.
Some people just don't have the depth.
Little Terry most certainly does, I see.
Maybe one day we'll be sharing *your* obscenely priced art on these walls.
Bet on it.
Bet on me!
All right, all right, let's get going. You need to get back to where you belong.

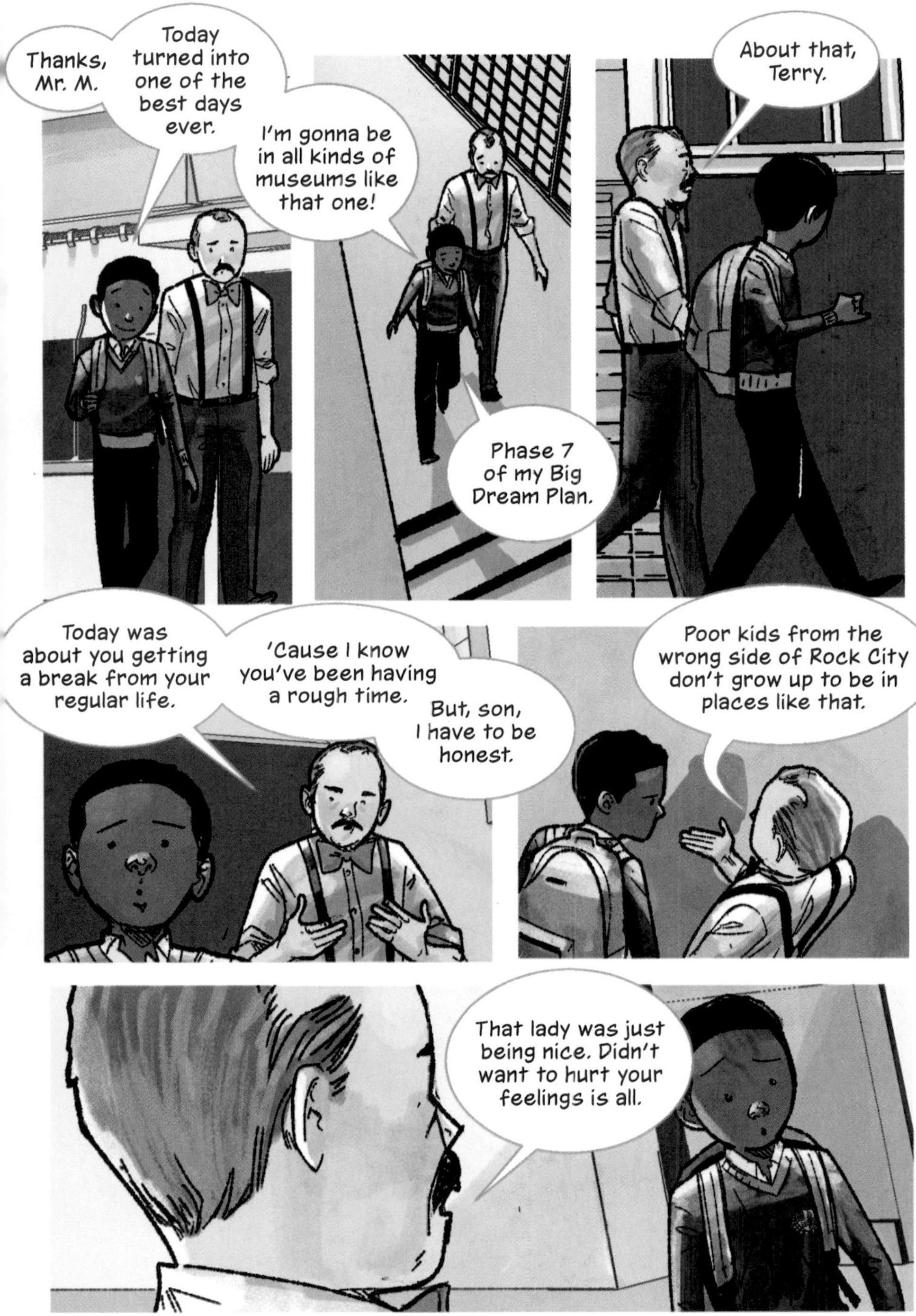

Thanks, Mr. M.
Today turned into one of the best days ever.
I'm gonna be in all kinds of museums like that one!
Phase 7 of my Big Dream Plan.
About that, Terry.
Today was about you getting a break from your regular life.
'Cause I know you've been having a rough time.
But, son, I have to be honest.
Poor kids from the wrong side of Rock City don't grow up to be in places like that.
That lady was just being nice. Didn't want to hurt your feelings is all.

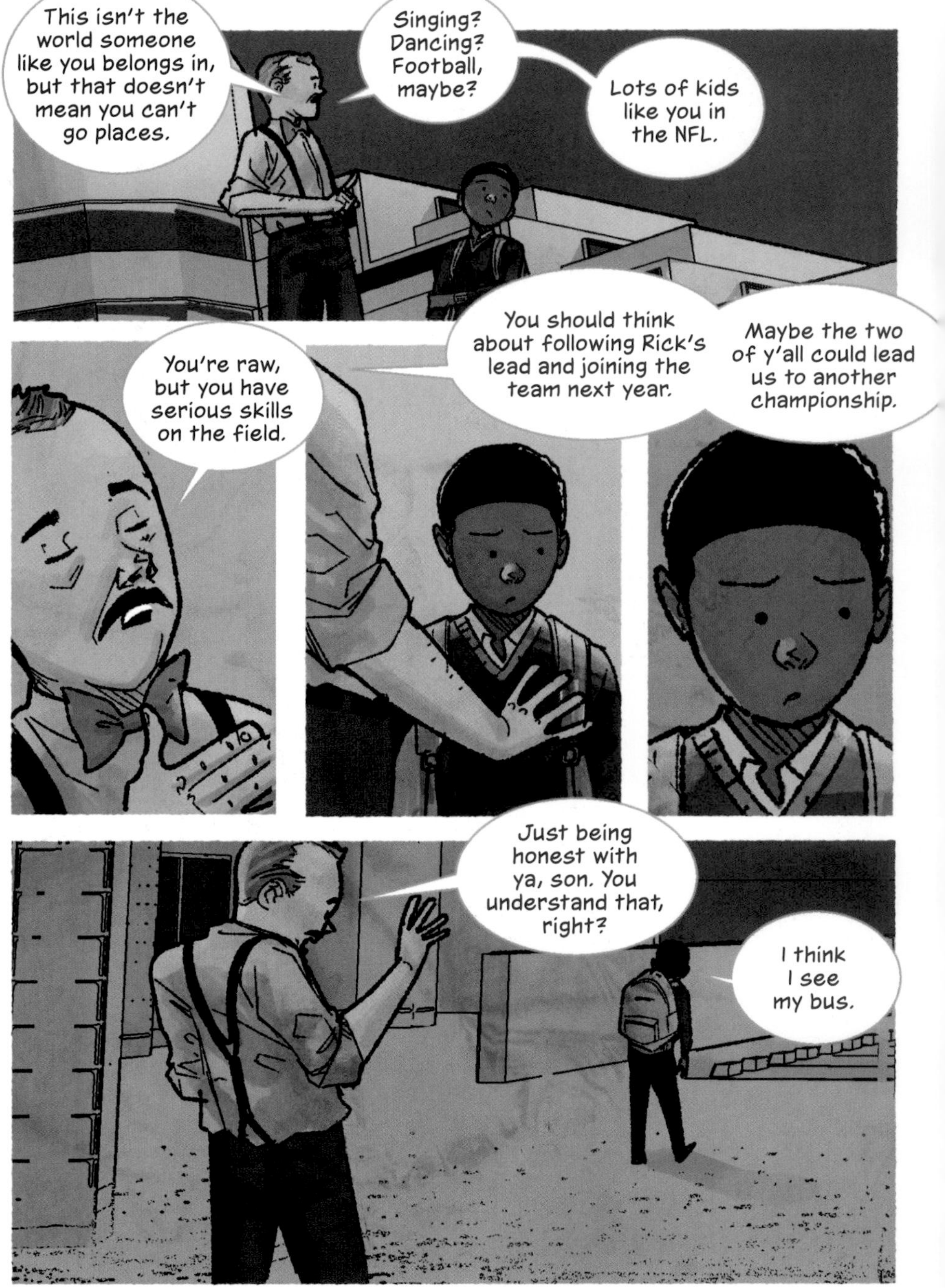
This isn't the world someone like you belongs in, but that doesn't mean you can't go places.
Singing? Dancing? Football, maybe?
Lots of kids like you in the NFL.
You're raw, but you have serious skills on the field.
You should think about following Rick's lead and joining the team next year.
Maybe the two of y'all could lead us to another championship.
Just being honest with ya, son. You understand that, right?
I think I see my bus.

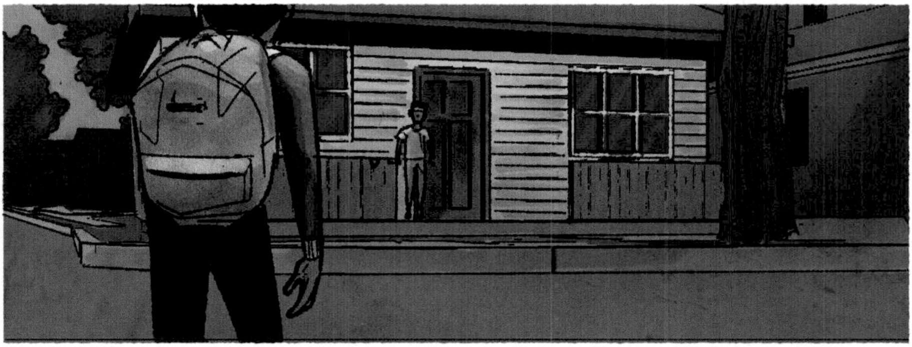

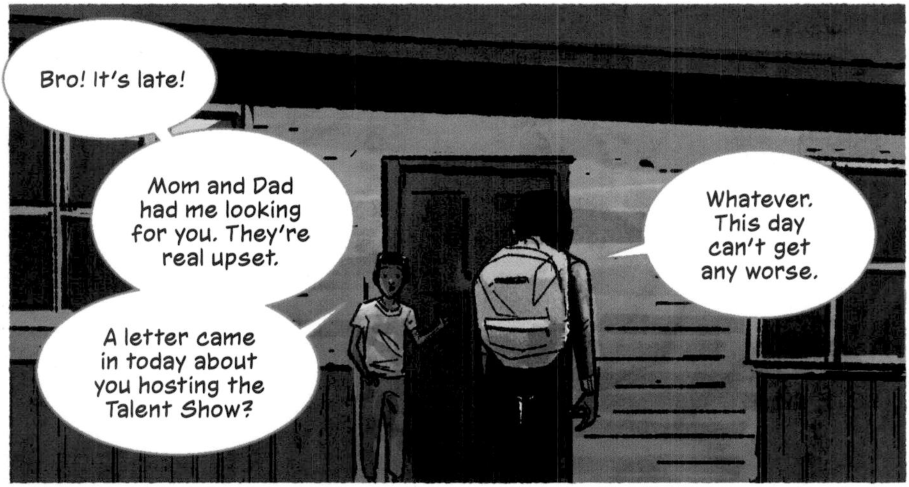
Bro! It's late!
Mom and Dad had me looking for you. They're real upset.
A letter came in today about you hosting the Talent Show?
Whatever. This day can't get any worse.

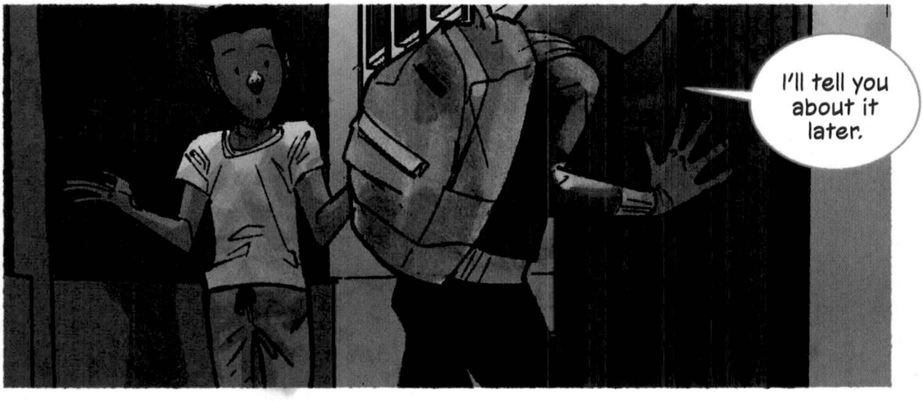
I'll tell you about it later.

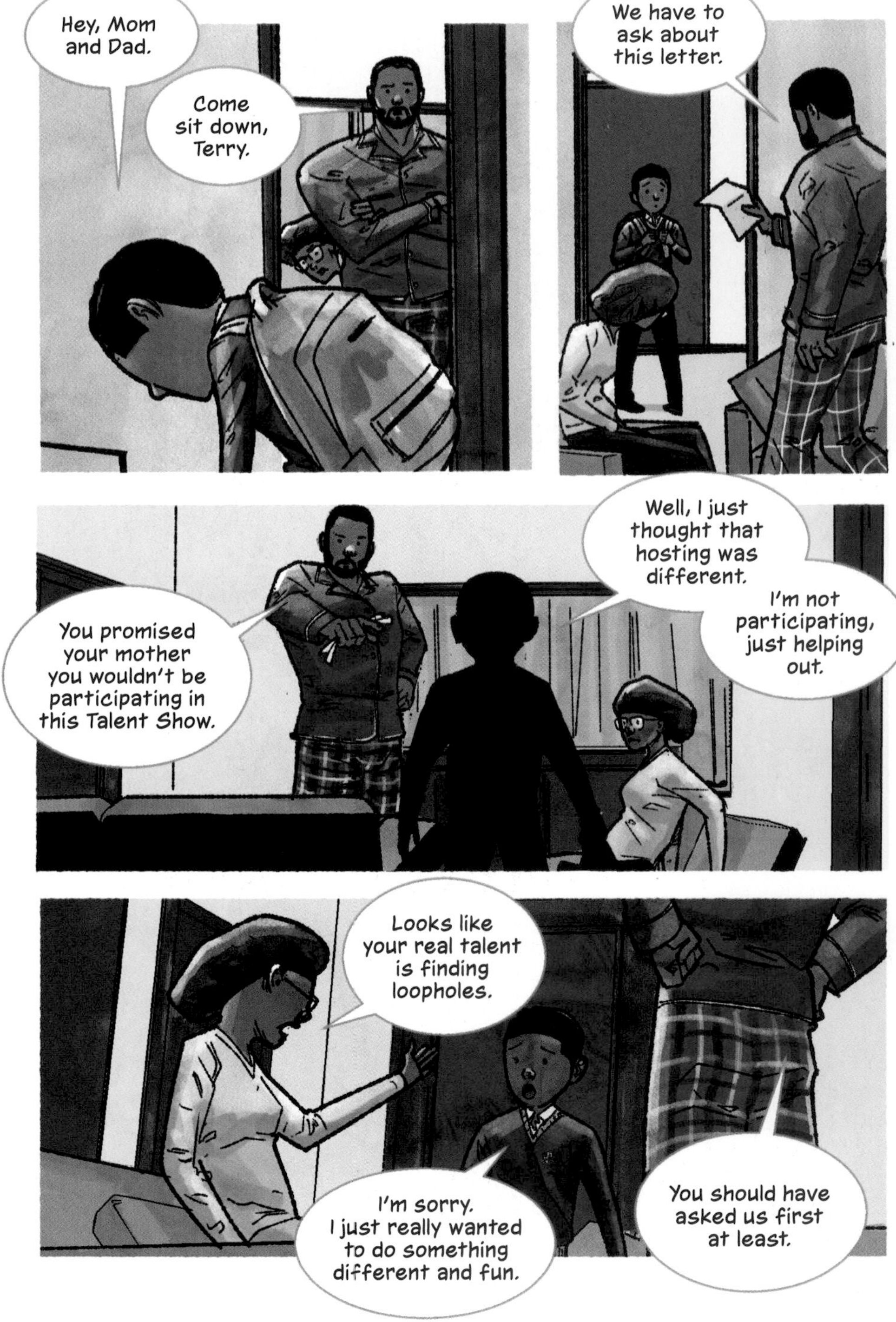
Hey, Mom and Dad.
Come sit down, Terry.
We have to ask about this letter.
You promised your mother you wouldn't be participating in this Talent Show.
Well, I just thought that hosting was different.
I'm not participating, just helping out.
Looks like your real talent is finding loopholes.
I'm sorry. I just really wanted to do something different and fun.
You should have asked us first at least.

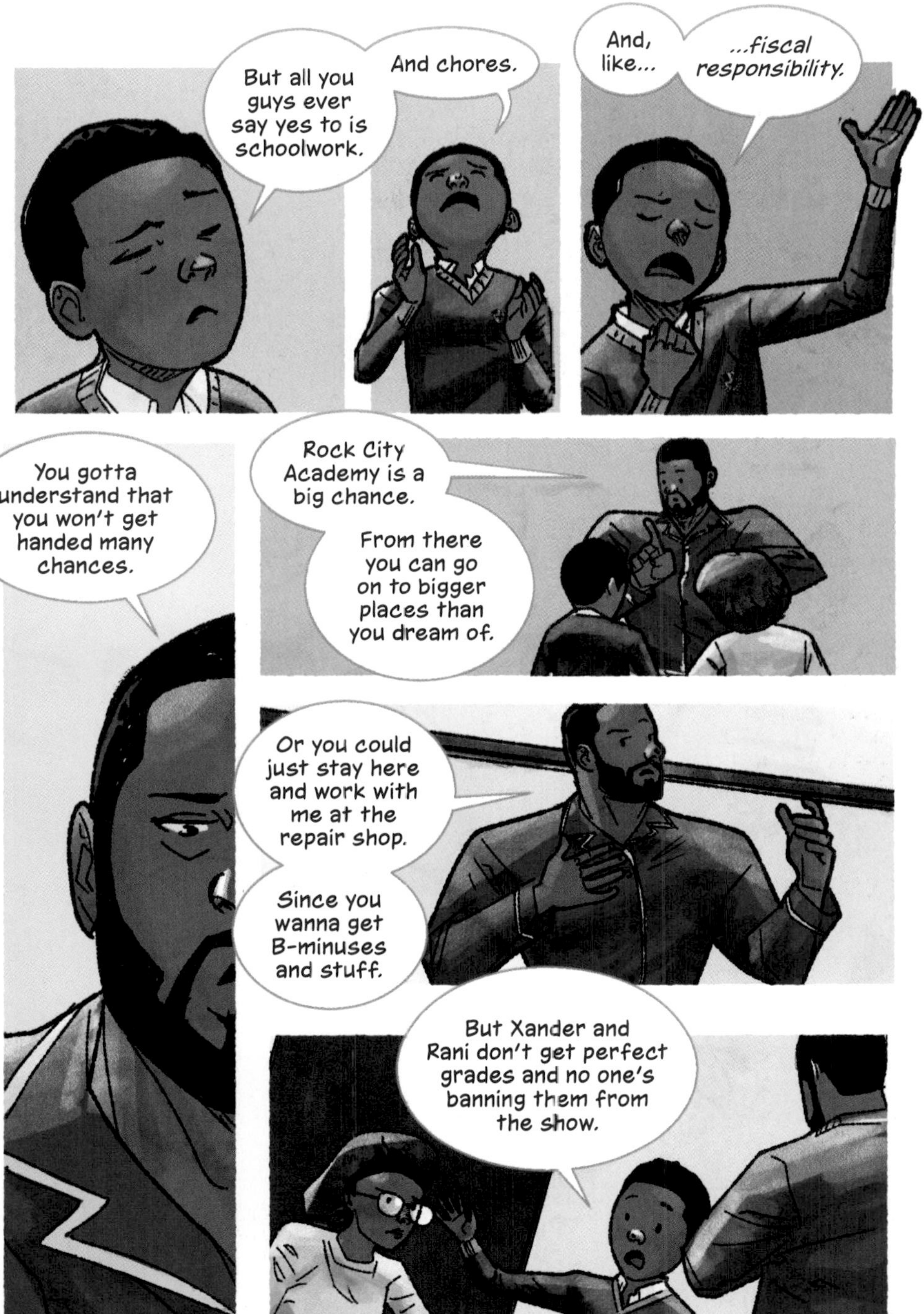
But all you guys ever say yes to is schoolwork.
And chores.
And, like...
...fiscal responsibility.
You gotta understand that you won't get handed many chances.
Rock City Academy is a big chance.
From there you can go on to bigger places than you dream of.
Or you could just stay here and work with me at the repair shop.
Since you wanna get B-minuses and stuff.
But Xander and Rani don't get perfect grades and no one's banning them from the show.

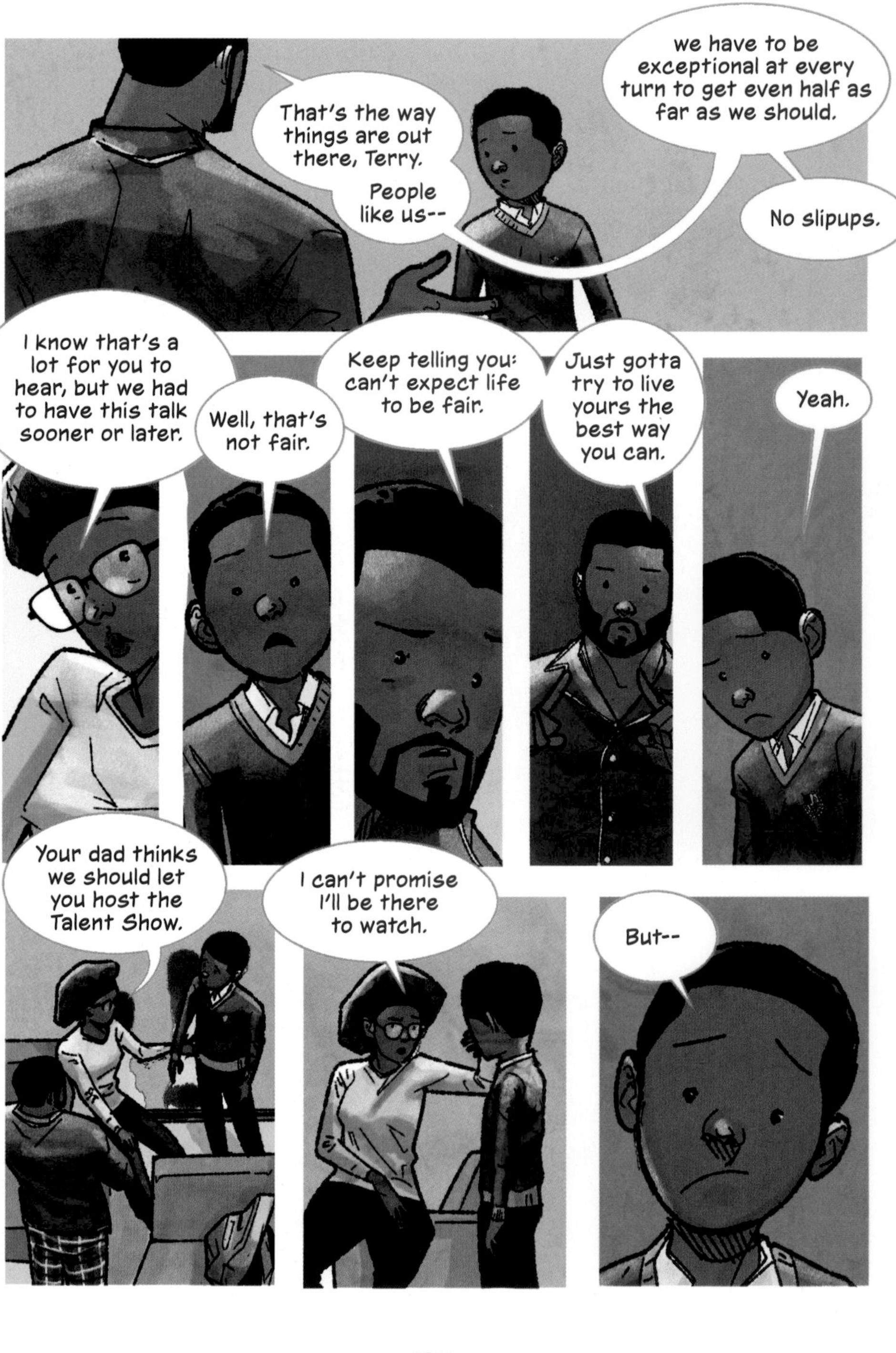
That's the way things are out there, Terry.
People like us--
we have to be exceptional at every turn to get even half as far as we should.
No slipups.
I know that's a lot for you to hear, but we had to have this talk sooner or later.
Well, that's not fair.
Keep telling you: can't expect life to be fair.
Just gotta try to live yours the best way you can.
Yeah.
Your dad thinks we should let you host the Talent Show.
I can't promise I'll be there to watch.
But--

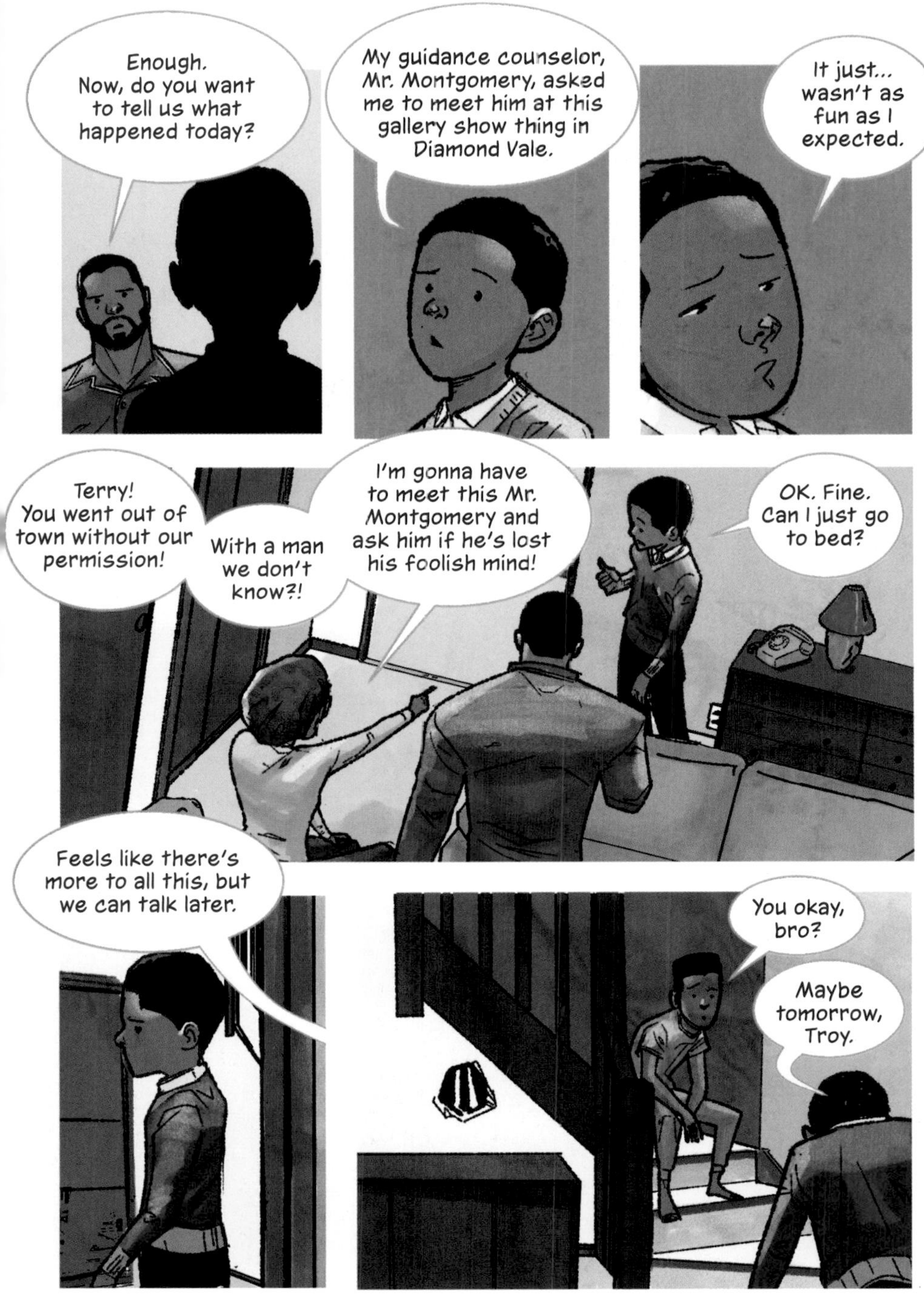

Enough. Now, do you want to tell us what happened today?
My guidance counselor, Mr. Montgomery, asked me to meet him at this gallery show thing in Diamond Vale.
It just... wasn't as fun as I expected.
Terry! You went out of town without our permission!
With a man we don't know?!
I'm gonna have to meet this Mr. Montgomery and ask him if he's lost his foolish mind!
OK. Fine. Can I just go to bed?
Feels like there's more to all this, but we can talk later.
You okay, bro?
Maybe tomorrow, Troy.

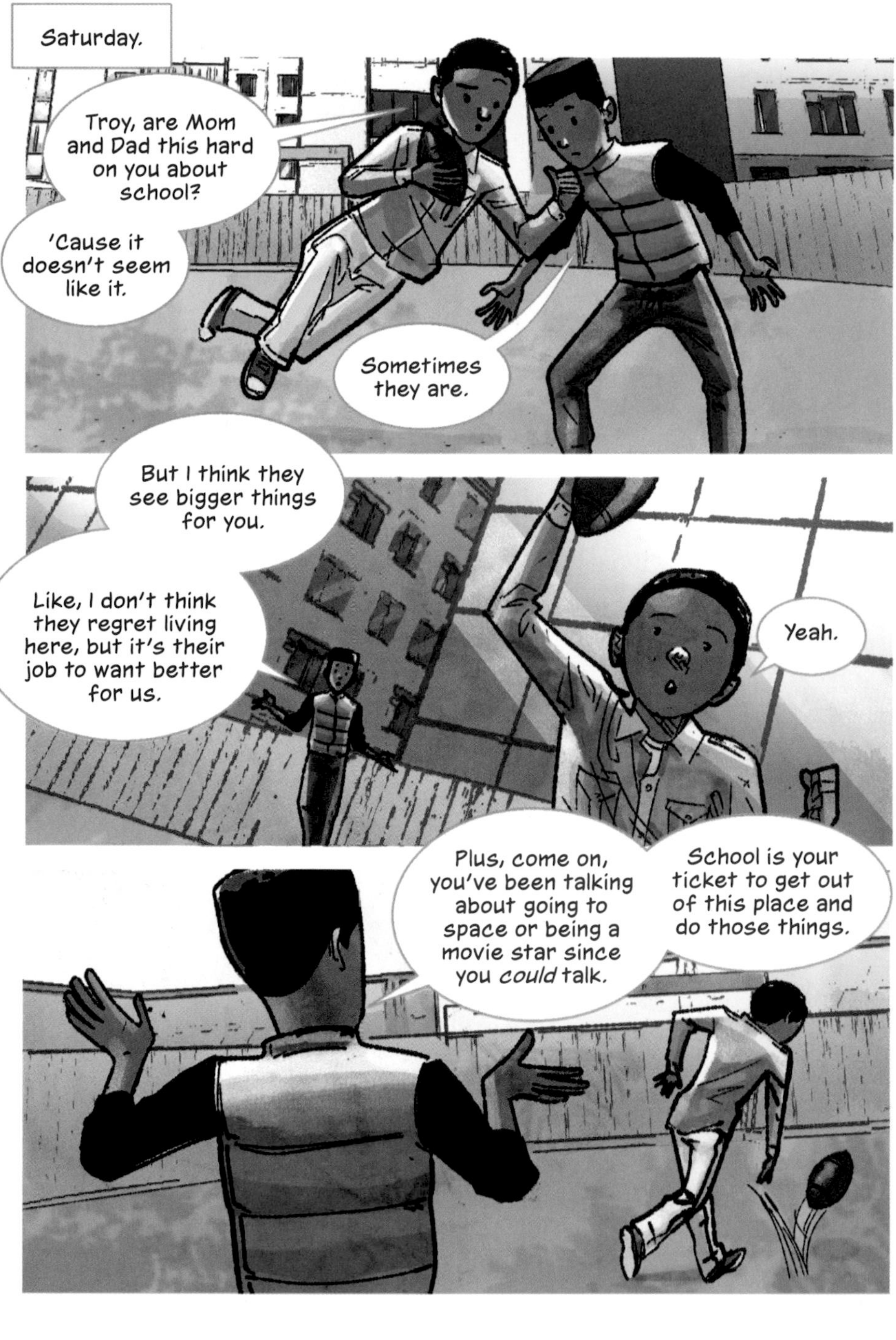
Saturday.
Troy, are Mom and Dad this hard on you about school?
'Cause it doesn't seem like it.
Sometimes they are.
But I think they see bigger things for you.
Like, I don't think they regret living here, but it's their job to want better for us.
Yeah.
Plus, come on, you've been talking about going to space or being a movie star since you *could* talk.
School is your ticket to get out of this place and do those things.

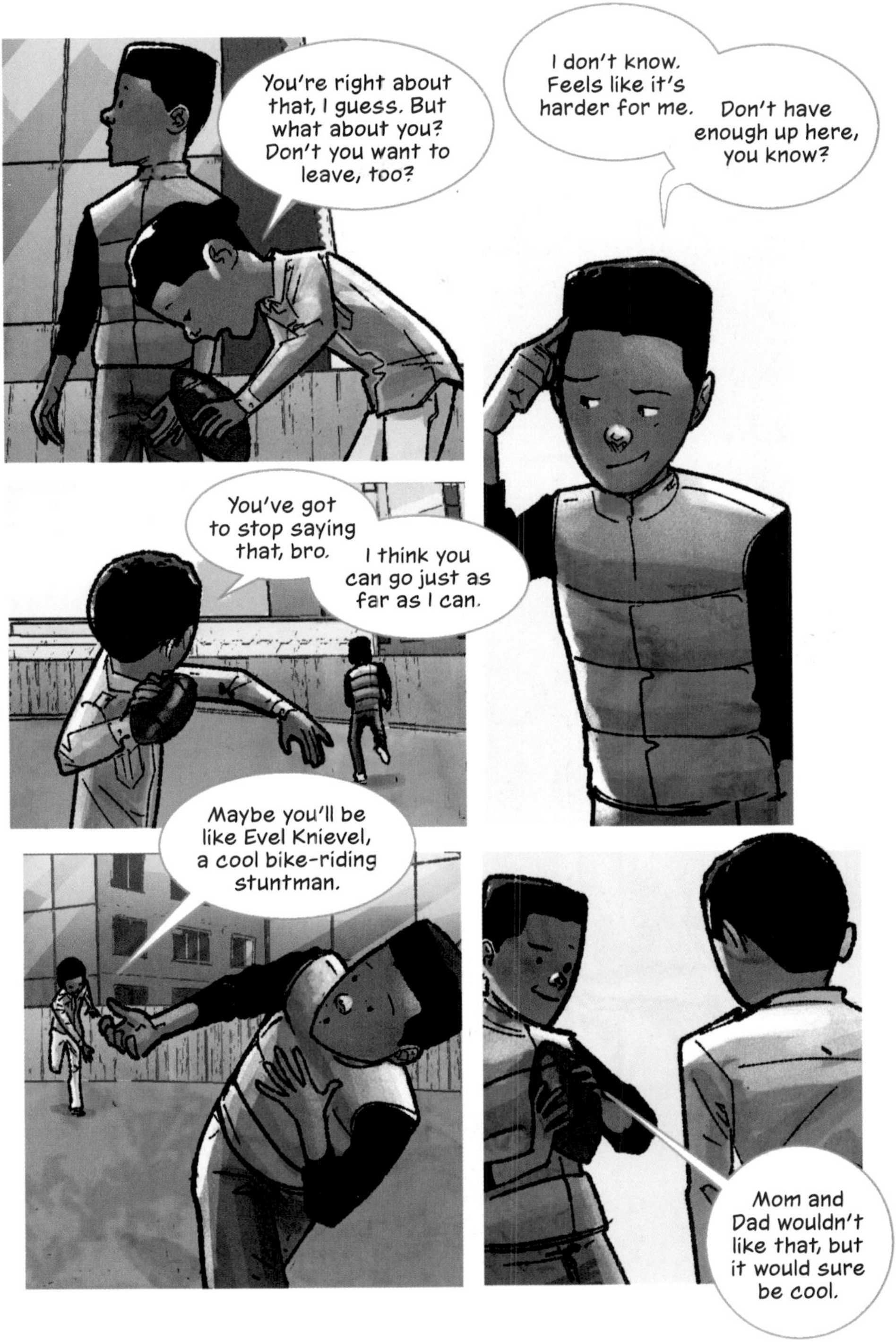
You're right about that, I guess. But what about you? Don't you want to leave, too?
I don't know. Feels like it's harder for me.
Don't have enough up here, you know?
You've got to stop saying that, bro.
I think you can go just as far as I can.
Maybe you'll be like Evel Knievel, a cool bike-riding stuntman.
Mom and Dad wouldn't like that, but it would sure be cool.

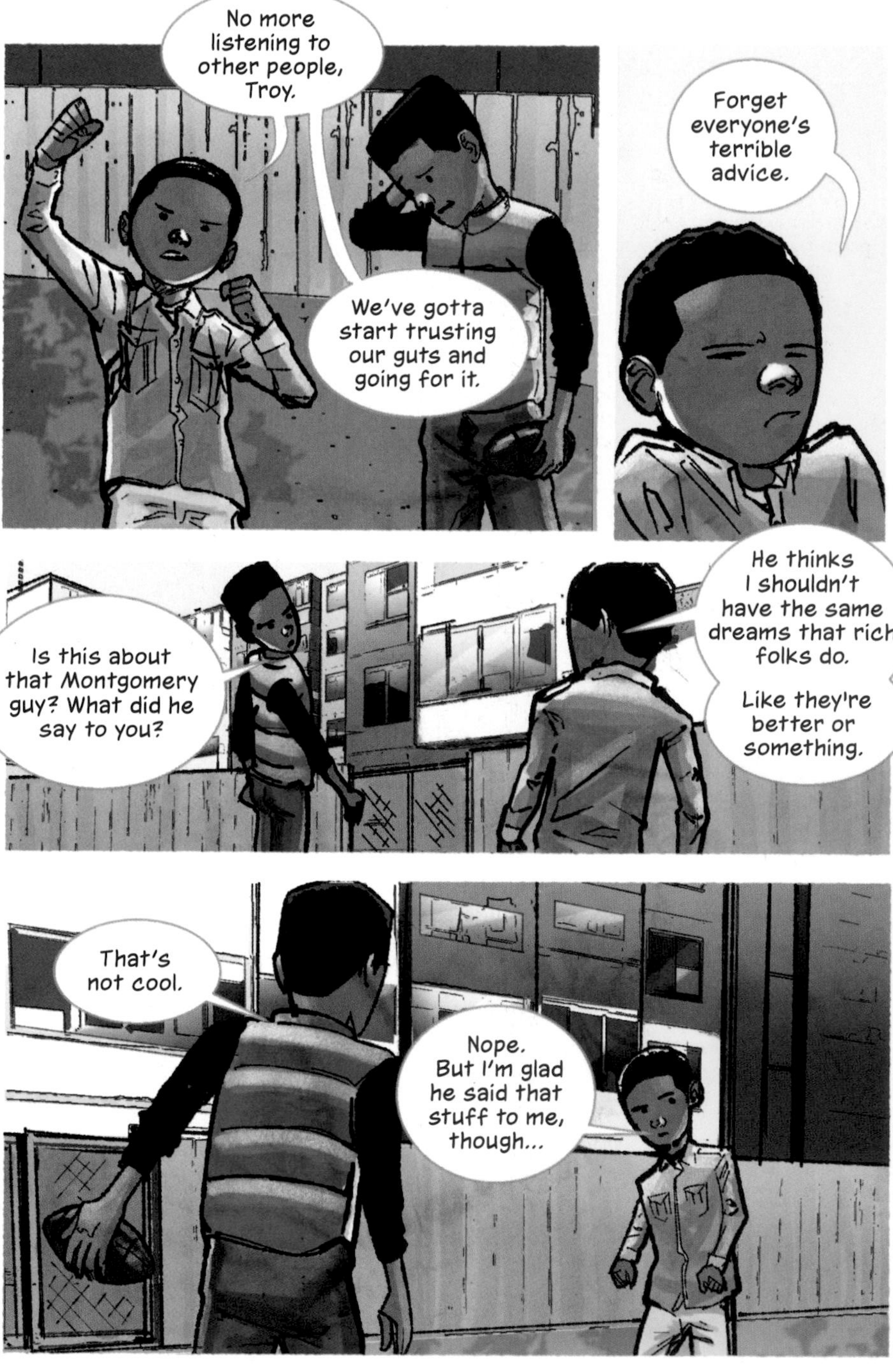
No more listening to other people, Troy.
We've gotta start trusting our guts and going for it.
Forget everyone's terrible advice.
Is this about that Montgomery guy? What did he say to you?
He thinks I shouldn't have the same dreams that rich folks do.
Like they're better or something.
That's not cool.
Nope. But I'm glad he said that stuff to me, though...

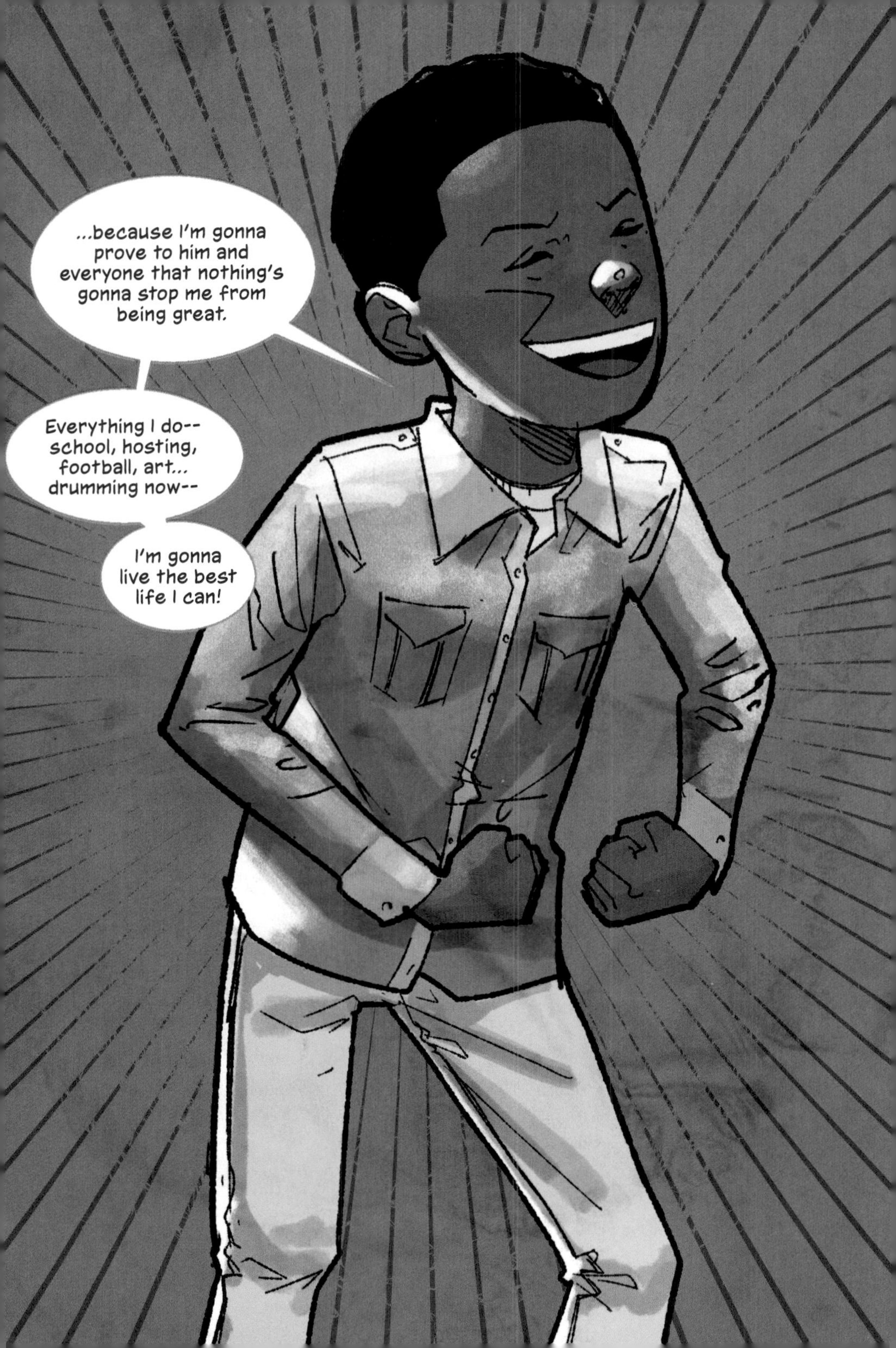
...because I'm gonna prove to him and everyone that nothing's gonna stop me from being great.
Everything I do--school, hosting, football, art... drumming now--
I'm gonna live the best life I can!

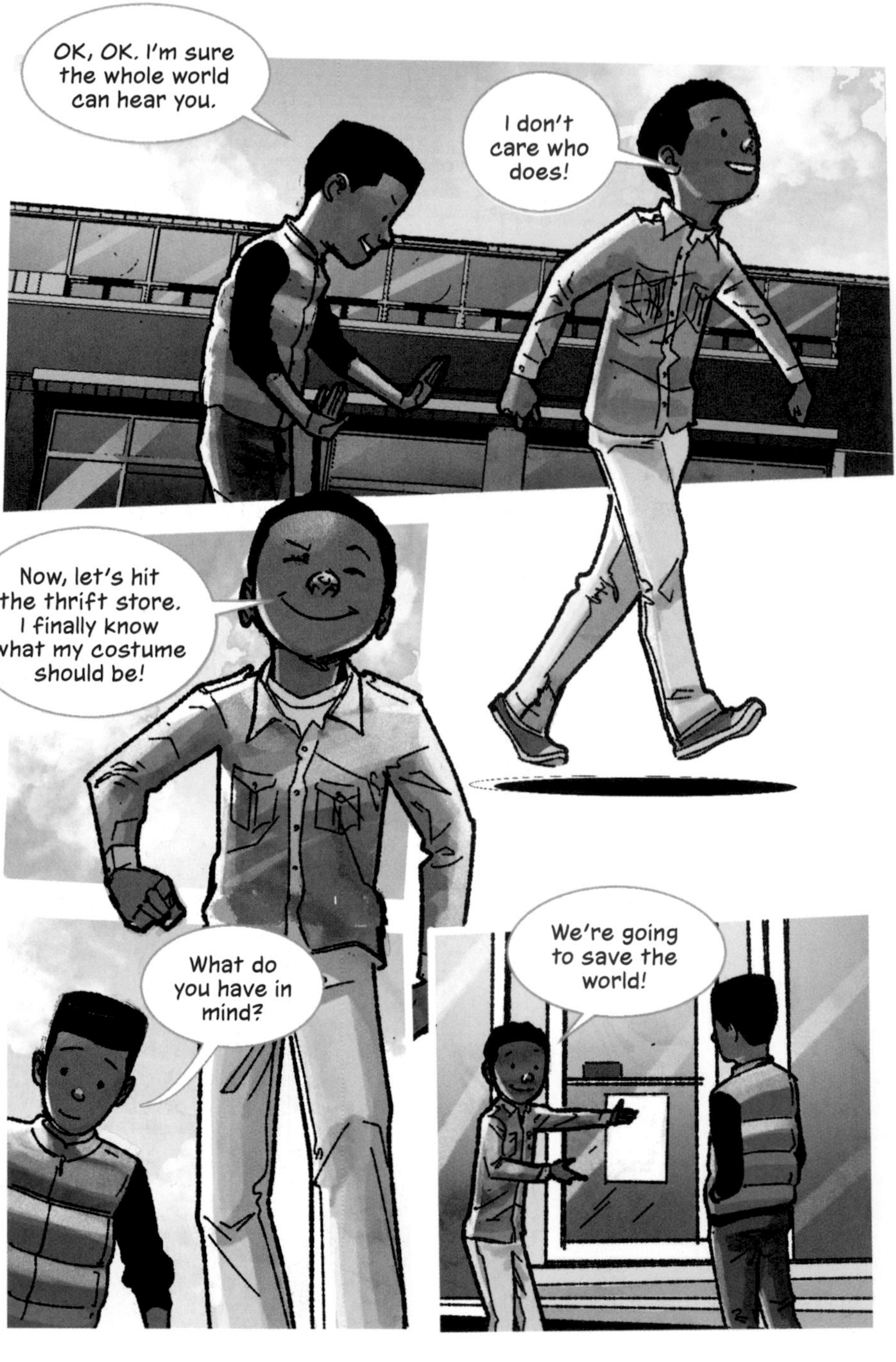
OK, OK. I'm sure the whole world can hear you.
I don't care who does!
Now, let's hit the thrift store. I finally know what my costume should be!
What do you have in mind?
We're going to save the world!

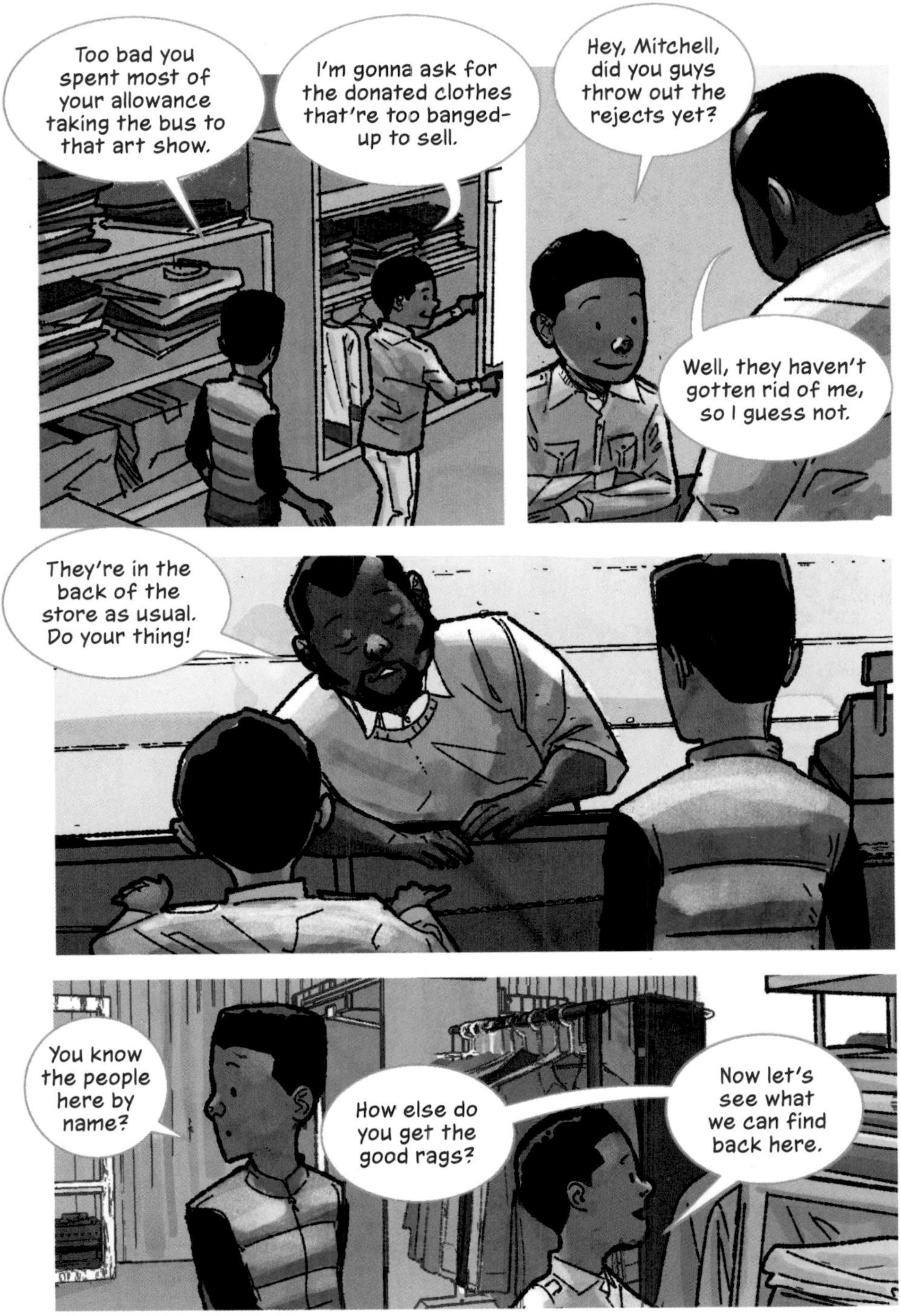
Too bad you spent most of your allowance taking the bus to that art show.
I'm gonna ask for the donated clothes that're too banged-up to sell.
Hey, Mitchell, did you guys throw out the rejects yet?
Well, they haven't gotten rid of me, so I guess not.
They're in the back of the store as usual. Do your thing!
You know the people here by name?
How else do you get the good rags?
Now let's see what we can find back here.

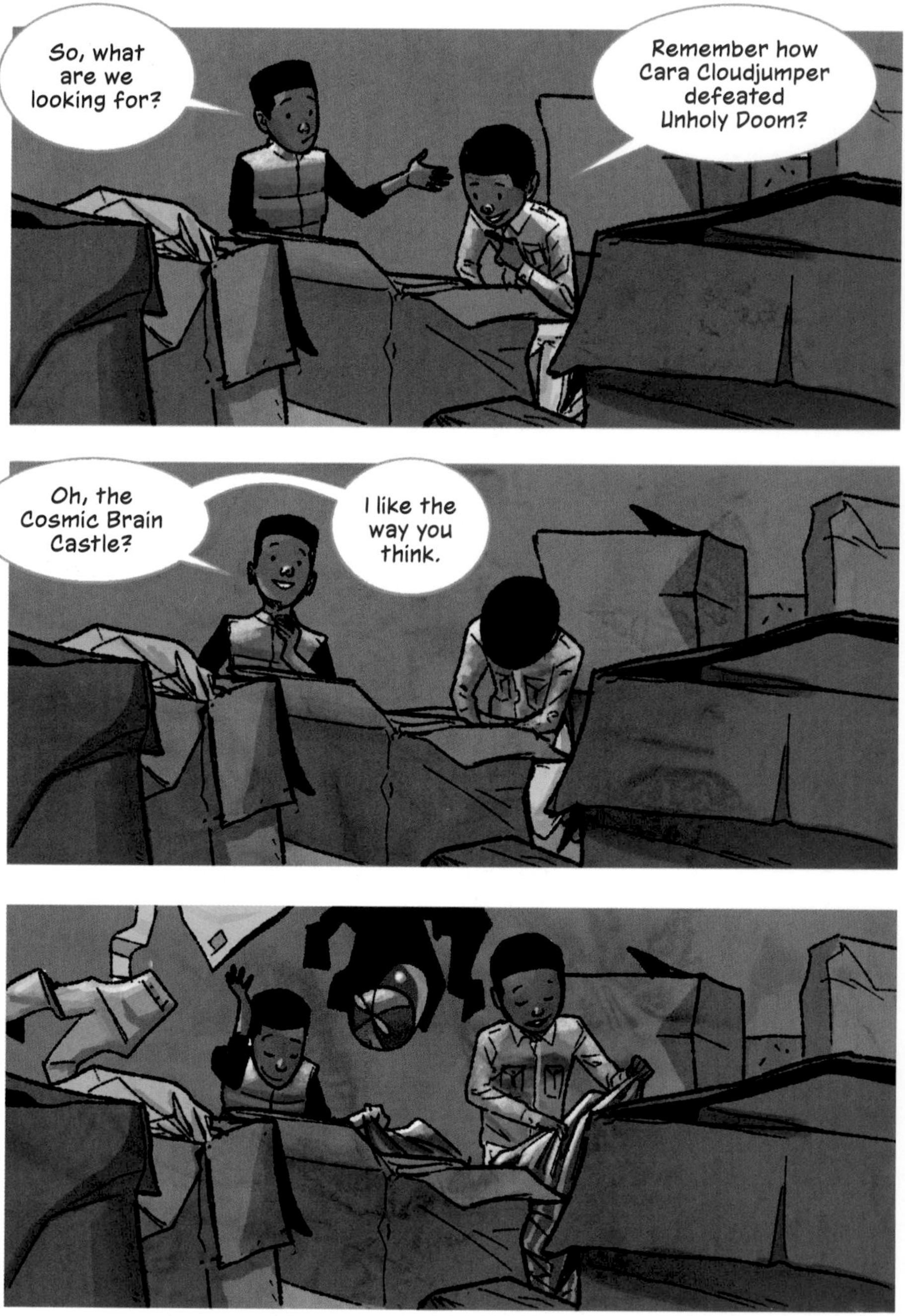
So, what are we looking for?
Remember how Cara Cloudjumper defeated Unholy Doom?
Oh, the Cosmic Brain Castle?
I like the way you think.

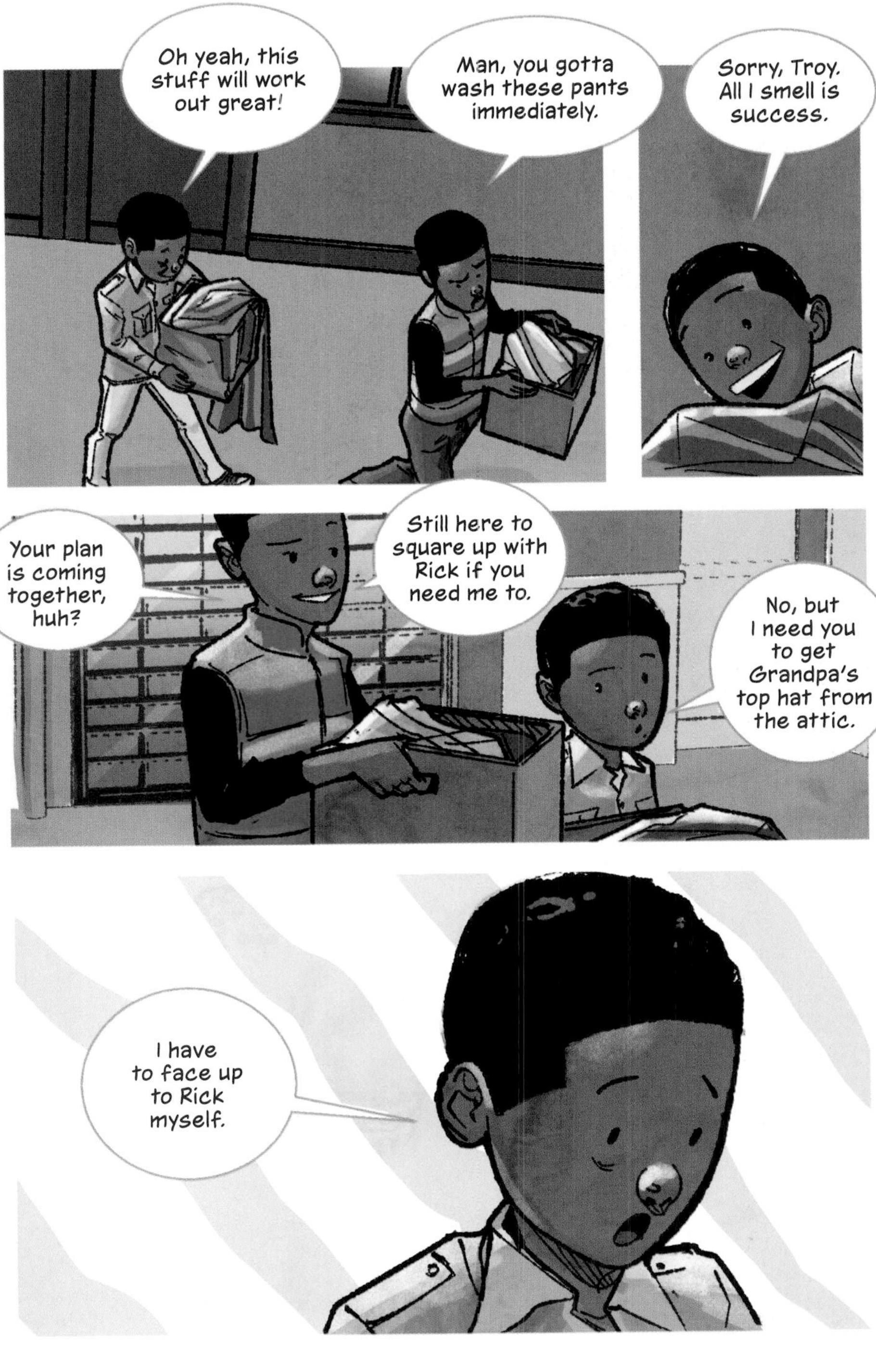
Oh yeah, this stuff will work out great!
Man, you gotta wash these pants immediately.
Sorry, Troy. All I smell is success.
Your plan is coming together, huh?
Still here to square up with Rick if you need me to.
No, but I need you to get Grandpa's top hat from the attic.
I have to face up to Rick myself.

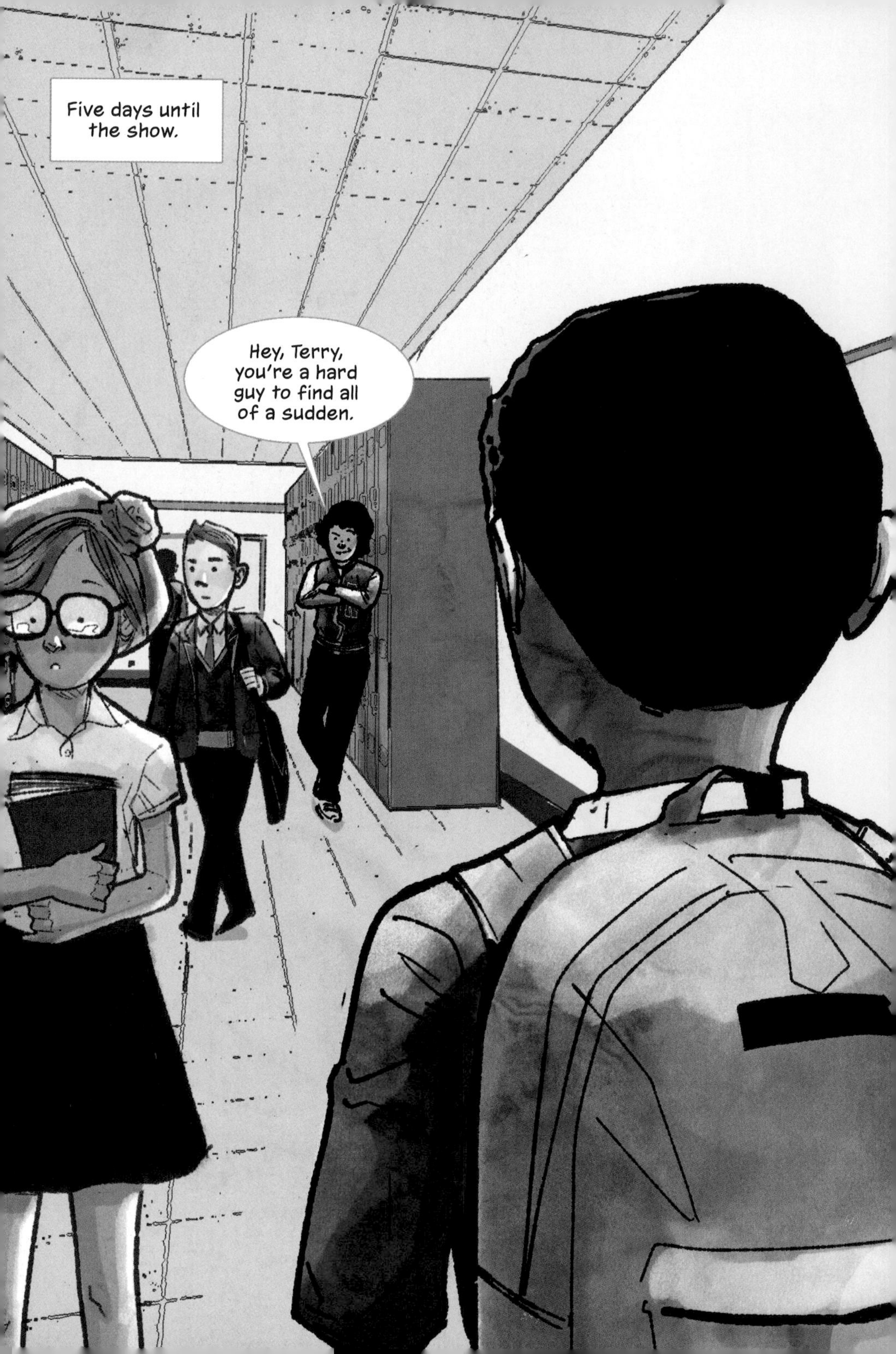
Five days until the show.
Hey, Terry, you're a hard guy to find all of a sudden.

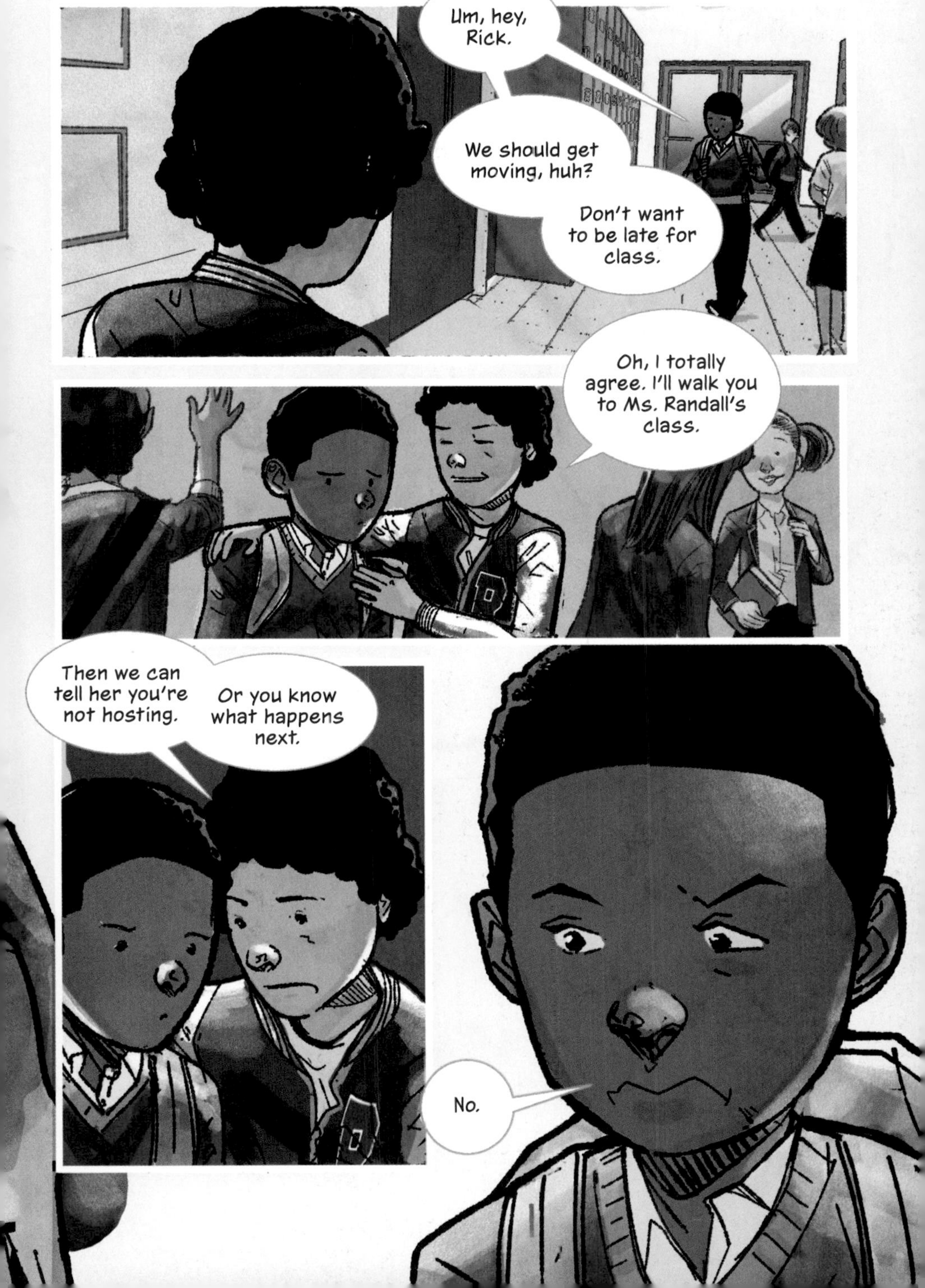
Um, hey, Rick.
We should get moving, huh?
Don't want to be late for class.
Oh, I totally agree. I'll walk you to Ms. Randall's class.
Then we can tell her you're not hosting.
Or you know what happens next.
No.

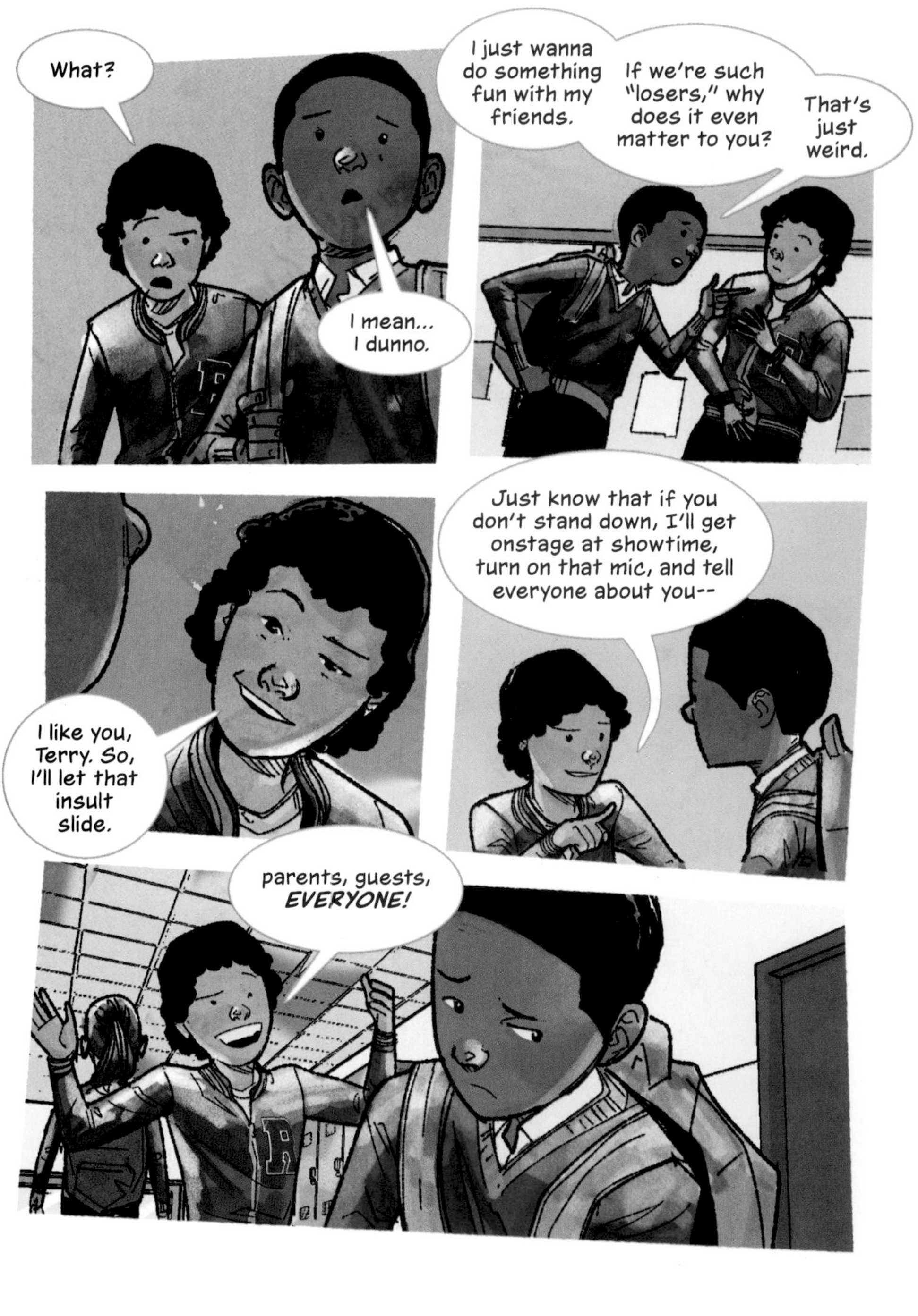
What?
I mean... I dunno.
I just wanna do something fun with my friends.
If we're such "losers," why does it even matter to you?
That's just weird.
I like you, Terry. So, I'll let that insult slide.
Just know that if you don't stand down, I'll get onstage at showtime, turn on that mic, and tell everyone about you--
parents, guests, *EVERYONE!*

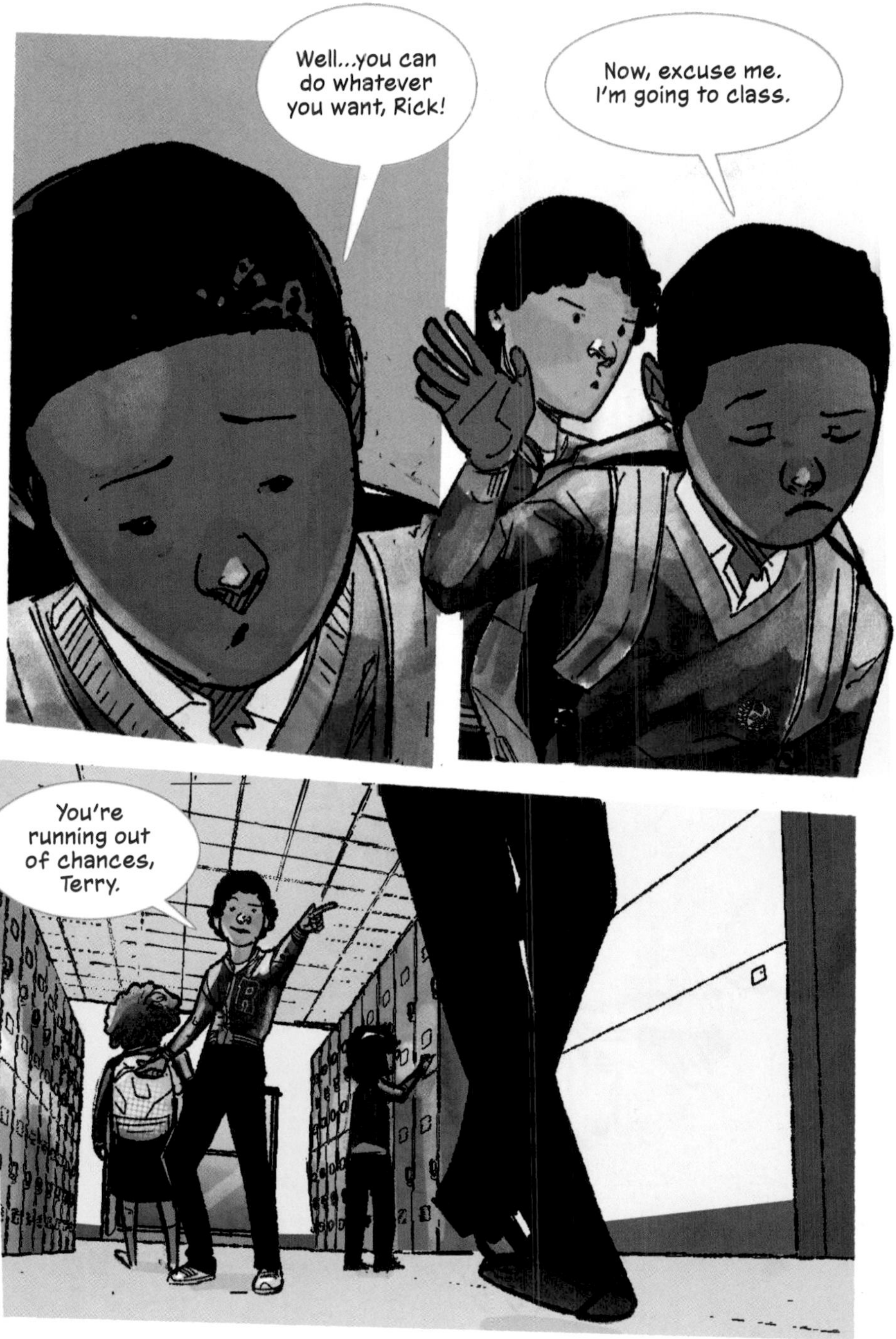
Well...you can do whatever you want, Rick!
Now, excuse me. I'm going to class.
You're running out of chances, Terry.

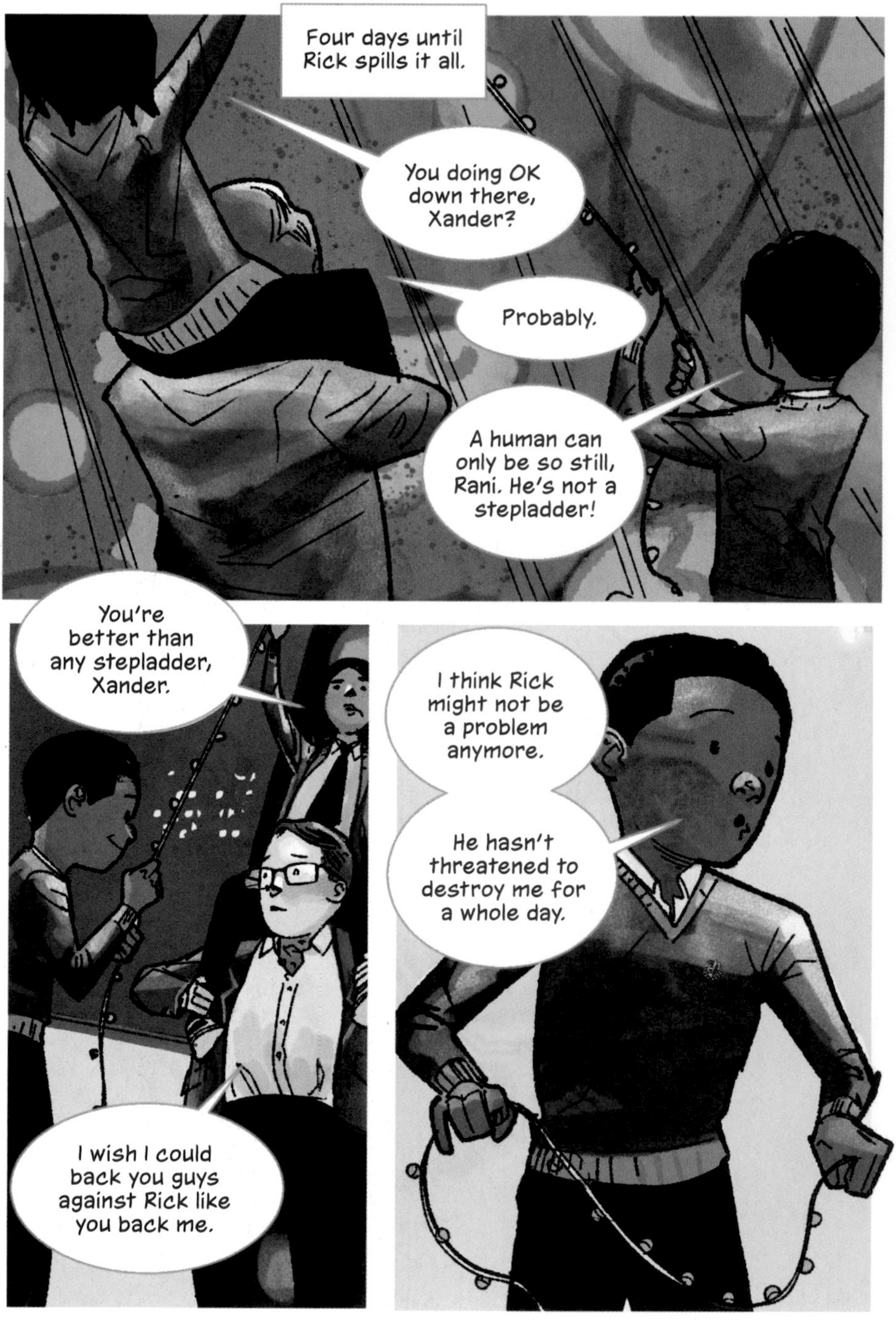
Four days until Rick spills it all.
You doing OK down there, Xander?
Probably.
A human can only be so still, Rani. He's not a stepladder!
You're better than any stepladder, Xander.
I wish I could back you guys against Rick like you back me.
I think Rick might not be a problem anymore.
He hasn't threatened to destroy me for a whole day.

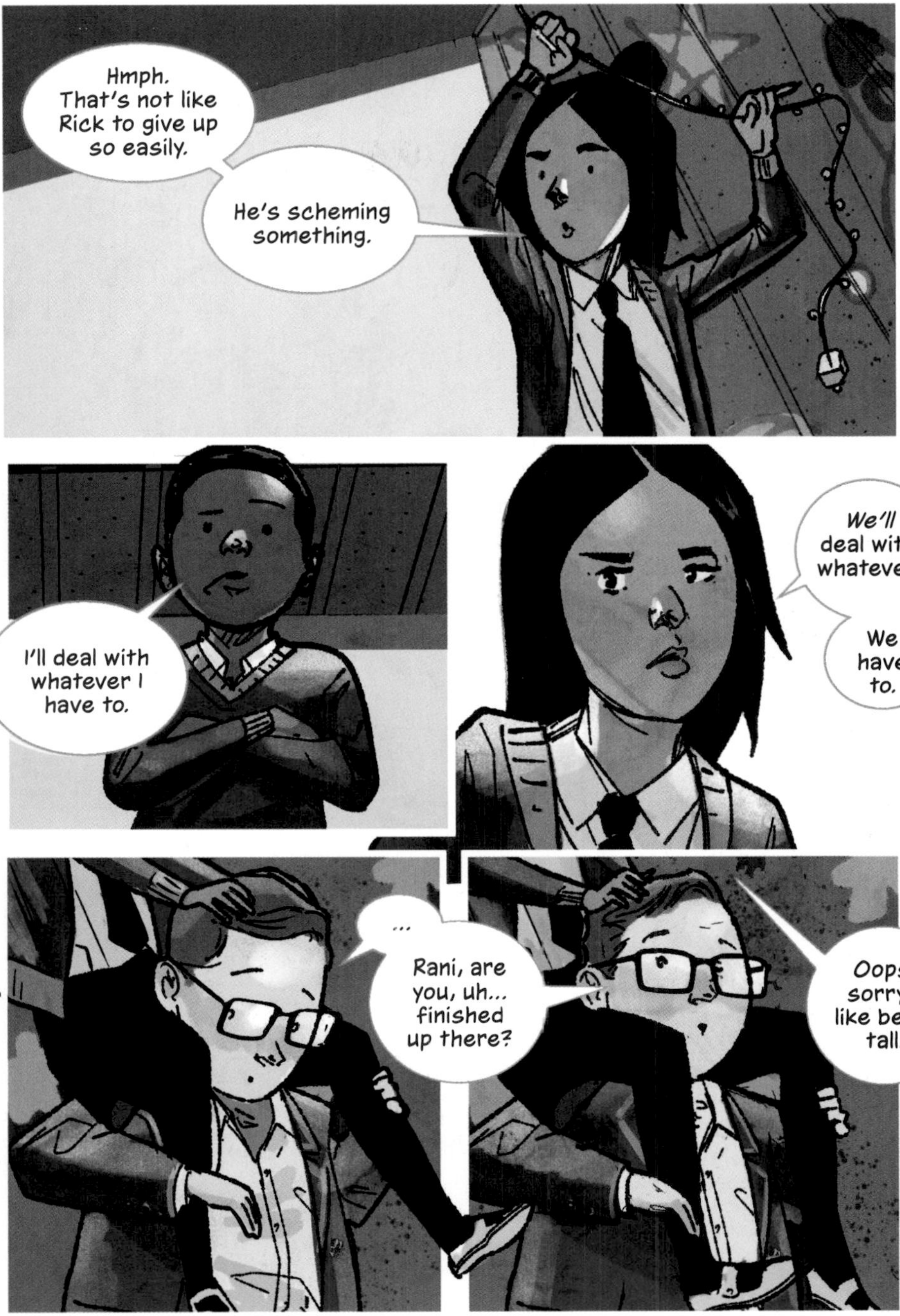
Hmph. That's not like Rick to give up so easily.
He's scheming something.
I'll deal with whatever I have to.
We'll deal with whatever.
We have to.
...
Rani, are you, uh... finished up there?
Oops, sorry. I like being tall.

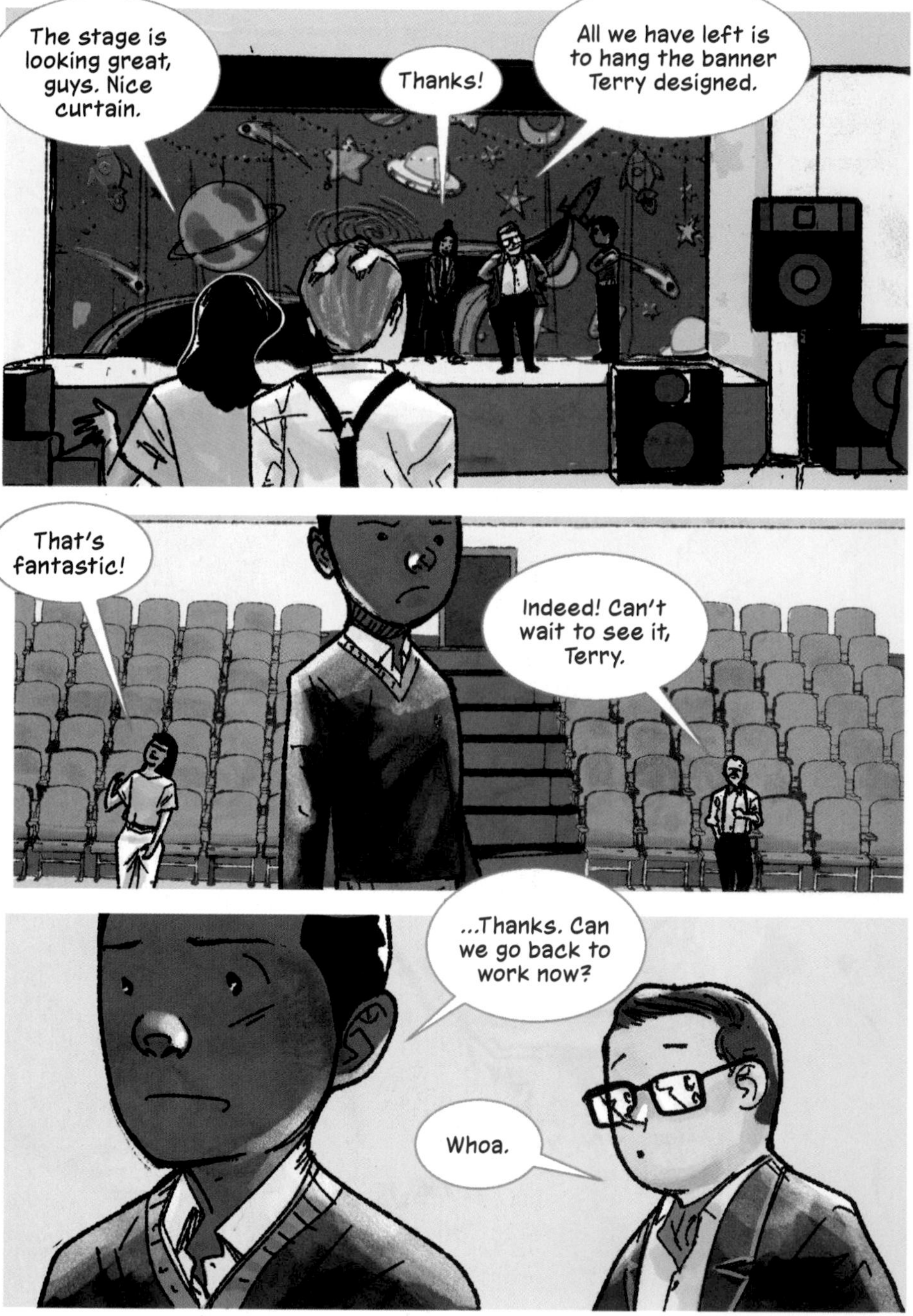
The stage is looking great, guys. Nice curtain.
Thanks!
All we have left is to hang the banner Terry designed.
That's fantastic!
Indeed! Can't wait to see it, Terry.
...Thanks. Can we go back to work now?
Whoa.

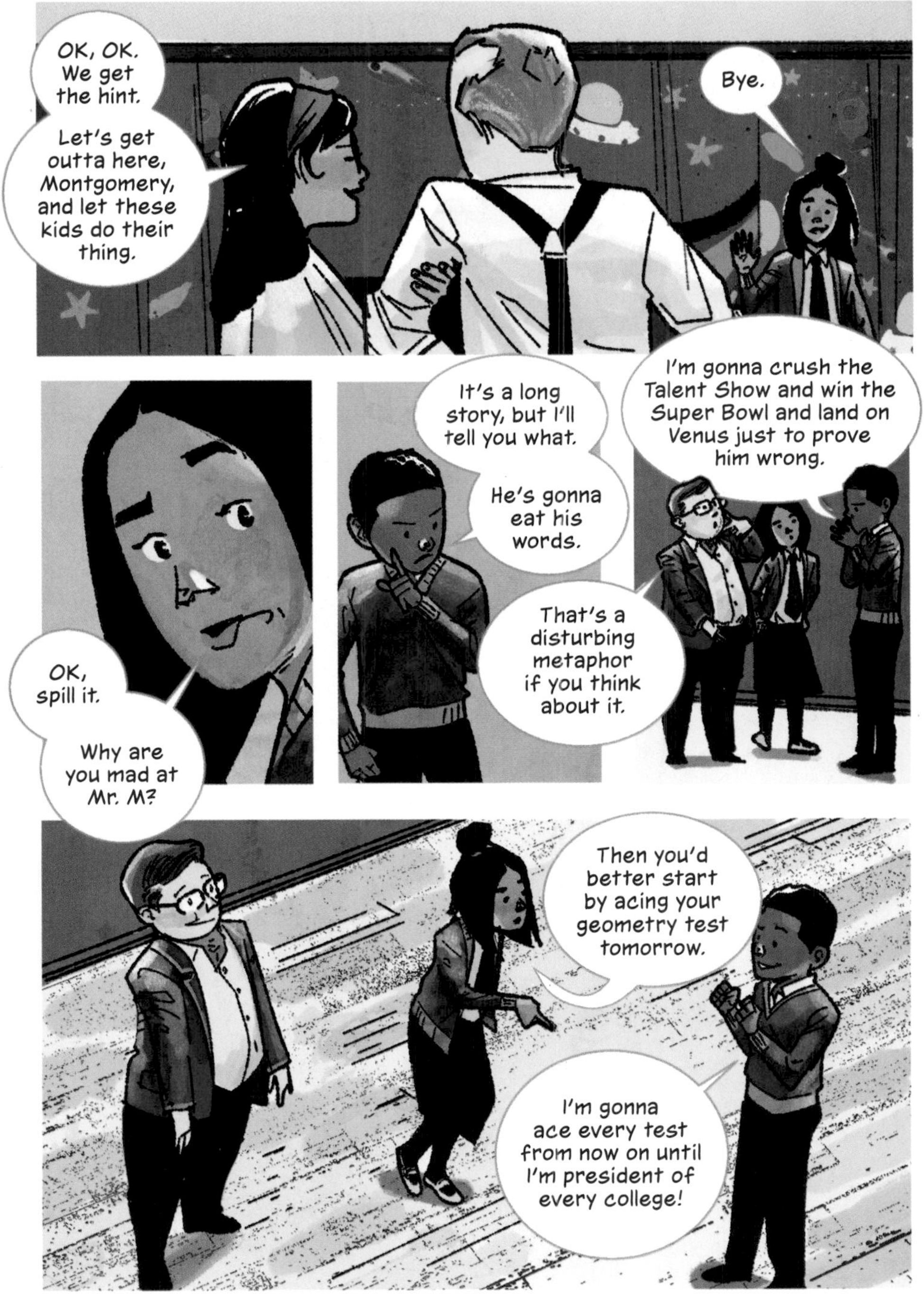
OK, OK. We get the hint.
Let's get outta here, Montgomery, and let these kids do their thing.
Bye.
OK, spill it.
Why are you mad at Mr. M?
It's a long story, but I'll tell you what.
He's gonna eat his words.
I'm gonna crush the Talent Show and win the Super Bowl and land on Venus just to prove him wrong.
That's a disturbing metaphor if you think about it.
Then you'd better start by acing your geometry test tomorrow.
I'm gonna ace every test from now on until I'm president of every college!

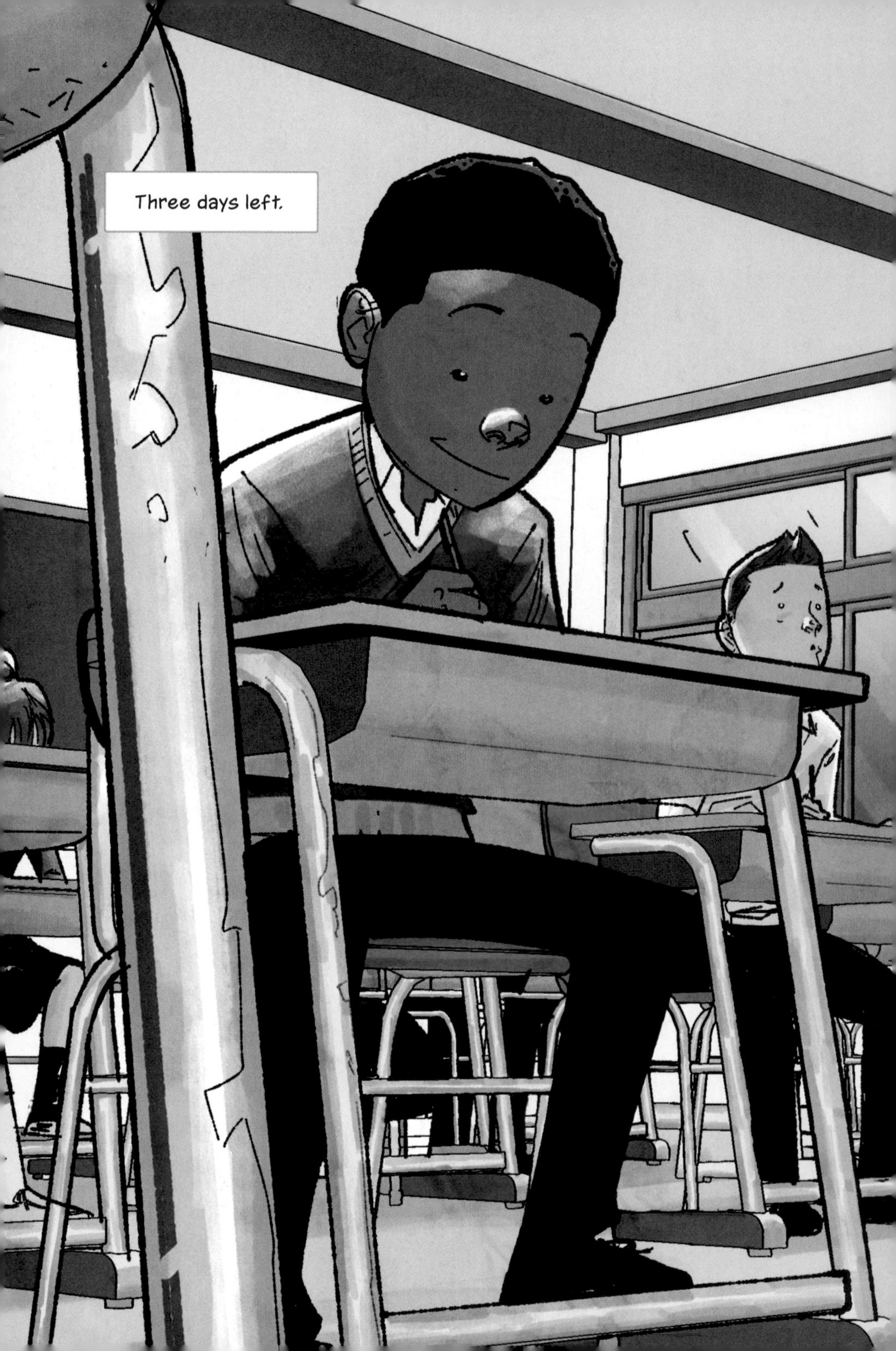
Three days left.

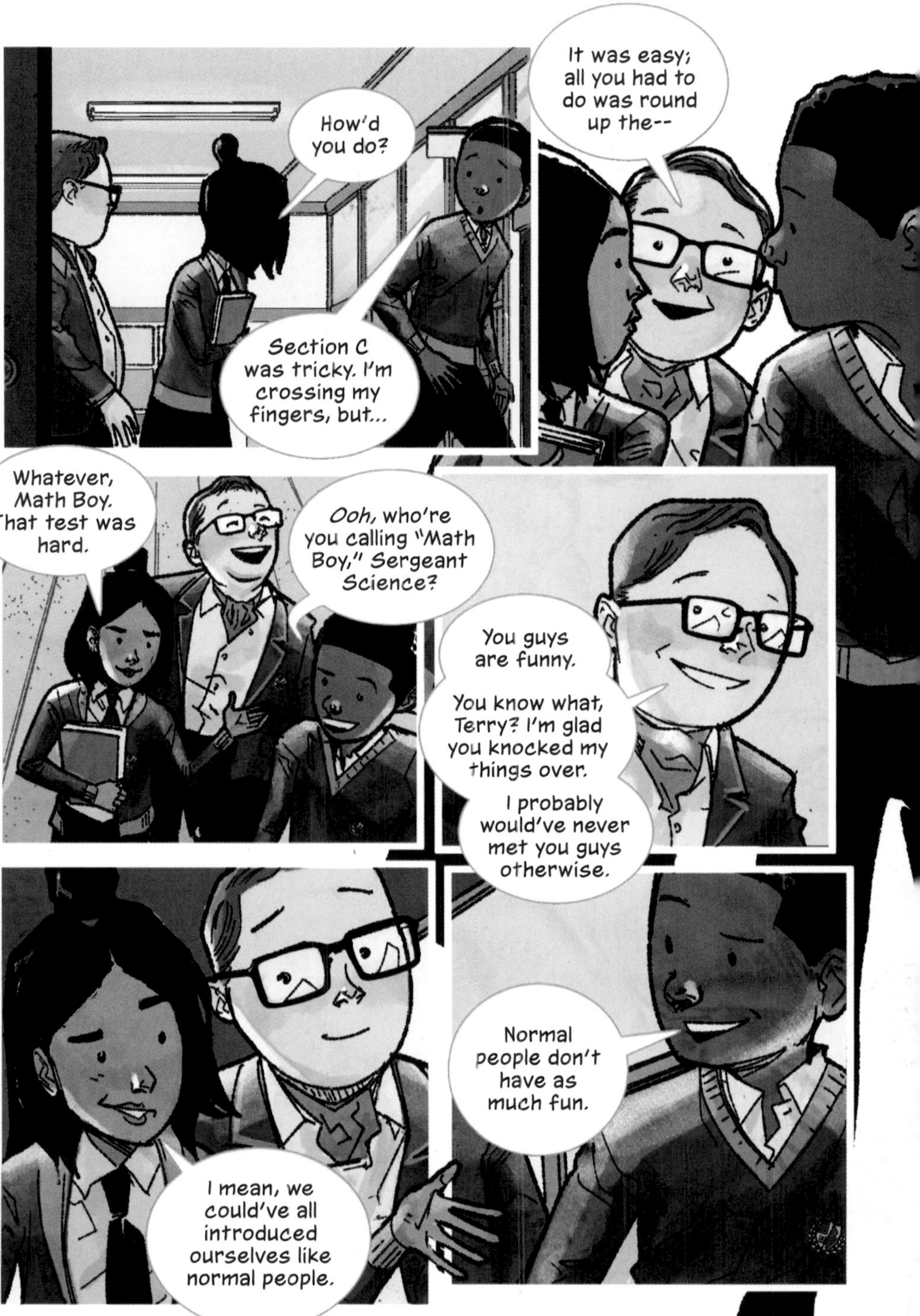
How'd you do?
Section C was tricky. I'm crossing my fingers, but...
It was easy; all you had to do was round up the--
Whatever, Math Boy. That test was hard.
Ooh, who're you calling "Math Boy," Sergeant Science?
You guys are funny.
You know what, Terry? I'm glad you knocked my things over.
I probably would've never met you guys otherwise.
I mean, we could've all introduced ourselves like normal people.
Normal people don't have as much fun.

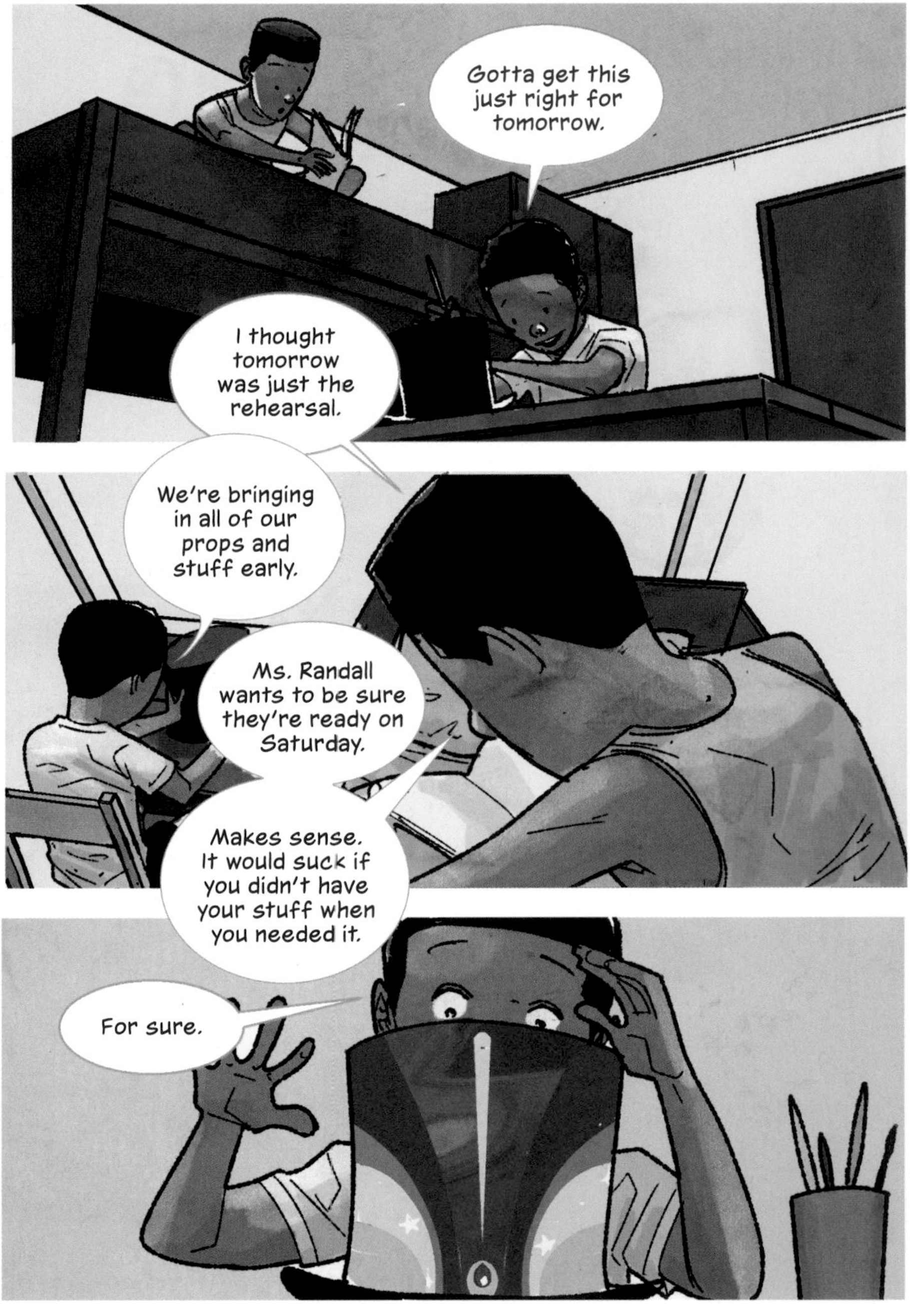

Gotta get this just right for tomorrow.
I thought tomorrow was just the rehearsal.
We're bringing in all of our props and stuff early.
Ms. Randall wants to be sure they're ready on Saturday.
Makes sense. It would suck if you didn't have your stuff when you needed it.
For sure.

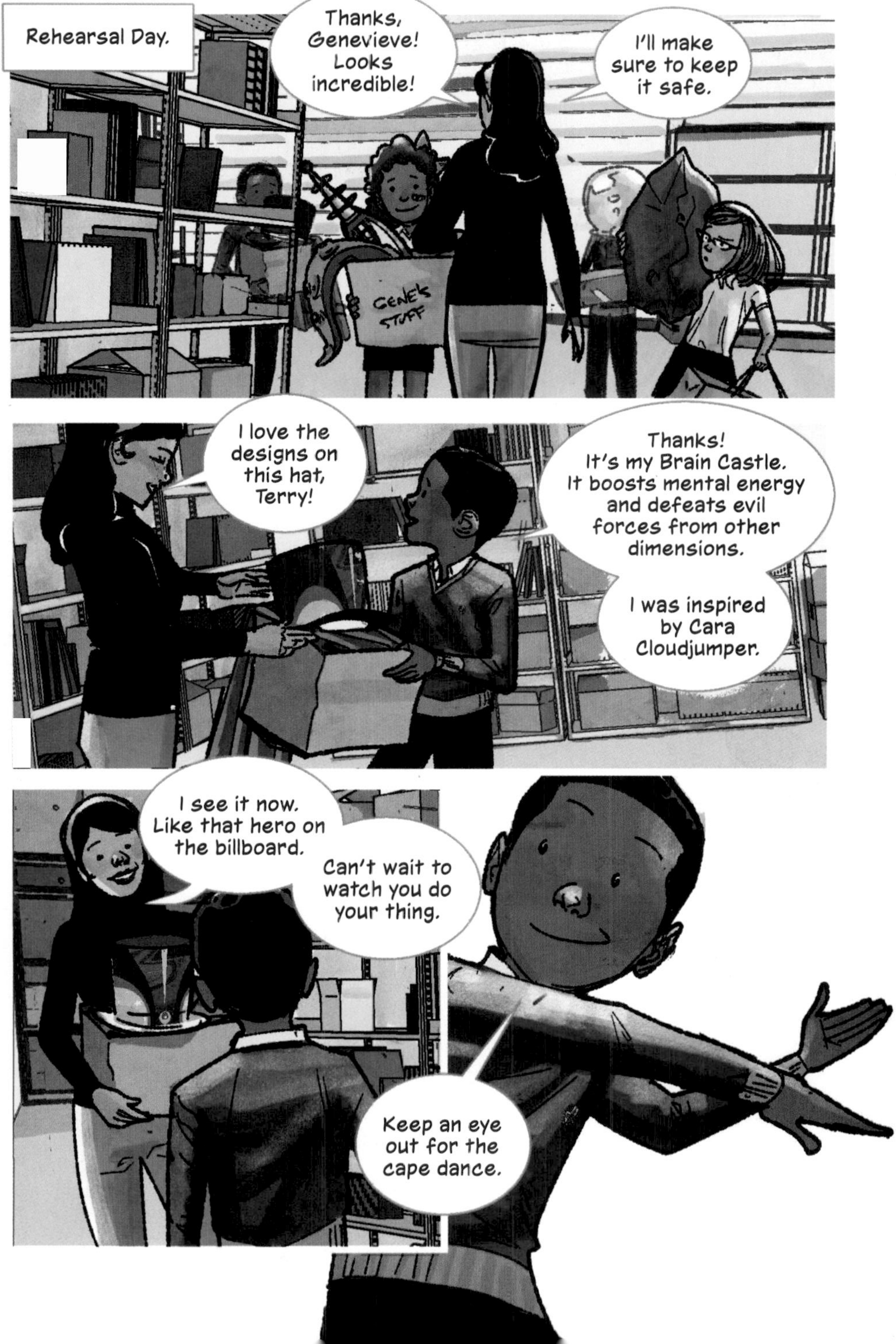
Rehearsal Day.
Thanks, Genevieve! Looks incredible!
I'll make sure to keep it safe.
GENE'S STUFF
I love the designs on this hat, Terry!
Thanks! It's my Brain Castle. It boosts mental energy and defeats evil forces from other dimensions.
I was inspired by Cara Cloudjumper.
I see it now. Like that hero on the billboard.
Can't wait to watch you do your thing.
Keep an eye out for the cape dance.

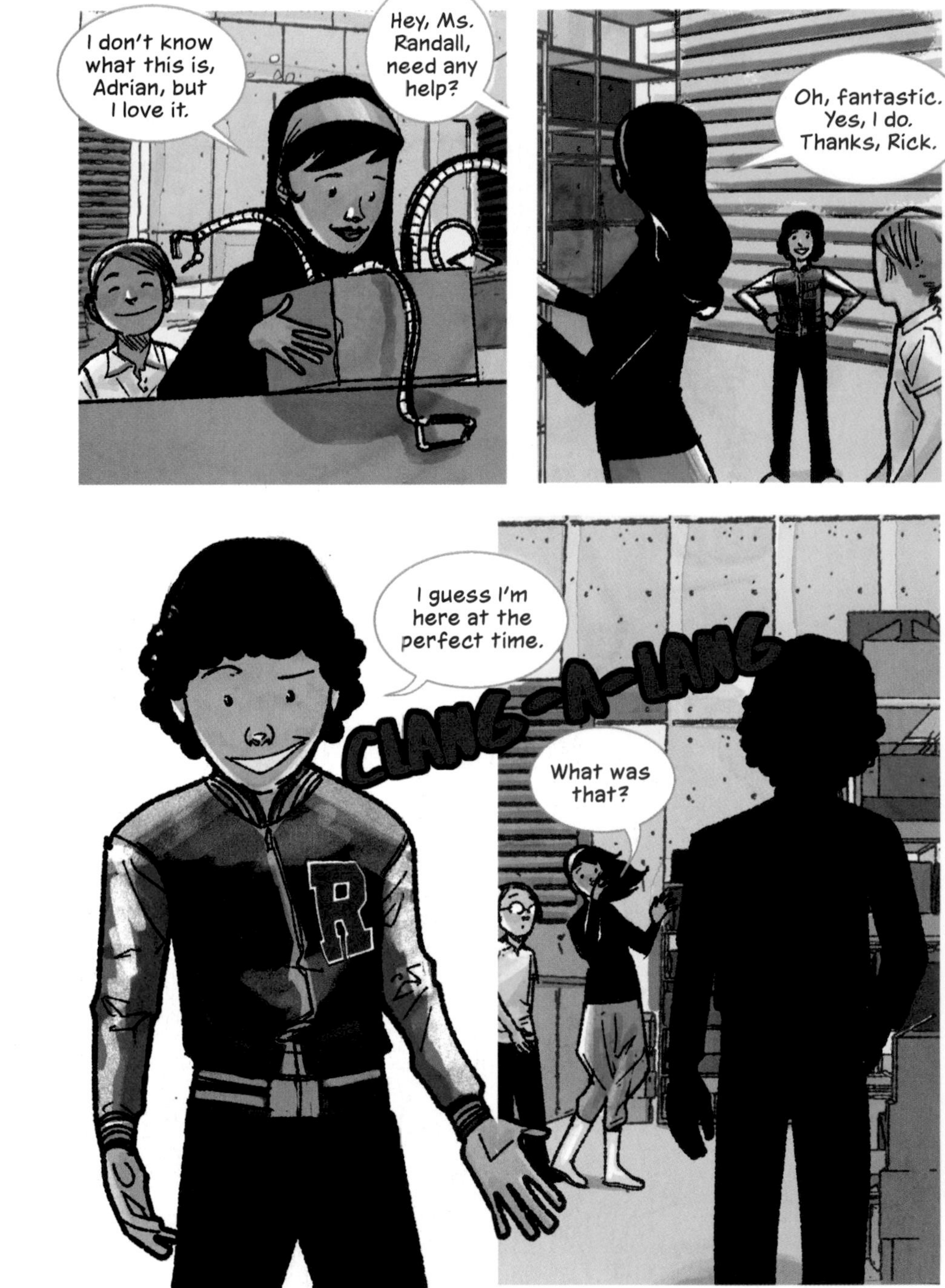
I don't know what this is, Adrian, but I love it.
Hey, Ms. Randall, need any help?
Oh, fantastic. Yes, I do. Thanks, Rick.
I guess I'm here at the perfect time.
CLANG-A-LANG
What was that?

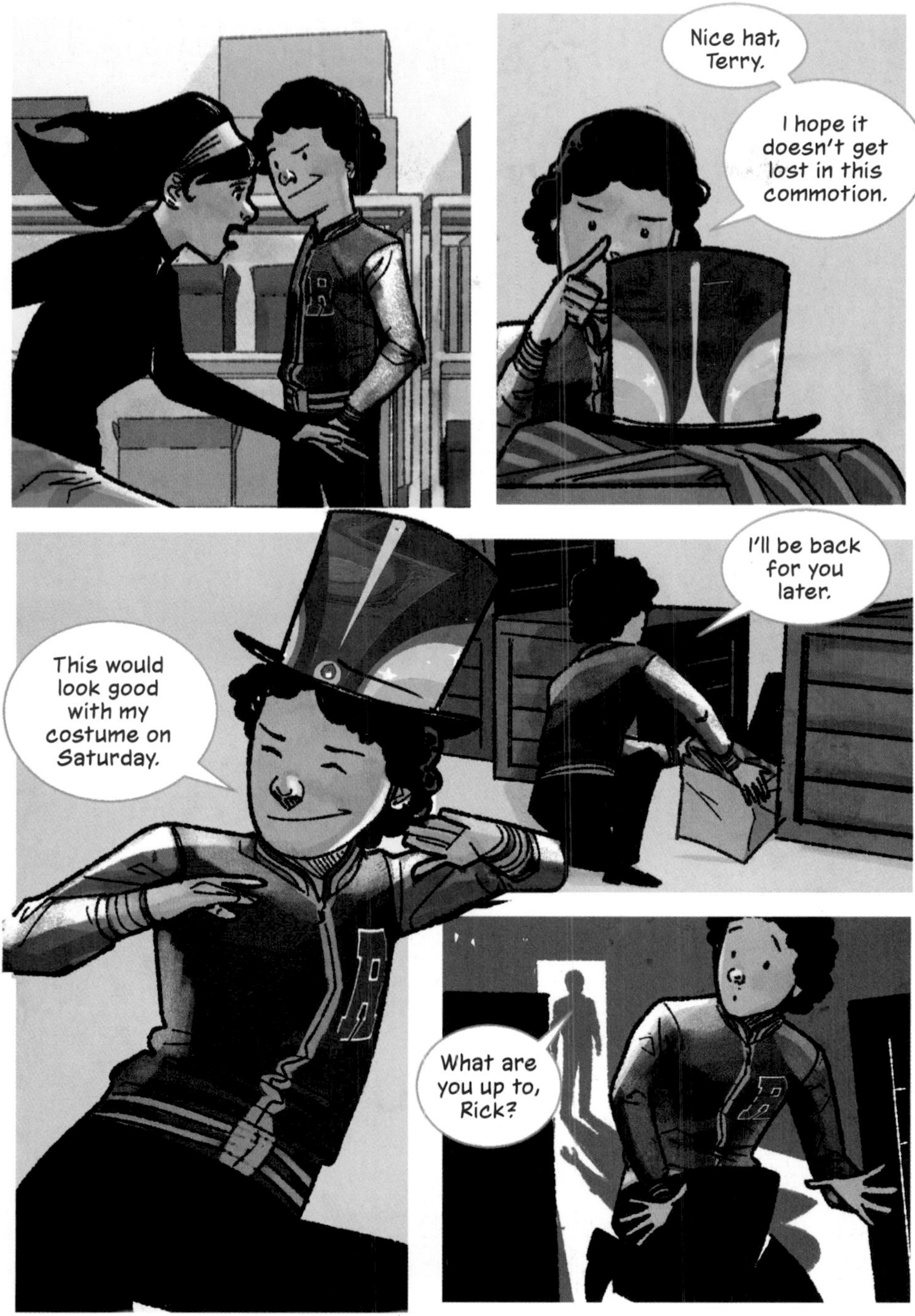
Nice hat, Terry.
I hope it doesn't get lost in this commotion.
This would look good with my costume on Saturday.
I'll be back for you later.
What are you up to, Rick?

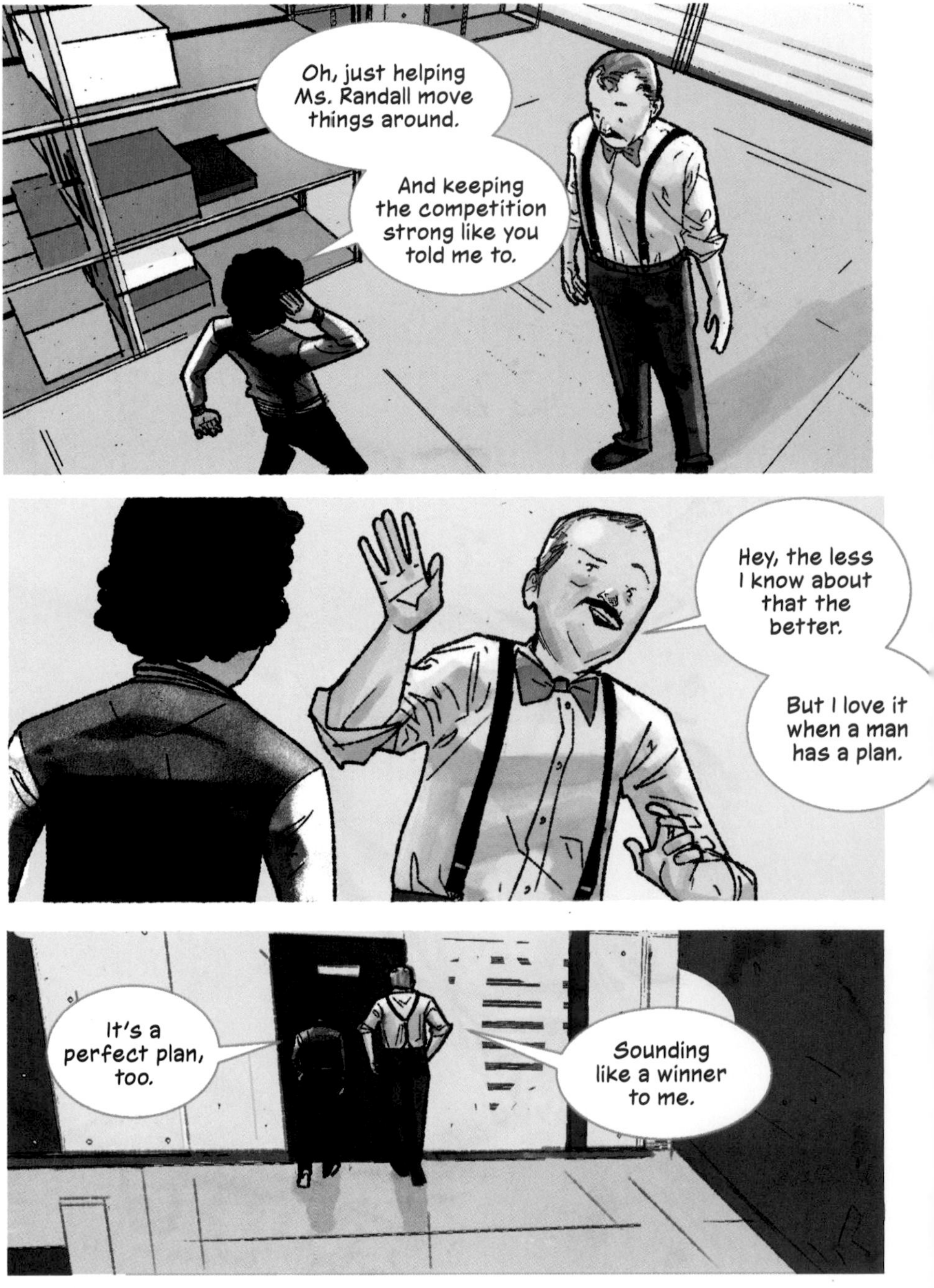
Oh, just helping Ms. Randall move things around.
And keeping the competition strong like you told me to.
Hey, the less I know about that the better.
But I love it when a man has a plan.
It's a perfect plan, too.
Sounding like a winner to me.

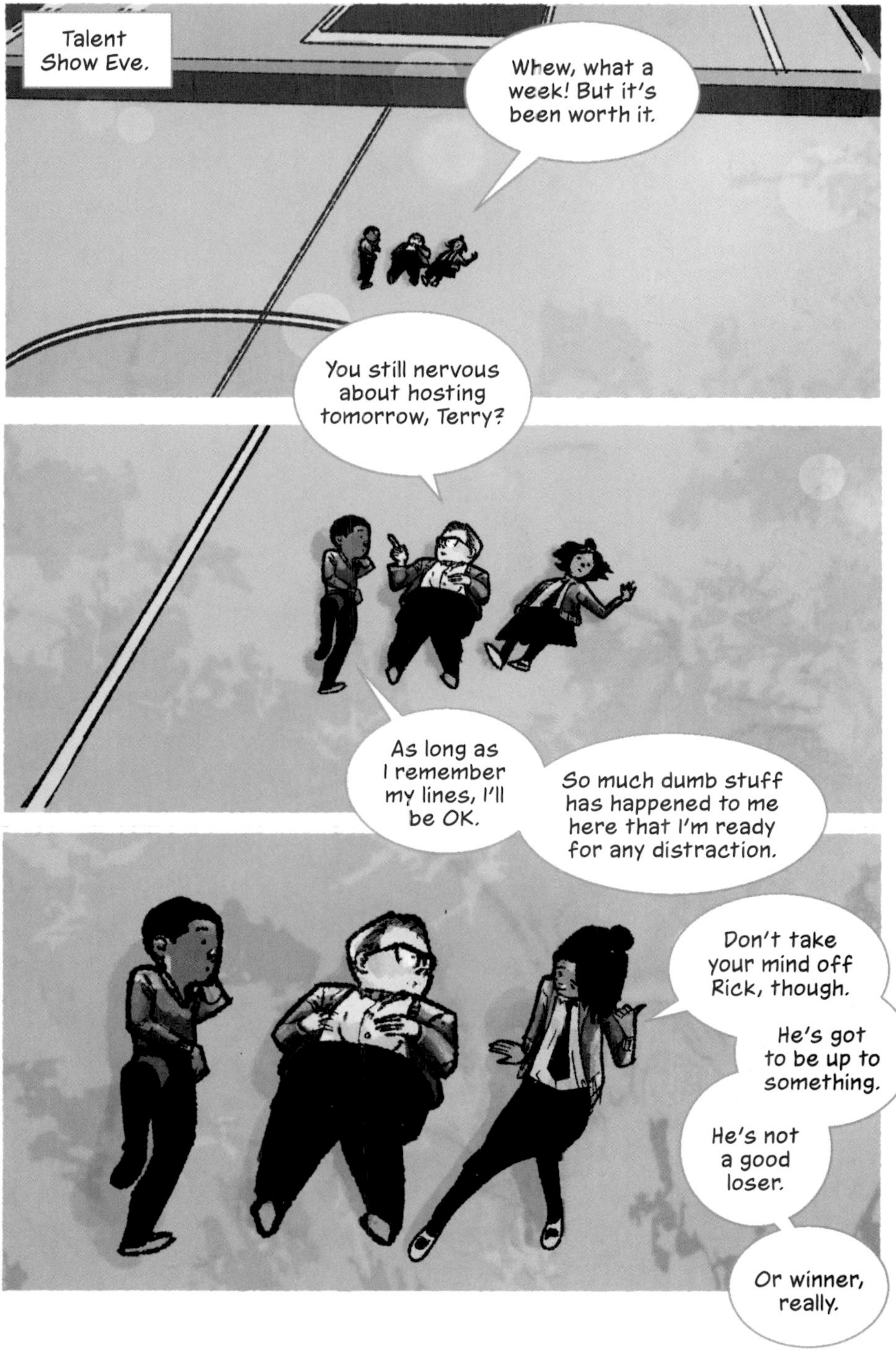
Talent Show Eve.
Whew, what a week! But it's been worth it.
You still nervous about hosting tomorrow, Terry?
As long as I remember my lines, I'll be OK.
So much dumb stuff has happened to me here that I'm ready for any distraction.
Don't take your mind off Rick, though.
He's got to be up to something.
He's not a good loser.
Or winner, really.

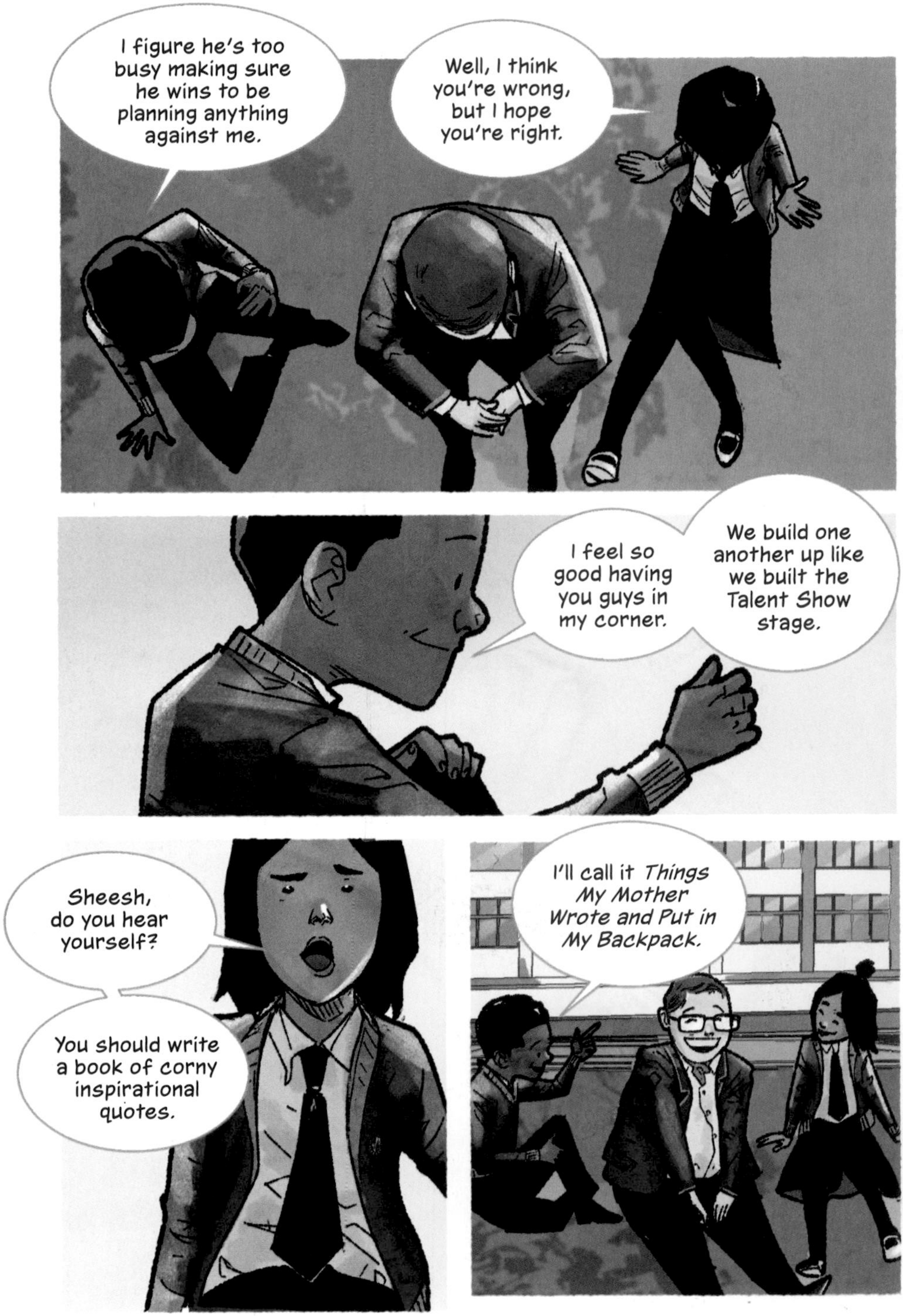
I figure he's too busy making sure he wins to be planning anything against me.
Well, I think you're wrong, but I hope you're right.
I feel so good having you guys in my corner.
We build one another up like we built the Talent Show stage.
Sheesh, do you hear yourself?
You should write a book of corny inspirational quotes.
I'll call it *Things My Mother Wrote and Put in My Backpack*.

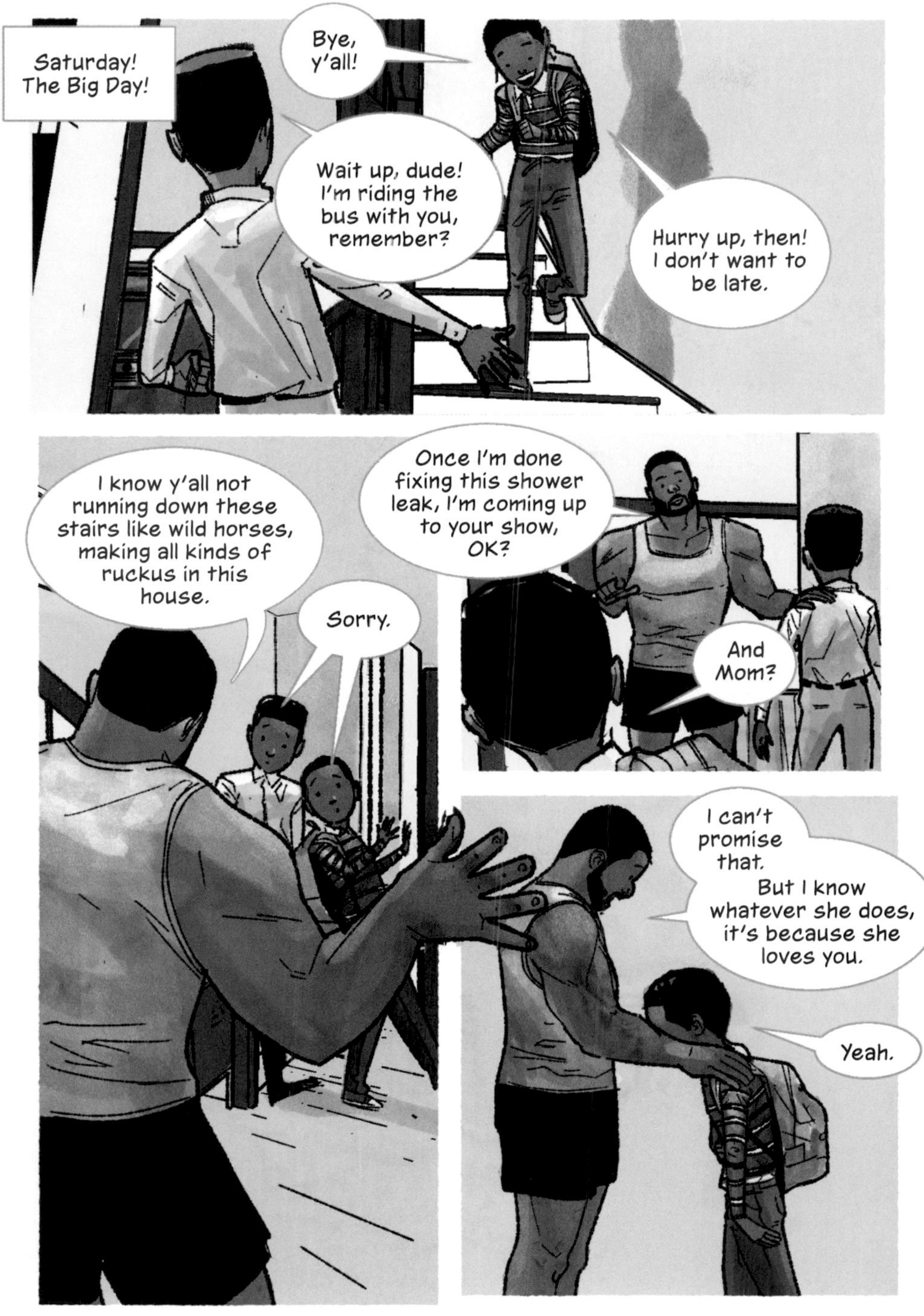
Saturday!
The Big Day!
Bye, y'all!
Wait up, dude! I'm riding the bus with you, remember?
Hurry up, then! I don't want to be late.
I know y'all not running down these stairs like wild horses, making all kinds of ruckus in this house.
Sorry.
Once I'm done fixing this shower leak, I'm coming up to your show, OK?
And Mom?
I can't promise that.
But I know whatever she does, it's because she loves you.
Yeah.

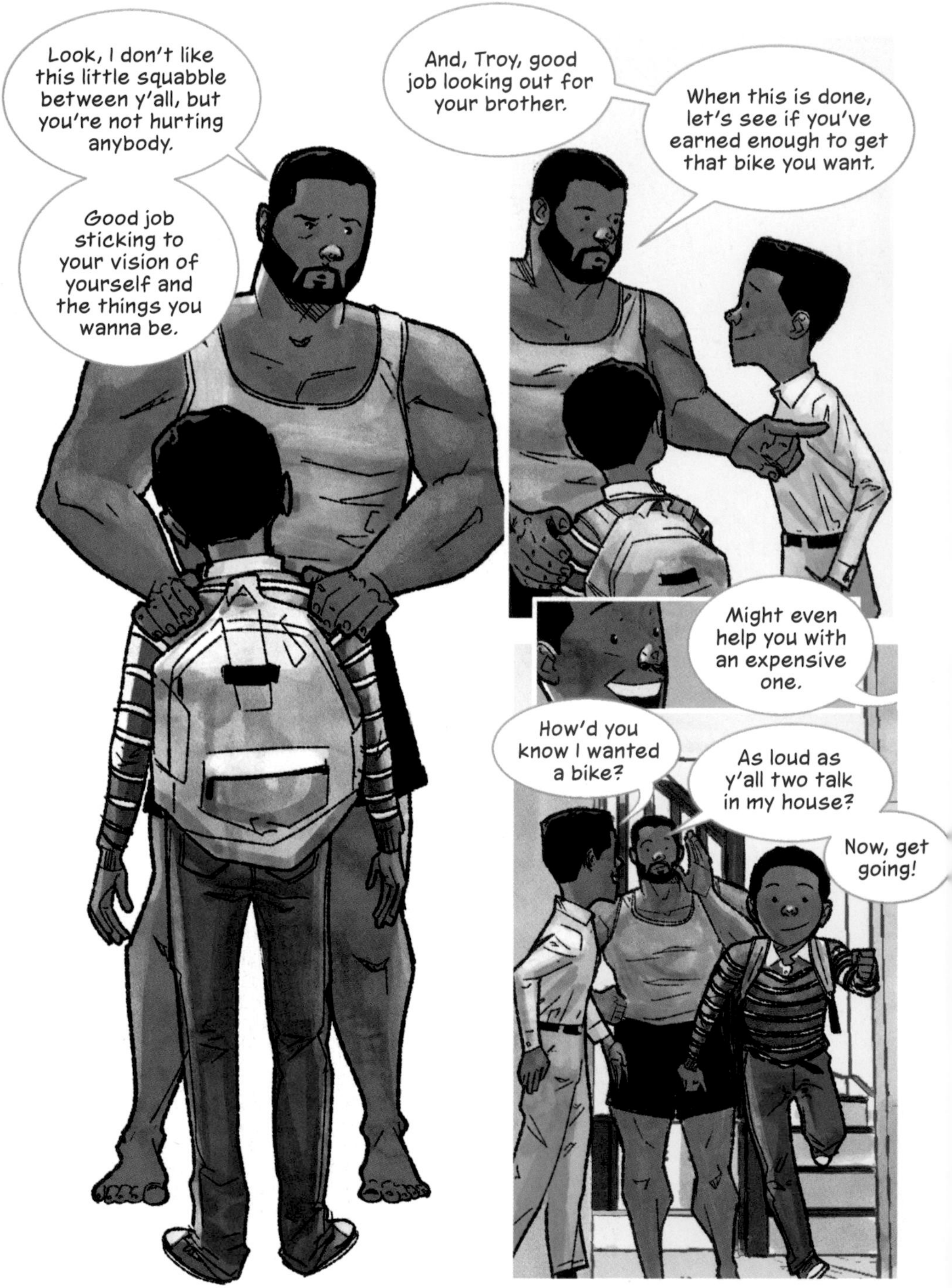
Look, I don't like this little squabble between y'all, but you're not hurting anybody.
Good job sticking to your vision of yourself and the things you wanna be.
And, Troy, good job looking out for your brother.
When this is done, let's see if you've earned enough to get that bike you want.
Might even help you with an expensive one.
How'd you know I wanted a bike?
As loud as y'all two talk in my house?
Now, get going!

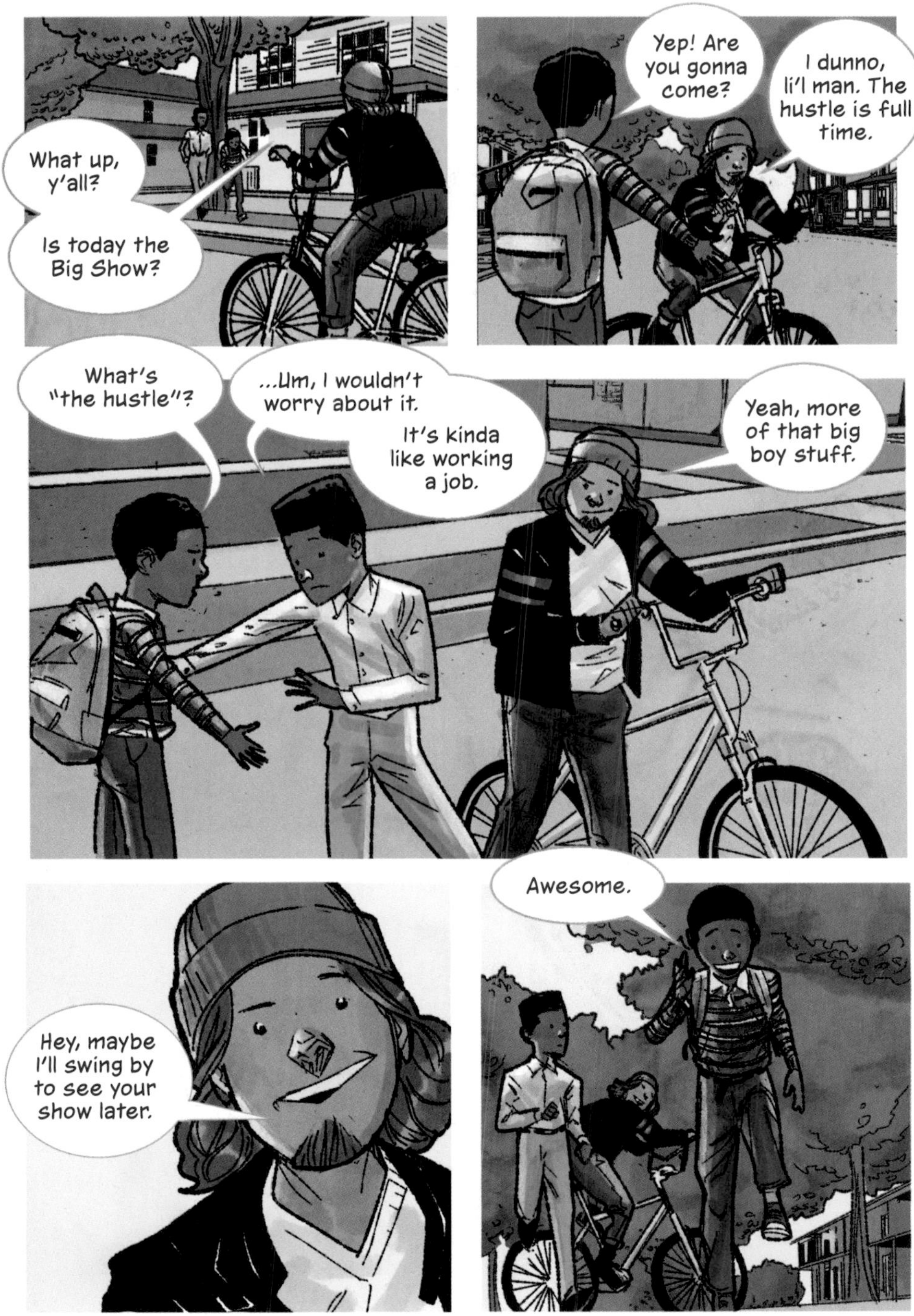
What up, y'all?
Is today the Big Show?
Yep! Are you gonna come?
I dunno, li'l man. The hustle is full time.
What's "the hustle"?
...Um, I wouldn't worry about it.
It's kinda like working a job.
Yeah, more of that big boy stuff.
Hey, maybe I'll swing by to see your show later.
Awesome.

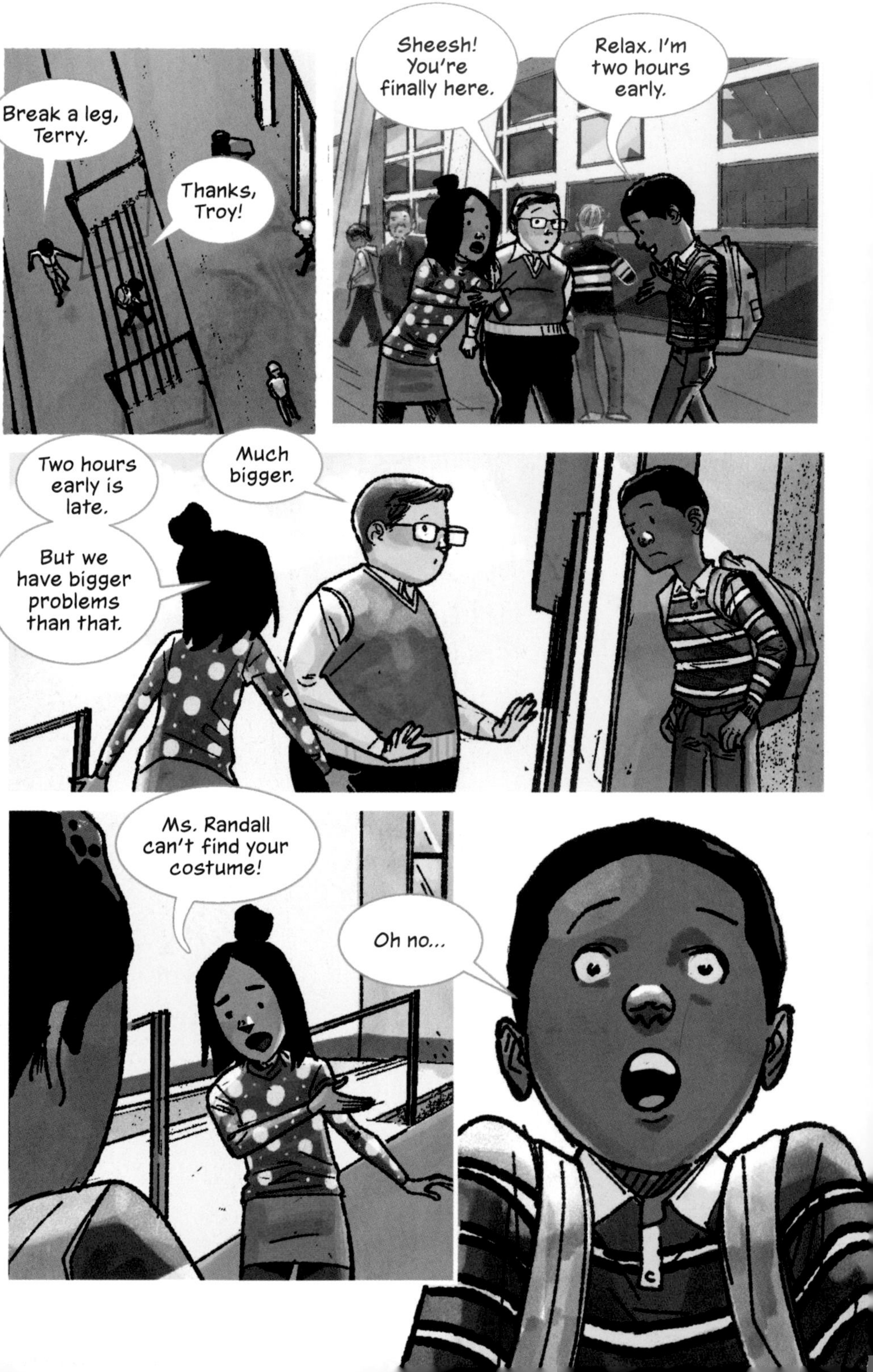
Break a leg, Terry.
Thanks, Troy!
Sheesh! You're finally here.
Relax. I'm two hours early.
Two hours early is late.
But we have bigger problems than that.
Much bigger.
Ms. Randall can't find your costume!
Oh no...

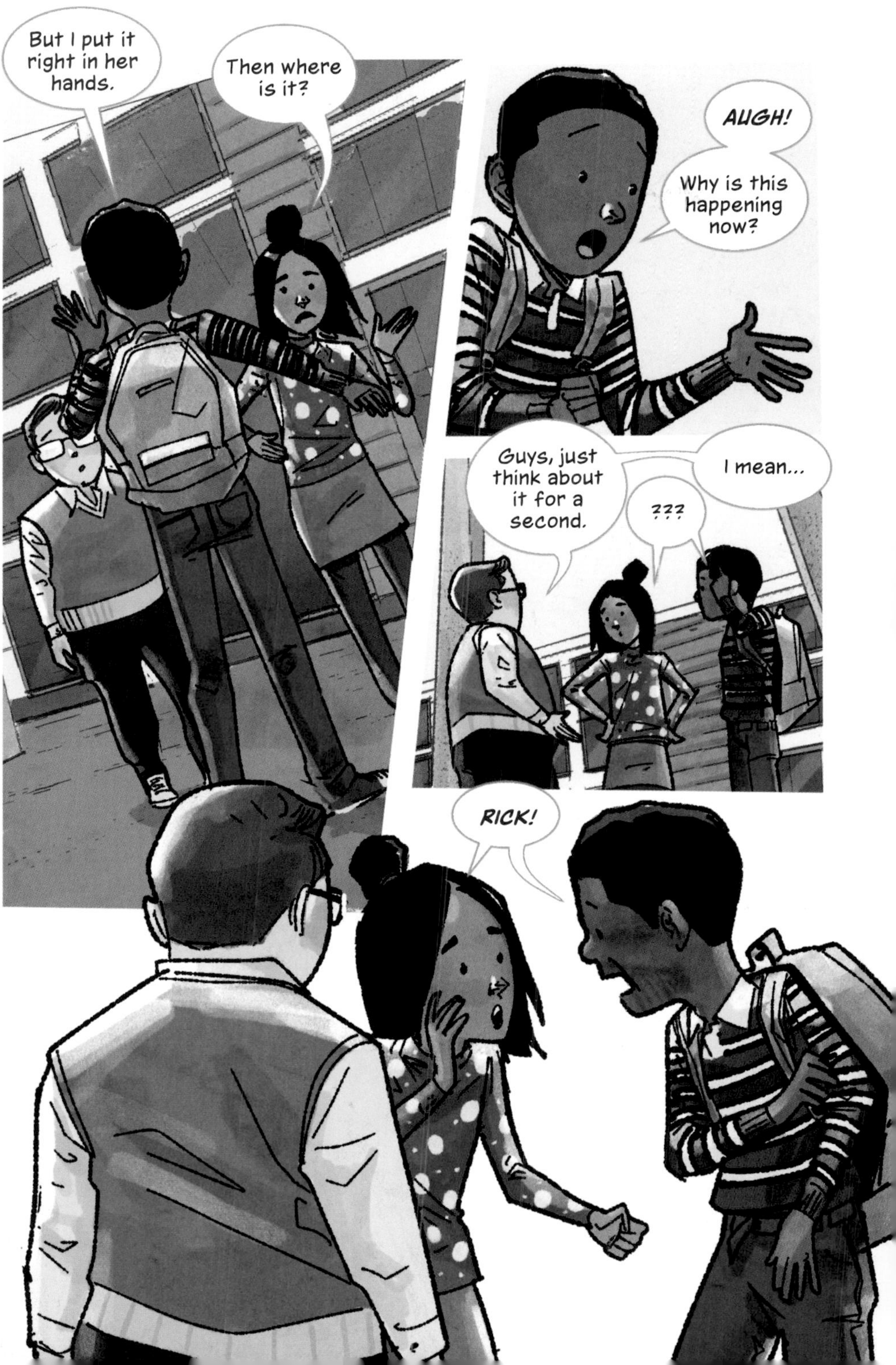
But I put it right in her hands.
Then where is it?
AUGH!
Why is this happening now?
Guys, just think about it for a second.
???
I mean...
RICK!

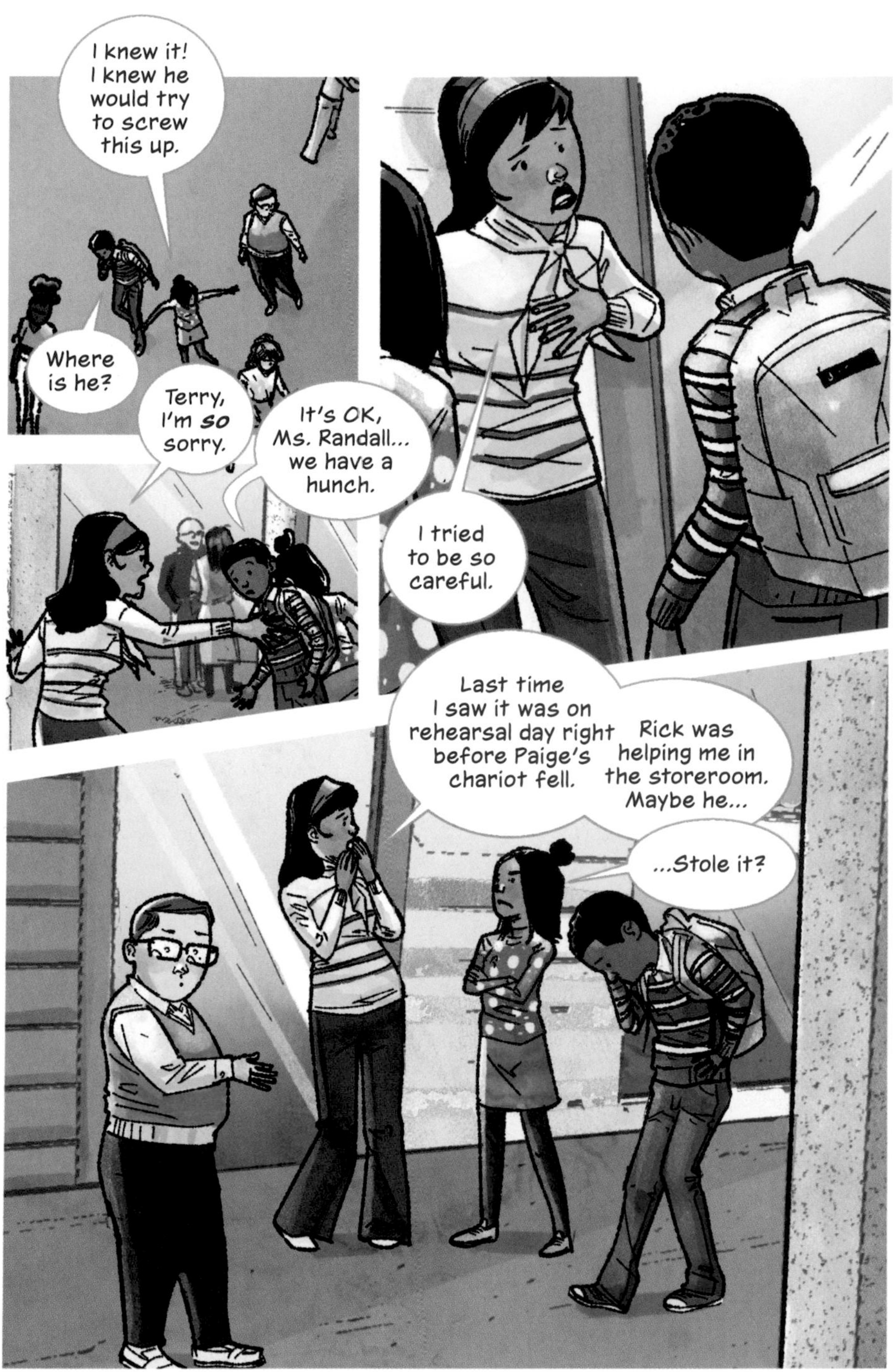
I knew it! I knew he would try to screw this up.
Where is he?
Terry, I'm **so** sorry.
It's OK, Ms. Randall... we have a hunch.
I tried to be so careful.
Last time I saw it was on rehearsal day right before Paige's chariot fell.
Rick was helping me in the storeroom. Maybe he...
...Stole it?

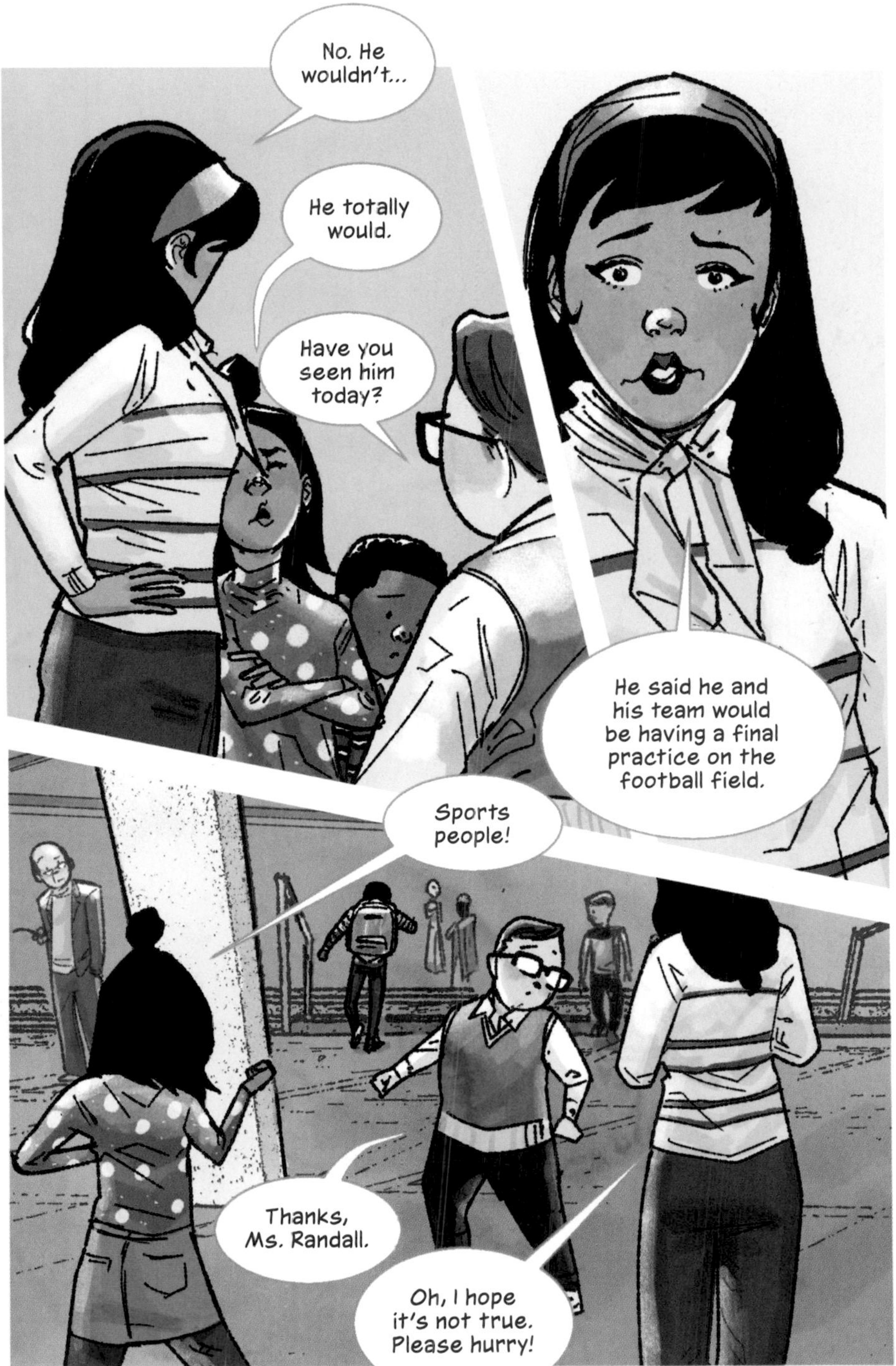
No. He wouldn't...
He totally would.
Have you seen him today?
He said he and his team would be having a final practice on the football field.
Sports people!
Thanks, Ms. Randall.
Oh, I hope it's not true. Please hurry!

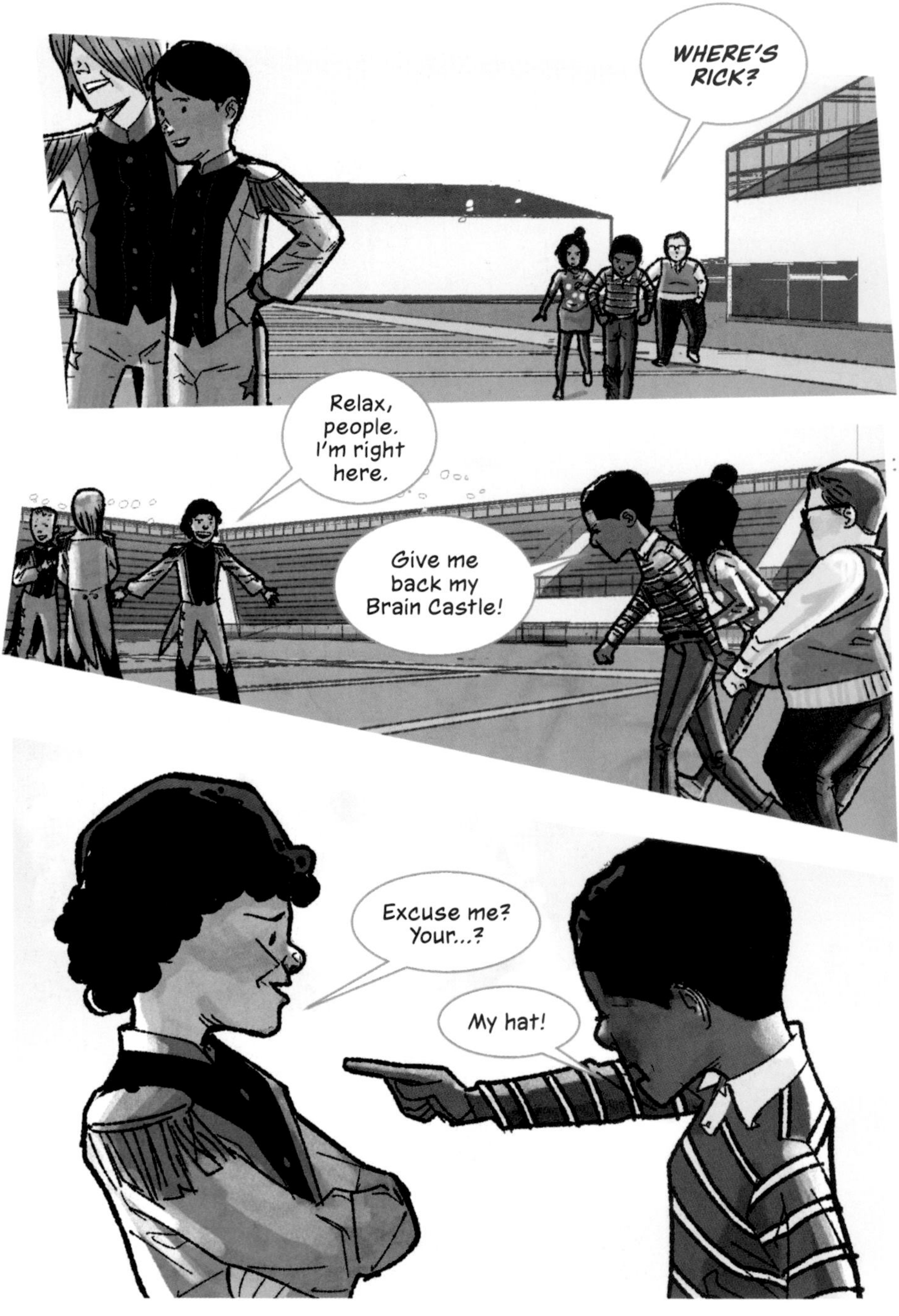
WHERE'S RICK?
Relax, people. I'm right here.
Give me back my Brain Castle!
Excuse me? Your...?
My hat!

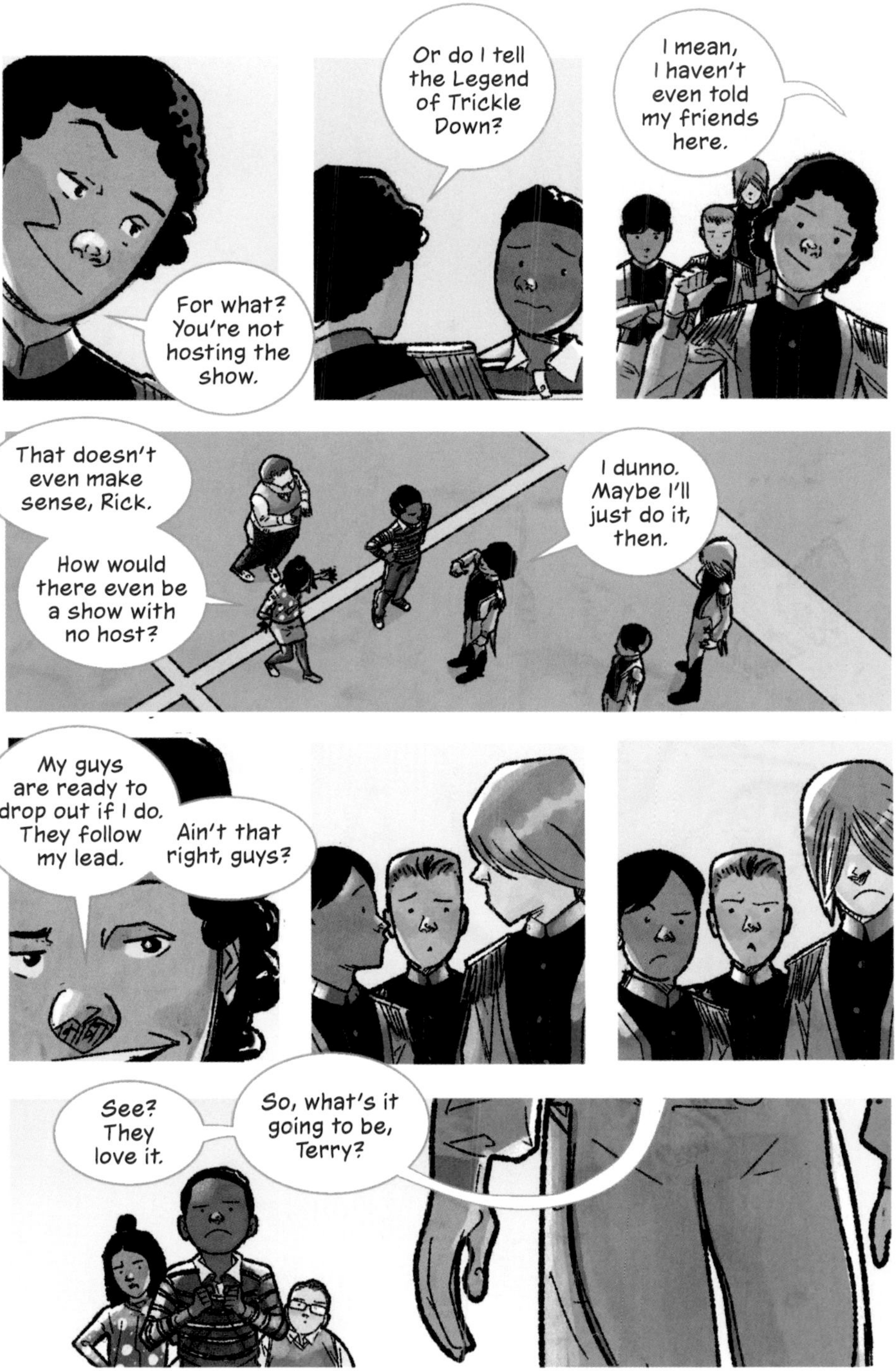
For what? You're not hosting the show.
Or do I tell the Legend of Trickle Down?
I mean, I haven't even told my friends here.
That doesn't even make sense, Rick.
How would there even be a show with no host?
I dunno. Maybe I'll just do it, then.
My guys are ready to drop out if I do. They follow my lead.
Ain't that right, guys?
See? They love it.
So, what's it going to be, Terry?

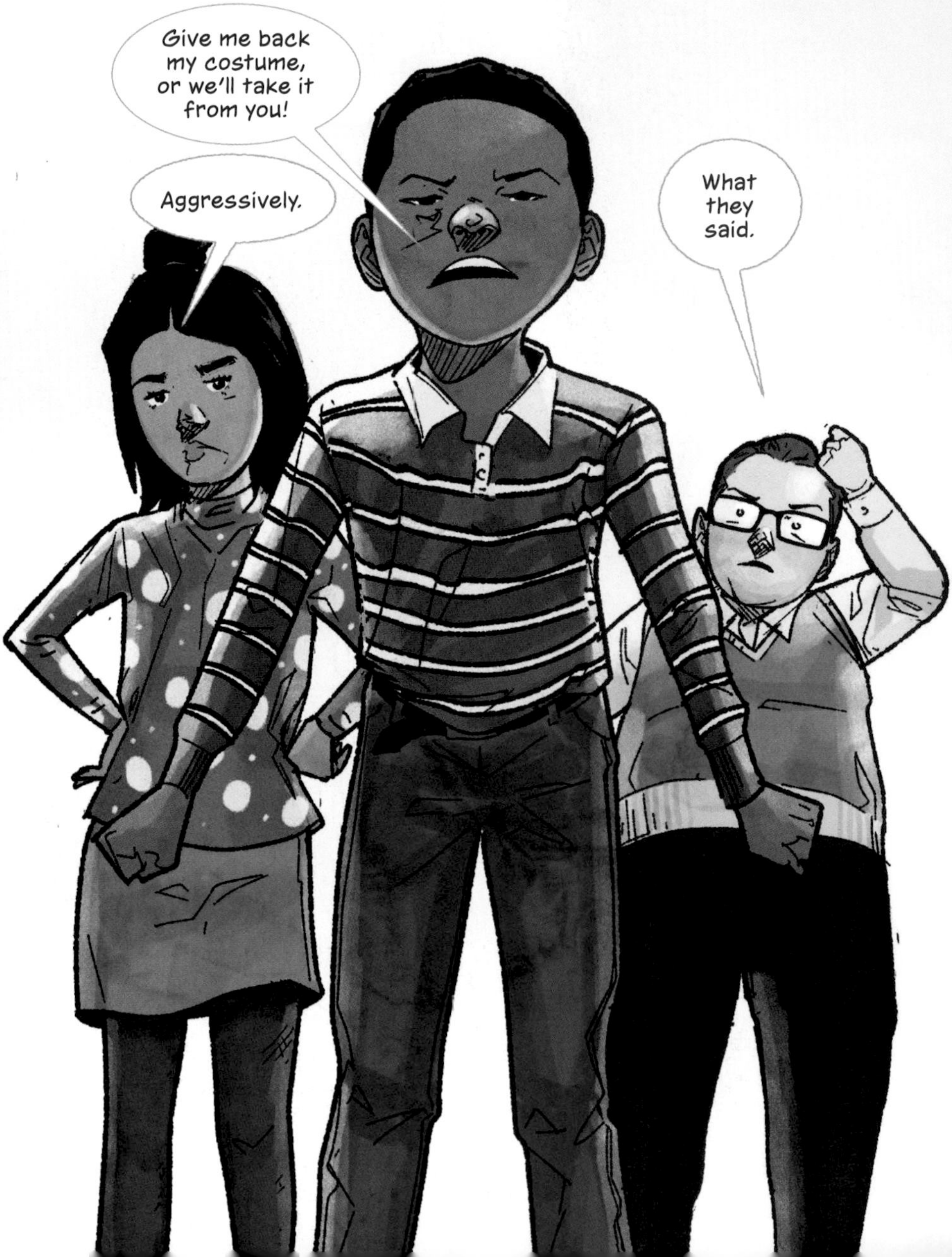
Give me back my costume, or we'll take it from you!
Aggressively.
What they said.

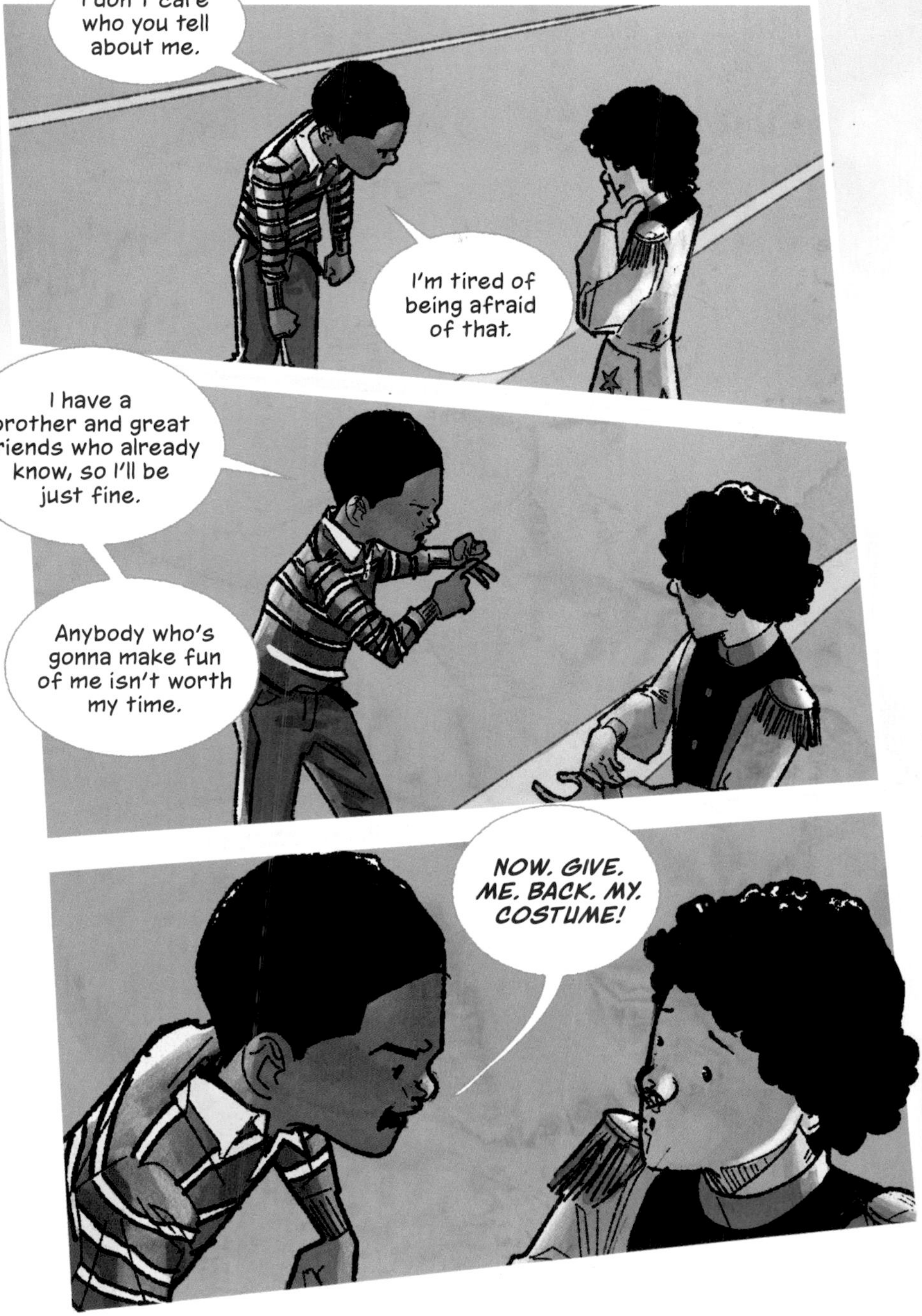
I don't care who you tell about me.
I'm tired of being afraid of that.
I have a brother and great friends who already know, so I'll be just fine.
Anybody who's gonna make fun of me isn't worth my time.
NOW. GIVE. ME. BACK. MY. COSTUME!

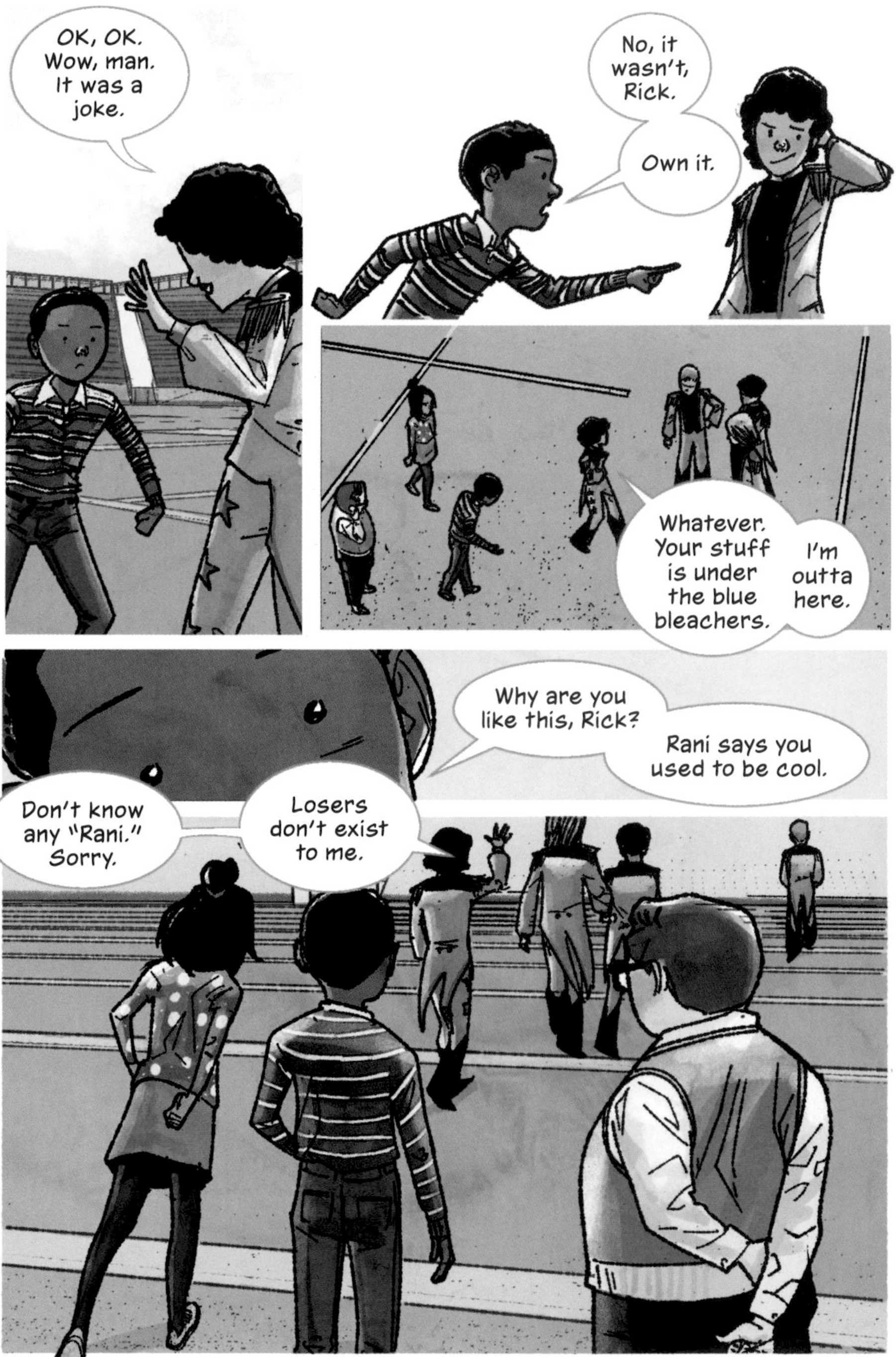
OK, OK. Wow, man. It was a joke.
No, it wasn't, Rick.
Own it.
Whatever. Your stuff is under the blue bleachers.
I'm outta here.
Why are you like this, Rick?
Rani says you used to be cool.
Don't know any "Rani." Sorry.
Losers don't exist to me.

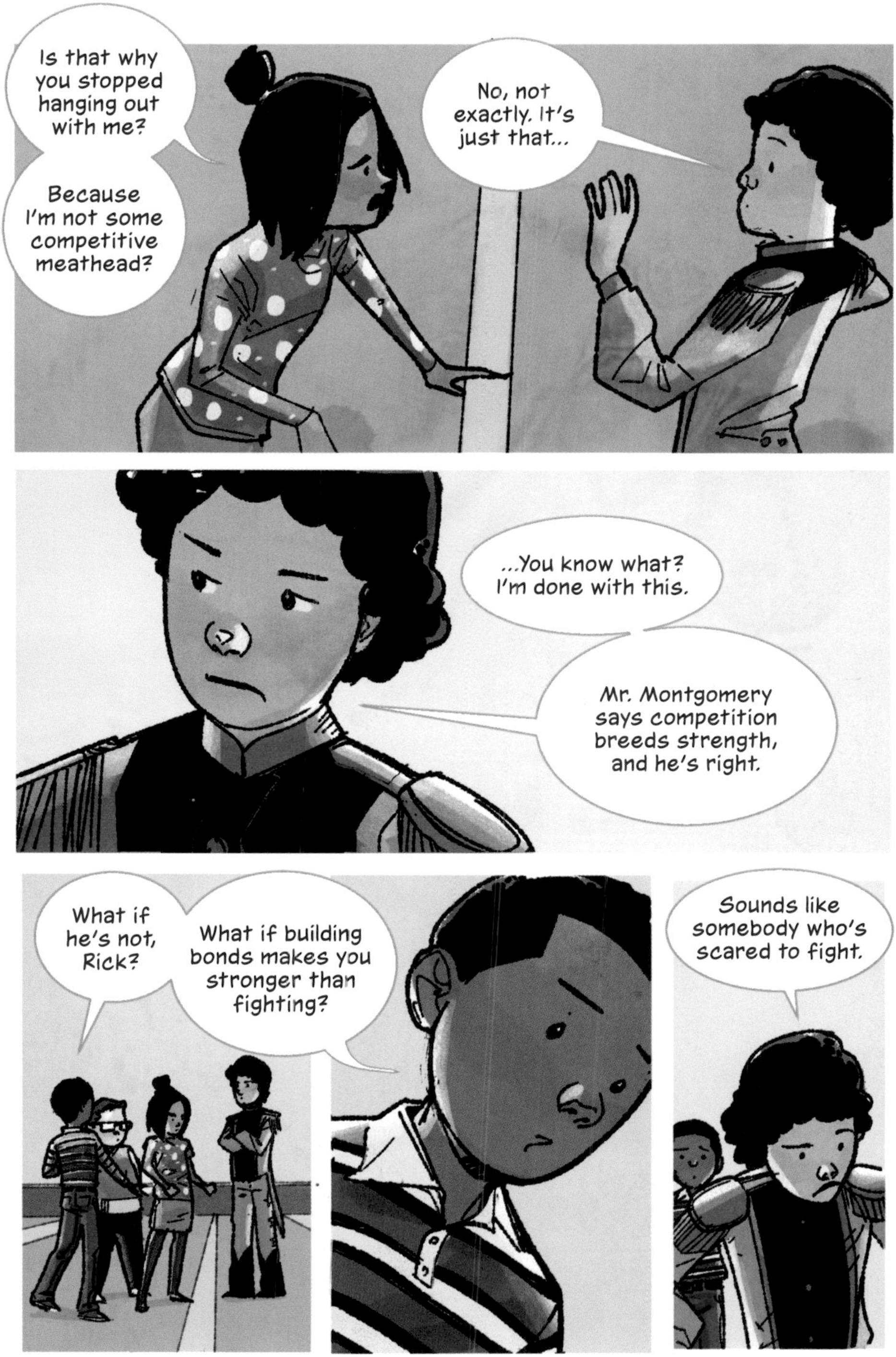
Is that why you stopped hanging out with me?
Because I'm not some competitive meathead?
No, not exactly. It's just that...
...You know what? I'm done with this.
Mr. Montgomery says competition breeds strength, and he's right.
What if he's not, Rick?
What if building bonds makes you stronger than fighting?
Sounds like somebody who's scared to fight.

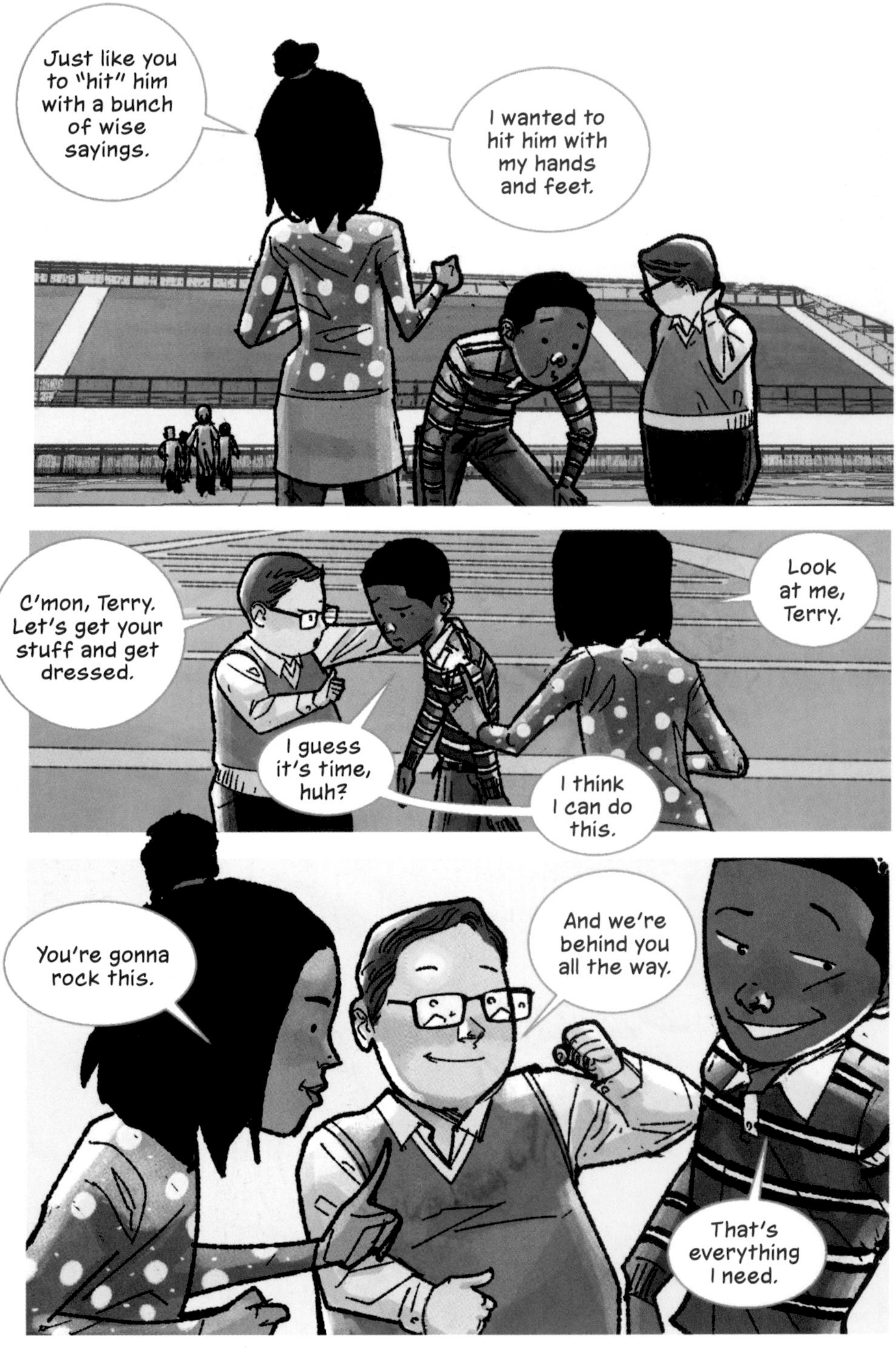
Just like you to "hit" him with a bunch of wise sayings.
I wanted to hit him with my hands and feet.
C'mon, Terry. Let's get your stuff and get dressed.
Look at me, Terry.
I guess it's time, huh?
I think I can do this.
You're gonna rock this.
And we're behind you all the way.
That's everything I need.

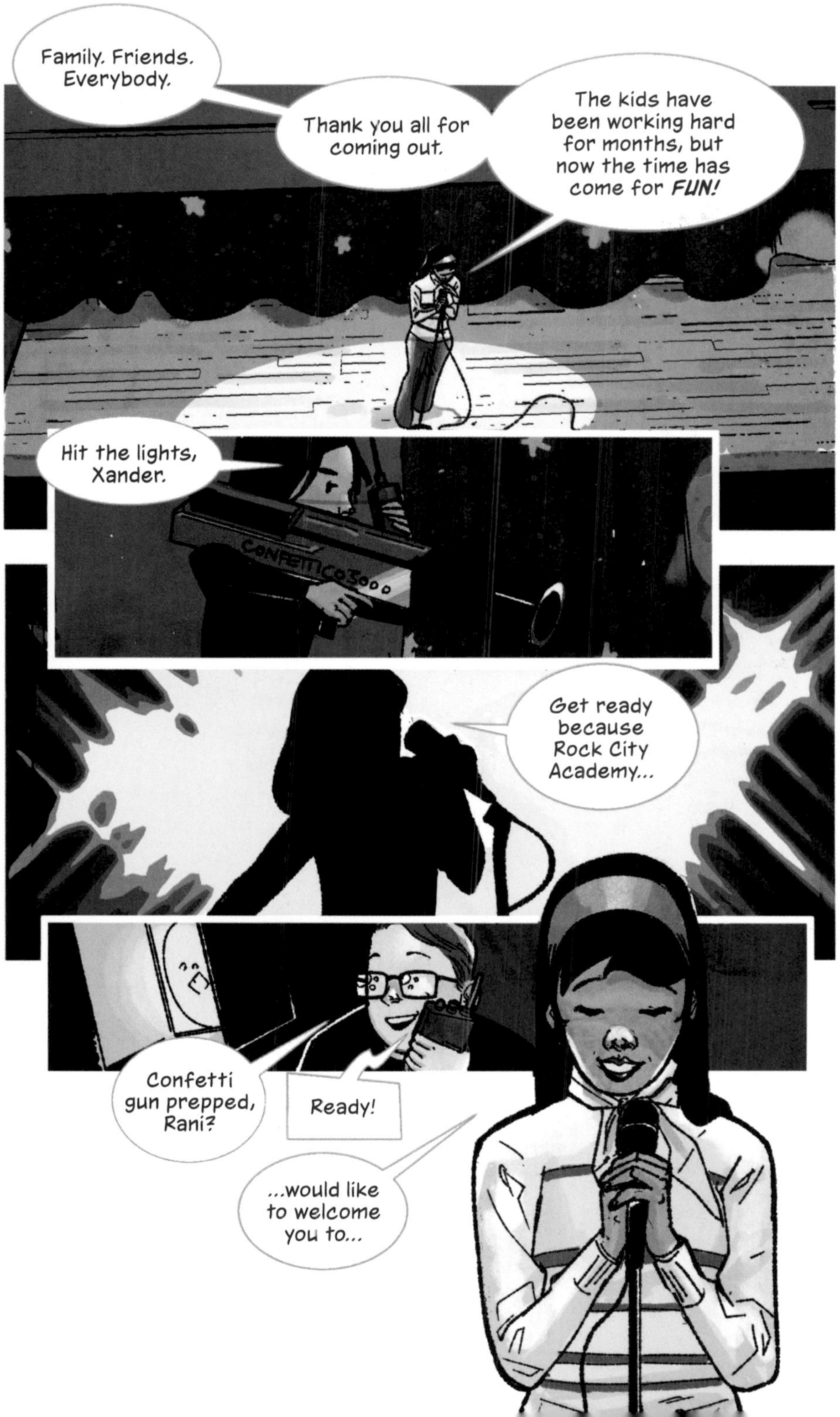
Family. Friends. Everybody.
Thank you all for coming out.
The kids have been working hard for months, but now the time has come for *FUN!*
Hit the lights, Xander.
CONFETTICO3000
Get ready because Rock City Academy...
Confetti gun prepped, Rani?
Ready!
...would like to welcome you to...

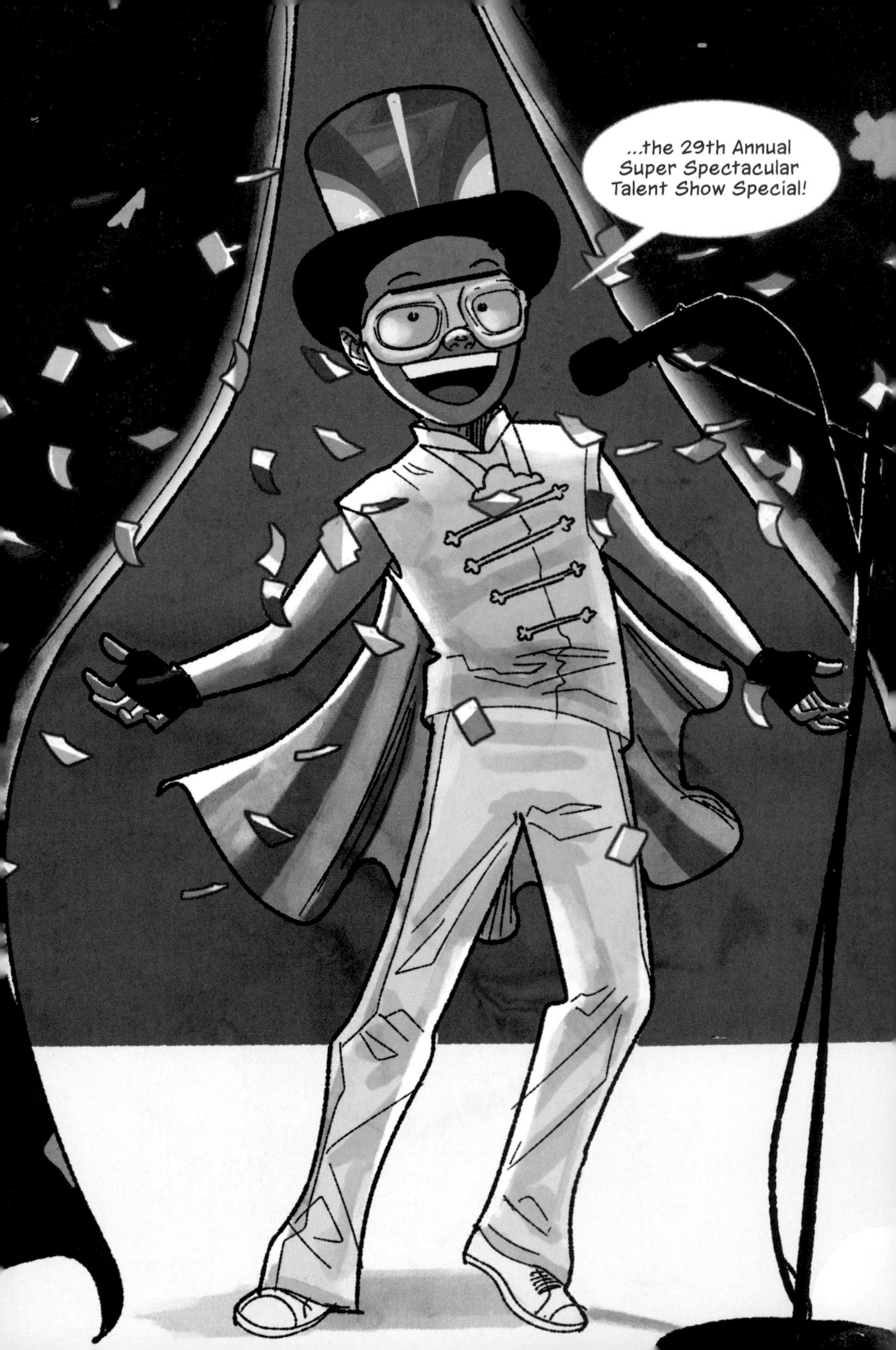
...the 29th Annual Super Spectacular Talent Show Special!

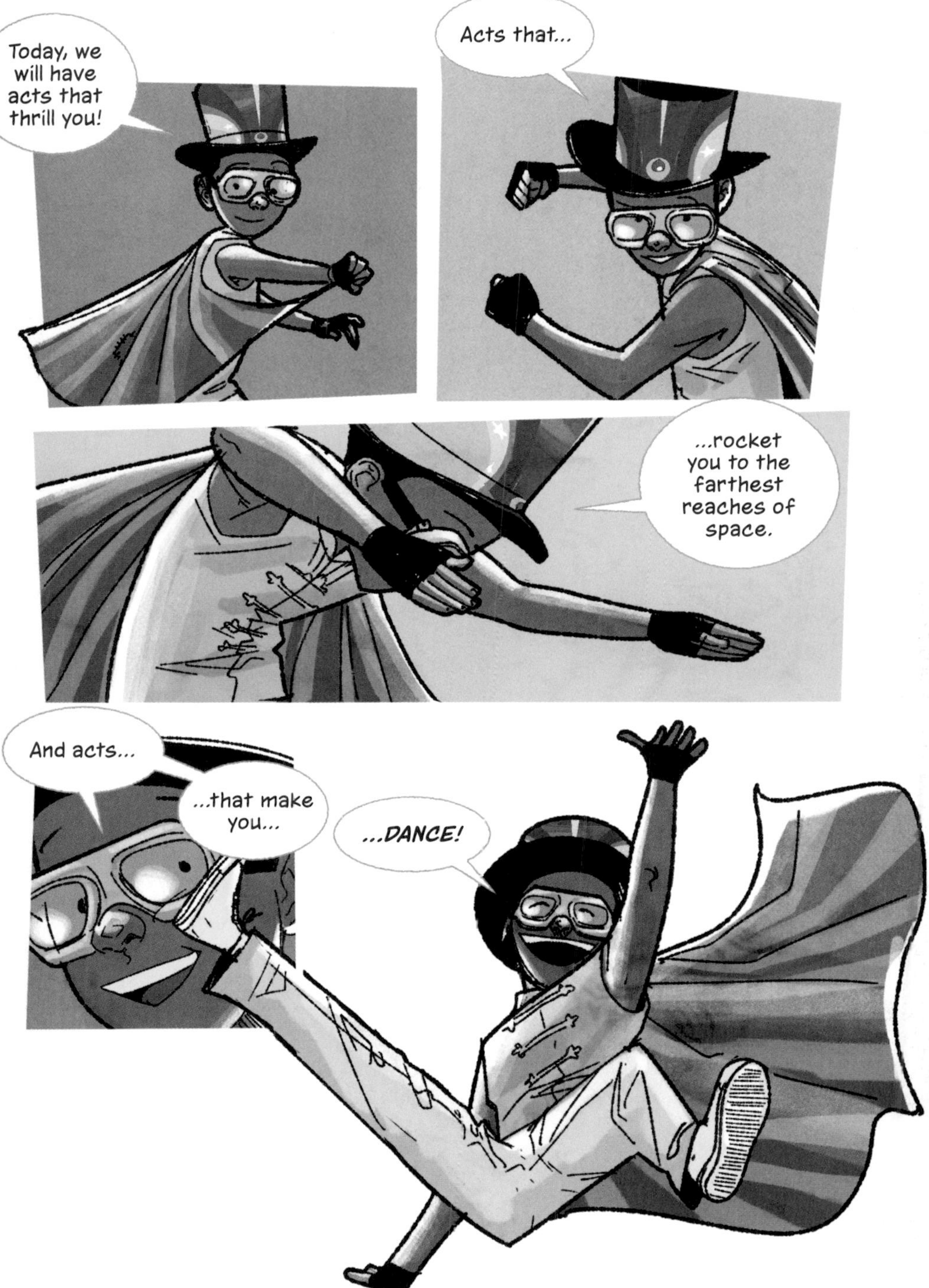
Today, we will have acts that thrill you!
Acts that...
...rocket you to the farthest reaches of space.
And acts...
...that make you...
...DANCE!

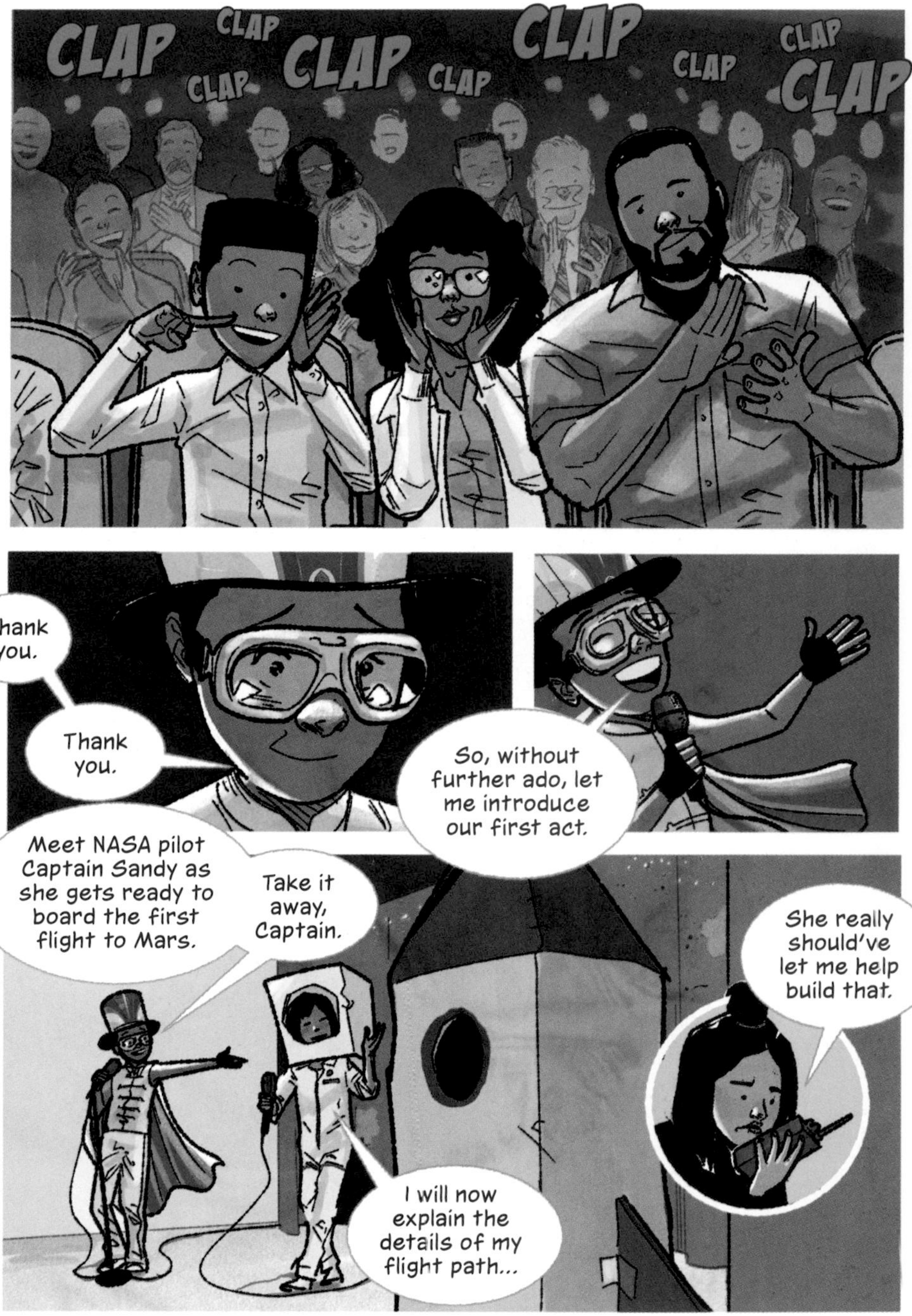
CLAP
CLAP
CLAP
CLAP
CLAP
CLAP
CLAP
CLAP
CLAP
Thank you.
Thank you.
So, without further ado, let me introduce our first act.
Meet NASA pilot Captain Sandy as she gets ready to board the first flight to Mars.
Take it away, Captain.
She really should've let me help build that.
I will now explain the details of my flight path...

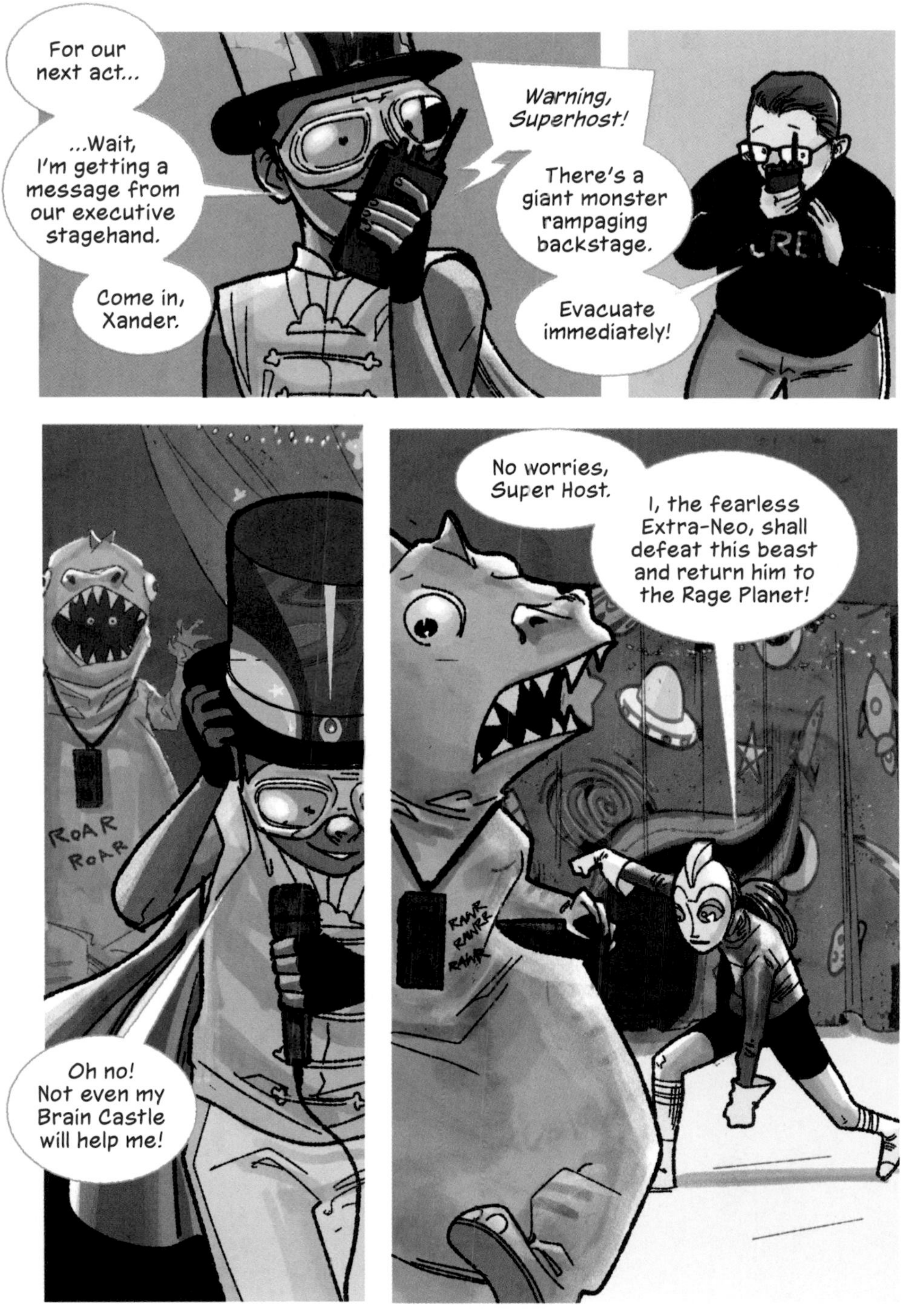

For our next act...
...Wait, I'm getting a message from our executive stagehand.
Come in, Xander.
Warning, Superhost!
There's a giant monster rampaging backstage.
Evacuate immediately!
RoAR RoAR
Oh no! Not even my Brain Castle will help me!
No worries, Super Host.
I, the fearless Extra-Neo, shall defeat this beast and return him to the Rage Planet!
RAWR RAWR RAWR

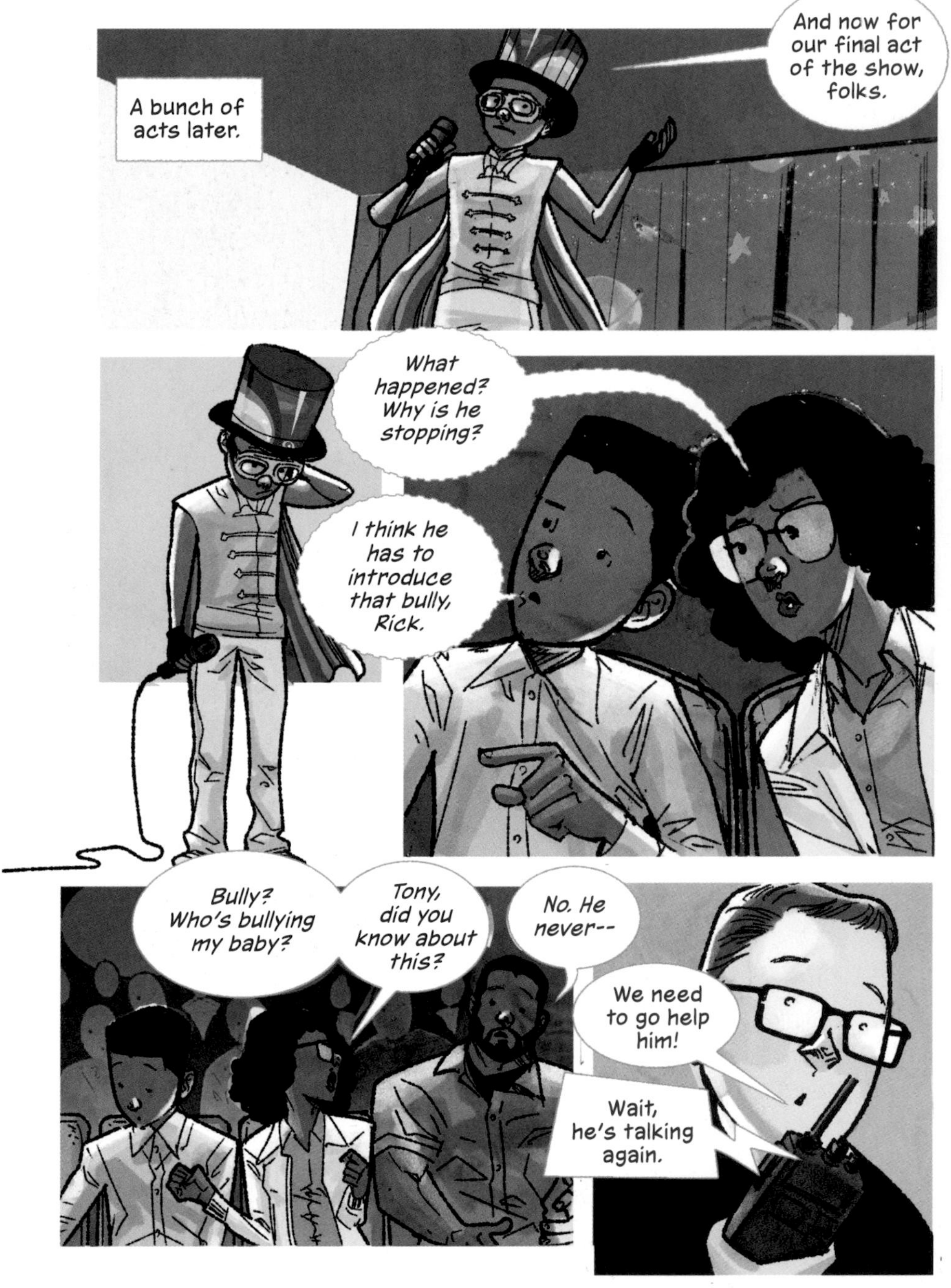
A bunch of acts later.
And now for our final act of the show, folks.
What happened? Why is he stopping?
I think he has to introduce that bully, Rick.
Bully? Who's bullying my baby?
Tony, did you know about this?
No. He never--
We need to go help him!
Wait, he's talking again.

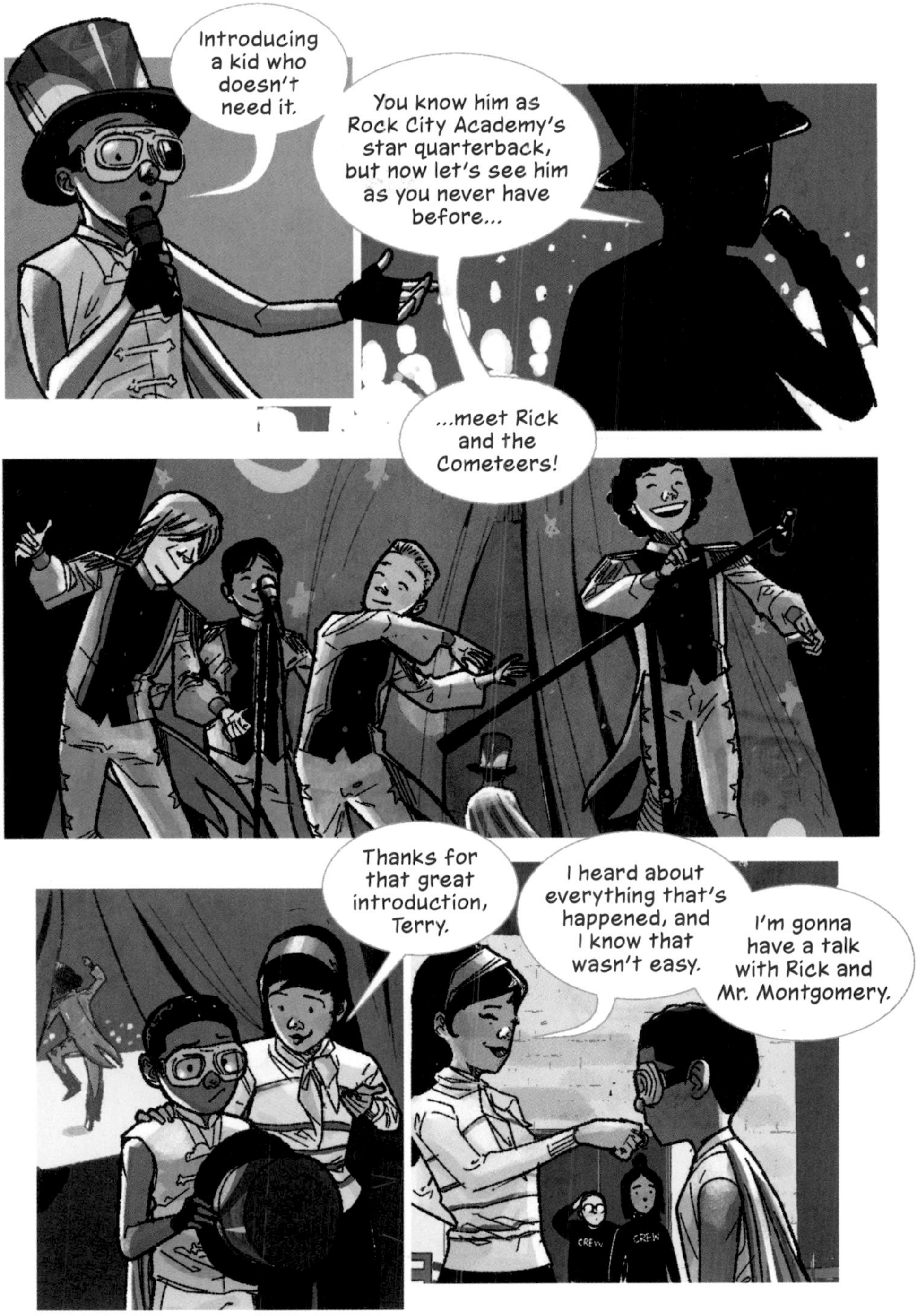
Introducing a kid who doesn't need it.
You know him as Rock City Academy's star quarterback, but now let's see him as you never have before...
...meet Rick and the Cometeers!
Thanks for that great introduction, Terry.
I heard about everything that's happened, and I know that wasn't easy.
I'm gonna have a talk with Rick and Mr. Montgomery.
CREW
CREW

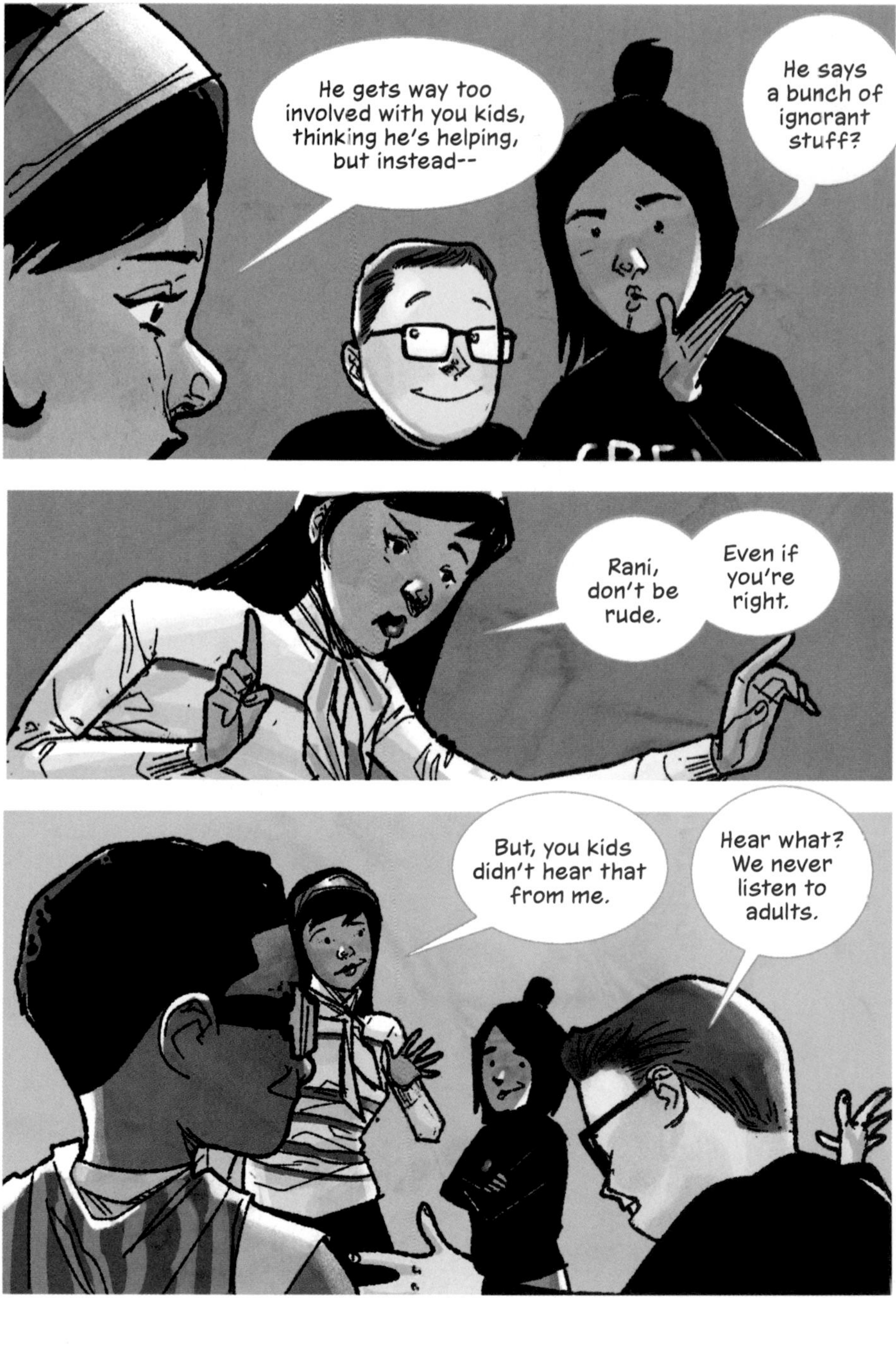
He gets way too involved with you kids, thinking he's helping, but instead--
He says a bunch of ignorant stuff?
Rani, don't be rude.
Even if you're right.
But, you kids didn't hear that from me.
Hear what? We never listen to adults.

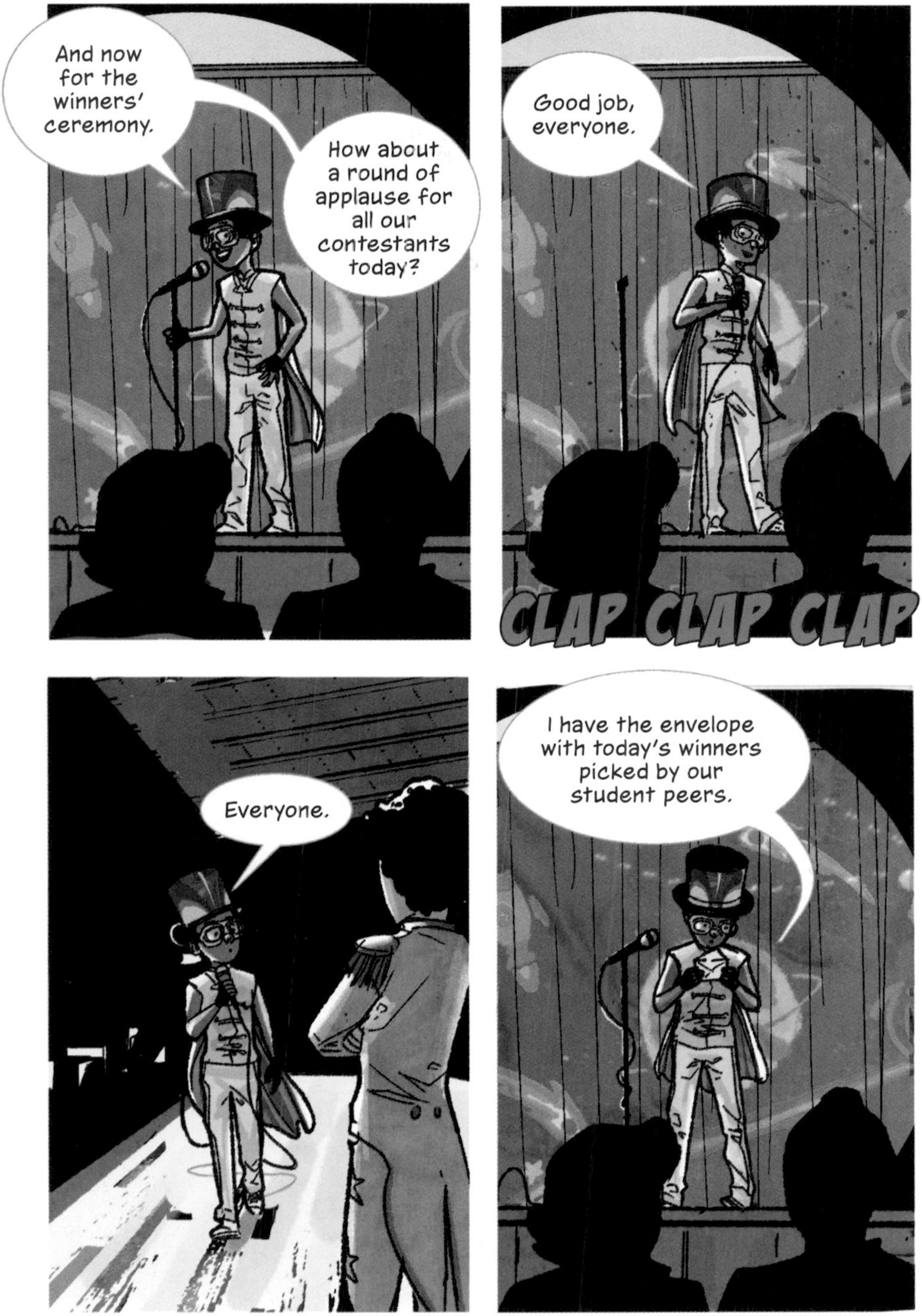
And now for the winners' ceremony.
How about a round of applause for all our contestants today?
Good job, everyone.
CLAP CLAP CLAP
Everyone.
I have the envelope with today's winners picked by our student peers.

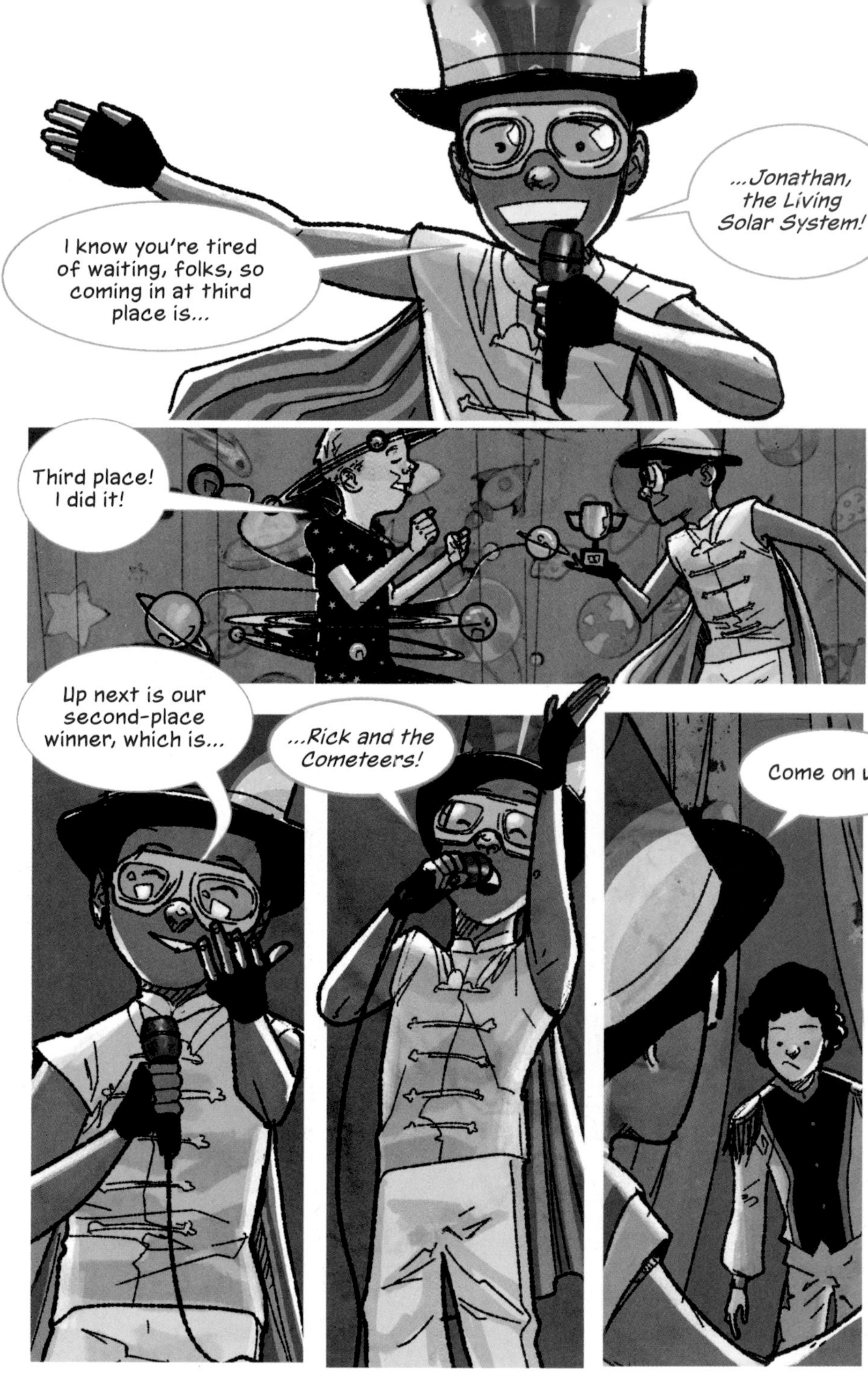
I know you're tired of waiting, folks, so coming in at third place is...
...Jonathan, the Living Solar System!
Third place! I did it!
Up next is our second-place winner, which is...
...Rick and the Cometeers!
Come on up.

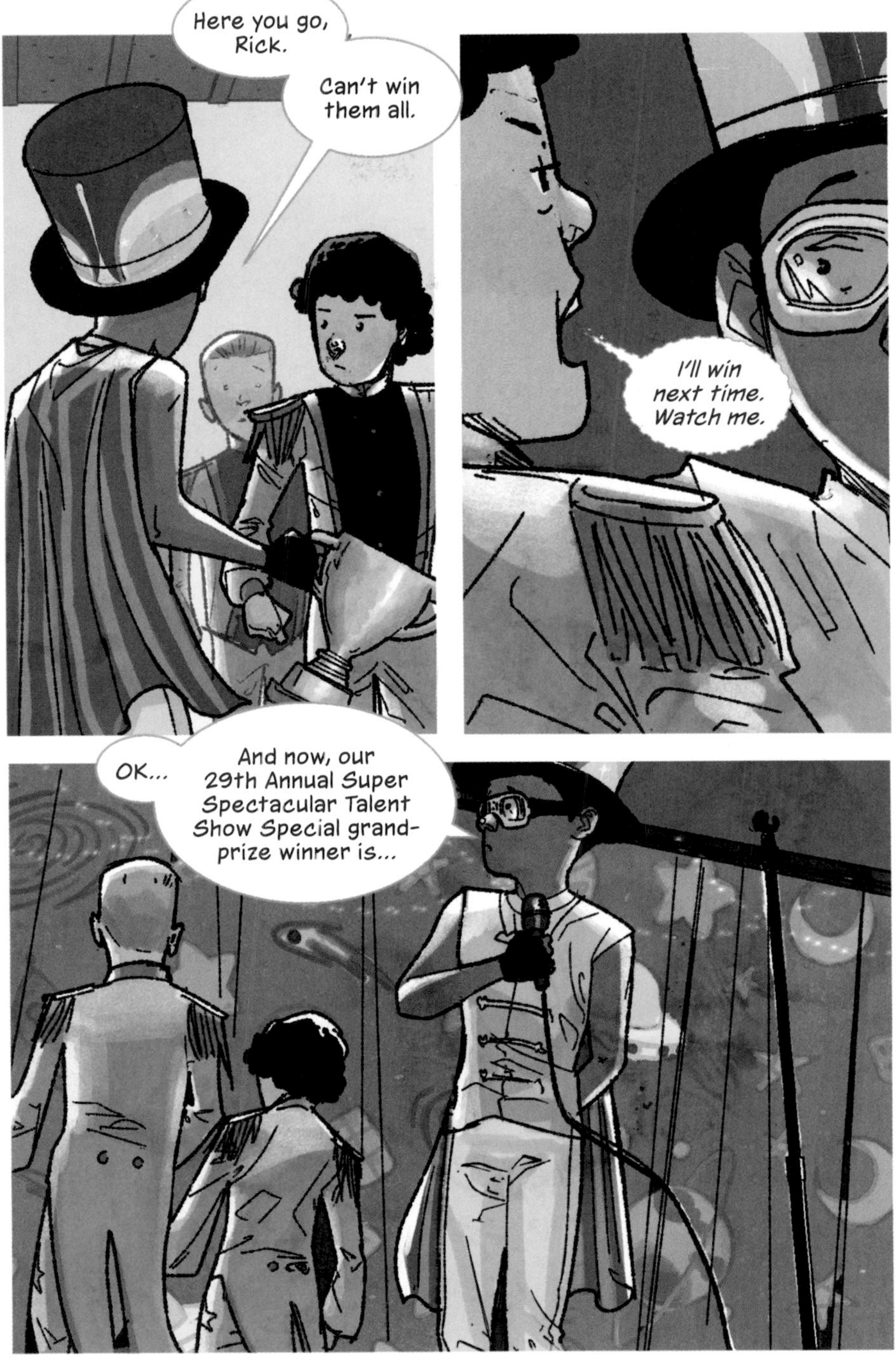
Here you go, Rick.
Can't win them all.
I'll win next time. Watch me.
OK...
And now, our 29th Annual Super Spectacular Talent Show Special grand-prize winner is...

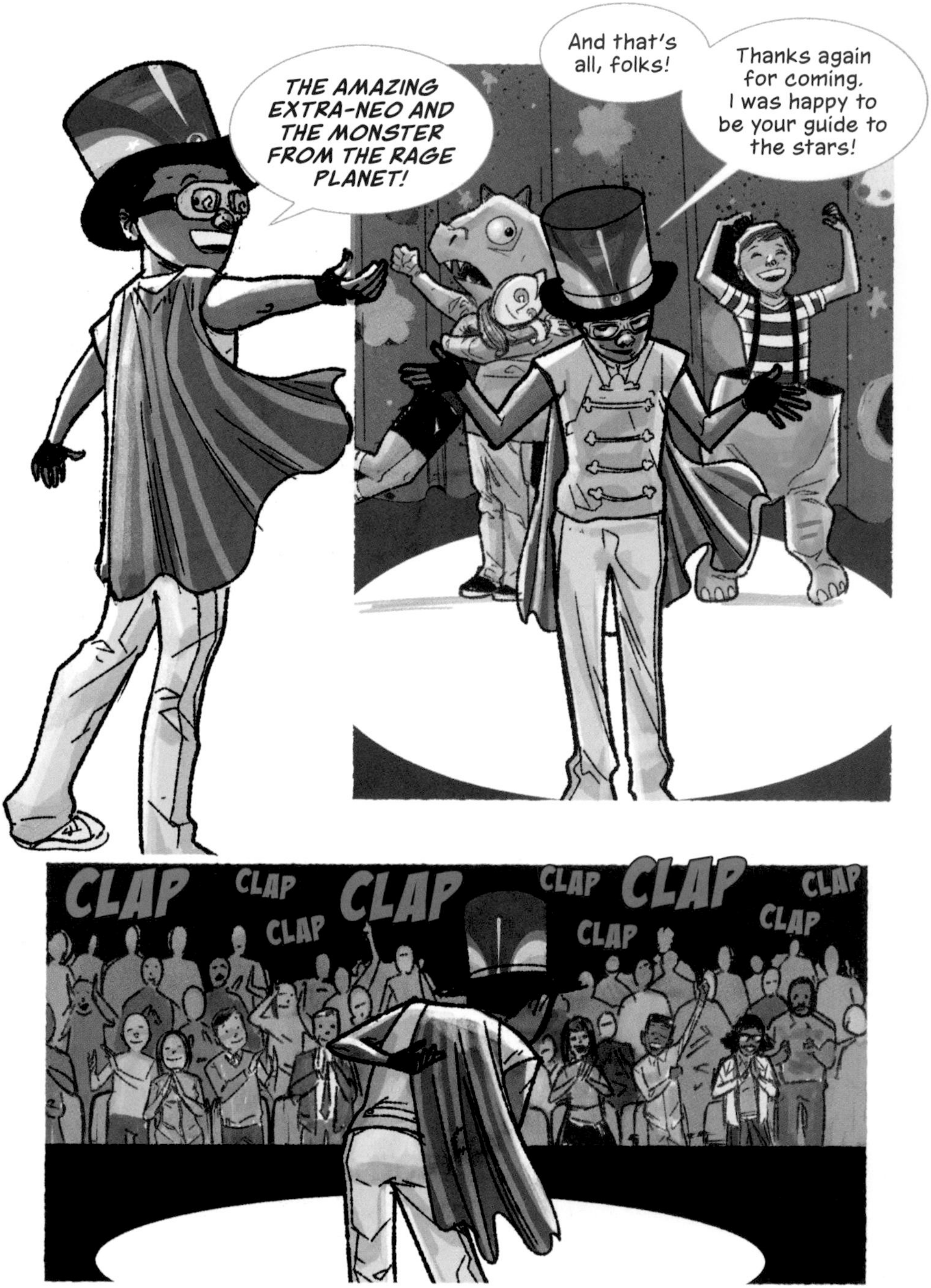
THE AMAZING EXTRA-NEO AND THE MONSTER FROM THE RAGE PLANET!
And that's all, folks!
Thanks again for coming. I was happy to be your guide to the stars!
CLAP
CLAP
CLAP
CLAP
CLAP
CLAP
CLAP
CLAP
CLAP

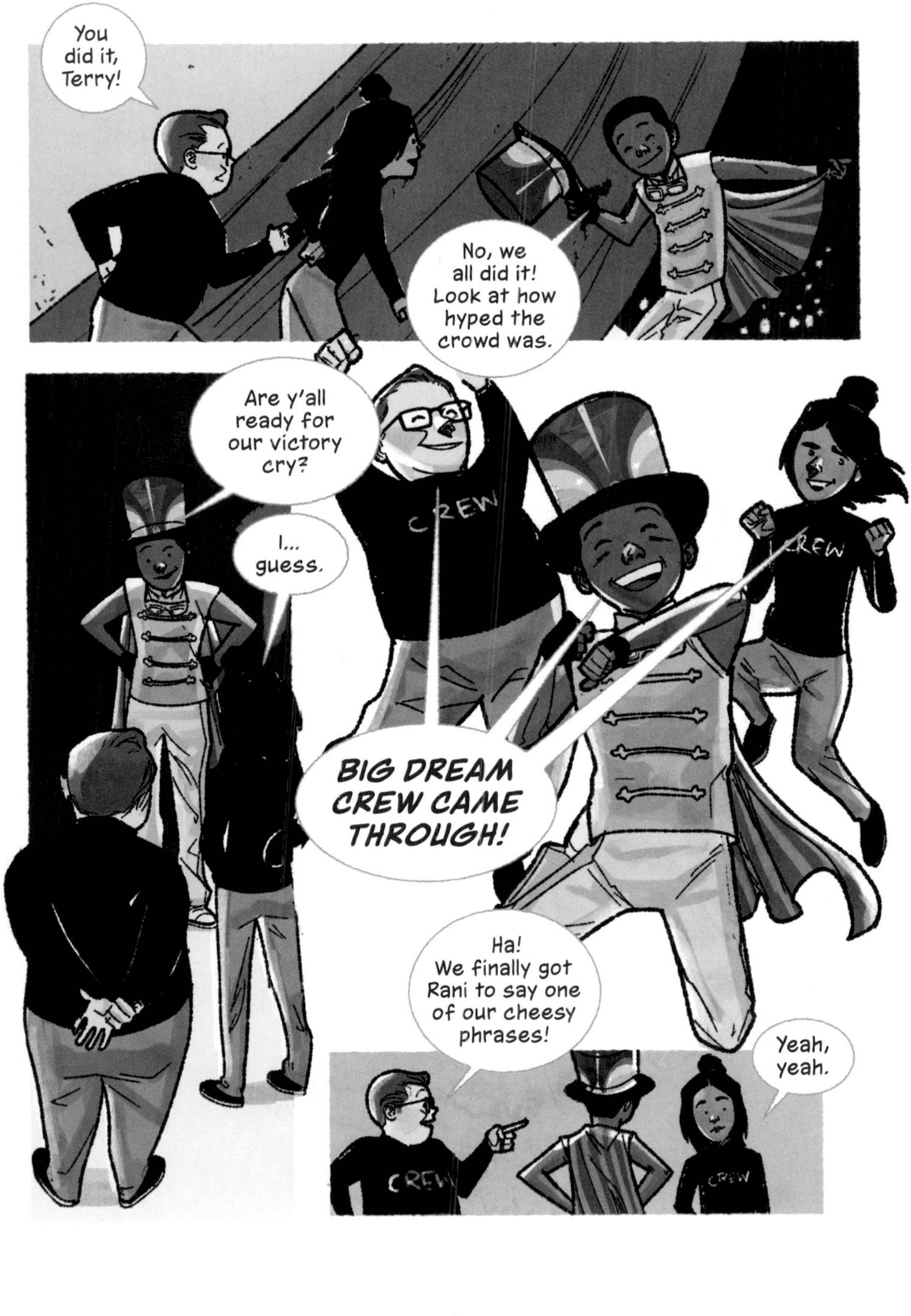

You did it, Terry!
No, we all did it! Look at how hyped the crowd was.
Are y'all ready for our victory cry?
I... guess.
BIG DREAM CREW CAME THROUGH!
CREW
Ha! We finally got Rani to say one of our cheesy phrases!
Yeah, yeah.

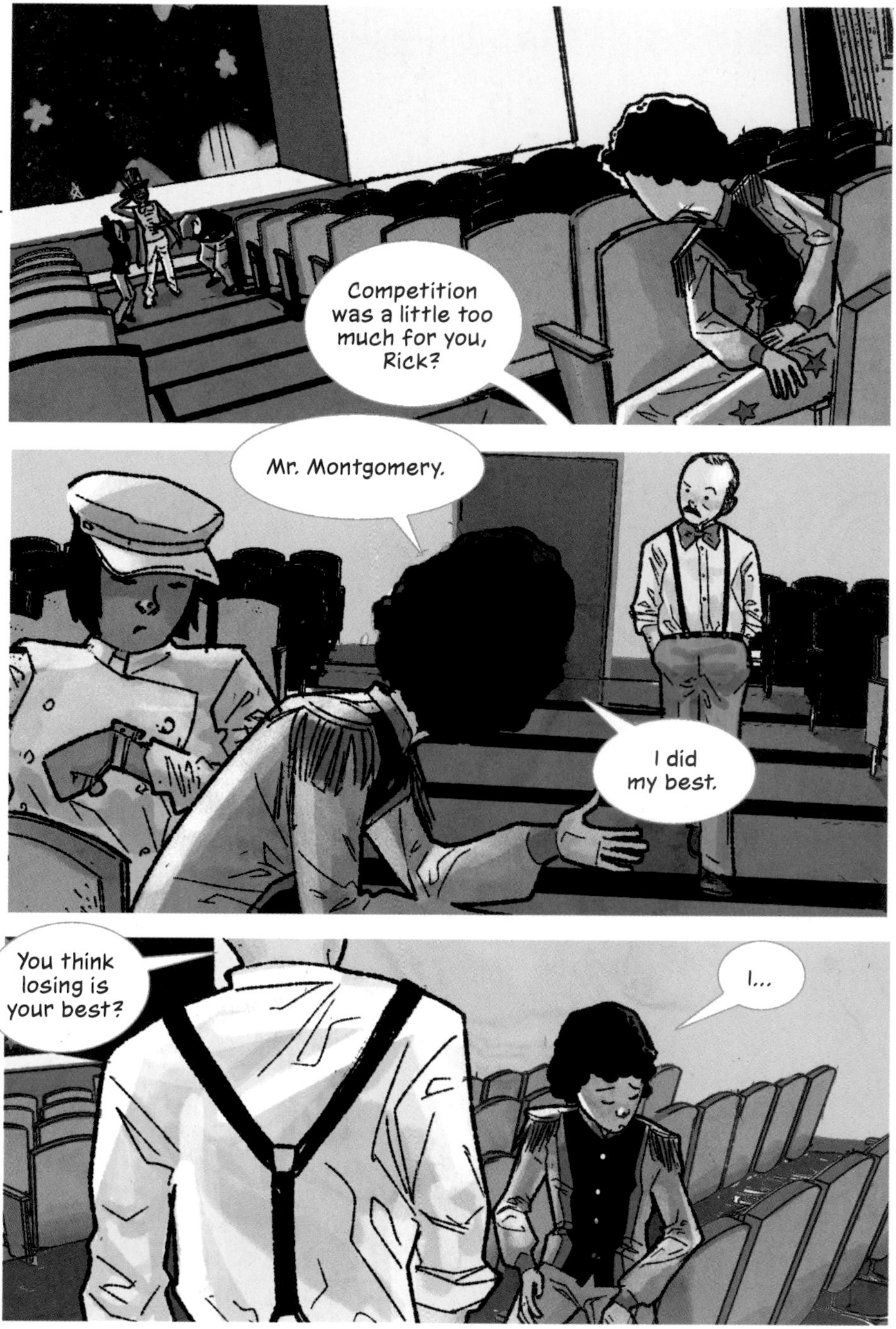
Competition was a little too much for you, Rick?
Mr. Montgomery.
I did my best.
You think losing is your best?
I...

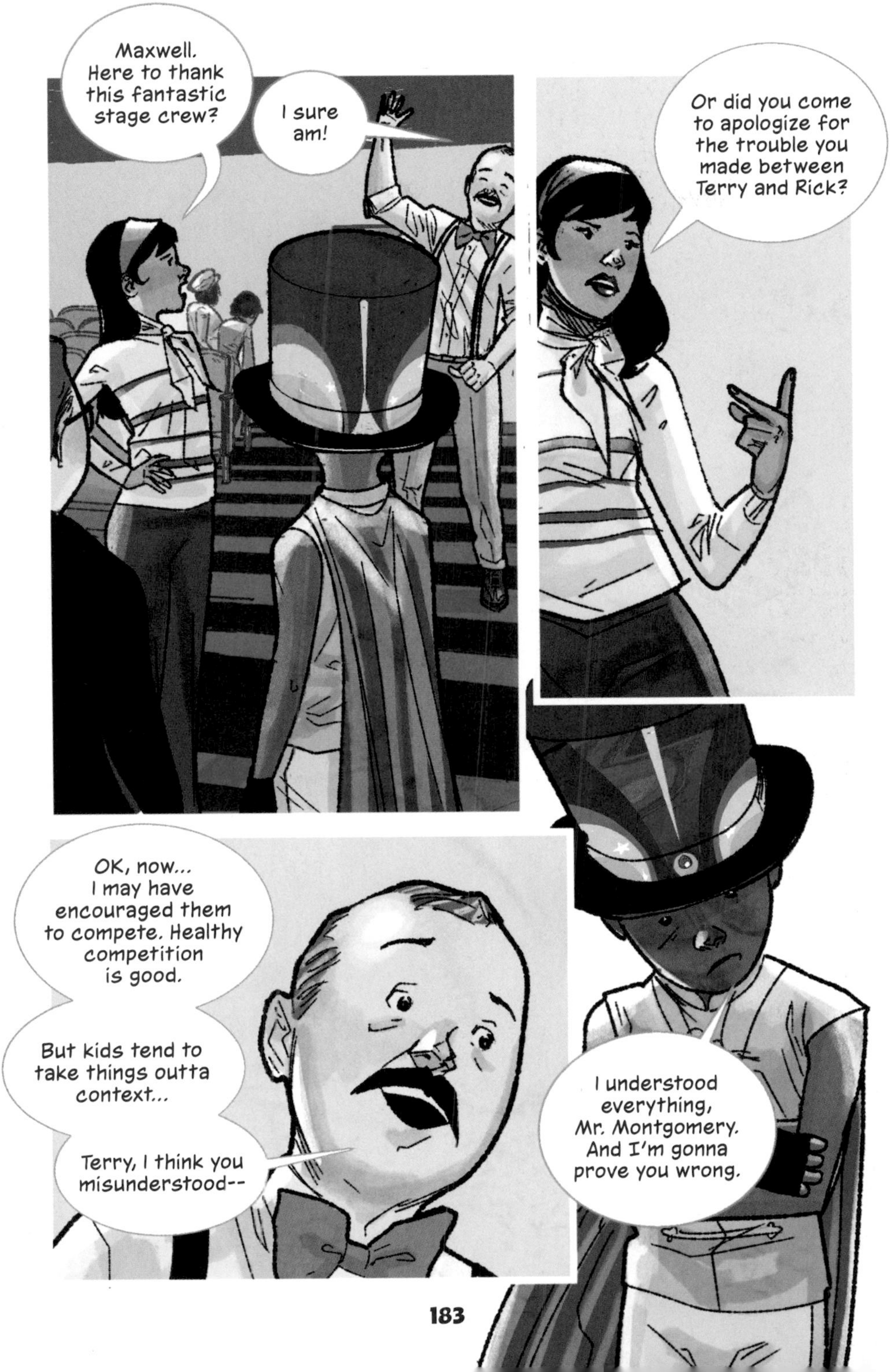
Maxwell. Here to thank this fantastic stage crew?
I sure am!
Or did you come to apologize for the trouble you made between Terry and Rick?
OK, now... I may have encouraged them to compete. Healthy competition is good.
But kids tend to take things outta context...
Terry, I think you misunderstood--
I understood everything, Mr. Montgomery. And I'm gonna prove you wrong.

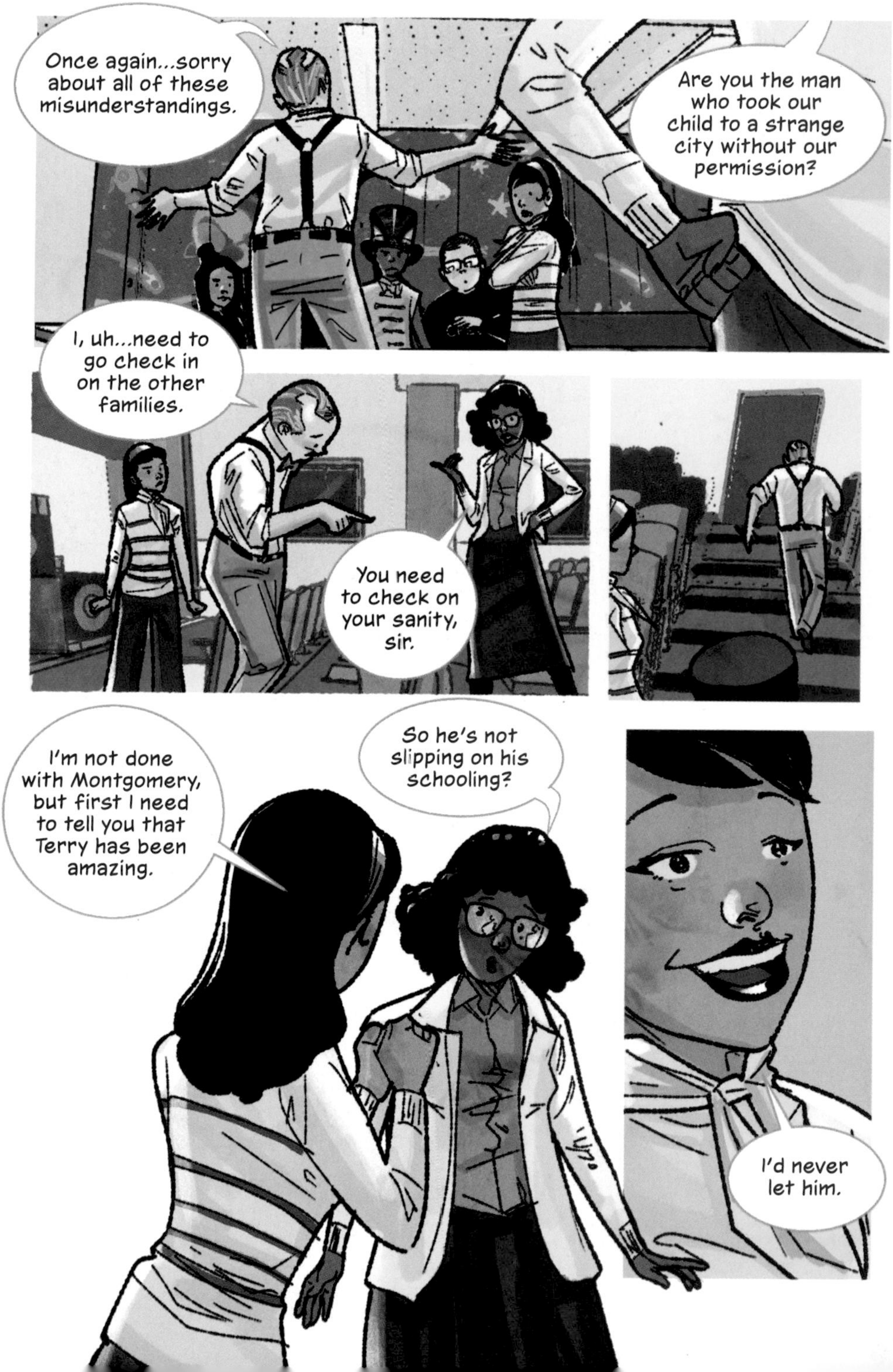
Once again...sorry about all of these misunderstandings.
Are you the man who took our child to a strange city without our permission?
I, uh...need to go check in on the other families.
You need to check on your sanity, sir.
I'm not done with Montgomery, but first I need to tell you that Terry has been amazing.
So he's not slipping on his schooling?
I'd never let him.

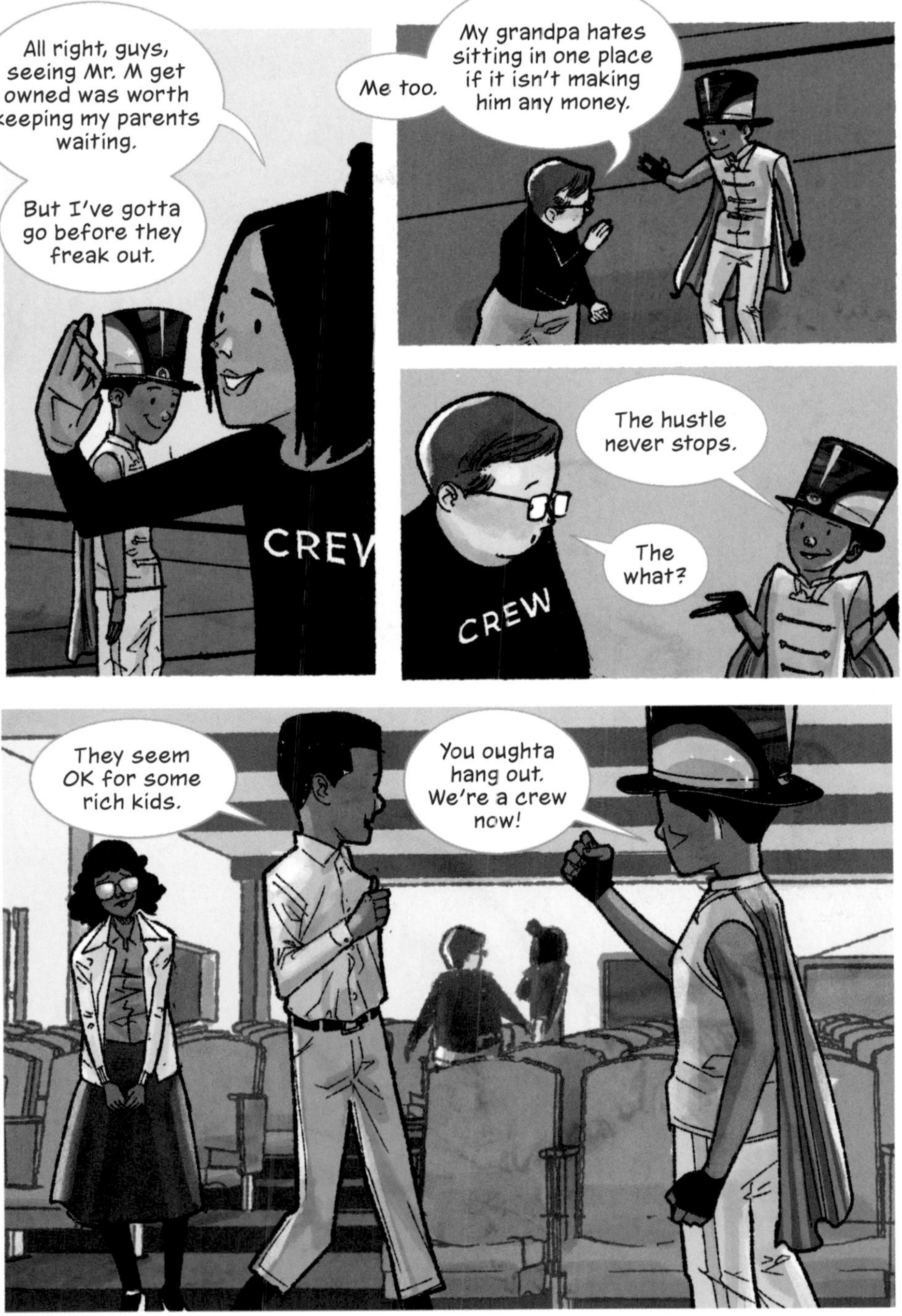
All right, guys, seeing Mr. M get owned was worth keeping my parents waiting.
But I've gotta go before they freak out.
CREW
Me too.
My grandpa hates sitting in one place if it isn't making him any money.
The hustle never stops.
The what?
CREW
They seem OK for some rich kids.
You oughta hang out. We're a crew now!

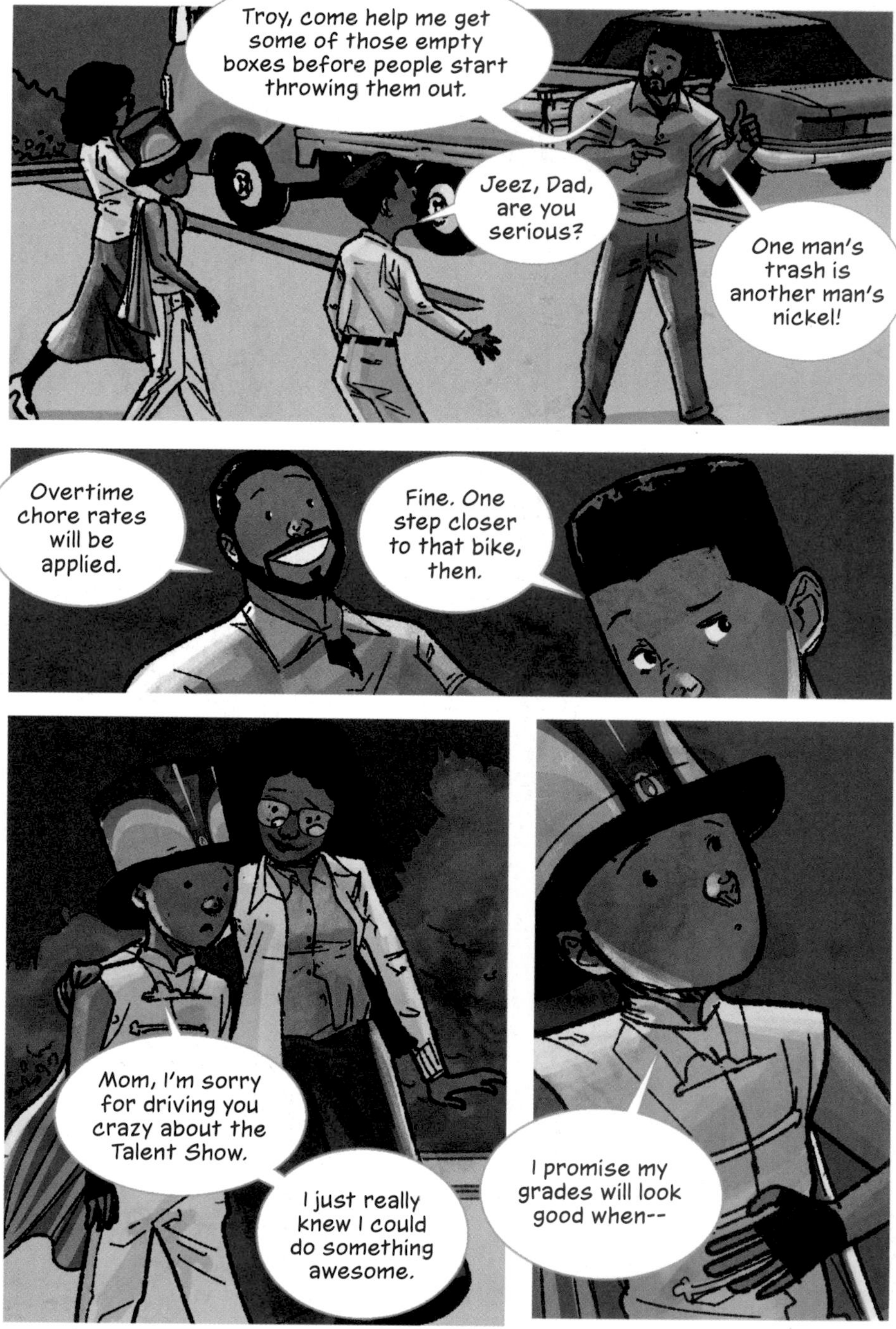
Troy, come help me get some of those empty boxes before people start throwing them out.
Jeez, Dad, are you serious?
One man's trash is another man's nickel!
Overtime chore rates will be applied.
Fine. One step closer to that bike, then.
Mom, I'm sorry for driving you crazy about the Talent Show.
I just really knew I could do something awesome.
I promise my grades will look good when--

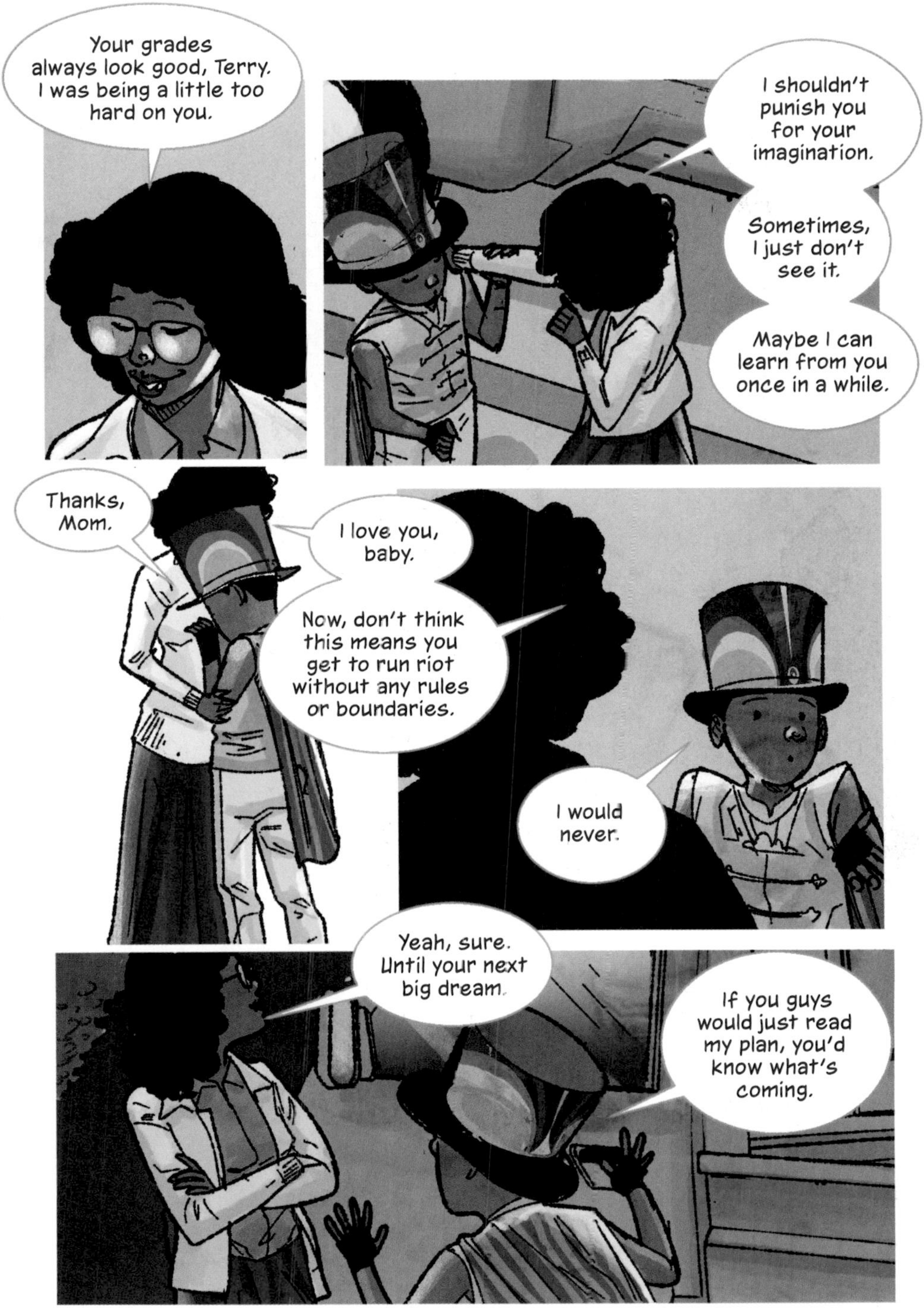
Your grades always look good, Terry. I was being a little too hard on you.
I shouldn't punish you for your imagination.
Sometimes, I just don't see it.
Maybe I can learn from you once in a while.
Thanks, Mom.
I love you, baby.
Now, don't think this means you get to run riot without any rules or boundaries.
I would never.
Yeah, sure. Until your next big dream.
If you guys would just read my plan, you'd know what's coming.

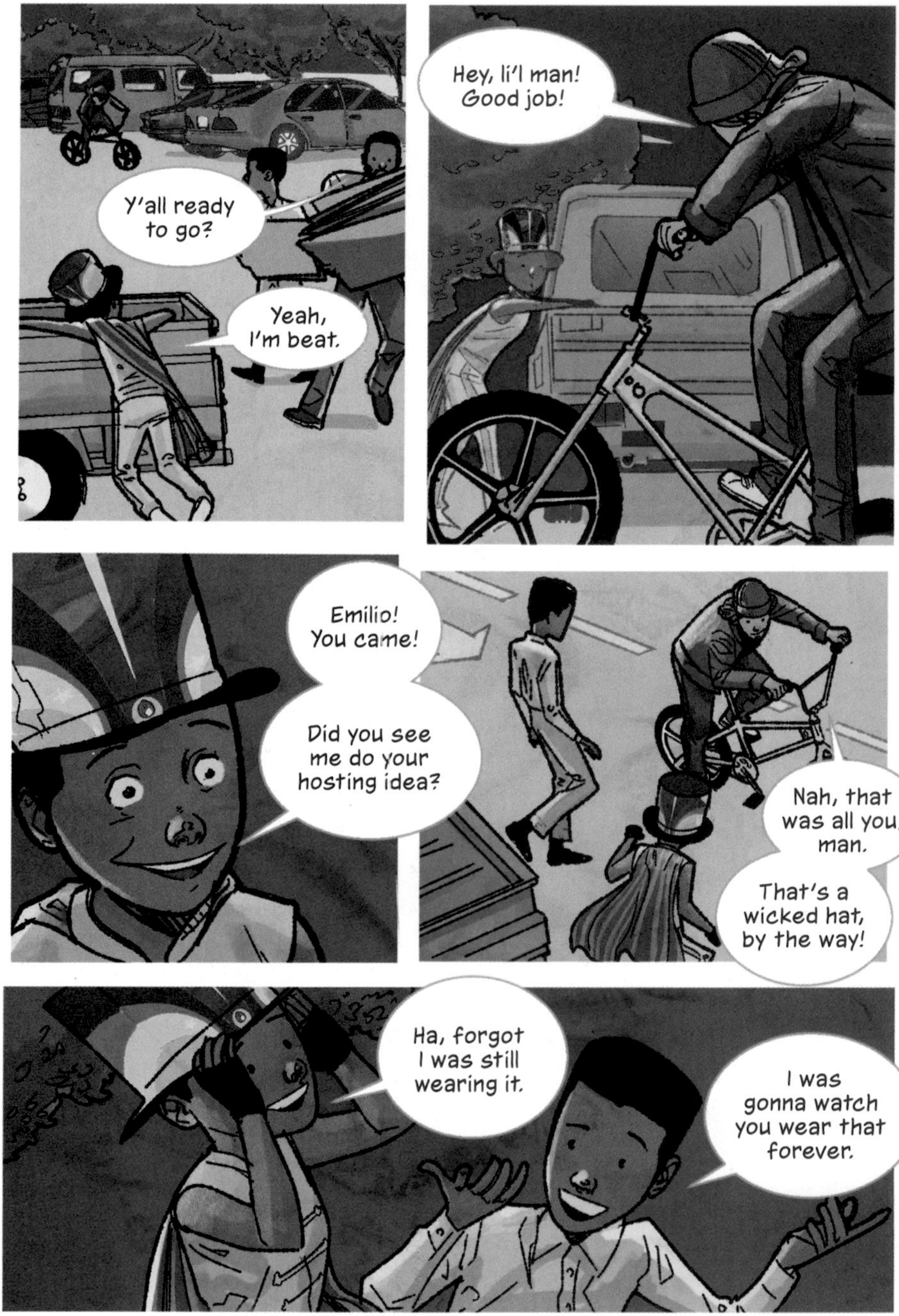
Y'all ready to go?
Yeah, I'm beat.
Hey, li'l man! Good job!
Emilio! You came!
Did you see me do your hosting idea?
Nah, that was all you, man.
That's a wicked hat, by the way!
Ha, forgot I was still wearing it.
I was gonna watch you wear that forever.

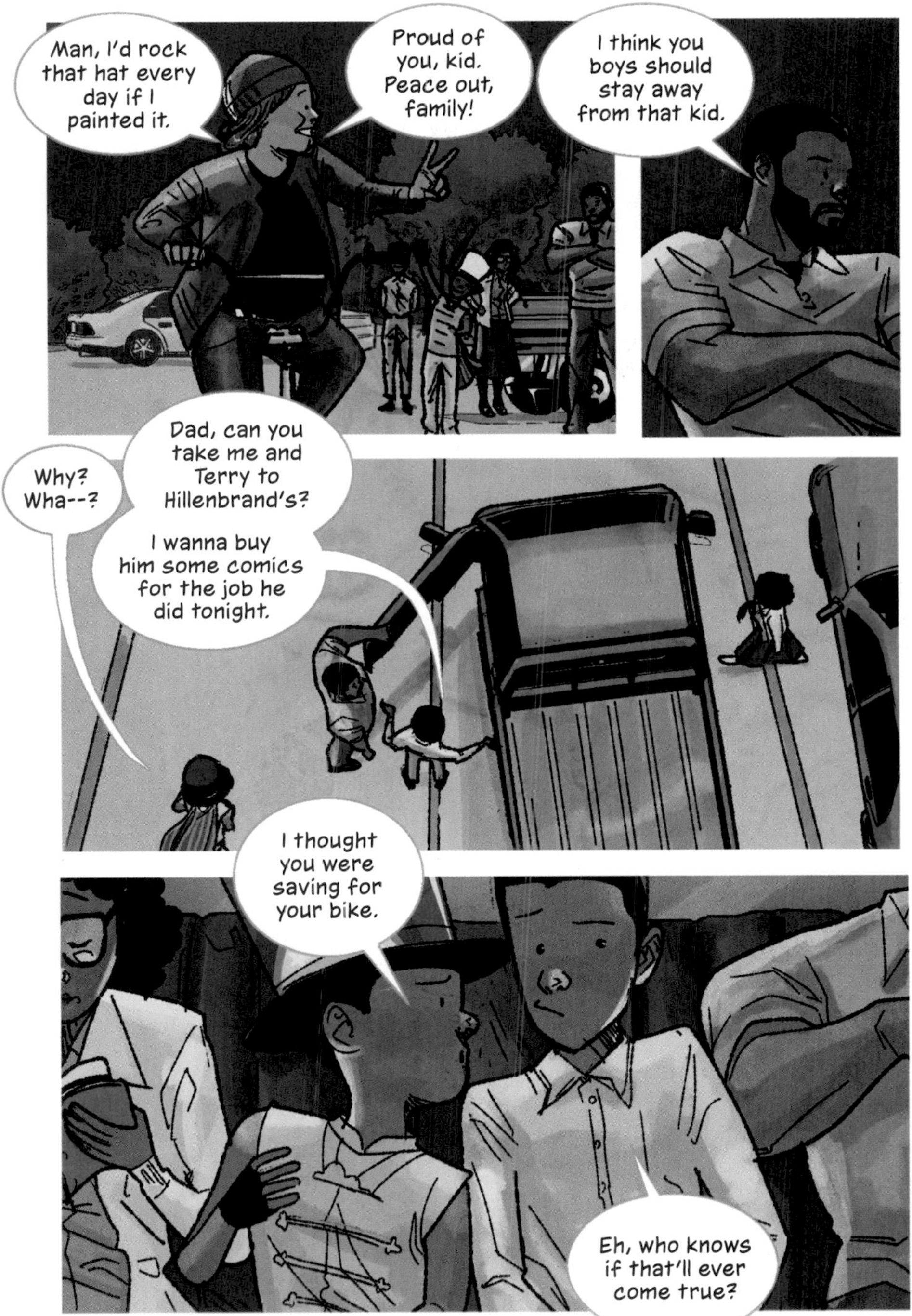

Man, I'd rock that hat every day if I painted it.
Proud of you, kid. Peace out, family!
I think you boys should stay away from that kid.
Why? Wha--?
Dad, can you take me and Terry to Hillenbrand's?
I wanna buy him some comics for the job he did tonight.
I thought you were saving for your bike.
Eh, who knows if that'll ever come true?

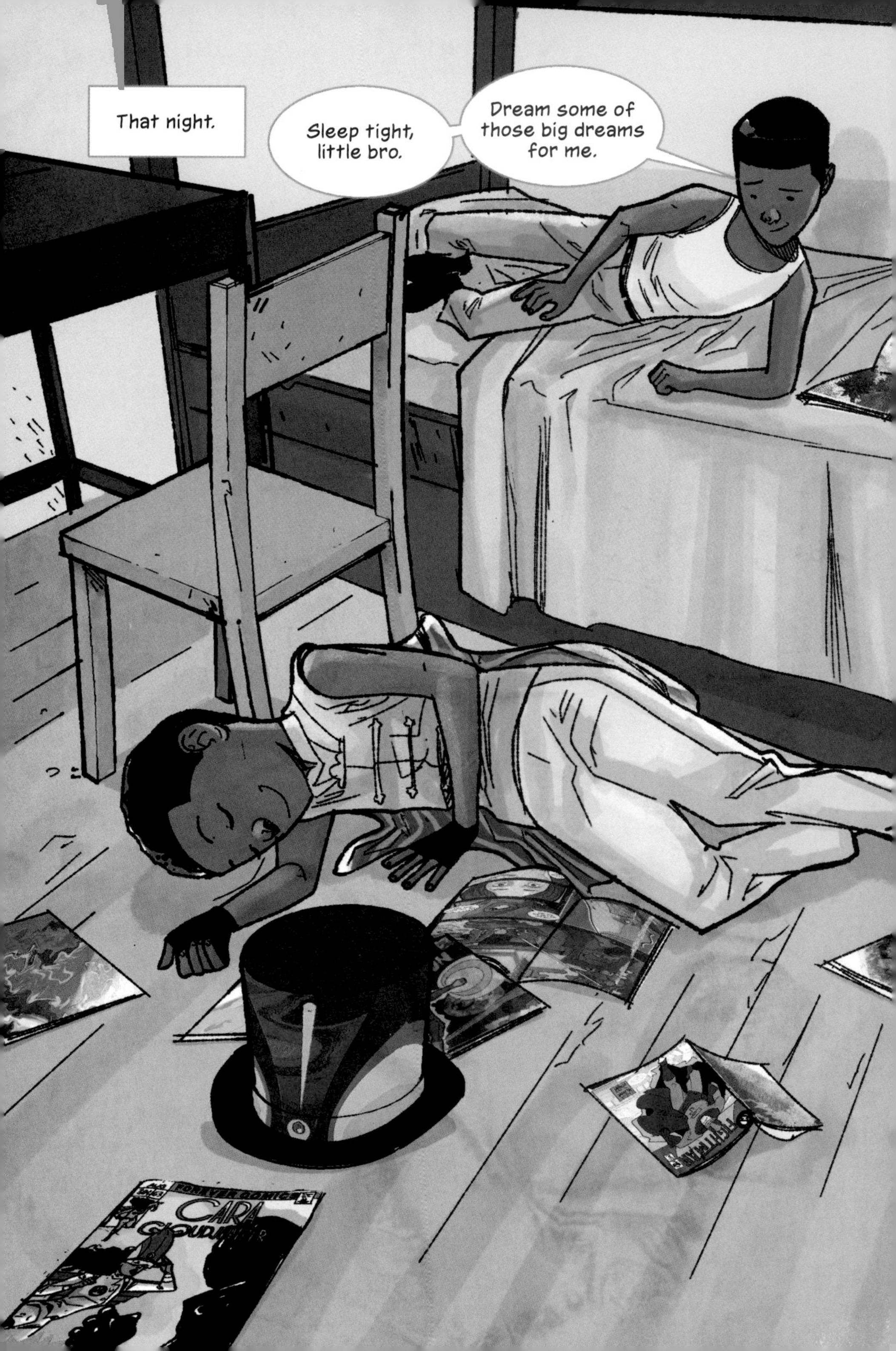
That night.
Sleep tight, little bro.
Dream some of those big dreams for me.

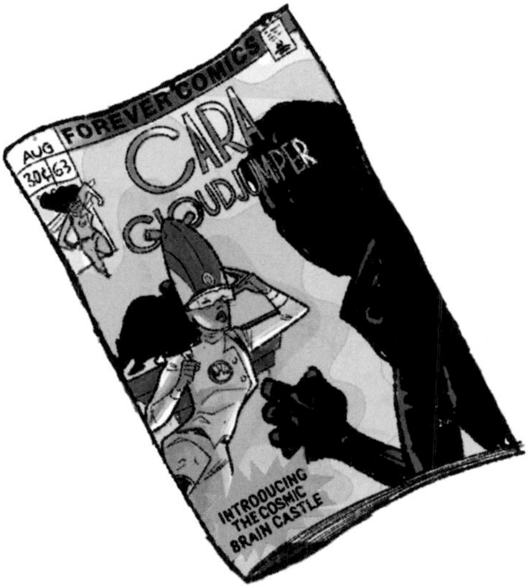
AUG
30¢ 63
FOREVER COMICS
CARA
CLOUDJUMPER
INTRODUCING
THE COSMIC
BRAIN CASTLE

Terry's Crew is a fictionalized version of my life. I grew up in Flint, Michigan, which is a *lot* like Rock City. Flint was changing very quickly in my early teens, as the auto industry, which provided the ways and means for most of its citizens, began to slowly fade away. But while that happened, my dreams kept getting bigger and bigger, and I was fortunate enough to attend a special school that encouraged all my talents—from art and dance all the way to science and sports. Most of the time I was asked to choose the one I liked best, but it was like choosing a favorite immediate family member: Each one held a special place in my heart.

I really did have an older streetwise friend like Emilio, who always looked out for me, encouraged me, and believed in me. I also loved to draw and paint, and having that outlet always fed an imaginative cycle where art was a pipeline to even more ideas—every one of which I wanted to see realized. I even really hosted my high school talent show, the precursor to hosting *America's Got Talent*—the biggest talent show in the world!

I also encountered great and supportive friends like Rani and Xander who I could trust to tell me the truth about my ideas and, more important, myself. What I loved about my school was that Black or white, rich or poor, artistic or athletic, we all contributed to one another's goals and dreams. Like Emilio would say, "You'll be whoever you let yourself be." My own Rock City Academy was where you were allowed to "let yourself be."

Now, that doesn't mean I didn't have obstacles. Most of the time I had to get out of my own way instead of trying to be cool by joking at others' expense or taking the bait of competing with others when I should have been creating with them. That always ended in disappointment. My parents were *very* strict, but in hindsight they just wanted to keep me out of the trouble plenty of my peers were getting into at the time...although it took me years to understand that. I also had some teachers who meant well but ended up not supporting me in the best way, like the professor who really did tell me I wasn't good enough to achieve my dreams. I may not have been good enough at the time, but I learned that most skills can be developed and achieved through hard work and patience. I found out things are not "you either have it or you don't," but rather "you can have it when it's earned," especially if you get good feedback from a great crew.

When I set out to write a book for young readers, I wanted to use my own experiences to share some of the lessons I've learned along the way (like Dream Big! Have a Crew!) and hopefully inspire those readers to keep going, even when things don't feel like they are working out.

Love,

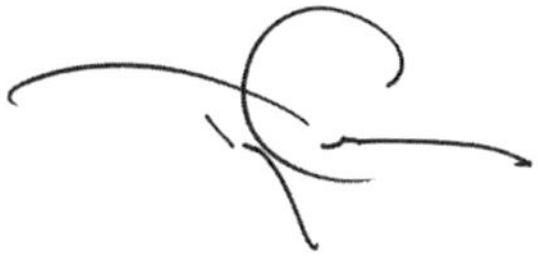

Terry

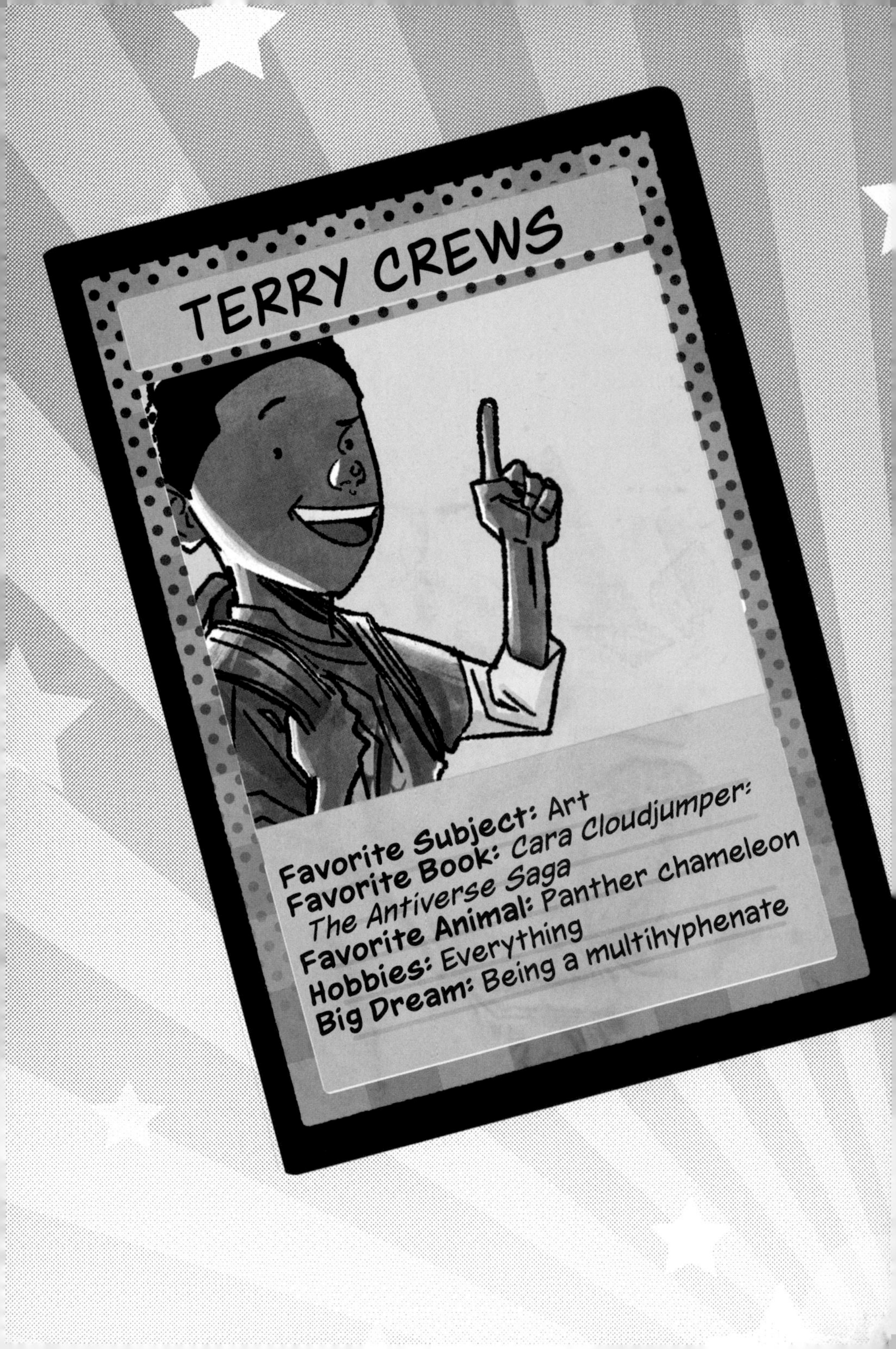
TERRY CREWS
Favorite Subject: Art
Favorite Book: Cara Cloudjumper: The Antiverse Saga
Favorite Animal: Panther chameleon
Hobbies: Everything
Big Dream: Being a multihyphenate

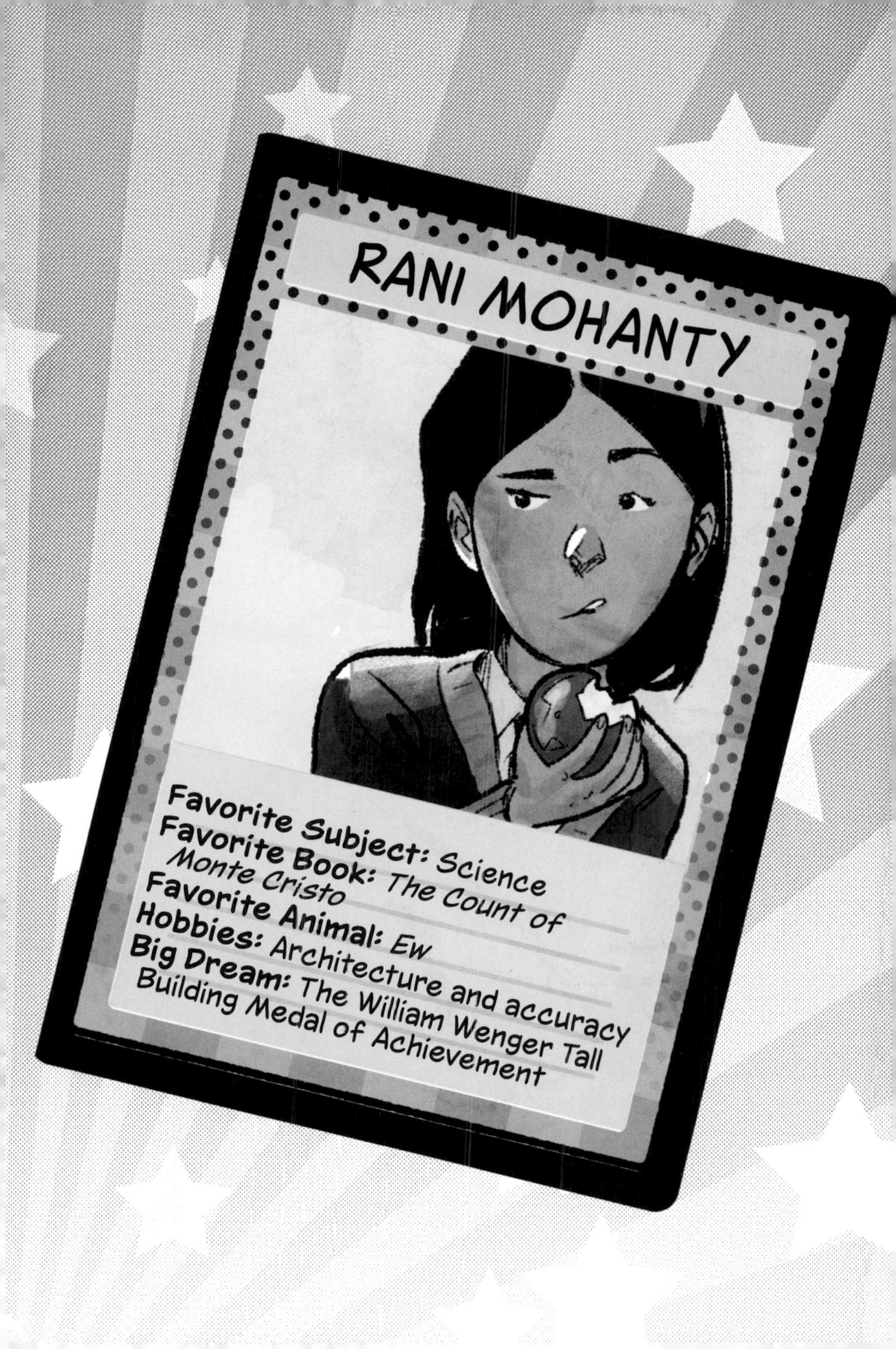
RANI MOHANTY
Favorite Subject: Science
Favorite Book: The Count of Monte Cristo
Favorite Animal: Ew
Hobbies: Architecture and accuracy
Big Dream: The William Wenger Tall Building Medal of Achievement

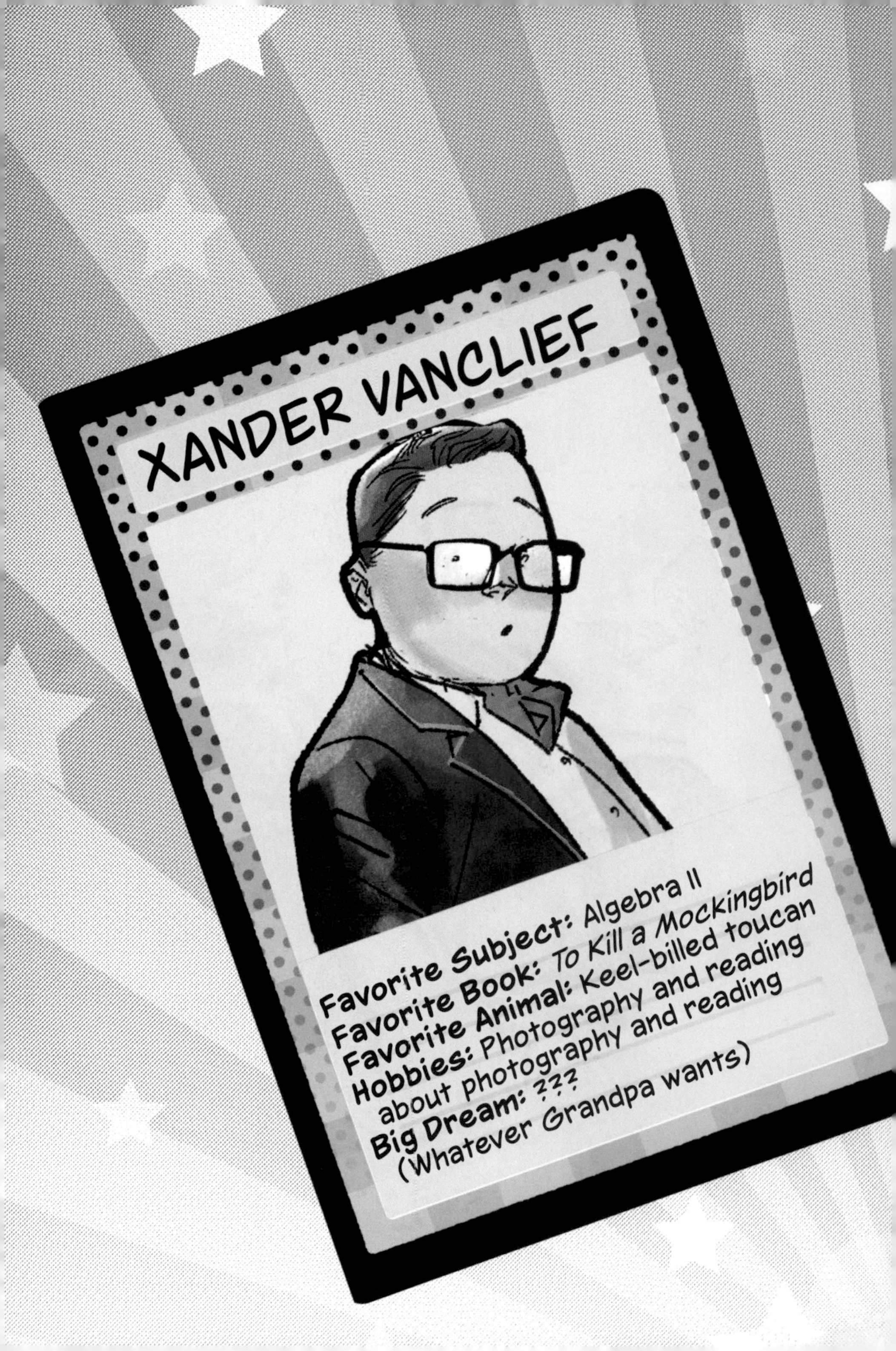
XANDER VANCLIEF
Favorite Subject: Algebra II
Favorite Book: To Kill a Mockingbird
Favorite Animal: Keel-billed toucan
Hobbies: Photography and reading about photography and reading
Big Dream: ??? (Whatever Grandpa wants)

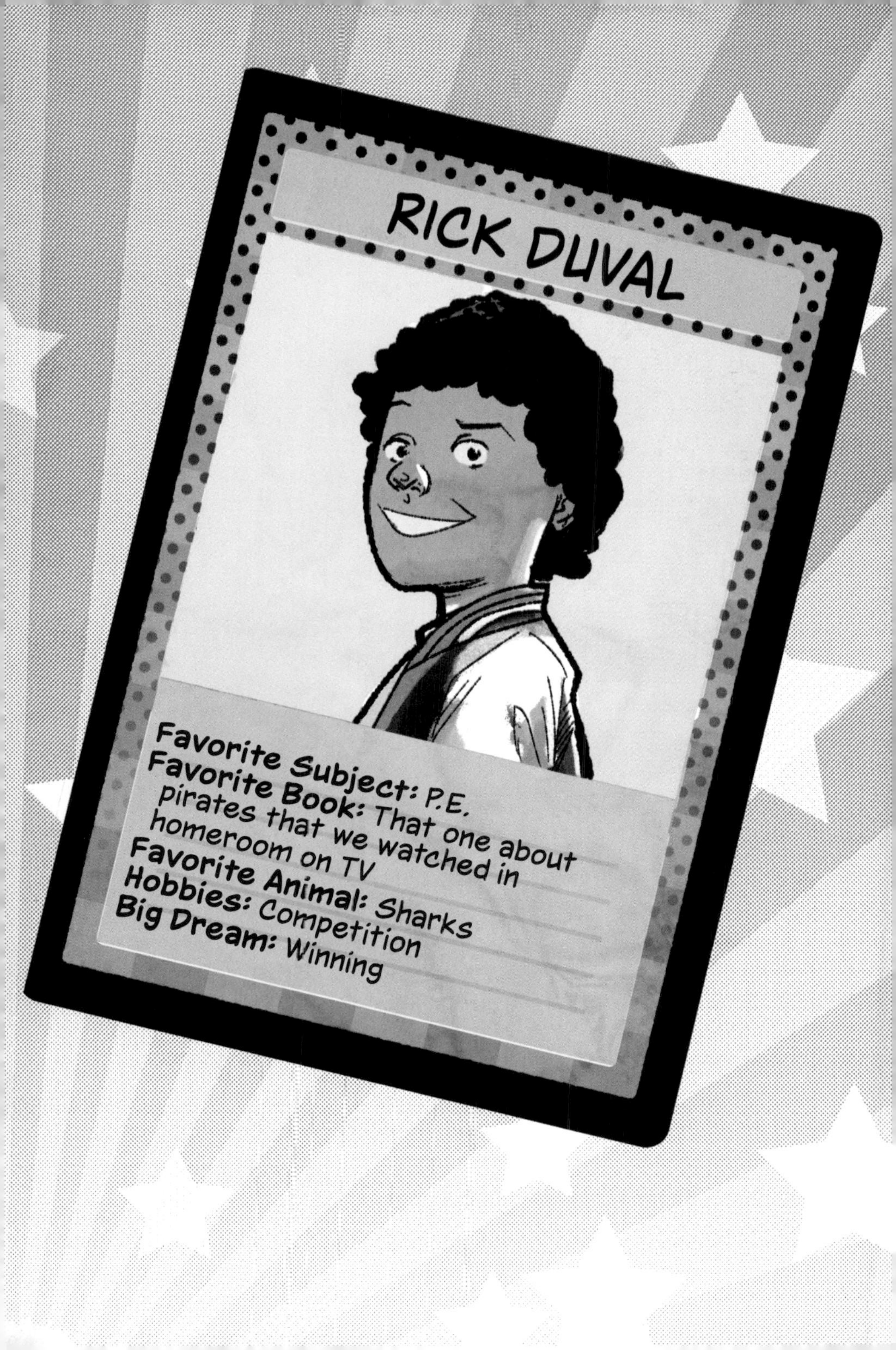
RICK DUVAL
Favorite Subject: P.E.
Favorite Book: That one about pirates that we watched in homeroom on TV
Favorite Animal: Sharks
Hobbies: Competition
Big Dream: Winning

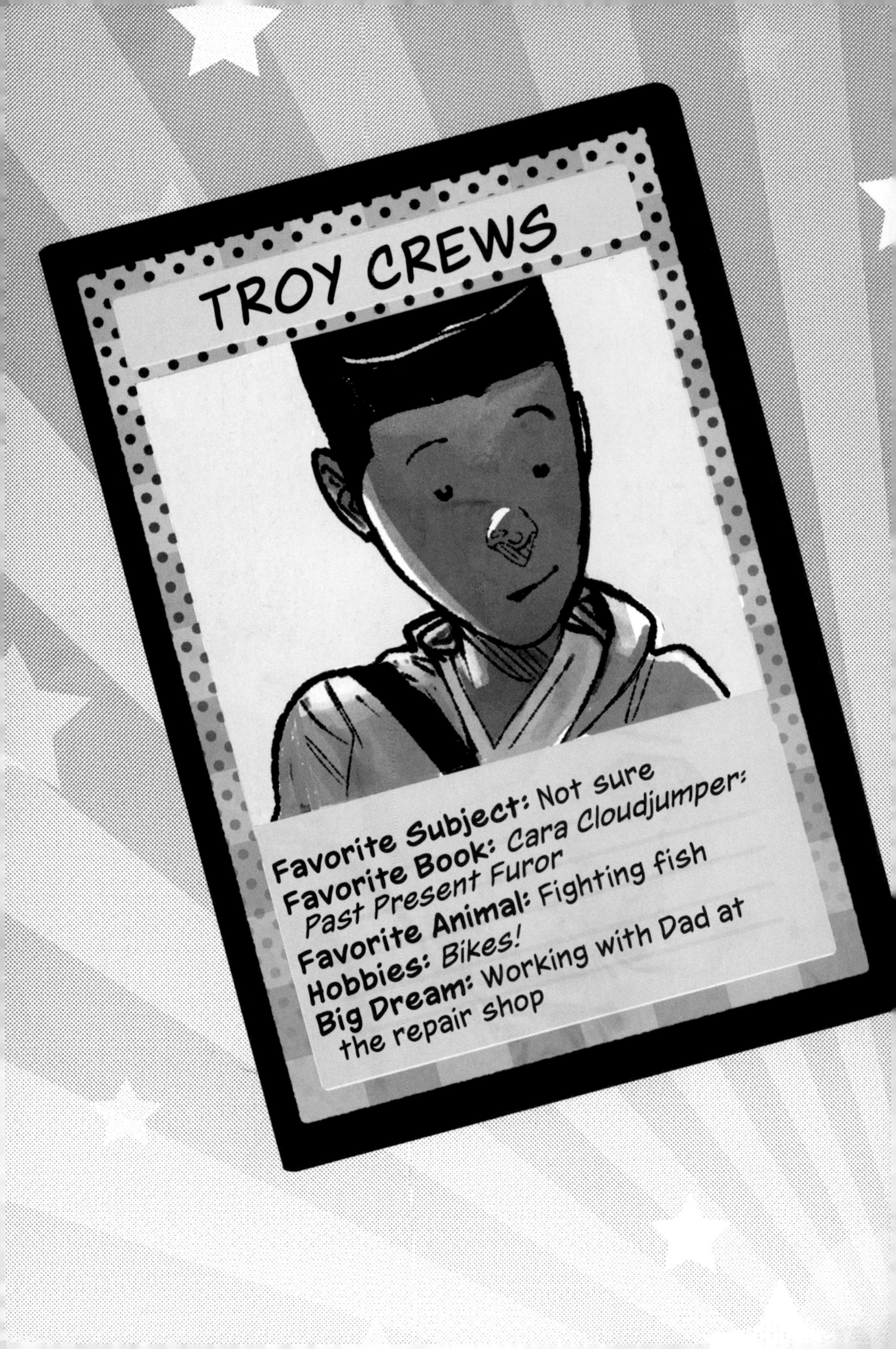
TROY CREWS
Favorite Subject: Not sure
Favorite Book: Cara Cloudjumper: Past Present Furor
Favorite Animal: Fighting fish
Hobbies: Bikes!
Big Dream: Working with Dad at the repair shop

I would like to thank my wife, Rebecca; my children, Naomi, Azriel, Tera, Wynfrey, and Isaiah; my granddaughter, Miley; my parents, Terry and Patricia Crews; my brother, Marcelle; and my sister, Micki.

Thanks also to my teacher Dwight Eichelberg and coach Lee Williams; to my agent, Albert Lee; manager, Troy Zien; and attorney, David Krintzman.

And finally, to my editor, Andrea Colvin, and this book's illustrator, Cory Thomas.

— TC

I want to thank my wife—the Dharma to my Greg (which is apparently a different show to *Will & Grace*). Throughout the long hours, sleepless nights, and hair loss, she has shown me so much love and encouragement. More than this book, I couldn't do life so fully without her. Thank you, Banakayi.

And to everyone who fed into me, supported me, guided me, and mocked my imposter syndrome—thank you, too. Ashelyn and Marlene and everyone who made me believe this could be a thing. You were right.

— CT

CORY THOMAS is a Trinidad-born illustrator, writer, and interesting man. In 2005, he began the newspaper comic strip *Watch Your Head*, and in 2013 began his journey into children's literature. Cory now lives in Atlanta, Georgia, with his wife, Netflix, and too many hats. He invites you to visit him at seethomas.com.

TERRY CREWS can be described in a lot of ways: author, action-movie hero, sitcom star, TV host, children's book illustrator, advertising pitchman, playable video game character, high-end furniture designer, and human rights activist. Crews is best known for his breakout roles on *Brooklyn Nine-Nine* and *Everybody Hates Chris*, hosting *America's Got Talent*, and his voicework in the animated films *Cloudy with a Chance of Meatballs 2* and *The Willoughbys*. *Terry's Crew* is his debut middle-grade graphic novel.